Boardroom
COLLECTION

February 2018

March 2018

April 2018

May 2018

June 2018

July 2018

Revenge in the Boardroom

ABBY GREEN

NINA HARRINGTON

CAT SCHIELD

MILLS & BOON

Published in Great Britain 2018
by Mills & Boon, an imprint of HarperCollins*Publishers*
1 London Bridge Street, London, SE1 9GF

Revenge in the Boardroom © 2018 Harlequin Books S.A.

Fonseca's Fury © 2015 Abby Green
Who's Afraid of the Big Bad Boss? © 2014 Nina Harrington
Unfinished Business © 2012 Catherine Schield

ISBN: 978-0-263-26624-5

09-0218

MIX
Paper from
responsible sources
FSC C007454

This book is produced from independently certified FSC™ paper to ensure responsible forest management.

For more information visit: www.harpercollins.co.uk/green

Printed and bound in Spain
by CPI, Barcelona

FONSECA'S FURY

ABBY GREEN

This is for Helen Kane – thanks for going to Dubai and letting me rent out your house and possibly the most idyllic office space in Dublin. And I do forgive you for leaving me behind in Kathmandu (on my birthday!) while you went off and romanced your own Mills & Boon hero! X

CHAPTER ONE

SERENA DEPIERO SAT in the plush ante-room and looked at the name on the opposite wall, spelled out in matt chrome lettering, and reeled.

Roseca Industries and Philanthropic Foundation.

Renewed horror spread through her. It had only been on the plane to Rio de Janeiro, when she'd been reading the extra information on the charity given to her by her boss, that she'd become aware that it was part of a much bigger organisation. An organisation run and set up by Luca Fonseca. The name Roseca was apparently an amalgamation of his father and mother's surnames. And Serena wasn't operating on a pay grade level high enough to require her to be aware of this knowledge before now.

Except here she was, outside the CEO's office, waiting to be called in to see the one man on the planet who had every reason to hate her guts. Why hadn't he sacked her months ago, as soon as she'd started working for him? Surely he must have known? An insidious suspicion took root: perhaps he'd orchestrated this all along, to lull her into a false sense of security before letting her crash spectacularly to the ground.

That would be breathtakingly cruel, and yet this man

owed her nothing but his disdain. She owed *him*. Serena
knew that there was a good chance her career in fundraising was about to be over before it had even taken
off. And at that thought she felt a spurt of panic mixed
with determination. Surely enough time had passed
now? Surely, even if this *was* some elaborate revenge
cooked up by Luca Fonseca as soon as he'd known she
was working for him, she could try to convince him
how sorry she was?

But before she could wrap her head around it any further a door opened to her right and a sleek dark-haired
woman dressed in a grey suit emerged.

'Senhor Fonseca will see you now, Miss DePiero.'

Serena's hands clenched tightly around her handbag.
She felt like blurting out, *But I don't want to see him!*

But she couldn't. As much as she couldn't just flee.
The car that had met her at the airport to deliver her
here still had her luggage in its boot.

As she stood up reluctantly a memory assailed her
with such force it almost knocked her sideways: Luca
Fonseca in a bloodstained shirt, with a black eye and a
split lip. Dark stubble shadowing his swollen jaw. He'd
been behind the bars of a jail cell, leaning against a
wall, brooding and dangerous. But then he'd looked up
and narrowed that intensely dark blue gaze on her, and
an expression of icy loathing had come over his face.

He'd straightened and moved to the bars, wrapping
his fingers around them almost as if he was imagining
they were her neck. Serena had stopped dead at the battered sight of him. He'd spat out, *'Damn you, Serena
DePiero, I wish I'd never laid eyes on you.'*

'Miss DePiero? Senhor Fonseca is waiting.'

The clipped and accented voice shattered Serena's

memory and she forced her feet to move, taking her past the unsmiling woman and into the palatial office beyond.

She hated that her heart was thumping so hard when she heard the door snick softly shut behind her. For the first few seconds she saw no one, because the entire back wall of the office was a massive window and it framed the most amazingly panoramic view of a city Serena had ever seen.

The Atlantic glinted dark blue in the distance, and inland from that were the two most iconic shapes of Rio de Janeiro: the Sugar Loaf and Christ the Redeemer high on Corcovado. In between were countless other tall buildings, right up to the coast. To say that the view was breathtaking was an understatement.

And then suddenly it was eclipsed by the man who moved into her line of vision. Luca Fonseca. For a second past and present merged and Serena was back in that nightclub, seeing him for the first time.

He'd stood so tall and broad against the backdrop of that dark and opulent place. Still. She'd never seen anyone so still, yet with such a commanding presence. People had skirted around him. Men suspicious, envious. Women lustful.

In a dark suit and open-necked shirt he'd been dressed much the same as other men, but he'd stood out from them all by dint of that sheer preternatural stillness and the incredible forcefield of charismatic magnetism that had drawn her to him before she could stop herself.

Serena blinked. The dark and decadent club faded. She couldn't breathe. The room was instantly stifling. Luca Fonseca looked different. It took her sluggish brain a second to function enough for her to realise that he looked different because his hair was longer, slightly unruly. And he had a dark beard that hugged his jaw. It made him look even more intensely masculine.

He was wearing a light-coloured open-necked shirt tucked into dark trousers. For all the world the urbane, civilised businessman in his domain, and yet the vibe coming from him was anything but civilised.

He crossed his arms over that massive chest and then he spoke. 'What the hell do you think you're doing here, DePiero?'

Serena moved further into the vast office, even though it was in the opposite direction from where she wanted to go. She couldn't take her eyes off him even if she wanted to.

She forced herself to speak, to act as if seeing him again wasn't as shattering as it was. 'I'm here to start working in the fundraising department for the global communities charity.'

'Not any more, you're not,' Fonseca said tersely.

Serena flushed. 'I didn't know you were…involved until I was on my way over here.'

Fonseca made a small sound like a snort. 'An unlikely tale.'

'It's true,' Serena blurted out. 'I had no idea the charity was linked to the Roseca Foundation. Believe me, if I'd had any idea I wouldn't have agreed to come here.'

Luca Fonseca moved around the table and Serena's eyes widened. For a big man, he moved with innate grace, and that incredible quality of self-containment oozed from every pore. It was intensely captivating.

He admitted with clear irritation, 'I wasn't aware that you were working in the Athens office. I don't micromanage my smaller charities abroad because I hire the best staff to do that for me—although I'm reconsidering my policy after this. If I'd known they'd hired you, of all people, you would have been let go long before now.'

His mouth twisted with recrimination.

'But I have to admit that I was intrigued enough to have you brought here instead of just leaving you at the airport until we could put you on a return flight.'

So he hadn't even known she was working for him. Serena's hands curled into fists at her sides. His dismissive arrogance set her nerves even more on edge.

He glanced at a big platinum watch on his wrist. 'I have a spare fifteen minutes before you are to be delivered back to the airport.'

Like an unwanted package. He was firing her.

He hitched a hip onto the corner of his desk, for all the world as if they were having a normal conversation amidst the waves of tension. 'Well, DePiero? What the hell is Europe's most debauched ex-socialite doing working for minimum wage in a small charity office in Athens?'

Only hours ago Serena had been buoyant at the thought of her new job. A chance to prove to her somewhat over-protective family that she was going to be fine. She'd been ecstatic at the thought of her independence. And now this man was going to ensure that everything she'd fought so hard for was for naught.

For years she had been the *enfant terrible* of the Italian party scene, frequently photographed, with reams of newsprint devoted to her numerous exploits which had been invariably blown out of proportion. Nevertheless, Serena knew well that there was enough truth behind the headlines to make her feel that ever-present prick of shame.

'Look,' she said, hating the way her voice had got husky with repressed emotion and shock at facing this blast from her past, 'I know you must hate me.'

Luca Fonseca smiled. But his expression was hard. 'Hate? Don't flatter yourself, DePiero, *hate* is a very inadequate description of my feelings where you are concerned.'

Another poisonous memory assailed her: a battered Luca, handcuffed by Italian police, being dragged bodily to an already loaded-up van, snarling, *'You set me up, you bitch!'* at Serena, who had been moments away from being handed into a police car herself, albeit minus the handcuffs.

They'd insisted on everyone being hauled in to the police station. He'd tried to jerk free of the burly police officers and that had earned him a thump to his belly, making him double over. Serena had been stupefied. Transfixed with shock.

He'd rasped out painfully, just before disappearing into the police van, 'She planted the drugs on *me* to save herself.'

Serena tried to force the memories out of her head. 'Mr Fonseca, I didn't plant those drugs in your pockets… I don't know who did, but it wasn't me. I tried to contact you afterwards…but you'd left Italy.'

He made a sound of disgust. 'Afterwards? You mean after you'd returned from your shopping spree in Paris? I saw the pictures. Avoiding being prosecuted for possession of drugs and continuing your hedonistic existence was all in a week's work for you, wasn't it?'

Serena couldn't avoid the truth; no matter how innocent she was, this man *had* suffered because of their brief association. The lurid headlines were still clear in her mind: *DePiero's newest love interest? Brazilian billionaire Fonseca caught with drugs after raid on Florence's most exclusive nightclub, Den of Eden.*

But before Serena could defend herself Luca was standing up and walking closer, making her acutely aware of his height and powerful frame. Her mouth dried.

When he was close enough that she could make out the dark chest hair curling near the open V of his shirt, he sent an icy look from her face to her feet, and then said derisively, 'A far cry from that lame excuse for a dress.'

Serena could feel heat rising at the reminder of how she'd been dressed that night. How she'd dressed most nights. She tried again, even though it was apparent that her attempt to defend herself had fallen on deaf ears. 'I really didn't have anything to do with those drugs. I promise. It was all a huge misunderstanding.'

He looked at her for a long moment, clearly incredulous, before tipping his head back and laughing so abruptly that Serena flinched.

When his eyes met hers again they still sparkled with cold mirth, and that sensual mouth was curved in an equally cold smile.

'I have to hand it to you—you've got some balls to come in here and protest your innocence after all this time.'

Serena's nails scored her palms, but she didn't notice. 'It's true. I know what you must think...'

She stopped, and had to push down the insidious

reminder that it was what *everyone* had thought. Erroneously.

'I didn't do those kinds of drugs.'

Any hint of mirth, cold or otherwise, vanished from Luca Fonseca's visage. 'Enough with protesting your innocence. You had Class A drugs in that pretty purse and you conveniently slipped them into my pocket as soon as it became apparent that the club was being raided.'

Feeling sick now, Serena said, 'It must have been someone else in the crush and panic.'

Fonseca moved even closer to Serena then, and she gulped and looked up. She felt hot, clammy.

His voice was low, seductive. 'Do I need to remind you of how close we were that night, Serena? How easy it must have been for you to divest yourself of incriminating evidence?'

Serena could recall all too clearly that his arms had been like steel bands around her, with hers twined around his neck. Her mouth had been sensitive and swollen, her breathing rapid. Someone had rushed over to them on the dance floor—some acquaintance of Serena's who had hissed, *'There's a raid.'*

And Luca Fonseca thought… He thought that during those few seconds before chaos had struck she'd had the presence of mind to somehow slip drugs onto his person?

He said now, 'I'm sure it was a move you'd perfected over the years, which was why I felt nothing.'

He stepped back and Serena could take a breath again. But then he walked around her, and her skin prickled. She was acutely aware of his regard and wanted to adjust her suit, which felt constrictive.

She closed her eyes and then opened them again,

turning around to face him. 'Mr Fonseca, I'm just looking for a chance—'

He held up his hand and Serena stopped. His expression was worse than cold now: it was completely indecipherable.

He clicked his fingers, as if something just occurred to him, and his lip curled. 'Of *course*—it's your family, isn't it? They've clipped your wings. Andreas Xenakis and Rocco De Marco would never tolerate a return to your debauched ways, and you're still *persona non grata* in the social circles who fêted you before. You and your sister certainly landed on your feet, in spite of your father's fall from grace.'

Disgust was etched on his hard features.

'Lorenzo DePiero will never be able to show his face again after the things he did.'

Serena felt nauseous. She of all people didn't need to be reminded of her father's corruption and many crimes.

But Luca wasn't finished. 'I think you're doing this under some sort of sufferance, to prove to your newfound family that you've changed… In return for what? An allowance? A palatial home back in Italy, your old stomping ground? Or perhaps you'll stay in Athens, where the stench of your tarnished reputation is a little less…pungent? After all, it's where you'll have the protection of your younger sister who, if I recall correctly, was the one who regularly cleaned up your messes.'

Fire raced up Serena's spine at hearing him mention her family—and especially her sister. A sense of protectiveness overwhelmed her. They were everything to her and she would never, ever let them down. They had saved her. Something this cold, judgmental man would never understand.

Serena was jet-lagged, gritty-eyed, and in shock at seeing this man again, and it was evident in her voice now, as she lashed back heatedly, 'My family have nothing to do with this. And nothing to do with *you*.'

Luca Fonseca looked at Serena incredulously. 'I'm sure your family have everything to do with this. Did you drop a tantalising promise of generous donations from them in return for a move up the career ladder?'

Serena flushed and got out a strangled-sounding, 'No, of course not.'

But the way she avoided his eyes told Luca otherwise. She wouldn't have had to drop anything but the most subtle of hints. The patronage of either her half-brother, Rocco De Marco, or her brother-in-law, Andreas Xenakis, could secure a charity's fortunes for years to come. And, as wealthy as he was in his own right, the foundation would always need to raise money. Disgusted that his own staff might have been so easily manipulated, and suddenly aware of how heated his blood was, Luca stepped back.

He was grim. 'I am not going to be a convenient conduit through which you try to fool everyone into thinking you've changed.'

Serena just looked at him, and he saw her long, graceful throat work, as if she couldn't quite get out what she wanted to say. He felt no pity for her.

She couldn't be more removed from the woman of his memory of seven years ago, when she'd been golden and sinuous and provocative. The woman in front of him now looked pale, and as if she was going for an interview in an insurance office. Her abundantly sexy white-blonde hair had been tamed into a staid chignon. And yet even that, and the sober dark suit, couldn't dim

her incredible natural beauty or those piercing bright
blue eyes.

Those eyes had hit him right in the solar plexus as
soon as she'd walked into his office, when he'd been
able to watch her unobserved for a few seconds. And
the straight trousers couldn't hide those famously long
legs. The generous swell of her breasts pushed against
the silk of her shirt.

Disgust curled through him to notice her like this.
Had he learnt nothing? She should be prostrating herself
at his feet in abject apology for turning his life upside
down, but instead she had the temerity to defend herself: *'My family have nothing to do with this.'*

His clear-headed focus was being eroded in this
woman's presence. Why was he even wondering anything about her? He didn't care what her nefarious moti-
vations were. He'd satisfied whatever curiosity he'd had.

He clenched his jaw. 'Your time is up. The car will
be waiting outside for your return to the airport. And I
do sincerely hope to never lay eyes on you again.'

So why was it so hard to rip his gaze *off* her?

Anger and self-recrimination coursed through Luca
as he stepped around Serena and stalked back to his
desk, expecting to hear the door open and close.

When he didn't, he spun round and spat out tersely,
'We have nothing more to discuss.'

The fact that she had gone paler was something that
Luca didn't like to acknowledge that he'd noticed. Or
his very bizarre dart of concern. No woman evoked concern in him. He could see her swallow again, that long,
graceful throat moving, and then her soft, husky voice,
with that slightest hint of an Italian accent, crossed the
space between them.

'I'm just asking for a chance. Please.'

Luca's mouth opened and closed. He was stunned. Once he declared what he wanted no one questioned him. Until now. And this woman, of all people? Serena DePiero had a less than zero chance of Luca reconsidering his decision. The fact that she was still in his office set his nerves sizzling just under his skin. Irritating him.

But instead of admitting defeat and turning round, the woman stepped closer. Further away from the door.

Luca had an urge to snarl and stalk over to her, to put her over his shoulder, physically remove her from his presence. But right then, with perfect timing, the memory of her lush body pressed against his, her soft mouth yielding to his forceful kiss, exploded into his consciousness and within a nano-second he was battling a surge of blood to his groin.

Damn her. Witch.

She was at the other side of his desk. Blue eyes huge, her bearing as regal as a queen's, reminding him effortlessly of her impeccable lineage.

Her voice was low and she clasped her hands together in front of her, knuckles white. 'Mr Fonseca, I came here with the best of intentions to do work for your charity, despite what you may believe. I'll do anything to prove to you how committed I am.'

Anger surged at her persistence. At her meek *Mr Fonseca.*

Luca uncrossed his arms and placed his hands on the table in front of him, leaning forward. '*You* are the reason I had to rebuild my reputation and people's trust in my charitable work—not to mention trust in my family's mining consortium. I spent months, *years*, undoing the damage of that one night. Debauchery is all very well and good, as you must know, but the stigma of possessing Class A drugs does tend to last. The truth is that once those pictures of us together in the nightclub surfaced I *had* no defence.'

It almost killed Luca now to recall how he had instinctively shielded Serena from the police and detectives who had stormed the club, which was when she must have taken the opportunity to plant the drugs on him.

He thought of the paparazzi pictures of her shopping in Paris while he'd been leaving Italy under a cloud of disgrace, and bitterness laced his voice. 'Meanwhile you were oblivious to the fallout, continuing your hedonistic existence. And after all that, you have the temerity to think that I would so much as allow your name to be mentioned in the same sentence as mine?'

If possible, she paled even more, displaying the genes she'd inherited from her half-English mother, a classic English rose beauty.

He straightened up. 'You disgust me.'

Serena was dimly aware that on some level his words were hurting her in a place that she shouldn't be feeling hurt. But something dogged deep inside had pushed her to plead. And she had.

His eyes were like dark, hard sapphires. Impervious to heat or cold or her pleas. He was right. He was the one man on the planet who would never give her a chance. She was delusional to have thought even for a second that he might hear her out.

The atmosphere in the office was positively glacial in comparison to the gloriously sunny day outside. Luca Fonseca was just looking at her. Serena's belly sank. He wasn't even going to say another word. He'd said everything. He'd just wanted to see her, to torture her. Make her realise just how much he hated her—as if she had been in any doubt.

She finally admitted defeat and turned to the door. There would be no reprieve. Hitching up her chin in a tiny gesture of dignity, she didn't glance back at him, not wanting to see that arctic expression again. As if she was something distasteful on the end of his shoe.

She opened the door, closed it behind her, and was met by his cool assistant who was waiting for her. And who'd undoubtedly been privy to the plans of her boss well before Serena had been. Silently she was escorted downstairs.

Her humiliation was complete.

Ten minutes later Luca spoke tersely into his phone. 'Call me as soon as you know she's boarded and the plane has left.'

When he'd terminated the call Luca swivelled around in his high-backed chair to face the view. His blood was still boiling with a mixture of anger and arousal. Why had he indulged in the dubious desire to see her face to face again? All it had done was show him his own weakness for her.

He hadn't even known she was on her way to Rio until his assistant had informed him; the significance of her arrival had only come to light far too late to do anything about it.

Serena DePiero. Just her name brought an acrid taste of poison to his mouth. And yet the image that accompanied her name was anything but poisonous. It was provocative. It was his first image of her in that night-club in Florence.

He'd known who she was, of course. No one could have gone to Florence and *not* known who the DePiero sisters were—famed for their light-haired, blue-eyed aristocratic beauty and their vast family fortune that stretched back to medieval times. Serena had been the media's darling. Despite her debauched existence, no matter what she did, they'd lapped it up and bayed for more.

Her exploits had been legendary: high-profile weekends in Rome, leaving hotels trashed and staff incandescent with rage. Whirlwind private jet trips to the Middle East on the whim of an equally debauched sheikh who fancied a party with his Eurotrash friends. And always pictured in various states of inebriation and loucheness that had only seemed to heighten her dazzling appeal.

The night he'd seen her she'd been in the middle of the dance floor in what could only be described as an excuse for a dress. Strapless gold lamé, with tassels barely covering the top of her toned golden thighs. Long white-blonde hair tousled and falling down her back and over her shoulders, brushing the enticing swell of a voluptuous cleavage. Her peers had jostled around her, vying for her attention, desperately trying to emulate her golden exclusiveness.

With her arms in the air, swaying to the hedonistic beat of music played by some world-class DJ, she had symbolised the very font of youth and allure and beauty. The kind of beauty that made grown men fall to their knees in wonder. A siren's beauty, luring them to their doom.

Luca's mouth twisted. He'd proved to be no better than any other mortal man when she'd lured him to his doom. He took responsibility for being in that club—

of course he did. But from the moment she'd sashayed over to stand in front of him everything had grown a little hazy. And Luca was not a person who got hazy. No matter how stunning the woman. His whole life was about being clear and focused, because he had a lot to achieve.

But her huge bright blue eyes had seared him alive, igniting every nerve-ending, blasting aside any concerns. Her skin was flawless, her aquiline nose a testament to her breeding. Her mouth had fascinated him. Perfectly sculpted lips. Not too full, not too thin, effortlessly hinting at a dark and sexy sensuality.

She'd said coquettishly, 'It's rude to stare, you know.'

And instead of turning on his heel in disgust at her reputation and her arrogance, Luca had felt the blood flow through his body, hardening it, and he'd drawled softly, 'I'd have to be blind not to be dazzled. Join me for a drink?'

She'd tossed her head and for a second Luca had thought he glimpsed something curiously vulnerable and weary in those stunning blue eyes, but it had to have been a trick of the strobing lights, because then she'd purred, 'I'd love to.'

The wisps of memory faded from Luca's mind. He hated it that even now, just thinking of her, was having an effect on his body. Seven years had passed, and yet he felt as enflamed by anger and desire as he had that night. A bruising, humiliating mix.

He'd just left Serena DePiero in no doubt as to what he thought of her. She'd effectively been fired from her job. So why wasn't there a feeling of triumph rushing through him? Why was there an unsettling, prickling feeling of...unfinished business?

And why was there the tiniest grudging sliver of admiration for the way she had not backed down from him and the way that small chin had tipped up ever so slightly just before she'd left?

CHAPTER TWO

THE HOTEL WAS a few blocks back from Copacabana beach. To say that it was basic was an understatement, but it was clean—which was the main thing. And cheap—which was good, considering Serena was living off her meagre savings from the last year. She took off her travelling clothes, which were well creased by now, and stepped into the tiny shower, relishing the luke-warm spray.

Her belly clenched minutely when she imagined Luca's reaction to her *not* leaving Rio but she pushed it aside. She'd been standing in line for the check-in when her sister had phoned her. Too heartsore to admit that she was coming home so soon, and suddenly aware that Athens didn't even really feel like home, Serena had made a spur-of-the-moment decision to tell a white lie and pretend everything was okay.

And, even though she'd hated lying—to her sister, of all people—she didn't regret it now. She was still angry at Luca Fonseca's easy dismissal of her, the way he'd toyed with her before kicking her out of his office.

It had been enough to propel her out of the airport and back into the city. She scrubbed her scalp with un-necessary force, not liking how turbulent her emotions still were after meeting him again, and she certainly didn't like admitting that he'd roused her to a kind of anger she hadn't felt in a long time. Angry enough to rebel...when she'd thought she'd left all that behind her.

When she emerged from the bathroom she had a towel hitched around her body and another one on her head, and was feeling no less disgruntled. She almost jumped out of her skin when a loud, persistent knocking came on her door.

Scrambling around to find something to put on, Serena called out to whoever it was to wait a second as she pulled on some underwear and faded jeans and a T-shirt. The towel fell off her head so her long hair hung damply down her back and over her shoulders.

She opened the door and it was as if someone had punched her in the stomach. She couldn't draw breath because Luca Fonseca was standing there, eyes shooting sparks at her, looking angrier than she'd ever seen him.

'What the hell are you doing here, DePiero?' he snarled.

Serena answered faintly, 'You seem to be asking me that a lot lately.'

And then the fright he'd just given her faded and the anger she'd been harbouring swelled back. Her hand gripped the door.

'Actually, I might ask the same of you—what the hell are *you* doing *here*, Fonseca?' Something occurred to her. 'And how on earth did you even know where I was?'

His mouth was a tight line. 'I told Sancho, my driver, to wait at the airport and make sure you got on the flight.'

The extent of how badly he'd wanted her gone hit

her. Her hand gripped the door even tighter. 'This is a free country, Fonseca. I decided to stay and do a little sightseeing, and as I no longer work for you I really don't think you have any jurisdiction here.'

She went to close the door in his face but he easily stopped her and stepped into the room, closing the door behind him and forcing her to take a step back.

His arctic gaze took in her appearance with derision and Serena crossed her arms over her braless chest, self-conscious.

'Mr Fonseca—'

'Enough with the *Mr Fonseca*. Why are you still here, Serena?'

His use of her name made something swoop inside her. She crossed her arms tighter. It reminded her bizarrely of how it had felt to kiss him in the middle of that dance floor. Dark and hot and intoxicating. No other man's kiss or touch had ever made her feel like that. She'd pulled back from him in shock, as if his kiss had incinerated her, right through to where she was still whole. *Herself.*

'Well?'

The curt question jarred Serena back to the present and she hated it that she'd remembered that feeling of exposure.

'I want to see Rio de Janeiro before going home.' As if she would confide that she also wanted to delay revealing the extent of her failure to her family for as long as possible.

Luca snorted indelicately. 'Do you have *any* idea where you are? Were you planning on taking a stroll along the beach later?'

Serena gritted her jaw. 'I was, actually. I'd invite

you to join me, but I'm sure you have better things to be doing.'

His sheer animal magnetism was almost overwhelming in the small space. The beard and his longer hair only added to his intense masculinity. Her skin prickled with awareness. She could feel her nipples tighten and harden against the barrier of her thin T-shirt and hated the unique way this man affected her above any other.

Luca was snarling again. 'Do you realise that you're in one of the most dangerous parts of Rio? You're just minutes from one of the worst *favelas* in the city.'

Serena resisted the urge to point out that that should please him. 'But the beach is just blocks away.'

Now he was grim. 'Yes, and no one goes near this end of the beach at night unless they're out to score some drugs or looking to get mugged. It's one of the most dangerous places in the city after dark.'

He stepped closer and his eyes narrowed on her speculatively.

'But maybe that's it? You're looking for some recreational enhancement? Maybe your family have you under their watch and you're relishing some freedom? Have you even told them you've been fired?'

Serena's arms fell to her sides and she barely noticed Luca's gaze dropping to her chest before coming up again. All she felt was an incredible surge of anger and hatred for this man and his perspicacity—even if it wasn't entirely accurate.

Disgusted at the part of her that wanted to try and explain herself to him, she spat out, 'What's the point?'

She stalked around Luca and reached for the door handle, but before she could turn it and open the door an arm came over her head, keeping the door shut. She turned and folded her arms again, glaring up at Luca, conscious of her bare feet and damp hair, trying desperately not to let his sheer physicality affect her.

'If you don't leave in five seconds I'll start screaming.'

Luca kept his arm on the door, semi caging Serena in. 'The manager will just assume we're having fun. You can't be so naive that you didn't notice this place rents rooms by the hour.'

Serena felt hot. First of all at thinking of this man making her scream with pleasure and then at her own naivety.

'Of course I didn't,' she snapped, feeling vulnerable. She scooted out from under Luca's arm and put some space between them.

Luca crossed his arms. 'No, I can imagine you didn't. After all, it's not what you're used to.'

Serena thought of the Spartan conditions of the rehab facility she'd been in in England for a year, and then of her tiny studio apartment in a very insalubrious part of Athens. She smiled sweetly. 'How would you know?'

Luca scowled then. 'You're determined to stay in Rio?'

Never more so than right now. Even if just to annoy this man. 'Yes.'

Luca looked as though he would cheerfully throttle her. 'The last thing I need right now is some eagle-eyed reporter spotting you out and about, clubbing or shopping.'

Serena bit back a sharp retort. He had no idea what her life was like now. Clubbing? Shopping? She couldn't imagine anything worse.

Her smile got even sweeter. 'I'll wear a Louis Vuitton bag over my head while I go shopping for the latest Chanel suit. Will that help?'

That didn't go down well. Blood throbbed visibly in Luca's temple. 'You leaving Rio would be an even bigger help.'

Serena unconsciously mimicked his wide-legged stance. 'Well, unless you're planning on forcibly removing me, that's not going to happen. And if you even try such a thing I'll call the police and tell them you're harassing me.'

Luca didn't bother to tell her that with far greater problems in the city the police would no doubt just ogle her pale golden beauty before sending her on her way. And that such a stunt would only draw the interest of the paparazzi, who followed him most days.

The very thought of her being spotted, identified and linked to him was enough to make him go cold inside. He'd had enough bad press and innuendo after what had happened in Italy to last him a lifetime.

An audacious idea was being formulated in his head. It wasn't one he particularly relished, but it seemed like the only choice he had right now. It would get Serena DePiero out of Rio more or less immediately, and hopefully out of Brazil entirely within a couple of days.

'You said earlier that you were looking for another chance? That you'd do anything?'

Serena went very still, those huge blue eyes narrowing on him. Irritation made Luca's skin feel tight. The room was too small. All he could see was her. When she'd dropped her arms his eyes had tracked hungrily to her breasts, and he could still recall the jut of those hard nipples against her T-shirt. She was naked underneath.

Blood pooled at his groin, making him hard. *Damn.*

'Do you want a chance or not?' he growled, angry at his unwarranted response. Angry that she was still here.

Serena blinked. 'Yes, of course I do.'

Her voice had become husky and it had a direct effect on Luca's arousal. This was a mistake—he knew it. But he had no choice. Damage limitation.

Tersely, he said, 'I run an ethical mining company. I'm due to visit the Iruwaya mines, and the tribe that lives near there, to check on progress. You can prove your commitment by coming with me, instead of the assistant I'd lined up, to take notes. The village is part of the global communities network, so it's not entirely unrelated.'

'Where is the village?'

'Near Manaus.'

Serena's eyes widened. 'The city in the middle of the Amazon?'

Luca nodded. Perhaps this would be all it would take? Just the thought of doing something vaguely like hard work would have her scrambling back. Giving in. Leaving.

As if to mock his line of thought, Serena looked at him with those huge blue eyes and said determinedly, 'Fine. When do we go?'

Her response surprised Luca—much as the fact that she'd chosen this rundown flea-pit of a hotel had surprised him. He'd expected her to check into one of Rio's five-star resorts. But then he'd figured that perhaps her family had her on a tight leash where funds were concerned.

Whatever. He cursed himself again for wondering about her and said abruptly, 'Tomorrow. My driver will pick you up at five a.m.'

Once again he expected her to balk, but she didn't. He swept his gaze over the minor explosion of clothes from her suitcase and the toiletries spread across the narrow bed. The fact that her scent was clean and sweet, at odds with the sultry, sexy perfume he remembered from before, was not a welcome observation.

He looked back to her. 'I'll have an assistant stop by with supplies for the trip within the hour. You won't be able to bring your case.'

That gaze narrowed again. Suspicious. 'Supplies?'

Luca faced her squarely and said, with only the slightest twinge to his conscience, 'Oh, didn't I mention that we would be trekking through the jungle to get to the village? It takes two days from the farthest outskirts of Manaus.'

Those blue eyes flashed. 'No,' she responded. 'You didn't mention that we would be trekking through the jungle. Is it even safe?'

Luca smiled, enjoying the thought of Serena bailing after half an hour of walking through the earth's largest insect and wildlife-infested hothouse. He figured that after her first brush with one of the Amazon's countless insect or animal species she'd give up the act. But for now he'd go along with it. Because if he didn't she'd be a loose cannon in Rio de Janeiro. A ticking publicity time bomb. At least this way she'd have to admit defeat and go of her own free will.

He made a mental note to have a helicopter standing by to extract her and take her to the airport.

'It's eminently safe, once you have a guide who knows what they're doing and where they're going.'

'And that's you?' she said flatly.

'Yes. I've been visiting this tribe for many years, and

exploring the Amazon for a lot longer than that. You couldn't be in safer hands.'

The look Serena shot him told him that she doubted that. His smile grew wider and he arched a brow. 'By all means you can say no, Serena, it's entirely up to you.'

She made a derisive sound. 'And if I say no you'll personally escort me to the airport, no doubt.'

She stopped and bit her lip for a moment, making Luca's awareness of her spike.

'But if I do this, and prove my commitment, will you let me take up the job I came for?'

Luca's smile faded and he regarded her. Once again that tiny grudging admiration reared its head. He ruthlessly crushed it.

'Well, as I'm almost certain you won't last two hours in the jungle it's a moot point. All this is doing is delaying your inevitable return home.'

Her chin lifted and her arms tightened over her chest. 'It'll take more than a trek and some dense vegetation to put me off, Fonseca.'

The early-morning air was sultry, and the dawn hadn't yet broken, so it was dark when Serena got out of the back of the chauffeur-driven car at the private airfield almost twelve hours later. The first person she saw was the tall figure of Luca, carrying bags into a small plane. Instantly her nerves intensified.

He barely glanced at her as she walked over behind the driver, who carried the new backpack she'd been furnished with. And then his dark gaze fell on her and her heart sped up.

'You checked out of the hotel?'

Good morning to you too, Serena said silently, and

cursed her helpless physical reaction. 'Yes. And my suitcase is in the car.'

Luca took her small backpack from the driver and exchanged a few words with him in rapid Portuguese. Then, as the driver walked away, Luca said, 'Your things will be left at my headquarters until you get back.'

The obvious implication of *you*—not *we*—was not lost on Serena, and she said coolly, 'I won't be bailing early.'

Luca looked at her assessingly and Serena was conscious of the new clothes and shoes she'd been given. Lightweight trousers and a sleeveless vest under a khaki shirt. Sturdy trekking boots. Much like what Luca was wearing, except his looked well worn, faded with time. Doing little to hide his impressive muscles and physique.

She cursed. Why did he have to be the one man who seemed to connect with her in a way she'd never felt before?

Luca, who had turned back to the plane, said over his shoulder, 'Come on, we have a flight slot to make.'

'Aye-aye, sir,' Serena muttered under her breath as she hurried after him and up the steps into the small plane. She was glad that she'd pulled her hair up into a knot on top of her head as she could already feel a light sweat breaking out on the back of her neck.

Luca told her to take a seat. He shut the heavy door and secured it.

As Serena was closing her seatbelt she saw him take his seat in the cockpit and gasped out loud, *'You're* the pilot?'

'Evidently,' he said drily.

Serena's throat dried. 'Are you even qualified?'

He was busy flicking switches and turning knobs. He threw back over his shoulder, 'Since I was eighteen. Relax, Serena.'

He put on a headset then, presumably to communicate with the control tower, and then they were taxiing down the runway. Serena wasn't normally a nervous flyer, but her hands gripped the armrests as the full enormity of what was happening hit her. She was on a plane, headed into the world's densest and most potentially dangerous ecosystem, with a man who hated her guts.

She had a vision of a snake, dropping out of a tree in front of her face, and shivered in the dry cabin air just as the small plane left the ground and soared into the dawn-filled sky. Unfortunately her spirits didn't soar with it, but she comforted herself that at least she wasn't arriving back in Athens with her tail between her legs...just yet.

Serena was very aware of Luca's broad-shouldered physique at the front of the plane, but as much as she wanted to couldn't quite drum up the antipathy she wanted to feel for him. After all, he had good reason to believe what he did about her—that she'd framed him.

Anyone else would have believed the same...except for her sister, who had just looked at her with that sad expression that had reminded Serena of how trapped they both were by their circumstances—and by Serena's helpless descent into addiction to block out the pain.

Their father had simply been too powerful. And Siena had been too young for Serena to try anything drastic like running away. By the time Siena had come of age Serena had been in no shape to do anything drastic. Their father had seen to that effectively. And they'd been too well known. Any attempt to run would have been ended within hours, because their father would have sent his goons after them. They'd been bound as effectively as if their father had locked them in a tower.

'*Serena.*'

Serena's attention came back to the small plane and she looked forward, to see Luca staring back to her impatiently. He must have called her a couple of times. She felt raw from her memories.

'What?'

'I was letting you know that the flight will take four hours.' He pointed to a bag on the floor near her and said, 'You'll find some information in there about the tribe and the mines. You should read up on them.'

He turned back to the front and Serena restrained herself from sticking her tongue out at him. She'd been bullied and controlled by one man for most of her life and she chafed at the thought of giving herself over to that treatment again.

As she dug for the documents she reiterated to herself that this was a means to an end. She'd chosen to come here with Luca, and she was going to get through it in one piece and prove herself to him if it was the last thing she did. She'd become adept in the past few years in focusing on the present, not looking back. And she'd need that skill now more than ever.

Just over four hours later Serena was feeling a little more in control of herself, and her head was bursting with information about where they were going. She was already fascinated and more excited about the trip, which felt like a minor victory in itself.

They'd landed in a private part of the airport and after a light breakfast, which had been laid out for them in a private VIP room, Luca was now loading bags and supplies into the back of a Jeep.

His backpack was about three times the size of hers. And there were walking poles. Nerves fluttered in Serena's belly. Maybe she was being really stupid. How on earth was she going to last in the jungle? She was a city girl... That was the jungle she understood and knew how to navigate.

Luca must have caught her expression and he arched a questioning brow. Instantly fresh resolve filled Serena and she marched forward. 'Is there anything I can do?'

He shut the Jeep's boot door. 'No, we're good. Let's go—we don't have all day.'

A short time later, as Luca navigated the Manaus traffic, which eventually got less crazy as they hit the suburbs, he delivered a veritable lecture to Serena on safety in the jungle.

'And whatever you do obey my commands. The jungle is perceived to be a very hostile environment, but it doesn't have to be—as long as you use your head and you're constantly on guard and aware of what's around you.'

A devil inside Serena prompted her to say, 'Are you always this bossy or is it just with me?'

To her surprise Luca's mouth lifted ever so slightly on one side, causing a reaction of seismic proportions in Serena's belly.

That dark navy glance slid to her for a second and he drawled, 'I instruct and people obey.'

Serena let out a small sound of disdain. That had

been her father's philosophy too. 'That must make life very boring.'

The glimmer of a smile vanished. 'I find that people are generally compliant when it's in their interests to gain something…as you yourself are demonstrating right now.'

There was an unmistakably cynical edge to his voice that had Serena's gaze fixed on his face. Not liking the fact that she'd noticed it, and wondering about where such cynicism stemmed from, she said, 'You offered me a chance to prove my commitment. That's what I'm doing.'

He shrugged one wide shoulder. 'Exactly my point. You have something to gain.'

'Do I, though?' Serena asked quietly, but Luca either didn't hear or didn't think it worth answering. Clearly the answer was *no*.

They were silent for the rest of the journey. Soon they'd left the city behind, and civilisation was slowly swallowed by greenery until they were surrounded by it. It gave Serena a very real sense of how ready the forest seemed to be to encroach upon its concrete rival given half a chance.

Her curiosity overcame her desire to limit her interaction with Luca. 'How did you become interested in these particular mines?'

One of his hands was resting carelessly on the wheel, the other on his thigh. He was a good driver—unhurried, but fast. In control. He looked at her and she felt very conscious of being in a cocoon-like atmosphere with nothing but green around them.

He returned his attention to the road. 'My grandfather opened them up when prospectors found bauxite.

The area was plundered, forest cleared, and the native Indians moved on to allow for a camp to be set up. It was the first of my family's mines…and so the first one that I wanted to focus on to try and undo the damage.'

Serena recalled what she'd read. 'But you're still mining?'

He frowned at her and put both hands on the wheel, as if that reminder had angered him. 'Yes, but on a much smaller scale. The main camp has already been torn down. Miners commute in and out from a nearby town. If I was to shut down the mine completely it would affect the livelihoods of hundreds of people. I'd also be doing the workers out of government grants for miners, education for their children, and so on. As it is, we're using this mine as a pilot project to develop ethical mining so that it becomes the standard.'

He continued. 'The proceeds are all being funnelled into restoring huge swathes of the forest that were cleared—they'll never be restored completely, but they can be used for other ends, and the native Indians who were taken off the land have moved back to farm that land and make a new living from it.'

'It sounds like an ambitious project.' Serena tried not to feel impressed. Her experience with her father had taught her that men could be masters in the art of altruism while hiding a soul so corrupt and black it would make the devil look like Mickey Mouse.

Luca glanced at her and she could see the fire of intent in his eyes—something she'd never seen in her father's eyes unless it was for his own ends. Greedy for more power. Control. Causing pain.

'It is an ambitious project. But it's my responsibility. My grandfather did untold damage to this country's natural habitat and my father continued his reckless destruction. I refuse to keep perpetuating the same mistake. Apart from anything else, to do so is to completely ignore the fact that the planet is intensely vulnerable.'

Serena was taken aback at the passion in his voice. Maybe he *was* genuine.

'Why do you care so much?'

He tensed, and she thought he wouldn't answer, but then he said, 'Because I saw the disgust the native Indians and even the miners had for my father and men like him whenever I went with him to visit his empire. I started to do my own research at a young age. I was horrified to find out the extent of the damage we were doing—not only to our country but on a worldwide scale—and I was determined to put an end to it.'

Serena looked at his stern profile, unable to stem her growing respect. Luca was turning the Jeep into an opening that was almost entirely hidden from view. The track was bumpy and rough, the huge majestic trees of the rainforest within touching distance now.

After about ten minutes of solid driving, deeper and deeper into the undergrowth, they emerged into a large clearing where a two-storey state-of-the-art facility was revealed, almost completely camouflaged to blend with the surroundings.

Luca brought the Jeep to a halt alongside a few other vehicles. 'This is our main Amazon operational research base. We have other smaller ones in different locations.' He looked at her before he got out of the Jeep. 'You should take this opportunity to use the facilities while we still have them.'

Serena wanted to scowl at the very definite glint of mockery in his eyes but she refused to let him see the flicker of trepidation she felt once again, when confronted with the reality of their awe-inspiring surroundings.

She was mesmerised by the dense foliage around them. She had that impression again that the forest was being held back by sheer will alone, as if given the slightest chance it would extend its roots and vines and overtake this place.

'Serena?'

Frowning impatiently, Luca was holding open the main door.

She walked in and he pointed down a corridor.

'The bathroom is down there. I'll meet you back here.'

When Serena found the bathroom and saw her own reflection in dozens of mirrors, she grimaced. She looked flushed and sweaty, and was willing to bet that if she made it to the end of the day she'd look a lot worse.

After throwing some water on her face and tying her hair back into a more practical plait she headed back, nerves jumping around in her belly at the prospect of the battle of wills ahead and her determination not to falter at the first hurdle.

When Serena joined Luca back outside he handed her the backpack. There was a long rubber hose coming from the inside of it to sit over one shoulder. He saw her look at it.

'That's your water supply. Sip little and often; we'll replenish it later.'

She put the pack on and secured it around her waist and over her chest. She was relieved to find that it didn't feel too heavy at all. And then she saw the size of

Luca's pack, which obviously held all their main supplies and had a tent rolled up at the bottom.

Her eyes widened when she saw what looked suspiciously like a gun in a holster on his waist. He saw her expression and commented drily, 'It's a tranquilliser gun.' He sent a thorough glance up and down her body and remarked, 'Tuck your trousers into your socks and make sure your shirtsleeves are down and the cuffs closed.'

Feeling more and more nervous, Serena did as he said. When she looked at him again, feeling like a child about to be inspected in her school uniform, he was cocking a dark brow over those stunning eyes.

'Are you sure about this? Now would be a really good time to say no, if that's your intention.'

Serena put her hands on her hips and hid every one of her nerves behind bravado. 'I thought you said we don't have all day?'

CHAPTER THREE

A COUPLE OF hours later Serena was blindingly aware only of stepping where Luca stepped—which was a challenge, when his legs were so much longer. Her breath was wheezing in and out of her straining lungs. Rivers of sweat ran from every pore in her body.

She was soaked through. And it was no consolation to see sweat patches showing on Luca's body too, because they only seemed to enhance his impressive physicality.

She hadn't known what to expect, what the rainforest would be like, but it was more humid than she'd ever imagined it could be. And it was *loud*. Screamingly loud. With about a dozen different animal and bird calls at any time. She'd looked up numerous times to see a glorious flash of colour as some bird she couldn't name flew past, and had once caught sight of monkeys high in the canopy, loping lazily from branch to branch.

It was an onslaught on her senses, and Serena longed to stop for a minute to try and assimilate it all, but she didn't dare say a word to Luca, who hadn't stopped since he strode into the jungle, expecting her to follow him. He'd sent only the most cursory of glances back—presumably to make sure she hadn't been dragged into the dense greenery by one of mythical beasts that were running rampant in her imagination.

Every time the undergrowth rustled near her she sped up a little. Consequently, when Luca stopped suddenly and turned, Serena almost ran into him and skidded to a halt only just in time.

She noticed belatedly that they were on the edge of a clearing. It was almost a relief to get out of the oppressive atmosphere of the forest and suck in some breaths. She put her hands on her hips and hoped she didn't look as if she was about to burst a blood vessel.

Luca extracted something from a pocket in his trousers. It looked like a slightly old-fashioned mobile phone, a little larger than the current models.

'This is a satellite phone. I can call the chopper and it'll be here in fifteen minutes. This is your last chance to walk away.'

On the one hand Serena longed for nothing more than to see the horizon fill up with a cityscape again. And to feel the blast of clean, cool water on her skin. She was boiling. Sweating. And her muscles were burning. But, perversely, she'd never felt more energised, in spite of the debilitating heat. And, apart from anything else, she had a fierce desire to show no weakness to this man. He was the only thing that stood between her and independence.

'I'm not going anywhere, Luca.'

A glimpse of something distinctly like surprise crossed his face, and a dart of pleasure made Serena stand tall. Even that small indication that she was proving to be not as easy a pushover as he'd clearly expected was enough to keep her rooted to the spot.

He looked down then, his attention taken by something, and then back up at her. A very wicked hint of a smile was playing about his mouth as he said, with a pointed look towards her feet, 'Are you absolutely sure?'

Serena looked down and her whole body froze with fear and terror when she saw a small black scorpion crawling over the toe of her boot with its tail curled high over its arachnid body.

Without any previous experience of anything so potentially dangerous, Serena fought down the fear and took her walking pole and gently nudged the scorpion off her shoe. It scuttled off into the undergrowth. Feeling slightly light-headed at what she'd just done, she looked back at Luca.

'Like I said, I'm not going anywhere.'

Luca couldn't stem a flash of respect. Not many others would have reacted to seeing a scorpion like that with such equanimity. Men included. And any woman he knew would have used it as an excuse to hurl herself into his arms, squeaking with terror.

But Serena was staring him down. Blue eyes massive. Something in his chest clenched for a moment, making him short of breath. In spite of being sweaty and dishevelled, she was still stunningly beautiful. Helen of Troy beautiful. He could appreciate in that moment how men could be driven to war or driven mad because of the beauty of one woman.

But not him.

Not when he knew first-hand just how strong her sense of self-preservation was. Strong enough to let another take the fall for her own misdeeds.

'Fine,' he declared reluctantly. 'Then let's keep going.'

He turned his back on the provocative view of a flushed-faced Serena and strode back into the jungle.

Serena sucked in a few last deep breaths, relishing the cleared space for the last time, and then followed Luca, unable to stem the surge of triumph that he was letting her stay. And as she followed him she tried not to wince at the way her boots were pinching at her ankles and toes, pushing all thoughts of pain out of her head. Here, she couldn't afford to be weak. Luca would seize on it like a predator wearing its quarry down to exhaustion.

Serena felt as if she was floating above her body slightly. Pain was affecting so many parts of her that it had all coalesced into one throbbing beat of agony. Her backpack, which had been light that morning, now felt as if someone had been adding wet sand to it while she walked.

They'd stopped only briefly and silently for a few minutes while Luca had doled out a protein bar and some figs he'd pulled from a nearby tree—which had incidentally tasted delicious. And then they'd kept going.

Her feet were mercifully numb after going through the pain barrier some time ago. Her throat was parched, no matter how much water she sipped, and her legs were like jelly. But Luca's pace was remorseless. And Serena was loath to call out with so much as a whisper.

And then he stopped, suddenly, and looked around him, holding up a compass. He glanced back at her and said, 'Through here—stick close to me.'

She followed where he led for a couple of minutes, and then cannoned into his backpack and gave a little yelp of surprise when he stopped again abruptly. He turned and steadied her with his big hands. Serena hadn't even realised she was swaying until he did that.

'This is the camp.'

Serena blinked. Luca took his hands away and she
didn't like how aware she was of that lack of touch.

Afraid he might see something she didn't want him
to, she stepped back.

'Camp?'

She looked around and saw a small but obviously
well-used clearing. She also noticed belatedly that the
cacophony that had accompanied them all day had si-
lenced now, and it was as if an expectant hush lay over
the whole forest. The intense heat was lessening slightly.

'It's so quiet.'

'You won't be saying that in about half an hour, when
the night chorus starts up.' He was unloading his backpack and said over his shoulder, 'Take yours off too.'

Serena let it drop from her aching body and almost
cried out with the relief. She felt as though she might
lift right out of the forest now that the heavy weight
was gone.

Luca was down on his haunches, extracting things
from his bag, and the material of his trousers was drawn
taut over his powerful thighs. Serena found it hard to
drag her gaze away, not liking the spasm of awareness
in her lower belly.

He was unrolling the tent, which looked from where
Serena was standing alarmingly *small*. Oblivious to her
growing horror, Luca efficiently erected the lightweight
structure with dextrous speed.

When the full enormity of its intimate size sank in,
Serena said in a hoarse voice, 'We're not sleeping in
that.'

Luca looked up from where he was driving a stake
into the ground with unnecessary force. 'Oh, yes, *we*
are, *minha beleza*—that is unless you'd prefer to take

your chances sleeping al fresco? Jaguars are prevalent in this area. I'm sure they'd enjoy feasting on your fragrant flesh.'

Tension, fear and panic at the thought of sharing such a confined space with him spiked in Serena as Luca straightened up. She put her hands on her hips. 'You're lying.'

Luca looked at her, impossibly dark and dangerous. 'Do you really want to take that chance?' He swept an arm out. 'By all means be my guest. But if the jaguars don't get you any number of thousands of insects will do the job—not to mention bats. While you're thinking about that I'm going to replenish our water supplies.'

He started to leave and then stopped.

'While I'm gone you could take out some tinned food and set up the camping stove.'

When he walked away Serena had to resist the cowardly urge to call out that she'd go with him. She was sure he was just scaring her. Even so, she looked around nervously and stuck close to the tent as she did as he'd instructed, muttering to herself under her breath about how arrogant he was.

When Luca returned, a short while later, Serena was standing by the tent, clearly waiting for his return with more than a hint of nervousness. He stopped in his tracks, hidden behind a tree. His conscience pricked him for having scared her before. And something else inside him sizzled. *Desire.*

His gaze wandered down and took in the clothes that were all but plastered to her body after a day of trekking through the most humid ecosystem on earth. Her body was clearly defined and she was all woman, with firm, generous breasts, a small waist and curvaceous hips.

The whole aim of bringing her here had been to make her run screaming in the opposite direction, as far away as possible from him, but she'd been with him all the way.

He could still recall the terror tightening her face when she'd seen the scorpion and yet she hadn't allowed it to rise. He'd pursued a punishing pace today, even for him, and yet every time he'd cast a glance back she'd been right there, on his heels, dogged, eyes down, assiduously watching where she stepped as he'd instructed. Sweat had dripped down over her jaw and neck, making him think of it trickling into the lush valley of her breasts, dewing her golden skin with moisture.

Damn her. He hated to admit that up to now he'd been viewing her almost as a temporary irritation—like a tick that would eventually fall off his skin and leave him alone—but she was proving to be annoyingly resilient. He certainly hadn't expected to be sharing his tent with her.

The Serena DePiero he'd pegged as a reckless and wild party girl out only for herself was the woman he'd expected. The one he'd expected to leave Rio de Janeiro as soon as she'd figured she was on a hiding to nothing.

But she hadn't left.

So who the hell was the woman waiting for him now, if she wasn't the spoiled heiress? And why did he even care?

Serena bit her lip. The light was fading fast and there was no sign of Luca returning. She felt intensely vulnerable right then, and never more aware of her puny insignificance in the face of nature's awesome grandeur and power. A grandeur that would sweep her aside in a second if it had half a chance.

And then the snap of a twig alerted her to his presence. He loomed out of the gloom, dark and powerful. Sheer, abject relief that she wasn't alone made her feel momentarily dizzy, before she reminded herself that she really hated him for scaring her earlier.

Luca must have caught something of her relief. 'Worried that I'd got eaten by a jaguar, princess?'

'One can but hope,' Serena said sweetly, and then scowled. 'And don't call me princess.'

Luca brushed past her and took in the camping stove, commenting, 'I see you can follow instructions, at least.'

Serena scowled even more, irritated that she'd done his bidding. Luca was now gathering up wood and placing it in a small clearing not far from the tent. Determined not to let him see how much he rattled her, she said perkily, 'Can I help?'

Luca straightened from dumping some wood. 'You could collect some wood—just make sure it's not alive before you pick it up.'

Serena moved around, carefully kicking pieces of twigs and wood before she picked anything up. One twig turned out to be a camouflaged beetle of some sort that scuttled off and almost made her yelp out loud.

When she looked to see if Luca had noticed, though, he was engrossed in building up an impressive base of large logs for the fire. It was dusk now, and the massive trees loomed like gigantic shadows all around them.

Serena became aware of the rising sound of the forest around them as the night shift of wildlife took over from the day shift. It grew and grew to almost deafening proportions—like a million crickets going off at once right beside her head before settling to a more harmonious hum.

She brought the last of the wood she'd collected over to the pile just as Luca bent down to set light to the fire, which quickly blazed high. Feeling was returning to her feet and they had started to throb painfully.

Luca must have seen something cross her face, because he asked curtly, 'What is it?'

With the utmost reluctance Serena said, 'It's just some blisters.'

Luca stood up. 'Come here—let me see them.'

The flickering flames made golden light dance over his shadowed face. For a second Serena was too transfixed to move. He was the most beautiful man she'd ever seen. With an effort she looked away. 'I'm sure it's nothing. Really.'

'Believe me, I'm not offering because I genuinely care what happens to you. If you have blisters and they burst then they could get infected in this humidity. And then you won't be able to walk, and I really don't plan on carrying you anywhere.'

Fire raced up Serena's spine. 'Well, when you put it so eloquently, I'd hate to become more of a burden than I already am.'

Luca guided her towards a large log near the fire. Sitting her down, he went down on his knees and pulled his bag towards him.

'Take off your boots.' His voice was gruff.

Serena undid her laces and grimaced as she pulled off the boots. Luca pulled her feet towards him, resting them on his thighs. The feel of rock-hard muscles under her feet made scarlet heat rush up through her body and bloom on her face.

She got out a strangled, 'What are you doing?'

Luca was curt. 'I'm trained as a medic—relax.'

Serena shut her mouth. She felt churlish; was there no end to his talents? She watched as he opened up a complicated-looking medical kit and couldn't help asking, 'Why did you train as a medic?'

He glanced at her swiftly before looking down again. 'I was on a visit to a village near a mine with my father when I was younger and a small boy started choking. No one knew what to do. He died right in front of us.'

Serena let out a breath. 'That's awful.'

A familiar but painful memory intruded before she could block it out. She'd seen someone die right in front of her too—it was seared onto her brain like a tattoo. Her defences didn't seem to be so robust here, in such close proximity to this man. She could empathise with Luca's helplessness and that shocked her...to feel an affinity.

Luca was oblivious to the turmoil being stirred up inside Serena with that horrific memory of her own. He continued. 'Not as awful as the fact that my father didn't let it stop him from moving the tribe on to another location, barely allowing the parents time to gather up their son's body. They were nothing to him—a problem to be got rid of.'

He was pulling down Serena's socks now, distracting her from his words and the bitterness she could hear in his voice. He sucked in a breath when he saw the angry raw blisters.

'That's my fault.'

Serena blinked. Had Luca just said that? And had he

sounded ever so slightly apologetic? Together with his obvious concern for others, it made her uncomfortable.

He looked at her, face unreadable. 'New boots. They weren't broken in. It's no wonder you've got blisters. You must have been in agony for hours.'

Serena shrugged minutely and looked away, self-conscious under his searing gaze. 'I'm no martyr, Luca. I just didn't want to delay you.'

'The truth is,' he offered somewhat sheepishly, 'I hadn't expected you to last this far. I would have put money on you opting out well before we'd even left Rio.'

Something light erupted inside Serena and for a moment their eyes met and locked. Her insides clenched hard and all she was aware of was how powerful Luca's muscles felt under her feet. He looked away then, to get something from the medical box, and the moment was broken. But it left Serena shaky.

His hands were big and capable. Masculine. But they were surprisingly gentle as he made sure the blisters were clean and then covered them with thick plasters.

He was pulling her socks back up over the dressings when he said, with an edge to his voice, 'You've said a couple of times that you didn't do drugs... You forget that I was there. I saw you.'

His blue gaze seemed to sear right through her and his question caught Serena somewhere very raw. For a moment she'd almost been feeling *soft* towards him, when he was the one who had marched her into the jungle like some kind of recalcitrant prisoner.

Anger and a sense of claustrophobia made her tense. He'd seen only the veneer of a car crash lifestyle which had hidden so much more.

She was bitter. 'You saw what you wanted to see.'

Serena avoided his eyes and reached for her boots, but Luca got there first. He shook them out and said tersely, 'You should always check to make sure nothing has crawled inside.'

Serena repressed a shudder at the thought of what that might be and stuck her feet back into the boots, but Luca didn't move away.

'What's that supposed to mean? *I saw what I wanted to see.*'

Getting angry at his insistence, she glared at him. The firelight cast his face into shadow, making him seem even more dark and brooding.

He arched a brow. 'I think I have a right to know— you owe me an explanation.'

Serena's chest was tight with some unnamed emotion. The dark forest around them made her feel as if nothing existed outside of this place.

Hesitantly, she finally said, 'I wasn't addicted to Class A drugs…I've never taken a recreational drug in my life.' She tried to block out the doubtful gleam in Luca's eyes. 'But I *was* addicted to prescription medication. And to alcohol. And I'll never touch either again.'

Luca finally moved back and frowned. Serena felt as if she could breathe again. Until he asked, 'How did you get addicted to medication?'

Serena's insides curdled. This came far too close to that dark memory and all the residual guilt and fear that had been a part of her for so long. At best Luca was mildly curious; at worst he hated her. She had no desire to seek his sympathy, but a rogue part of her wanted to knock his assumptions about her a little.

'I started taking prescribed medication when I was five.'

Luca's frown deepened. 'Why? You were a child.'

His clear scepticism made Serena curse herself for being so honest. This man would never understand if she was to tell him the worst of it all. So she feigned a lightness she didn't feel and fell back on the script that her father had written for her so long ago that she couldn't remember *normal*.

She gave a small shrug and avoided that laser-like gaze. 'I was difficult. After my mother died I became hard to control. By the time I was twelve I had been diagnosed with ADHD and had been on medication for years. I became dependent on it—I liked how it made me feel.'

Luca sounded faintly disgusted. 'And your father... he sanctioned this?'

Pain gripped Serena. He'd not only sanctioned it, he'd made sure of it. She shrugged again, feeling as brittle as glass, and smiled. But it was hard. She forced herself to look at Luca. 'Like I said, I was hard to control. Wilful.'

Disdain oozed from Luca. 'Why are you so certain you're free of the addiction now?'

She tipped her chin up unconsciously. 'When my sister and I left Italy, after my father...' She stalled, familiar shame coursing through her blood along with anger. 'When it all fell apart we went to England. I checked into a rehab facility just outside London. I was there for a year. Not that it's any business of yours,' she added, immediately regretting her impulse to divulge so much.

Luca's expression was indecipherable as he stood up, and he pointed out grimly, 'I think our personal history makes it my business. You need to prove to me you can be trusted—that you will not be a drain on resources and the energy of everyone around you.'

Boots on, Serena stood up in agitation, her jaw tight with hurt and anger. She held up a hand. 'Whoa— judgemental, much? And you base this on your vast knowledge of ex-addicts?'

His narrow-minded view made Serena see red. She put her hands on her hips.

'Well?'

Tension throbbed between them as they glared at each other for long seconds. And then Luca bit out, 'I base it on an alcoholic mother who makes checking in and out of rehab facilities a recreational pastime. That's how I have a unique insight into the addict's mind. And when she's not battling the booze or the pills she's chasing her next rich conquest to fund her lifestyle.'

Serena felt sick for a moment at the derision in his voice. The evidence of just how personal his judgement was appeared entrenched in bitter experience.

Luca stepped back. 'We should eat.'

Serena's anger dissipated as she watched Luca turn away abruptly to light the camping stove near the fire. She reeled with this new knowledge of his own experience. And reeled at how much she'd told him of herself with such little prompting. She felt relieved now that she hadn't spilled her guts entirely.

No wonder he'd come down on her like a ton of bricks and believed the worst. Still…it didn't excuse him. And she told herself fiercely that she *didn't* feel a tug of something treacherous at the thought of him coping with an alcoholic parent. After all, she still bore the guilt of her sister having to deal with *her*.

Suddenly, in light of that conversation, she felt too raw to sit in Luca's company and risk that insightful mind being turned on her again. And fatigue was creeping over her like a relentless wave.

'Don't prepare anything for me. I'm not feeling hungry. I think I'll turn in now.'

Luca looked up at her from over his shoulder. He seemed to bite back whatever he was going to say and shrugged. 'Suit yourself.'

Serena grabbed her backpack and went into the tent, relieved to see that it was more spacious inside than she might have imagined. She could only do a basic toilette, and after taking off her boots and rolling out her sleeping bag carefully on one side of the tent she curled up and dived into the exhausted sleep of oblivion.

Anything to avoid thinking about the man who had comprehensively turned her world upside down in the last thirty-six hours and come far too close to where she still had so much locked away.

CHAPTER FOUR

THE FOLLOWING MORNING Luca heard movement from
the tent and his whole body tensed. When he'd turned
in last night Serena had been curled up in a ball inside
her sleeping bag, some long hair trailing in tantalising golden strands around her head, her breathing deep
and even. And once again he'd felt the sting of his conscience at knowing she'd gone to bed with no food, and
her feet rubbed raw from new boots.

What she'd told him the previous evening had
shocked him. She'd been taking medication since she
was a child. Out of control even then. It was so at odds
with the woman she seemed to be now that he almost
couldn't believe it.

She'd sounded defiant when she'd told him that she'd
been addicted by the age of twelve. Something inside
him had recoiled with disgust at the thought. It was one
thing to have a mother who was an addict as an adult.
But a *child*?

Serena had given him the distinct impression that
even then she'd known what she was doing and had revelled in it. But even as he thought that, something about
the way she'd said it niggled at him. It didn't sit right.

Was she telling the truth?

Why would she lie after all this time? an inner voice pointed out. And if she hadn't ever done recreational drugs then maybe she really hadn't planted them on him that night… He didn't like the way the knowledge sank like a stone in his belly.

The crush and chaos of the club that night came back to him and a flash of a memory caught him unawares: Serena's hand slipping into his. He'd looked down at her and she'd been wide-eyed, her face pale. That had been just before the Italian police had separated them roughly and searched them.

The memory mocked him now. He'd always believed that look to have been Serena's guilt and pseudo-vulnerability, knowing what she'd just done. But if it hadn't been guilt it had been something far more ambiguous. It made him think of her passionate defence when he'd questioned her trustworthiness. And why on earth did that gnaw at him now? Making him feel almost guilty?

The flaps of the tent moved and the object of his thoughts emerged, blinking in the dawn light. She'd pulled her hair up into a bun on top of her head, and when that blue gaze caught his, Luca's insides tightened. He cursed her silently—and himself for bringing her here and putting questions into his head.

For possibly being innocent of the charges he'd levelled against her.

She straightened up and her gaze was wary. 'Morning.'

Her voice was sleep-rough enough to tug forcibly at Luca's simmering desire. She should look creased and dishevelled and grimy, but she looked gorgeous. Her skin was as dewy and clear as if she'd just emerged from a spa, not a night spent in a rudimentary tent in the middle of the jungle.

He thrust a bowl of protein-rich tinned food towards her. 'Here—eat this.'

There was the most minute flash of something in her eyes as she acknowledged his lack of greeting, but she took the bowl and a spoon and sat down on a nearby log to eat, barely wincing at the less than appetising meal. Yet another blow to Luca's firmly entrenched antipathy.

He looked at her and forced himself to ignore that dart of guilt he'd just felt—to remember that thanks to his mother's stellar example he knew all about the mercurial nature of addicts. How as soon as you thought they truly were intent on making a change they went and did the exact opposite. From a young age Luca had witnessed first-hand just how brutal that lack of regard could be and he'd never forgotten it.

Serena looked up at him. She'd finished her meal, and Luca felt slightly winded at the intensity of her gaze. He reached down and took the bowl and handed her a protein bar. His voice gruff, which irritated him, he said, 'Eat this too.'

'But I'm full now. I—'

Luca held it out and said tersely, 'Eat it, Serena. I can't afford for you to be weak. We have a long walk today.'

Serena's eyes flashed properly at that, and she stood up with smooth grace and took the bar from his outstretched hand. Tension bristled and crackled between them.

Serena cursed herself for thinking, *hoping* that some kind of a truce might have grown between them. And she cursed herself again for revealing what she had last night.

Luca was cleaning up the camp, packing things away, getting ready to move on. When she'd woken a while ago it had taken long seconds for her to realise where she was and with whom. A sense of exultation had rushed through her at knowing they were still in the jungle and that she'd survived the first day, that she hadn't shown Luca any weakness.

Then she'd remembered the gentleness of his hands on her feet and had felt hot. And then she'd got hotter, acknowledging that only extreme exhaustion had knocked her out enough to sleep through sharing such an intimate space with him.

Before Luca might see some of that heat in her expression or in her eyes, Serena busied herself with rolling up the sleeping bags and starting to take down the tent efficiently.

'Where did you learn to do that?' came Luca's voice, its tone incredulous.

Serena barely glanced at him, prickling. 'We used to go on camping trips while we were in rehab. It was part of the programme.'

She tensed, waiting for him to be derisive or to ask her about it, but he didn't. He just went and started unpegging the other side of the tent. Serena hadn't shared her experience of rehab with anyone—not even her sister. Even though her sister had been the one who had sacrificed almost everything to ensure Serena's care, working herself to the bone and putting herself unwittingly at the mercy of a man she'd betrayed years before and who had come looking for revenge.

Against the odds, though, Siena and Andreas had fallen in love and were now blissfully happy, with a toddler and a baby. Sometimes their intense happiness made Serena feel unaccountably alienated, and she hated herself for the weakness. But it was the same with her half-brother Rocco and his wife and children. If she'd never believed in love or genuine happiness theirs mocked her for it every time she saw them.

Without even realising it was done, she saw the camp was cleared and Luca was handing Serena her backpack.

He arched a brow. 'Ready?'

Serena took the pack and nodded swiftly, not wanting Luca to guess at the sudden vulnerability she felt to be thinking of her family and their very natural self-absorption.

She put on the pack and followed Luca for a few steps until he turned abruptly. 'How are your feet?'

Serena frowned and said, with some surprise, 'They're fine, actually.'

Luca made an indeterminate sound and carried on, and Serena tried not to fool herself that he'd asked out of any genuine concern.

As they walked the heat progressed and intensified to almost suffocating proportions. When they stopped briefly by a small stream in the afternoon Serena almost wept with relief to be able to throw some cool water over her face and head. She soaked a cloth handkerchief and tied it around her neck.

It was only a short reprieve. Luca picked up the punishing pace again, not even looking to see if Serena was behind him. Irritation rose up inside her. Would he even notice if she was suddenly pulled by some animal into the undergrowth? He'd probably just shrug and carry on.

After another hour any feeling of relief from the

stream was a distant memory and sweat dripped down her face, neck and back. Her limbs were aching, her feet numb again. Luca strode on, though, like some kind of robot, and suddenly Serena felt an urge to provoke him, needle him. Force him to stop and face her. Acknowledge that she had done well to last this far. Acknowledge that she might be telling the truth about the drugs.

She called out, 'So, are you prepared to admit that I might be innocent after all?'

She got her wish. Luca stopped dead in his tracks and then, after a long second, slowly turned around. His eyes were so dark they looked black. He covered the space between them so fast and silently that Serena took an involuntary step backwards, hating herself for the reflexive action.

He looked infinitely dangerous, and yet perversely Serena didn't feel scared. She felt something far more ambiguous and hotter, deep in her pelvis.

'To be quite frank, I don't think I even care any more whether or not you did it. The fact is that my involvement with you made things so much worse. *You* were enough to turn the incident into front-page news and put certainty into people's minds about my guilt—because they all believed that *you* did drugs, and that I was either covering for you or dealing to you. So, innocent bystander or not—as you might have been—I still got punished.'

Serena swallowed down a sudden and very unwelcome lump in her throat. She recognised uncomfortably that the need for this man to know she was innocent was futile or worse. 'You'll never forgive me for it, will you?'

His jaw clenched, and just then a huge drop of water landed on her face—so large that it splashed.

Luca looked up and cursed out loud.

'What? What is it?' Serena asked, her tension dissolving to be replaced by a tendril of fear.

Luca looked around them and bit out, 'Rain. *Damn.* I'd hoped to make the village first. We'll have to shelter. Come on.'

Even before he'd begun striding away again the rain was starting in earnest, those huge drops cascading from the sky above the canopy. Serena hurried after him to try and keep up. Within seconds, though, it was almost impossible to see a few feet in front of her nose. Genuine panic spiked. She couldn't see Luca any more. And then he reappeared, taking her hand, keeping her close.

The rain was majestic, awesome. Deafening. But Serena was only aware of her hand in Luca's. He was leading them through the trees, off the path to a small clearing. The ground was slightly higher here. He let her go and she saw him unrolling a tarpaulin. Catching on quickly, she took one end and tied it off to a nearby sapling while Luca did the same on the other side, creating a shelter a few feet off the ground.

He laid out another piece of tarpaulin under the one they'd tied off and shouted over the roar of the rain, 'Get underneath!'

Serena slipped off her pack and did so. Luca joined her seconds later. They were drenched. Steam was rising off their clothes. But they were out of the worst of the downpour. Serena was still taken aback at how quickly it had come down.

They sat like that, their breaths evening out, for

long minutes. Eventually she asked, 'How long will it last?'

Luca craned his neck to look out, his arms around his knees. He shrugged one wide shoulder. 'Could be minutes—could be hours. Either way, we'll have to camp out again tonight. The village is only a couple of hours away, but it'll be getting dark soon—too risky.'

At the thought of another night in the tent with Luca, flutters gripped Serena's abdomen. He was pulling something out of a pocket and handed her another protein bar. Serena reached for it with her palm facing up, but before she could take it Luca had grabbed her wrist and was frowning.

She was distracted by his touch for a moment—all she felt was *heat*—and then he was saying, 'What are those marks? Did you get them here?'

He was inspecting her palm and pulling her other hand towards him to look at that, too. Far too belatedly Serena panicked, and tried to pull them back, but he wouldn't let her, clearly concerned that it had happened recently.

She saw what he saw: the tiny criss-cross of old, silvery scars that laced her palms.

As if coming to that realisation, he said, 'They're old.' He looked at her, stern. '*How* old?'

Serena tried to jerk her hands away but he held them fast. Her breath was choppy now, with a surge of emotion. And with anger that he was quizzing her as if she'd done something wrong.

She said reluctantly, 'They're twenty-two years old.'

Luca looked at her, turning towards her. '*Deus*, what *are* they?'

Serena was caught by his eyes. They blazed into hers,

seeking out some kind of truth and justice—which she was coming to realise was integral to this man's nature. It made him see the world in black and white, good and bad. And she was firmly in the bad category as far as he was concerned.

But just for once, Serena didn't want to be. She felt tired. Her throat ached with repressed emotions, with all the horrific images she held within her head, known only to her and her father. And he'd done his best to eradicate them.

A very weak and rogue part of her wanted to tell Luca the truth—much like last night—in some bid to make him see that perhaps things weren't so black and white. And even though an inner voice told her to protect herself from his derision, she heard the words spill out.

'They're the marks of a bamboo switch. My father favoured physical punishment.'

Luca's hands tightened around hers and she held back a wince. His voice was low. 'How old were you?'

Serena swallowed. 'Five—nearly six.'

'What the hell….?'

Luca's eyes burned so fiercely for a moment that Serena quivered inwardly. She took advantage of the moment to pull her hands back, clasping them together, hiding the permanent stain of her father's vindictiveness.

Serena could understand Luca's shock. Her therapist had been shocked when she'd told *her*.

She shrugged. 'He was a violent man. If I stepped out of line, or if Siena misbehaved, I'd be punished.'

'You were a *child*.'

Serena looked at Luca and felt acutely exposed, recalling just how her childhood had been so spectacularly snatched away from her, by far worse than a few scars on her palms.

She noticed something then, and seized on it weakly. 'The rain—it's stopped.'

Luca just looked at her for a long moment, as if he hadn't ever seen her before. It made Serena nervous and jittery.

Eventually he said, 'We'll make camp here. Let's set it up.'

Serena scrambled inelegantly out from under their makeshift shelter. The jungle around them was steaming from the onslaught of precipitation. It was unbearably humid…and uncomfortably sultry.

As she watched, Luca uncoiled himself, and for a moment Serena was mesmerised by his sheer masculine grace. He looked at her too quickly for her to look away.

He frowned. 'What is it?'

Serena swallowed as heat climbed up her chest. She blurted out the first thing she could think of. 'Thirsty— I'm just thirsty.'

Luca glanced around them and then strode to a nearby tree and tested the leaves. 'Come here.'

Not sure what to expect, Serena walked over. Luca put a hand on her arm and it seemed to burn right through the material.

He manoeuvred her under the leaf and said, 'Tip your head back—open your mouth.'

Serena looked at him and something dark lit his eyes, making her belly contract.

'Come on. It won't bite.'

So she did, and Luca tipped the leaf so that a cascade of water fell into her mouth, cold and more refreshing than anything she'd ever tasted in her life. She coughed slightly when it went down the wrong way, but couldn't stop her mouth opening for more. The water trickled over her face, cooling the heat that had nothing to do with the humid temperature.

When there were only a few drops left, she straightened up again. Luca was watching her. They were close—close enough that all Serena would have to do would be to step forward and they'd be touching.

And then, as if reading her mind and rejecting her line of thought, Luca stepped back, letting her arm go. 'We need to change into dry clothes.'

He walked away and Serena felt ridiculously exposed and shaky. What was *wrong* with her?

Luca was taking clothes out of his pack. He straightened up and his hands went to his shirt, undoing the buttons with long fingers. A sliver of dark muscled chest was revealed, the shadow of chest hair. And Serena was welded to the spot. She couldn't breathe.

Finally sense returned. Her face hot with embarrassment, she hurried to her own bag and concentrated on digging out her own change of clothes. The last thing she needed was to let Luca Fonseca into the deepest recesses of her psyche. But, much to her irritation, she couldn't forget the way he'd looked when he'd held her hands out for inspection, or the look in his eyes just now, when she fancied she'd seen something carnal in their depths, only for him to mock her for her fanciful imagination.

Luca was feeling more and more disorientated as he pulled on fresh clothes with rough hands. *Deus.* He'd almost backed Serena into the tree just now and covered her open mouth with his, jealous of the rainwater trickling between those plump lips.

And what about those scars on her hands? The silvery marks criss-crossing the delicate pale skin? He hadn't been prepared for the surge of panic when he'd seen them—afraid she'd been marked by something on the trail—or the feeling of rage when she'd told him so flatly who had done it.

He'd met her father once or twice at social events and had never liked the man. He had cold, dead dark eyes, and the superior air of someone used to having everything he wanted.

He didn't like to admit it, but the knowledge that he'd been violent didn't surprise Luca. He could picture the man being vindictive. Malevolent. But to his own daughters? The blonde, blue-eyed heiresses everyone had envied?

Luca knew Serena was changing behind him. He could hear the soft sounds of clothes being taken off and dropped. And then there was silence for a long moment. Telling himself it was concern, but knowing that it stemmed from a much deeper desire, Luca turned around.

Her back was to him and her legs were revealed in all their long shapely glory as she stripped off her trousers. High-cut pants showed off a toned length of thigh. Firm but curvy buttocks. When she stripped down to her bra he wanted to go over and undo it, slip his hands around her front to cup the generous swells and feel her arch into him.

He was rewarded with a burgeoning erection within seconds—no better than a pre-teen ogling a woman dressing in a changing room.

The snap of her belt around her hips broke Luca out of his trance and, angry with himself, he turned away and pulled on his own trousers. The light was falling rapidly now, and Luca had been so fixated on Serena that he was risking not having the camp set up in time.

But when he turned around again, about to issue a curt command, the words died on his lips. To his surprise Serena was already unrolling the tent and staking it out, her long ponytail swinging over her shoulder.

He cursed her silently, because he was losing his footing with this woman—fast.

Serena was sitting on a log on the opposite side of the fire to Luca a short time later, after they'd eaten their meagre meal. The tent stood close by, and she couldn't stop a surge of ridiculous pride that she'd put it up herself. He'd expected her to flee back to civilisation at the slightest hint of work or danger, but here she was, day two and surviving—if not thriving. The feeling was heady, and it made her relish her newfound independence even more.

However, none of that could block out the mortification when she thought of earlier and how close she'd come to betraying her desire for him...

She caught Luca's eye across the flickering light of the fire and he asked, 'What's the tattoo on your back?'

She went still. He must have seen the small tattoo that sat just above her left shoulderblade earlier, when she'd been changing. The thought of him looking at her made her feel hot.

The tattoo was so personal to her, she didn't want to tell him. Reluctantly, she finally said, 'It's a swallow. The bird.'

'Any significance?'

Serena almost laughed. As if she'd divulge *that* to him! He'd definitely fall off his log laughing.

She shrugged. 'It's my favourite bird. I got it done a few years ago.' *The day she'd walked out of the rehab clinic, to be precise.*

She avoided Luca's gaze. Swallows represented resurrection and rebirth... Luca would hardly look that deeply into its significance, but still... She had the uncanny sense that he might and she didn't like it.

She really wanted to avoid any more probing into her life or her head. She stood up abruptly, making Luca look up, his dark gaze narrowing on her. 'I'm going to turn in now.' She sounded too husky. Even now her body trembled with awareness, just from looking at his large rangy form relaxed.

Luca stirred the fire, oblivious to her heated imaginings. 'I'll let you get settled.'

Serena turned away and crawled into the tent, pulling off her boots, but leaving her clothes on. Then she felt silly. Luca hadn't given her the slightest hint that he felt any desire for her whatsoever, and she longed to feel cooler. She took off her shirt and stripped down to her panties, and pulled the sleeping bag around her.

She prayed that sleep would come as it had last night, like a dark blanket of oblivion, so she wouldn't have to hear Luca come in and deal with the reality that he slept just inches away from her and probably resented every moment.

Luca willed his body to cool down. He didn't like how off-centre Serena was pushing him. Making him desire her; wonder about her. Wanting to know more. She was surprising him.

He'd been exposed to the inherent selfishness of his mother and women in general from a very early age, so it was not a welcome sensation thinking that he might have misjudged her.

Lovers provided him with physical relief and an escort when he needed it. But his life was not about women, or settling down. He had too much to do to undo all the harm his father and grandfather had caused. He had set himself a mammoth task when his father had died ten years ago: to reverse the negative impact of the name Fonseca in Brazil, which up till then had been synonymous with corruption, greed and destruction.

The allegations of his drug-taking had come at the worst possible time for Luca—just when people had been beginning to sit up and trust that perhaps he *was* different and genuine about making a change. It was only now that he was back in that place.

And the person who could reverse all his good work was only feet away from him. He had to remember that. Remember who she was and what she had the power to do to him. Even if she *was* innocent, any association with her would incite all that speculation again.

Only when Luca felt sure that Serena must be asleep did he turn in himself, doing his best to ignore the curled-up shape inside the sleeping bag that was far too close to his for comfort. He'd really *not* expected to have to share this tent with anyone, and certainly not with Serena DePiero for a second night in a row.

But as he lay down beside her he had to acknowledge uncomfortably that there was no evidence of the spoilt ex-wild-child. There wasn't one other woman he could think of, apart from those whose life's work it was to study the Amazon, who would have fared better than her over the past couple of days. And even some of those would have run screaming long before now, back to the safety of a research lab, or similar.

He thought of her putting up the tent, her tongue caught between her teeth as she exerted herself, sweat dripping down her neck and disappearing into the tantalising vee of her shirt. Gritting his jaw tightly, Luca sighed and closed his eyes. He'd accused her of not lasting in the jungle, but it was he who craved the order of civilisation again—anything to dilute this fire in his blood and put an end to the questions Serena kept throwing up.

A couple of hours later Luca woke, instantly alert and tensed, waiting to hear a sound outside. But it came from inside the tent. *Serena.* Moaning in her sleep in Italian.

'Papa...no, per favore, non che... Siena, aiutami.'

Luca translated the last word: *help me.* There was something gutturally raw about her words, and they were full of pain and emotion. Her voice cracked then, and Luca's chest squeezed when he heard her crying.

Acting on instinct, Luca reached over and touched her shoulder.

Almost instantly she woke up and turned her head. *'Ché cosa?'*

Something about the fact that she was still speaking Italian made his chest tighten more. 'You were dreaming.' He felt as if he'd invaded her privacy.

Serena went as tense as a board. He could see the bright glitter of those blue eyes in the gloom.

'Sorry for waking you.'

Her voice was thick, her accent stronger. He felt her pull abruptly away from his hand as she curled up again. Her hair was a bright sliver of white-gold and his body grew hot as he thought of it trailing over his naked chest as she sat astride him and took him deep into her body.

Anger at the wanton direction of his thoughts, at how easily she got under his skin and how she'd pulled away just now, almost as if he'd done something wrong, made him say curtly, 'Serena?'

She said nothing, and that wound him up more. A moment ago he'd been feeling sorry for her, disturbed by the gut-wrenching sound of those sobs. But now memories of his mother and how she'd use her emotions to manipulate the people around her made Luca curse himself for being so weak.

It made his voice harsh. 'What the hell was *that* about?'

Her voice sounded muffled. 'I said I was sorry for waking you. It was nothing.'

'It didn't sound like nothing to me.'

Serena turned then, those eyes flashing, her hair bright against the dark backdrop of the tent. She said tautly, 'It was a dream, okay? Just a bad dream and I've already forgotten it. Can we go to sleep now, please?'

Luca reacted viscerally to the fact that Serena was all but spitting at him, clearly in no need of comfort whatsoever. She pressed his buttons like no one else, and all he could think about right then was how much he wanted her to submit to him—anything to drown out all the contradictions she was putting in his head.

He reached out and found her arms, pulled her into him, hearing her shocked little gasp.

'Luca, what are you doing?'

But the defensive tartness was gone out of her voice.

He pulled her in closer, the darkness wrapping around them but failing to hide that bright blue gaze or the gold of her hair. The slant of her stunning cheekbones.

She wasn't pulling away.

Luca's body was on fire. From somewhere he found his voice and it sounded coarse, rough. 'What am I doing?'

'*This…*'

And then he pulled her right into him and his mouth found hers with unerring precision. Her breasts swelled against his chest—in outrage? He didn't know, because he was falling over the very thin edge of his control.

When he felt her resistance give way after an infinitesimal moment, triumph surged through his body. He couldn't think any more, because he was swept up in the decadent darkness of a kiss that intoxicated him and reminded him of only one other similar moment… with her…seven years before.

CHAPTER FIVE

SERENA WAS STILL in shock at finding herself in Luca's arms with his mouth on hers. When he'd woken her at first, she'd had an almost overwhelming instinctive need to burrow close to him, the tentacles of that horrible nightmare clinging like slimy vines to her hot skin.

And then she'd realised just who she was with—just who was precipitating such weak feelings of wanting to seek strength and comfort. Luca Fonseca, of all people? And that dream… She hadn't had it for a long time—not since she'd been in rehab. And to be having it again, *here*, was galling. As if she was going backwards. Not forwards. And it was all his fault, for getting under her skin.

Fresh anger made her struggle futilely against Luca's superior strength even after she'd let the hot tide of desire take her over, revealing how much she wanted him. She pulled back, ripping her mouth from his, mortified to find herself breathing harshly, her breasts moving rapidly against the steel wall of his chest, nipples tight and stinging.

Her body and her mind seemed to be inhabiting two different people. Her body was saying *Please don't stop* and her head was screaming *Stop now!*

'What is it, *minha beleza?*'

The gravelly tone of Luca's voice rubbed along her nerve-endings, setting them alight. Traitors.

'Do you really think this is a good idea?'

Dammit. She sounded as if she wanted him to convince her that it was, her voice all breathy.

His eyes were like black pits in his face and Serena was glad she couldn't make out their expression. She half expected Luca to come to his senses and recoil, but instead he seemed to move even closer. His hands slipped down her arms and came around her back, making her feel quivery at how light his touch was—and yet it burned.

'Luca…?'

'Hmm…?'

His mouth came close again and his lips feathered a kiss to her neck. Liquid fire spread through Serena's pelvis. *Damn him.*

She swallowed, her body taking over her mind, making her move treacherously closer to that huge hard body.

'I don't think this is a good idea. We'll regret it.'

Luca pulled back for a moment and said throatily, 'You think too much.'

And then he was covering her mouth with his again, and any last sliver of defence or righteous anger at how vulnerable he made her feel drained away. She was drowning in his strength. Mouth clinging to his, skin tightening all over as he coaxed her lips apart to explore deeper with his tongue. His kiss seven years ago had seared itself onto her memory like a brand. This was like being woken from a deep sleep. She'd never really enjoyed kissing or being touched by men...until him. And now this.

Barely aware of the fact that Luca was pulling down the zips of their sleeping bags, she only knew that there was nothing between them now, and that he was pulling her on top of him so her breasts were crushed against his broad chest.

Both hands were on her head, fingers thrust deep into her hair, and Luca positioned her so that he could plunder her mouth with devastating skill. Serena could feel herself getting damp between her legs.

Luca drew back for a moment and Serena opened her eyes, breathing heavily. With a smooth move he manoeuvred them so that Serena was on her back and loomed over her. He looked wild, feral. Exactly the way she imagined the marauding Portuguese *conquistadores* must have looked when they'd first walked on this land.

He smoothed some hair behind her ear and Serena's breath grew choppier. Her fingers itched to touch him, to feel that chest, so when his head lowered to hers again her hands went to the buttons of his shirt and undid them, sliding in to feel the dense musculature of his chest.

She was unable to hold back a deep sound of satisfaction as her hands explored, revelling in his strength. She dragged her fingers over his chest, sliding over the ridges of his muscles, a nail grazing a flat hard nipple. Her mouth watered. She wanted to taste it.

His beard tickled her slightly, but that was soon forgotten as his tongue thrust deep, making her arch up against him. He was pulling down the strap of her vest, taking with it her bra strap, exposing the slope of her breast.

When Luca pulled back again she was gasping for breath. She looked up, but everything was blurry for a moment. She could feel Luca's fingers reach inside the lace cup of her bra, brushing enticingly close to where her nipple was so hard it ached. He pulled it down and Serena felt her breast pop free of the confinement. Luca's gaze was so hot she could feel it on her bare skin.

He breathed out. *'Perfeito…'*

His head came down, and with exquisite finesse he flicked his tongue against that tip, making Serena's breath catch and her hips move of their own volition. He flicked it again, and then slowly expored the hard flesh, before placing his whole mouth around it and suckling roughly.

Serena cried out. Her hands were on his head, in his hair. She'd never felt anything like this in her life. Sex had been something to block out, to endure, an ineffective form of escape…not something to revel in like this.

His hand was on her trousers now, undoing her button, lowering the zip. There was no hesitation. She wanted this with an all-consuming need she'd never experienced before. His hand delved under her panties as his mouth still tortured her breast.

When his fingers found the evidence of her desire he tore his mouth away. She could see his eyes glitter almost feverishly as he stroked her intimately, releasing her damp heat. Serena whimpered softly, almost mindless, her hips jerking with reaction.

'You want me.'

His words sliced through the fever in her brain.

Serena bit her lip. She was afraid to speak, afraid of what might spill out. Luca was a master torturer. With his hand he forced her legs apart as much as they could go, and then he thrust a finger deep inside, where she was slick and hot. She gasped.

'Say it, Serena.'

He sounded fierce now, his finger moving intimately against her. *Oh, God…* She was going to come. Like this. In a tent in the middle of nowhere. Just from this man touching her…

Feeling vulnerable far too late, Serena tried to bring her legs together—but Luca wouldn't let her. She could see the determination on his face. The lines stark with desire and hunger. One finger became two, stretching her, filling her. She gasped, her hands going to his shoulders.

The heel of his hand put exquisite pressure on her clitoris. She was unable to stop her hips from moving, rolling, seeking to assuage the incredible ache that was building. And then his fingers moved faster, deeper, making Serena's muscles tighten against him.

'Admit you want me…*dammit*. You're almost coming. *Say it.*'

Serena was wild now, hands clutching at him. He was looking down at her. She knew what was stopping the words being wrenched from her: the fact that Luca seemed so intent on pushing her over the edge when *he* appeared to be remarkably in control. The fact that she suspected he just wanted to prove his domination over her.

But she couldn't fight it. She needed it—*him*—too badly.

'I do…' she gasped out, the words torn from her as her body reached its crescendo against the relentless rhythm of Luca's wicked hand and fingers. 'I do…want you…*damn you.*'

And with those last guttural words she went as taut as a bowstring as the most indescribably pleasurable explosion racked her entire body and broke it apart into a million pieces before letting it float back together again.

Serena had orgasmed before. But never like this. With such intensity...losing herself in the process.

Luca's brain had melted into a pool of lust and heat. Serena's body was still clamping around his fingers and he ached to be embedded within her, so that the inferno in his body might be assuaged.

But something held him back—had held him back from replacing his hand with his erection. At some point he'd become aware that he needed this woman on a level that surpassed anything he'd ever known before.

And, worse, he needed to know that she felt it too. So making her admit it, making her *come*, had become some kind of battle of wills. She'd confounded him since she'd turned up in his office, just days ago, and this felt like the first time he'd been able to claw back some control. By making her lose hers.

But now, as he extricated his hand and her body jerked in reaction, it felt like an empty triumph. Luca pulled back and gritted his jaw at the way his body rejected letting Serena go. He pulled on his shirt, feeling wild. Undone.

Serena was moving, pulling her clothes together. He saw her hands shaking and wanted to snarl. Where was the insouciant, confident woman he remembered meeting that night in Florence? She bore no resemblance to this woman, who was almost *impossibly* shy.

Luca lay back, willing down the throbbing heat in his blood. Cursing the moment he'd ever laid eyes on

Serena DePiero. She went still beside him, and even that set his nerves on edge. Sizzling.

Eventually she said hesitantly, 'You didn't...'

She trailed off. But he knew what she'd meant to say, and suddenly her unbelievable hesitance pushed him over another edge. He'd cursed this woman for a long time for sending his life into turmoil, and yet again she was throwing up another facet of her suddenly chameleon-like personality. The most in control he'd felt around her since she'd come back into his life had been just now—when she'd been surrendering to him even though she'd obviously hated it.

He would have her—completely. In his bed. On his terms. Would reveal this hesitant shyness to be the sham that it was.

And then, when he'd had her, sated himself, he would be able to walk away and leave her behind for good. One thing was certain: he'd wanted her since the moment he'd laid eyes on her, and not even his antipathy for her had put a dent in that need. If he didn't have her he'd be haunted for ever. And no woman, however alluring, retained any hold over him once he'd had her.

He came up on one elbow and looked down, saw her eyes flash blue as she looked at him. Her mouth was swollen.

Luca forced down the animalistic urge to take her there and then. He was civilised. He'd spent years convincing people that he wasn't his lush of a mother or his corrupt father.

'No, I didn't.'

He saw her frown slightly. 'Why didn't you...?'

He finished for her, 'Make love to you?'

Serena nodded her head, pulling the sleeping bag

back up over her body. Luca resisted the urge to yank it back down. *Control.*

His jaw was hard. 'I didn't make love to you, Serena, because I have no protection with me. And when we do make love it will be in more comfortable surroundings.'

He sensed her tensing.

'Don't be so sure I want to make love to you, Luca.'

He smiled and felt ruthless. '*Minha beleza*, don't even *try* to pretend that you would have objected to making love here and now. I felt your body's response and it didn't lie. Even if you don't like it.'

She opened her mouth and he reached out and put a finger to her lips, stopping her words.

'Don't even waste your breath. After that little performance you're mine as surely as if I'd stamped a brand on your body.'

She smacked his hand away, hard enough to sting. 'Go to hell, Luca.'

Luca curbed the desire to show Serena in a more subtle way that what he said was true, but it was true that he didn't have protection, and he knew that if he touched her again he wouldn't be able to stop himself.

So he lay down and closed his eyes, just saying darkly, 'Not before I take you with me, *princesa*.'

The fact that he could sense Serena fuming beside him only made him more determined to shatter her control again.

She would be his.

The following day Serena was galvanised on her walk—largely by the depth of her humiliation and her hatred for Luca. She glared at his back as he strode ahead of her and mentally envisaged a jaguar springing from the jungle to swallow him whole.

She couldn't get the lurid images out of her head—the way she'd so completely and without hesitation capitulated to Luca's lovemaking. The way he'd played her body like a virtuoso played a violin. The way he'd controlled her reactions while maintaining his own control.

His words mocked her: *'After that little performance you're mine.'* She felt like screaming. Unfortunately it had been no performance—which was galling, considering that for most of her life she'd perfected the performance of a spoilt, reckless heiress.

But on a deeper level what had happened last night with Luca terrified her.

For as long as she could remember there had been a layer between her and the world around her and she was still getting used to that layer being gone. She'd first tasted freedom when her father had disappeared and they'd been left with nothing. It had been too much to deal with, sending her spiralling into a hedonistic frenzy, saved only by her sister taking her to England and to rehab.

Since then she'd learnt to deal with being free; not bearing the constant weight of her father's presence. Her job, becoming independent, was all part of that process. Even if she still harboured deep secrets and a sense of guilt.

But when Luca had been touching her last night—watching her, making her respond to his touch—her sense of freedom had felt very flimsy. Because he'd also been touching a part of her that she hadn't yet given room to really breathe. Her emotions. Her yearning for what her sister had: a life and happiness.

And the fact that Luca had brought that to the surface made her nervous and angry. All she was to him was a conquest. A woman he believed had betrayed him. A woman he wanted to slake his desire with.

A woman he didn't like, even if he ever conceded that she might be innocent.

She'd known that the night they'd met first. He'd had a gleam of disdain in his eyes that he'd barely concealed even as she saw the burn of desire.

And yet, damn him, since she'd walked into his office the other day it was as if everything was brighter, sharper. More intense. *Bastard.*

Serena crashed into Luca's back before she'd even realised she'd been so preoccupied she hadn't noticed he'd stopped. She sprang back, scowling, and then noticed that they were on a kind of bluff, overlooking a huge cleared part of the forest.

To be out from under the slightly oppressive canopy was heady for a moment. Ignoring Luca, Serena studied the view. She could see that far away in the distance the land had been eviscerated. Literally. Huge chunks cut out. No trees. And what looked like huge machines were moving back and forth, sun glinting off steel.

Forgetting that she hated Luca for a moment, because unexpected emotion surged at seeing the forest plundered like this, she asked, a little redundantly, 'That's the mine?'

Luca nodded, his face stern when she sneaked an illicit glance.

'Yes, that's my family's legacy.'

And then he pointed to a dark smudge much closer. 'That's the Iruwaya tribe's village there.'

Serena shaded her eyes until she could make out

what looked like a collection of dusty huts and a clearing. Just then something else caught her eye: a road leading into the village and a bus trundling along merrily, with bags and crates hanging precariously from its roof along with a few live chickens.

It took a few seconds for the scene to compute and for Serena's brain to make sense of it. Slowly she said, 'The village isn't isolated.'

'I never said it was totally isolated.'

The coolness of Luca's tone made Serena step back and look up at him, her blood rapidly rising again. 'So why the hell have we been trekking through a rainforest to get to it?' She added, before he could answer, 'You never said anything about it being optional.'

Luca crossed his arms. 'I didn't offer an option.'

'My God,' Serena breathed. 'You really did do this in a bid to scare me off... I mean, I know you did, but I stupidly thought...'

She trailed off and backed away as the full significance sank in. Her stupid feeling of triumph for putting up the tent last night without help mocked her now. She'd known Luca hated her, that he wanted to punish her...but she hadn't believed for a second that there had been any other way of getting to this village.

All this time he must have been alternating between laughing his head off at her and cursing her for being so determined to stick it out. And then amusing himself by demonstrating how badly she wanted him.

Luca sighed deeply and ran a hand through his hair. 'Serena, this *is* how I'd planned to come to the village, but I'll admit that I thought you would have given up and gone home long before now.'

His words fell on deaf ears. Serena felt exposed, humiliated. She shook her head. 'You're a bastard, Luca Fonseca.'

Terrified of the emotion rising in her chest, she turned and blindly walked away, not taking care to look where she was going.

She'd landed on her hands and knees, the breath knocked out of her, before she realised she'd tripped over something. It also took a moment for her to register that the black ground under her hands was moving.

She sprang back with a small scared yelp just as Luca reached her and hauled her up, turning her to face him.

'Are you okay?'

Still angry with him, Serena broke free. And then she registered a stinging sensation on her arm, and on her thigh. She looked down stupidly, to see her trousers ripped apart from her fall, and vaguely heard Luca curse out loud.

He was pulling her away from where she'd tripped and ripping off her shirt, but Serena was still trying to figure out what had happened—and that was when the pain hit in two places: her arm and her leg.

She cried out in surprise at the shock of how excruciating it was.

Luca was asking urgently, 'Where is it? Where's the pain?'

Struggling, because it was more intense than anything she'd ever experienced, Serena got out thickly, 'My arm…my leg.'

She was barely aware of Luca inspecting her arm, her hands, and then undoing her trousers to pull them down roughly, inspecting her thigh where it was burning. He was brushing something off her and cursing again.

She struggled to recall what she'd seen. Ants. They'd just been ants. It wasn't a snake or a spider.

Luca was doing a thorough inspection of both legs and then moving back up to her arms. In spite of the pain she struggled to get out, 'I'm fine—it's nothing, really.'

But she was feeling nauseous now, with a white-hot sensation blooming outwards from both limbs. She was also starting to shake. Luca pulled her trousers back up. She wasn't even registering embarrassment that he'd all but stripped her.

She tried to take a step, but the pain when she moved almost blinded her. And suddenly she was being lifted into the air against a hard surface. She wanted to tell Luca to put her down but she couldn't seem to formulate the words.

And then the pain took over. There was a sense of time being suspended, loud voices. And then it all went black.

'Serena?'

The voice penetrated the thick warm blanket of darkness that surrounded her. And there was something about the voice that irritated her. She tried to burrow away from it.

'*Serena.*'

'What?' She struggled to open her eyes and winced at the light. Her surroundings registered slowly. A rudimentary hut of some kind. She was lying down on something deliciously soft. And one other thing registered: mercifully…the awful, excruciating pain was gone.

'Welcome back.'

That voice. Deep and infinitely memorable. And not in a good way.

It all came back.

She turned her head to see Luca looking at her with a small smile on his face. *A smile.* He was sitting down near the bed she lay on.

She croaked out, 'What happened?'

His smile faded, and it must have been a trick of the light but she could have sworn he paled slightly. 'You got stung. Badly.'

Serena recalled the ground moving under her hands and shuddered delicately. 'But they were just ants. How could ants do that?'

Luca's mouth twisted. 'They were bullet ants.'

Serena frowned. 'Should that mean anything to me?'

He shook his head. 'Not really, but they deliver a sting that is widely believed to be the most painful on record of any biting insect—like the pain of a bullet. I've been bitten once or twice; I know exactly what it's like.'

Serena felt embarrassed. 'But I passed out like some kind of wimp.'

Luca had a funny look on his face.

'The fact that you were semi-conscious till we reached the village and kept fighting to walk was a testament to your obviously high pain threshold.'

She lifted her arm and looked at it. There was only a very faint redness where she'd been bitten. All that pain and not even a scratch left behind? She almost felt cheated. And then she thought of what he'd said and her arm dropped.

'Wait a second—you carried me all the way here?'

He nodded. There was a scuffling sound from nearby

and thankfully Luca's intense focus moved off her. She looked past him to see some small curious faces peeping around the door. He said something to them and they disappeared, giggling and chattering.

Luca turned back. 'They're fascinated by the golden-haired *gringa* who arrived unconscious into their village a few hours ago.'

Serena was very disorientated by this far less antagonistic Luca. Feeling self-conscious, she struggled to sit up, moving back the covers on the bed.

But Luca rapped out, 'Stay there! You're weak and dehydrated. You're not going anywhere today, or this evening. The women have prepared some food and you need to drink lots of water.'

Luca stood up, and his sheer size made Serena feel dizzy enough to lie down again. As if by magic some smiling women appeared in the doorway, holding various things. Luca ushered them in and said to Serena over their heads, 'I have to go to the mines. I'll be back later. You'll be looked after.'

Weakly, Serena protested, 'But I'm supposed to be taking notes…'

Something flashed in Luca's eyes but he just said, 'Don't worry about that. There'll be time tomorrow, before we have to leave.'

'Before we have to leave.' She felt a lurch in her belly and an awful betraying tingle of anticipation as to what might happen once they did leave this place.

The following morning, early, Luca was trying not to keep staring at Serena, who sat at the end of a long table in the communal eating hut. She was wearing a traditional smock dress, presumably given to her by one of the women to replace her own clothes, and the simple design might have been haute couture, the way she wore it with such effortless grace.

A small toddler, a girl, was sitting on Serena's lap and staring up at her with huge, besotted brown eyes. She'd been crying minutes before, and Serena had bent down to her level and cajoled her to stop crying, lifting her up and settling her as easily as if she was her mother.

Now she was eating her breakfast—a manioc-based broth—for all the world acting as if it was the finest caviar, giving the little girl morsels in between her own mouthfuls. She couldn't have looked more innocent and pure if she'd tried, tugging remorselessly on his conscience.

A mixture of rage and sexual frustration made Luca's whole body tight. The remnants of the panic he'd felt the previous day when she'd been so limp in his arms after being stung still clung to him. She'd been brave. Even though he knew he was being completely irrational, he couldn't stop lambasting her inwardly for not behaving as he expected her to.

Their eyes met and caught at that moment and he saw her cheeks flush. With desire? Or anger? Or a mixture of both like him? Suddenly her significance wasn't important any more—who she was, what she'd done. Or not done. He wanted her, and she would pay for throwing his life out of whack not once but twice.

Resolve filling his body, he stood up and said curtly, 'We're leaving for the mines in ten minutes.'

He didn't like the way he noticed how her arm tightened around the small girl almost protectively, or how seeing a child on her lap made him feel. All sorts of things he'd never imagined feeling in his life—ever.

Her chin tipped up. 'I'll be ready.'

Luca left before he did something stupid, like take up his phone and ask for the helicopter to come early so that he could haul her back to Rio and douse this fire in his blood as soon as possible.

CHAPTER SIX

A FEW HOURS later Serena was back in her own clothes, now clean, and sitting cross-legged beside Luca in the hut of the tribal elders. She was still smarting from the intensity of his regard that morning at breakfast. As if he'd been accusing her of something. Her suspicions had been reinforced when he'd said, with a definitely accusatory tone, on their journey to the mines, 'You were good with that little girl earlier.'

Serena had swallowed back the tart urge to apologise and explained, 'I have a nephew just a little bit older. We're very close.'

She hadn't liked being reminded of that vulnerability—that from the moment she'd held Siena's son, Spiro, he and Serena had forged an indelible bond and her biological clock had started ticking loudly.

For someone who had never seen the remotest possibility of such a domestic idyll in her life, she was still surprised at how much she craved it.

And she hated it that she'd barely slept a wink in the hut because she'd missed knowing Luca's solid bulk was just inches away. She dragged her attention back to what she was meant to be focusing on: writing notes as fast as Luca translated what he wanted taken down.

They'd spent the morning at the mines and she'd seen how diplomatic he had to be, trying to assuage the fears of the miners about losing their jobs, while attempting to drag the mine and its administration into the twenty-first century and minimise further damage to the land. It was a very fine balancing act.

When he was being diplomatic and charming he was truly devastating. It gave Serena a very strong sense of just how seductive he could be if...if he actually liked her. The thought of that made her belly swoop alarmingly.

He turned to her now. 'Did you get that?'

She looked at the notes quickly. 'About coming up with ideas to actively promote and nurture growth in the local economy?'

He nodded. But before he turned back to the tribal leader Serena followed an impulse and touched his arm. He frowned at her, and she smiled hesitantly at the man Luca was talking to before saying, 'Could I make a suggestion?'

He drew back a few inches and looked at her. His entire stance was saying, *You?*

Serena fought off the urge to hit him and gritted her teeth. 'Those smock dresses that the women make—I haven't seen them anywhere else. Also, the little carvings that the children have been doing... I know that this village is twinned with another one, and they have monthly fair days when they barter goods and crops and utilise their skills and learn from each other...but what about opening it up a bit—say, having a space in Rio, or Manaus, a charity shop that sells the things they make here. And in the other village. A niche market, with the money coming back directly to the people.'

'That's hardly a novel idea,' Luca said coolly.

Serena refused to be intimidated or feel silly. 'Well, if it's not a new concept why hasn't one of these shops been mentioned anywhere in your literature about the charity? I'm not talking about some rustic charity shop. I'm talking about a high-end finish that'll draw in discerning tourists and buyers. Something that'll inspire them to help conserve the rainforest.'

Luca said nothing for a long moment, and then he turned back to the chief and spoke to him rapidly. The man's old, lined face lit up and he smiled broadly, nodding effusively.

Luca looked back to Serena, a conciliatory gleam in his eyes. 'I'll look into it back in Rio.'

The breath she hadn't even been aware of holding left her chest and she had to concentrate when the conversation started again. Finally, when Luca and the chief had spoken for an hour or so, they got up to leave. The old man darted forward with surprising agility to take Serena's hand in his and pump it up and down vigorously. She smiled at his effervescence.

Following Luca out into the slightly less intense late-afternoon heat, she could see a Jeep approach in the distance.

Luca looked at his watch. 'That'll be our lift to the airfield. We need to pack our stuff up.'

He looked at her and must have seen something that Serena had failed to disguise in time.

His eyes glinted with something indefinable. 'I thought you'd welcome the prospect of civilisation again?'

'I do,' Serena said quickly, avoiding his look. But the truth was that she didn't…exactly. Their couple of days in the rainforest…the otherworldly pace of life in the village…it had soothed something inside her. And she realised that she would miss it.

Afraid Luca might see that, she folded her arms and said, 'Are you going to give me a chance?' And then quickly, before he could interject, 'I think I deserve it. I don't want to go home yet.'

Luca looked at her. She could see the Jeep coming closer, stopping. She held her breath. His gaze narrowed on her and became…*hot*. Instantly Serena felt something spike. Anticipation.

He came closer, blocking out the Jeep arriving, the village behind him.

'I've no intention of letting you go home.'

Serena's arms clenched tighter. She didn't like the way her body reacted to that implacable statement and what it might mean. 'You're giving me a trial period?'

Luca smiled, and it made Serena's brain fuzzy.

'Something like that. I told you I wanted you, Serena. And I do. In my bed.'

Anger spiked at his arrogant tone, even as her pulse leapt treacherously. 'I'm not interested in becoming your next mistress, Fonseca. I'm interested in working.'

Luca's eyes flashed at her use of 'Fonseca'. 'I'll give you a two-week trial. Two weeks of working in the charity by day and two weeks in my bed by night.'

Serena unclenched her arms, her hands in fists by her sides, hating the betraying sizzle in her blood. Had she no self-respect?

'That's blackmail.'

Luca shrugged, supremely unconcerned. 'Call it what you want. That's the only way you'll get your trial.'

Serena swallowed a caustic rush of tangled emotions

along with the betraying hum of desire. 'And what about your precious reputation? If people see us together? What then?'

Luca moved closer. Serena's words struck him somewhere deep inside. What *was* he doing? he asked himself. All he knew was that the things that had been of supreme importance to him for a long time no longer seemed as important. There was only here and now and this woman. And *heat*. And need.

Yet he wasn't losing sight of what had driven him for all these years completely. He was cynical enough to recognise an opportunity when it arose. Having Serena on his arm would mean news, and news would mean focus on the things close to his heart. Like his foundation.

He said now, 'I have every intention of people seeing us together. You see, I've realised that seven years is like seven lifetimes in the media world. You're old news. And if anyone does make something of it I'm quite happy for you to be seen by my side as someone intent on making up for her debauched past by doing charity work. Everyone loves a redemption story, after all. And in the meantime I get what I want—which is *you*. You owe me, Serena. You don't think I'm going to give you a two-week trial without recompense, do you?'

Serena just looked at him. She was too stunned to say anything. What Luca had said was so...*cold*. And yet all she could feel was *hot*. She should be slapping him across the face and taking a bus back to Manaus and the next flight home. Maybe that was what he was doing? Calling her bluff. Goading her. She couldn't imagine that he didn't have a string of willing mistresses back in Rio.

But that only made something very dark rise up: jealousy.

'We leave in fifteen minutes.'

With that he turned and strode away, as if he hadn't just detonated a bomb between them. She watched him incredulously, and then stalked to the small hut.

As she packed up her small backpack a few minutes later she alternated between the longing to to find Luca and deliver that slap to his face which he so deserved and pausing to remember how it had felt when he'd kissed her and touched her the other night.

She'd never really enjoyed sex; it had been another route to oblivion which had invariably ended in disappointment and an excoriating sense of self-disgust.

But Luca... It was as if he was able to see right through to her deepest self, to the part of her that was still innocent, untainted by what she'd seen and experienced as a child...

'Ms DePiero?'

Serena whirled around to see a young man in the doorway of the hut.

'Senhor Fonseca is waiting for you at the Jeep.'

Serena muttered something about coming and watched the man walk away. Something inside her solidified. She could leave and go home, lose any chance of a job with the charity and start all over again. Concede defeat. Or...if she was going to admit to herself that she wanted Luca too...she could be as strategic as him.

But if she was going to stay and submit to his arrogant demands then it would be on *her* terms, and she would gain from it too.

Luca sent a wary glance to Serena, who was sitting on the other side of the plane. She was looking out of the window, so he couldn't see her expression, but he would guess that it was as stony as it had been when she'd got into the Jeep and on the silent journey to the private airfield near the airport.

He wasn't flying the plane this time. Ostensibly so he could catch up on work, but for possibly the first time in his life he couldn't focus on it.

All he could focus on was Serena, and the tense lines of her slim body, and wonder what that stony silence meant. He knew he deserved it. He was surprised she hadn't slapped him back at the village. He'd seen the moment in her expression when she'd wanted to.

He'd never behaved so autocratically with a woman in his life. If he wanted a woman he seduced her and took her to bed, and they were never under the impression that he was in the market for more than that.

But this was Serena DePiero. From the first moment he'd ever seen her he'd been tangled up into knots. The last few days had shown him a vastly different woman from the one he'd met before…and yet hadn't he seen something of this woman in her eyes that night in the club? He didn't like to admit that he *had* seen that moment of vulnerability.

His conscience pricked him. *He'd all but blackmailed her.* He wasn't so deluded that he couldn't acknowledge uncomfortably that it had been a crass attempt on his behalf to get her where he wanted her without having to let her know how badly he needed to sate this hunger inside him.

He opened his mouth to speak to her just as she turned her head to look at him and those searing blue eyes robbed him of speech. She looked determined.

'I've been thinking about your…proposal.'

Luca's conscience hit him again. He winced inwardly. Never had he imagined that she would be so diplomatic when he'd been such a bastard. 'Serena—'

She held up a hand. 'No, let me speak.'

He closed his mouth and didn't like the flutter of panic at the thought that he might just have completely mismanaged this. She could leave now and he'd never see her again.

'If I agree to stay and do this trial for two weeks... If I do well—prove that I'm capable...and...' She stopped, a dark flush staining her cheeks before she continued. 'If I agree to what you said...then I want you to assure me that you'll give me a job—whether it's here or back in Athens. A proper contracted, paying job for the charity.'

The relief that flowed through Luca was unsettling and heady. His conscience still struck him, but he was too distracted to deal with it.

He held out a hand towards Serena and growled, 'Come here.'

The flush on her cheeks got pinker. 'Luca—'

'Come here and I'll tell you.'

He saw her bite her lip, the dart of her pink tongue. After a few seconds her hands went to her belt and she undid it and pushed herself up and out of her seat. As soon as she was within touching distance Luca had closed a hand around her wrist and tugged her so that she fell onto his lap with a soft *ooph*.

'Luca, what are you—?'

He couldn't help himself. He covered her mouth with his and stopped her words. A very dangerous kind of relief flowed through him. She would be his. She wasn't leaving. Her arms crept around his neck after a moment of resistance. Her mouth softened under his. And when he swept his tongue along hers, and she sighed, he could have howled with triumph.

Before he lost it completely he drew back, his breathing laboured. He touched a hand to her jaw, cupping it, running a finger along its delicate line. He looked into her eyes and said, 'Yes, I'll give you a job.'

He could feel Serena's breath making her chest shudder against him. The pressure in his groin intensified.

'I want a signed agreement, Luca, that you'll keep your word.'

Indignation made anger flare. 'You don't trust me?' It had all been about him not trusting *her*. Luca had never considered her not trusting *him*, and it didn't sit well.

Serena's lush mouth compressed. She didn't answer directly, she said, 'A promise on paper, Luca, or I'll leave as soon as we touch down.'

Any feeling of triumph or any sense of control slipped out of Luca's grasp. His hands were around Serena's hips, holding her to him, and as much as he wanted to push her back, tell her that no woman dictated to him…he couldn't. The taste of her was on his tongue and, dammit, it wasn't enough. Not yet.

So he finally bit out, 'Fine.'

Serena took in the frankly mind-boggling three-hundred-and-sixty-degree view of Rio de Janeiro outside the glass walls of the penthouse apartment. It was at the top of the building she'd come to that first day.

She turned to face Luca. 'This is your apartment?'

He was watching her intently and inclined his head. 'Yes, but I only use it if I'm working late, or for entertaining clients after meetings.'

Or for entertaining mistresses?

Suddenly she didn't feel half as sure as she had on the plane, when Luca had pulled her into his lap to kiss her. Now her doubts and insecurities were back. Luca affected her...too much.

She crossed her arms. 'I can't stay here. It's inappropriate.'

Luca stifled an inelegant snort. 'This from the woman who was photographed at her debs in an exclusive Paris hotel in a bathtub full of champagne while dressed in a priceless gown?'

Serena flushed, recalling her father's malevolent smile and even more malevolent tone of voice: *'Good girl. We wouldn't want people to think you're becoming boring, now, would we?'*

Serena chose to ignore Luca's comment. 'What about the apartment I was meant to stay in? The one for staff?'

'It's no longer available; someone else took your place there.'

'Well, that's hardly my fault, is it?' she retorted hotly.

Luca's jaw firmed. 'It's either here, Serena, or if you insist, the charity will be put to the expense of finding you somewhere else.'

'No!' she shot out, aghast. 'But it's just—'

He cut in coolly. 'You're staying here. I'm sure you can put up with it for two weeks.'

This was what she was afraid of. He made her emotions and blood pressure see-saw out of control.

Luca looked at Serena and narrowed his gaze. She was skittish, nervy. A million miles from the woman who had melted in his arms just a short time before.

'Serena, what is it?'

She was angry, her cheeks growing pink. 'I've agreed

to sleep with you to get a job—how do you think that makes me feel?'

Luca's conscience pricked but he pointed out, 'You're not sleeping with me yet.'

She went redder.

Luca felt something give inside him and ran a hand through his hair impatiently. 'Look, I behaved like a boor earlier. The very least you deserve is a trial period. I would have given it to you anyway.'

She looked at him, surprised, and it affected him more than he'd like to admit.

'You would? And what about a job?'

Luca schooled his features. 'That depends on your trial period—as it would for anyone else.'

He moved closer then, and put his hands on her upper arms. 'And you are *not* sleeping with me to get a job. You're sleeping with me because it's what you want. What we *both* want.'

She just looked at him, and something desperate rose inside Luca. He ground out, 'The door is behind me, Serena. You can walk out right now if that's what you want and you'll still get your trial.'

For an infinitesimal moment she said nothing, and he was reminded of telling her where the door was before, willing her to use it. Now he'd launch an army if she tried to leave. He had to consciously stop his hands from gripping her arms tight, as if he could restrain her from walking out. He could see her throat work as she swallowed. Her eyes were wide, pupils as black as night.

She opened her mouth and he kept his eyes off the seductive temptation of those soft lips. He needed to hear this too badly. Needed her to stay.

'Serena...'

Her tongue moistened those lips. Luca's pulse jumped.

Her voice was husky. 'I just want a chance.'

The tension in Luca's body spiked. *Damn her.* 'And? What else?'

She turned her head away and bitterness laced her voice. 'You know I want you. In the tent…you made me show you. You humiliated me.'

Luca's chest was tight enough to hurt. An alien sensation. He cursed softly and felt as if some layer of himself was being stripped away when he admitted, 'Do you know how hard it was for me to stop myself from taking you that night?'

Those blue eyes locked with his. She whispered, 'You made me feel as if you just wanted to prove your dominance over me.'

Luca tipped her chin up with a finger and felt her jaw clench. He smiled, and it was wry. 'You credit me with far too much forethought. I needed to hear you say it…that you wanted me. You made *me* feel that much out of control.'

Instantly something flashed in those piercing eyes— something that made some of Luca's tightness ease.

'You're so in control. It's almost scary.'

Now Luca was the one to grit his jaw as he recognised that no one had ever said that to him before—certainly not a woman. Serena's gaze seemed to see right through him to where he stood as a small boy, witnessing the awesome power parents had to rip your life apart. He knew his desire for control and respectability stemmed from that chaotic, messy, tumultuous moment. And here he was, skating far too close to the edges of losing it all again. And yet…he couldn't walk away.

He said, with quiet conviction, 'If I was to kiss you right now you'd see how thin the veneer of my control is, believe me.'

Something hot flared in the bright blue depths and he stifled a groan of pure need. But he would not take her now, like this, after trekking in a jungle for days, when they were both dizzy with fatigue.

It was the hardest thing in the world, but he let her go and stepped back. 'I have work to catch up on—some conference calls to make. And I'm sure you'll appreciate a night in a real bed again. My assistant will be here in the morning to take you down to the charity offices where you'll be working. And tomorrow evening I'm taking you to a charity function.'

Serena's heart palpitated with a mixture of relief and disappointment. So he wasn't staying tonight? And then shame lanced her that she hadn't been strong enough just to walk away. That a part of her wanted to explore what this man was offering, almost more than she wanted to prove herself or ensure her independence.

The last three and a half years had been all about finding and nurturing an inner strength she'd never known she had. But Luca made her feel weak, and it scared her. But not enough to turn away from him. Damn him.

'Okay.'

Luca said nothing for a long moment and then he said quietly, '*Boa noite,* Serena. *Até amanha.*'

Till tomorrow.

He turned and walked away and the slick, modern apartment was immediately cavernous without him. They'd only spent four days together but it felt like a lifetime. Serena battled the urge to flee, once again questioning her rationale... But her decision to stay had nothing to do with being rational. That had fled out of the window as soon as Luca had pulled her onto his lap on the plane and kissed her witless.

Doubts and fears melted away. She wasn't going anywhere. She couldn't.

As soon as that registered in her body fatigue and exhaustion hit her like a freight train. Along with the realisation that she had hot water at her disposal and could finally wash.

Pushing all thoughts of Luca and what the immediate future held out of her head, she unpacked, took the longest and most delicious shower she'd ever had in her life, fell face-down onto an indescribably soft bed, and sank into oblivion.

Luca stood at the window of his office a floor below the apartment. Rio was a carpet of twinkling golden lights as far as the eye could see. He spoke into the mobile he held to his ear.

His voice was tight. 'Let's just say that I have my doubts about whether she did it or not, and I'd appreciate your help in finding out.' There was a pause, and then Luca said curtly, 'Look, Max, if it's too much trouble—' He sighed. 'Okay, yes. And, thanks, I appreciate it.'

Luca cut the connection and threw his phone down on the table behind him. It bounced off and hit the carpeted floor. He ignored it and turned back to the view. Any conversation with his brother drove his blood pressure skywards. He knew that Max didn't blame Luca specifically for the fact that they'd been split up the way they had between their parents...but guilt festered inside Luca even now. He was the elder twin and he'd always felt that responsibility keenly.

Pushing thoughts of his brother aside, Luca hated to admit it, but he felt altered in some way. As if some alchemy had taken place in his head and body since he'd stood looking at this view the last time—just before Serena had arrived almost a week ago.

He scowled at his fanciful thoughts. There was no alchemy. It was physical attraction, pure and simple. It had been between them from the moment their eyes had first locked. And now he was going to sate it. That was all.

The fact that he was prepared to allow Serena De-Piero to sign an agreement which would potentially offer her employment with his company for the foreseeable future, *and* to be seen with her in public, were things that he pushed to the deepest recesses of his mind.

He focused instead on the increasing anticipation in his blood and his body at the knowledge that soon this ever-present hunger would be assuaged.

CHAPTER SEVEN

THE FOLLOWING EVENING Serena waited on the outdoor terrace that wrapped around the entire apartment, a ball of nerves in her gut. The fact that Luca had said he was taking her to a charity function had been conveniently forgotten when she'd succumbed to exhaustion the previous evening—and in the whirlwind of the day she'd just had.

She'd woken early and had some breakfast just before his sleek assistant Laura had arrived, cracking a minute smile for once. She'd handed Serena a sheaf of papers and hot embarrassment had risen up when she'd seen it was the contract assuring her of work if she completed her trial period successfully. The contract she'd demanded.

To her relief there was no mention of the more personal side of their agreement. Luca's cool efficiency was scary.

After she'd signed, Laura had taken her down to the first floor, where the offices for the charity were based, and introduced her to the staff. Serena had spent such a pleasant day with the friendly Brazilians, who had been so nice and patient with her rudimentary Portuguese that she'd almost fooled herself into forgetting what else awaited her.

But she couldn't ignore it any longer. Not when she'd returned to the apartment to find a stylist and a troupe of hair and make-up people waiting to transform her for Luca's pleasure. Or *delectation* might be a better word. She felt like something that should be on display.

An entire wardrobe of designer clothes seemed to have materialised by magic during the day, and this whole process brought back so many memories of her old life—when her father had insisted on making sure his daughters had the most desirable clothes…for the maximum effect.

The thought of the evening ahead made her go clammy. Right now, weakly, she'd take a jungle full of scorpions, snakes, bullet ants and even an angry Luca Fonseca over the social jungle she was about to walk into.

And then she drew herself up tall. She was better than this. Was she forgetting what she'd survived in the past few years? The intense personal scrutiny and soul-searching? The constant invasion of her privacy as she'd faced her demons in front of strangers? And not only that—she'd survived the jungle with Luca, who'd been waiting for her to falter at every step.

Although right now that didn't feel so much of a triumph as a test of endurance that she was still undergoing. They'd exchanged the wild jungle for the so-called civilised jungle. And this time the stakes were so much higher.

At that moment the little hairs all over her body stood up a nano-second before she heard a noise behind her. She had no time to keep obsessing over whether or not she'd picked out the right dress. Squaring her shoulders, and drawing on the kind of reserves that she hadn't had to call on in years, Serena turned around.

For a second she could only blink to make sure she wasn't dreaming. Her ability to breathe was severely compromised. Memories of Luca seven years ago slammed into her like a punch to the gut. Except this Luca was infinitely harder, more gorgeous.

'You've shaved...' Serena commented faintly. But those words couldn't do justice to the man in front of her, dressed in a classic tuxedo, his hard jaw revealed in all its obduracy, the sensual lines of his mouth even more defined.

His thick dark hair was shorter too, and Serena felt an irrational spurt of jealousy for whoever had had his or her hands on his head.

She was too enflamed and stunned by this vision of Luca to notice that his gaze had narrowed on her and a flush had made his cheeks darken.

'You look...incredible.'

Luca's eyes felt seared, right through to the back. She was a sleek, beautiful goddess. All he could see at first was bare skin, arms and shoulders. And acres of red silk and gold, sparkling with inlaid jewels. A deep V drew his eye effortlessly to luscious curves. There was some embellishment on the shoulders and then the dress fell in a swathe of silk and lace from her waist to the floor. He could see the hint of one pale thigh peeping out from the luxurious folds and had to grit his jaw to stop his body from exploding.

She'd pinned her hair back into a low bun at the base of her neck. It should have made the outfit look more demure than if her hair had been around her shoulders in a silken white-golden tumble, but it didn't. It seemed to heighten the provocation of the dress.

Luca registered then that she looked uncomfortable.

Shifting minutely, those long fingers were fluttering near the V of the dress, as if to try and cover it up. The woman Luca had seen in Florence had been wearing a fraction of this much material and revelling in it.

She was avoiding his eye, and that made Luca move closer. She looked up and his pulse fired. He came close enough to smell her clean, fresh scent. Suddenly it felt as if he hadn't seen her in a month, when it had been just a day. A day in which he'd had to restrain himself from going down to the charity offices.

Danger.

He ignored it.

He might have expected her scent to be overpowering, overtly sensual, but it was infinitely more subtle.

Familiar irritation that she was proving to be more difficult to grasp than quicksilver made him say brusquely, 'What's wrong? The dress? You don't like it?'

She looked up at him and need gripped Luca so fiercely that his whole body tensed. But something very cynical followed. He'd had an entire wardrobe of clothes delivered to the apartment—and she wasn't happy?

Her eyes flashed. 'No, it's not the dress.' Her voice turned husky. 'The dress is beautiful. But what were you thinking, sending all those clothes? I'm not your mistress, and I don't want to be treated like one.'

Surprise lanced him, but he recovered quickly. 'I thought you'd appreciate being prepared for a public event.'

Serena looked down and muttered, 'You mean public humiliation.'

Something shifted in Luca's chest. He tipped up her chin, more concerned than he liked to admit by her uneasiness. Colour stained her pale cheeks and Luca almost gave in to the beast inside him. *Almost*. With a supreme effort he willed it down. 'What I said before… about exposing you to public scrutiny…that won't happen, Serena. I won't let it.'

Her eyes were wide. *Wounded*? Her mouth thinned. 'Isn't that part of the plan, though? A little revenge?'

Luca winced inwardly. What did this woman do to him? She called to his most base instincts and he could be as cruel as his father ever had been. Shame washed through him.

He shook his head, something fierce erupting inside him. 'I'm taking you out because I want to be seen with you, Serena.'

As he said it he realised it was true. He genuinely wanted this. To have her on his arm. And it had very little to do with wanting to punish her. At the thought of adverse public reaction a protective instinct nearly bowled him over with its force.

Before he could lose his footing completely, he took her by the hand and said gruffly, 'We should leave or we'll be late.'

In the lift something caught his eye, and he looked down to see Serena's other hand clutching a small bag which matched her dress. Her knuckles were white, and when his gaze travelled up he could see the tension in her body and jaw.

The lift jerked softly to a halt and almost against his will Luca found his hand going to the small of Serena's back to touch her. The minute his hand came into contact with the bare, warm, silky skin left exposed by the backless design she tensed more.

He frowned as something had dawned on him. 'Are you…*nervous*?'

Serena's eyes flashed with some indefinable emotion and she quickly stepped out of the open doors of the elevator, away from his touch, avoiding his narrowed gaze.

'Don't be ridiculous. It's just been a while since I've gone to anything like this, that's all.'

Luca sensed that there was a lot more to it than that, but he gestured for her to precede him out of the building, realising too late what awaited them outside when a veritable explosion of light seemed to go off in their faces. Without even realising what he was doing he put his arm around Serena and curved her into his body, one hand up to cover her face, as they walked quickly to his car, where a security guard held the passenger door open.

In the car, Serena's heart was pumping so hard she felt light-headed. The shock of that wall of paparazzi when she hadn't seen it in so long was overwhelming. And she couldn't help the fierce pain of betrayal. Everything Luca had just said was lies...and she hated that she wouldn't have expected it of him.

She was a sap. Of *course* he was intent on—

Her hand was taken in a firm grip. She clenched her jaw and looked at Luca in the driver's seat. His face was dark...*with anger*?

'Serena, I had nothing to do with that. They must have been tipped off.'

He looked so grim and affronted that Serena felt something melt inside her. Felt a wish to believe him.

'It won't happen again.'

She took her hand from Luca's and forced a smile. 'Don't worry about it.'

The imprint of Luca's body where he'd held her so close was still making her treacherous skin tingle all over. The way he'd drawn her into him so protectively had unsettled her. She'd felt unprotected for so long that it was an alien sensation. Maybe he *hadn't* planned it. She recalled him biting off a curse now, as if he'd been as surprised as her...

Once they'd left the paparazzi behind she pushed a button to lower her window, relishing the warm evening Rio breeze and the tang of the sea.

'Are you okay?'

Serena nodded. 'Fine—just needed some air.'

The setting sun was bathing the sky in a pink glow, and from somewhere distant Serena could hear cheers and clapping.

She looked at Luca. 'What's that?'

Luca's mouth twitched. 'Every evening sunset-worshippers applaud another stunning sunset from the beaches.'

Serena couldn't take her eyes off the curve of Luca's mouth. 'I love that idea,' she breathed. 'I'd like to see the sunset.'

She quickly looked away again, in case that dark navy gaze met hers when she felt far too exposed. Her cheeks were still hot from that moment when she'd been captivated by the way he filled out his suit so effortlessly. The obviously bespoke material did little to disguise his sheer power, flowing lovingly over defined muscles.

'Where do you live when you don't stay at the apartment?' Serena blurted out the first thing she could think of to try and take her mind off Luca's physicality.

He glanced at her, his hands strong on the wheel of the car.

'I have a house in Alto Gavea—it's a district in the Tijuca Forest, north of the lake…'

She sneaked a look. 'Is it your family home? Where you grew up?'

He shook his head abruptly, and when he answered his voice was tight. 'No, we lived out in the suburbs. My parents wouldn't have approved of living so near to the beaches and *favelas*.'

Serena thought of what he'd told her about his parents so far and asked, 'You weren't close to them?'

His mouth twisted. 'No. They split up when we were six, and my mother moved back to her native Italy.'

Serena had forgotten about that Italian connection. 'You said *we*… Do you have brothers and sisters?'

She could sense his reluctance to answer, but they weren't going anywhere fast in the evening traffic. Luca sighed. 'Yes, I have a twin brother.'

Serena's eyes widened. 'Wow—a twin? That's pretty amazing.' Her mind boggled slightly at the thought of *two* Lucas.

He slid her a mocking look and said, 'We're non-identical. He lives in Italy; he moved there with our mother after the divorce.'

Serena processed this and turned in her seat to face him. 'Wait…you mean you were split up?'

The thought of anyone splitting her and Siena up at that young age made her go cold. Siena had been the only anchor in her crazy world.

Luca faced forward, his voice emotionless. 'Yes, my parents decided that each would take one of us. My mother chose me to go to Italy with her, but when my brother got upset she swapped us and took him instead.'

Serena gasped as that scenario sank in. 'But that's...
horrific. And your father just let her?'

Luca looked at her, face hard. 'He didn't care which
son he got as long as he got one of us to be his heir.'

Serena knew what it was to grow up under a cruel
tyrant, but this shocked even her. 'And are you close
now? You and your brother?'

Luca shrugged minutely. 'Not particularly. But he
was the one who bailed me out of jail, and he was the
one who arranged for the best legal defence to get me
out of Florence and back to Rio, avoiding a lengthy
trial and jail time.'

His expression hardened to something infinitely
cynical.

'A hefty donation towards "the preservation of
Florence" was all it took to get the trial mysteriously
dismissed. That money undoubtedly went to corrupt
officials—one of whom was probably your father—
but I was damned if I was going to hang for a crime I
wasn't even responsible for. But they wouldn't clear me
completely, so every time I fly to Europe now I come
under the radar of Europe's law enforcement agencies.'

Serena felt cold. She turned back to the front, staring unseeingly out of the window, knowing it was futile
to say anything. She'd protested her innocence till she
was blue in the face, but Luca was right—his association with her *had* made things worse for him.

They were turning into a vast tree-lined driveway
now, which led up to a glittering colonial-style building. When Luca pulled up, and a valet parker waited
for him to get out, Serena took several deep breaths to
calm her frayed nerves.

Luca surprised her by not getting out straight away.

He turned to her. 'I'm not interested in the past any more, Serena. I'm interested in the here and now.'

Serena swallowed. Something fragile seemed to shimmer between them…tantalising. And then he got out of the car and she sucked in another shaky breath.

He came around and opened her door, extended a hand to help her out. She took it, and when his gaze tracked down her body and lingered on her breasts a pulse throbbed between her legs.

He tucked her arm into his as they moved forward and joined similarly dressed couples entering a glittering doorway lit by hundreds of small lights. It was a scene Serena had seen a million times before, but never heightened like this. Never *romantic*.

She asked herself as Luca led her inside, greeting someone in Portuguese, if they really could let the past go. Or was that just what Luca was willing to say so that he could bed her and then walk away, with all that resentment still simmering under the surface?

'Do you think you could crack a smile and not look as if you're about to be subjected to torture?'

Serena glanced at Luca, who had a fixed social smile on his face. She sent up silent thanks that he couldn't read her thoughts and said sweetly. 'But this *is* torture.'

Something flared in his eyes—surprise?—and then he said, 'Torture it may well be, but a few hours of social torture is worth it if it means that a *favela* gets a new free school staffed by qualified teachers.'

Serena felt immediately chastened. 'Is that what this evening's ball is in aid of?'

Luca looked at her assessingly. 'Among some other causes. The global communities charity too.'

Serena thought of that sweet little girl in the village—a million miles away from here…and yet *not*.

'I'm sorry,' she said huskily. 'You're right—it *is* worth it.'

Serena missed Luca's speculative look because a waiter was interrupting them with a tray of champagne. Luca took a glass and looked at her when she didn't.

She shook her head quickly and said to the waiter, 'Do you have some sparkling water, please?'

The waiter rushed off and Luca frowned slightly. 'You really don't drink any more?'

Serena's belly clenched. 'No, I really don't.' She made a face. 'I never liked the taste of alcohol anyway. It was more for the effect it had on me.'

'What was that?'

She looked at him. 'Numbing.'

The moment stretched between them…taut. And then the attentive waiter returned with a glass of water on a tray for Serena. She took it gratefully. Luca was getting too close to that dark place inside her.

To her relief someone came up then, and took his attention, but just as Serena felt hopeful that he might forget about her she felt her heart sink and jump in equal measure when she felt him reach for her hand and tug her with him, introducing her to the man.

Luca was finding it hard to concentrate on the conversation around him when he usually had no problem. Even if he *was* with a woman. He was aware of every tiny movement Serena made in that dress, and acutely aware of the attention she was attracting.

He was also aware that she seemed ill at ease. He'd expected her to come back into this kind of environment and take to it like the proverbial duck to water, but when they'd first come in she'd looked *pained*. It was just like in the jungle, when she'd proved him resoundingly wrong in his expectations of her.

Now her head was bent towards one of the executive team who managed his charities abroad, and they were engaged in an earnest conversation when Luca would have fully expected Serena to look bored out of her brains.

At that moment her head tipped back and she laughed at something the other woman had said. Luca couldn't breathe, and the conversation stopped around them as she unwittingly drew everyone's eye. She literally... *sparkled*, her face transformed by her wide smile. She was undeniably beautiful...and Luca realised he'd never seen true beauty till that moment.

His chest felt tight as he had a vision of what he'd subjected her to: dragging her into the jungle on a forced trek. She'd endured one of the most painful insect bites in the world. She'd stayed in a rustic village in the depths of the Amazon without blinking. She'd endeared herself to the tribespeople without even trying. It had taken him *years* to be accepted and respected.

And the miners—some of the hardest men in Brazil—weathered and rough as they came—they'd practically been doffing their caps when Serena had appeared with him, as if she was royalty.

Luca could see the crowd moving towards the ballroom and took Serena's hand in his. She looked at him with that smile still playing about her mouth and a sense of yearning stronger than anything he'd ever felt kicked him in the solar plexus. A yearning to be the cause of such a smile.

As if she was reading his mind her smile faded on cue.

'Come on—let's dance,' Luca growled, feeling unconstructed. Raw.

He tugged Serena in his wake before he remembered that he didn't even *like* dancing, but right now he needed to feel her body pressed against his or he might go crazy.

When they reached the edge of the dimly lit dance floor Luca turned and pulled her with him, facing her. The light highlighted her stunning bone structure. That effortlessly classic beauty.

Unbidden, he heard himself articulate the question resounding in his head. 'Who *are* you?'

She swallowed. 'You know who I am.'

'Do I really?' he asked, almost angry now. 'Or is this all some grand charade for the benefit of your family, so you can go back to doing what you love best—being a wild society princess?'

Serena went pale and pulled free of Luca's embrace, saying angrily, 'I've told you about me but you still don't have the first clue, Luca. And as for what I love best? You'll never know.'

She turned and was walking away, disappearing into the vast lobby, before Luca realised that he was struck dumb and immobile because no woman had ever walked away from him before.

Cursing under his breath, he followed her, but when he got to the lobby there was no sign of a distinctive red dress or a white-blonde head. The way she'd stood out in the crowd mocked him now. His gut clenched with panic.

He got to the open doors, where people were still arriving. He spotted the valet who had taken his car and accosted him, asking curtly, 'The woman I came with—have you seen her?'

The valet gulped, visibly intimidated by Luca. 'Yes. Sir. I just saw her into a taxi that had dropped off some guests.'

Luca swore so volubly that the valet's ears went red. He stammered, 'Do—do you want your car?'

Luca just looked at him expressively and the young man scurried off.

They were on a hill overlooking the city. Luca looked out onto the benignly twinkling lights of Rio and the panic intensified. He recalled Serena saying she wanted to see the sunset... Would she have gone to the beach? At this time of night?

Panic turned to fear. He took out his phone and made a call to Serena's mobile but it was switched off. Rio was a majestic city, but at night certain areas were some of the most dangerous on earth. Where the *hell* had she gone?

Serena stalked into the apartment and the door slammed behind her with a gratifyingly loud bang. She was still shaking with anger, and her emotions were bubbling far too close to the surface for comfort.

She kicked off her shoes and made her way out to the terrace, taking deep breaths. Damn Luca Fonseca. It shouldn't matter what he thought of her...but after everything they'd been through she'd foolishly assumed that he'd come to see that she *was* different.

This was the real her. A woman who wanted to work and do something worthwhile, and never, ever insulate herself against life again. The girl and the young woman she'd been had been born out of the twisted machinations of her father.

Her hands wrapped around the railing. Self-disgust rose up inside her. To think that she was willing to go to bed with a man who thought so little of her. Where was the precious self-esteem she'd painstakingly built up again?

She knew where… It had all dissolved in a puddle of heat as soon as Luca came within feet of her. And yet she knew that wasn't entirely fair—he'd treated her as his exact equal in the jungle, and earlier, in the charity offices, she'd been surprised to find that he'd already put in motion discussions on her idea for a high-end tourist shop showcasing products from the villages and credited her with the plan.

She heard a sound behind her and tensed. Panic washed through her. She wasn't ready to deal with Luca yet. But reluctantly she turned around to see him advancing on her, his face like thunder, as long fingers pulled at his bow-tie.

She still got a jolt of sensation to see him clean-shaven. It should have made him look more urbane. It didn't.

CHAPTER EIGHT

LUCA THREW ASIDE his bow-tie just before he came onto the terrace and bit out, 'Where the hell were you? I've been all over the beachfronts looking for you.'

His anger escalated when he saw Serena put her hands on her hips and say defiantly, 'What was it? Did you think I'd hit some nightclub? Or that I'd gone to find some late-night pharmacy so I could score some meds?'

Luca stopped. He had to acknowledge the relief that was coursing through his veins. She was here. She was safe. But the rawness he felt because she'd walked out on him and looked so upset when he'd suggested she was acting out a charade was still there.

An uncomfortable truth slid into his gut like a knife. Perhaps this *was* her. No charade. No subterfuge.

And just like that, Luca was thrown off-centre all over again.

He breathed deeply. 'I'm sorry.'

Serena was surprised. She blinked. 'Sorry for what?'

Honesty compelled Luca to admit, 'For what I said at the function. I just… *You*…'

He looked away and put his hands on his hips. Suddenly it wasn't so hard to say what he wanted to say— as if something inside him had given way.

He dropped his hands, came closer and shook his head. 'You confound me, Serena DePiero. Everything I thought I knew about you is wrong. The woman who came to Rio, the woman who survived the jungle, the woman who gave those villagers the kind of courtesy not many people ever give them…she's someone I wasn't expecting.'

Serena's ability to think straight was becoming compromised. Emotion was rising at hearing this admission and knowing what it must be costing him.

Huskily she said, 'But this *is* me, Luca. This has always been me. It was just…buried before.' Then she blurted out, 'I'm sorry for running off. I came straight here. I wouldn't have gone near the beaches—not after what you said. I do have *some* street-smarts, you know.'

Luca moved closer. 'I panicked. I thought of you being oblivious to the dangers.'

Now Serena noticed how pale Luca was. *He'd been worried about her.* He hadn't assumed she'd gone off the rails. The anger and hurt drained away, and something shifted inside her. A kind of tenderness welled up. *Dangerous.*

She had to physically resist the urge to go to him and touch his jaw. Instead she said, 'I'm here…safe.'

His hands landed on her hips and he tugged her into him. She was shorter without her heels. He made her feel delicate. Her skin was tingling now, coming up in goosebumps in spite of the warm air. Emboldened by his proximity, and what he'd just said, she lifted her own hands and pushed Luca's jacket apart and down his arms.

He let go of her so that it could fall to the ground.

Without saying anything, Luca took her by the hand and led her into the apartment, stepping over his coat.

Serena let herself be led. She'd never felt this connection with anyone else, and a deep-rooted surge of
desire to reclaim part of her sexuality beat like a drum
in her blood.

Yet when Luca led her into what she assumed was
his bedroom, because of its stark, masculine furnishings, trepidation gripped her. Perhaps she was being
a fool? Reading too much into what he'd said? Didn't
men say *anything* to get women into bed? There was
so much in her past that she was ashamed of, that she
hadn't made peace with, and Luca seemed to have an
unerring ability to bring all of those vulnerabilities to
the fore. What would happen when he possessed her
completely?

Her hand tightened around Luca's and he stopped by
the bed and turned to face her. Serena blurted out the
first thing she could think of, as if to try and put some
space between them again. 'I lost my virginity when I
was sixteen…does that shock you?'

He shrugged, his expression carefully veiled, 'Should
it? I lost mine at sixteen too—when one of my father's
ex-mistresses seduced me.'

Serena's desperation rose, in spite of her shock at
what he'd just revealed so flatly. 'It's what men expect,
though, isn't it? For their lovers to be somehow…in-
nocent?'

Luca made a face. 'I like my lovers to be experienced. I've no desire to be some wide-eyed virgin's
first time.'

A wide-eyed virgin she certainly was *not*. Innocence
had been ripped from her too early.

Luca pulled her closer and heat pulsed into Serena's
lower body. She could feel his arousal between them,

thick and hard. It scattered painful thoughts and she welcomed it like a coward.

'I want you, Serena, more than I've ever wanted anyone. I've wanted you from the first moment I laid eyes on you...'

For a heady moment Serena felt an overwhelming sense of power. She reassured herself that the emotions rising inside her were transitory; sex had never touched her emotionally before, so why should it now?

When he reached for her Serena curled into him without even thinking about it. It felt like the most necessary thing. The world dropped away and it was just them in this tight embrace, hearts thudding, skin hot.

His fingers spread out over her back, making her nipples harden almost painfully against the material of the dress. And then he lowered his head and his mouth was on hers, fitting like the missing piece of a jigsaw puzzle. Serena's lips opened to his on a sigh, tongues touching and tasting, stroking intimately. Her hands wound up around his neck, fingers tugging the short strands of hair, exploring, learning the shape of his skull.

Luca's wicked mouth and tongue made her strain to get even closer. After long, drugging moments he drew back, breathing harshly. Serena had to struggle to open her eyes.

'I want to see you,' he muttered thickly. 'Take down your hair.'

Serena felt as if she was in a dream. Had she, in fact, had this dream more often than once in the past seven years? She lifted her hand to the back of her head, feeling incredibly languid, and removed the discreet pin. Her hair tumbled around her shoulders, making her nerve-ends tingle even more.

Luca reached out and ran his fingers through it, then fisted it in one hand as the other reached around her to draw her into him again, kissing her with ruthless passion, tongue thrusting deep.

Serena's legs were starting to wobble. Luca's mouth was remorseless, sending her brain into a tailspin.

His hands came to the shoulders of her dress and pulled with gentle force, so the material slipped down her arms, loosening around her chest. She broke away from his mouth and looked up into dark pools of blue, feeling insecure.

Her arms came up against her breasts. Luca drew back and gently tugged them away, pulling the front of the dress down, leaving her bared to him.

She wore no bra, and Luca's gaze was so hot her skin sizzled. He reached out a hand and cupped the weight of one breast, a thumb moving over one puckered nipple. She bit her lip to stop from moaning out loud.

And then Luca put his hands on her hips and pulled her into him, hard enough to make her gasp, and replaced his thumb with his mouth, suckling on that hard peak roughly, making her back arch.

His erection was insistent against her and Serena's hips moved of their own volition.

Luca lifted his head. *'Feiticeira.'*

Her tongue felt heavy in her mouth, 'What does that mean?'

'Witch,' Luca replied succinctly.

And he kissed her again before her mind could catch up with the fact that his hands were now pushing her dress down over her hips so that it fell to the floor in a silken swish.

He put one hand between their bodies and Serena

held her breath when he explored down over her belly and lower, until he was gently pushing her legs apart so that he could feel for himself how ready she was.

Serena felt gauche, but wanton, as Luca moved his hand between her legs, over her panties. She lowered her head to his shoulder when her face got hot, and her breathing grew harsher when his wicked fingers moved against her insistently.

He slipped a finger under the gusset of her panties and touched her, flesh to flesh. Serena bit her lip hard enough to make tears spring into her eyes. She wanted to clamp her thighs together—the sensation was too much—but Luca's hand was too strong.

Her legs finally gave way and she collapsed back onto the bed, heart thumping erratically.

Luca started to undo his shirt, revealing that broad and exquisitely muscled chest. A smattering of dark hair covered his pectorals, leading down in a silky line under his trousers to where she could see the bulge of his arousal.

Serena's brain melted and she welcomed it. She didn't want to think or analyse—only feel.

His hands moved to his trousers and he undid them and pushed them down, taking his underwear with them. His erection was awe-inspiring. Long and thick and hard, a bead of moisture at the tip.

'Seven years, Serena,' he said throatily, 'For seven years I've wanted you above any other woman. No one came close to how I imagined this.'

She looked up at him, taken aback. She watched as he reached for something in a drawer in the side table. He rolled protection over his length. There was something unashamedly masculine about the action.

'Lie back,' he instructed gruffly.

Serena did, glad he was giving instructions because she couldn't seem to formulate a single coherent thought.

Luca curled his fingers under the sides of her panties and gently took them off. Now she was naked. And even though she'd been naked in front of men before it had never felt like this. As if she was being reborn.

Luca came down over her on strong arms, their bodies barely touching. He kissed her, and those broad shoulders blocked everything out. Serena reached up, desperate for contact again, her hands touching his chest and moving down the sides of his body, reaching around to his back, sliding over taut, sleek muscles.

Luca broke away. 'You're killing me. I need you… *now*. Spread your legs for me.'

Serena's entire body seemed to spasm at that husky entreaty. She moved her legs apart and Luca came down over her, his body pressing against hers. She could feel the thick blunt head of him pushing against her, seeking entrance.

She opened her legs wider, every cell in her body straining towards this union. Aching for it. She looked up at him, her whole body on the edge of some unknown precipice.

As if some lingering tension shimmering between them had just dissolved, Luca thrust in, hard and deep, and Serena cried out at the exquisite invasion.

It was sore…he was so big…but even as she had that thought the pain was already dissipating to be replaced by a heady sensation of fullness.

'Serena?'

She opened her eyes. Luca was frowning. She hadn't realised that she was biting her lip.

He started to withdraw. 'I've hurt you.'

There was a quality to his voice Serena had never heard before. She gripped him tight with her thighs, trapping him. 'No,' she said huskily. 'You're not hurting me... It's...been a while.'

He stopped, and for an infinitesimal moment Serena thought he was going to withdraw completely. But then he slowly thrust in again and relief rushed through her.

Luca reached under her back, arching her up into him more as he kept up a steady rhythm that made it hard to breathe. She could feel her inner muscles tight around him, saw his gritted jaw, the intense look of concentration on his face.

Luca pressed a searing kiss to her mouth before trailing his lips down, closing them over one nipple and then the other, forcing Serena's back to arch again as spasm after spasm of tiny pleasures rushed through her core.

She locked her feet around the back of Luca's body and he went deeper, but she couldn't break free of that sliver of control that kept her bound, kept her from soaring to the stars. A blinding flash of insight hit her like a smack in the face: she recognised now why she couldn't let go in this moment of intense intimacy—the reason why she'd never let herself feel this deeply before—it was because she'd always been too afraid of losing control.

Which was ironic. But being out of control on drink and medication had been—perversely—*within* her control. This wasn't. This was threatening to wrench her out of herself in a way that was frankly terrifying.

A small sob of need escaped Serena's mouth as that elusive pinnacle seemed to fade into the distance. The turmoil in her chest and body was burning her. But she couldn't let go—even as she heard a guttural sound coming from Luca's mouth and felt his body tense within her before deep tremors shook his big frame and his body thrust against her with the unconscious rhythm of his own release.

She felt hollowed out, unsatisfied.

Luca withdrew from her body, breathing harshly, and Serena winced minutely as her muscles relaxed their tight grip. As soon as Luca released her from the prison of his arms she felt the need to escape and left the bed.

She barely heard him call her name as she shut the bathroom door behind her, locking it. Her legs were shaking and tears burned the back of her eyes as the magnitude of what had just happened sank in. There was something fundamentally flawed, deep inside her. She'd been broken so long ago that she couldn't function normally now. And Luca had to be the one to demonstrate this to her. The ignominy was crushing.

Serena blindly reached into the shower and turned the spray to hot, stepping underneath and lifting her face up to the rush of water. Her tears slid and fell, silent heaves making her body spasm as she let it all out.

She heard banging on the door, her name. She called out hoarsely, 'Leave me alone, Luca!'

And then, mercifully, silence.

Serena sank down onto the floor of the shower as the water beat relentlessly down over her body. She drew her knees up to her chest and dropped her head onto them and tried to tell herself that what had just happened *wasn't* as cataclysmic as she thought it was.

* * *

Luca looked at the locked door. He wasn't used to feeling powerless, but right now he did. He cursed volubly, knowing it wouldn't be heard because he could hear the spray of the shower and something that sounded suspiciously like a sob.

His chest hurt. Was she crying? Had he hurt her?

Luca cursed again and paced. He went to his wardrobe and took out some worn jeans, pulled them on, paced again.

Dammit. No woman had ever reacted like that after making love with him. Running to the bathroom. *Crying.* And yet…

Had he really made love to Serena? Luca asked himself derisively. Or had he been so overcome with lust that he'd not taken any notice of the fact that she clearly hadn't been enjoying herself?

He winced now when he thought of how tight she'd been. And her husky words…*It's…been a while.* To be so tight he'd guess a lot longer than 'a while'. Which meant what? That her reputation for promiscuity was severely flawed, for a start. And she'd been awkward, slightly gauche. Not remotely like the practised seductress he might have expected.

He'd seen how her face had tightened, become inscrutable. She'd shut her eyes, turned her head away… But Luca had been caught in the grip of a pleasure so intense that he'd been unable to hold himself back, releasing himself into her with a force unlike anything he'd known before.

For the first time in his memory Luca was facing the very unpalatable fact that he'd behaved with all the finesse of a rutting bull.

The spray of the shower was turned off and Luca became tense. He felt a very real urge to flee at the prospect of facing Serena now. But that urge stemmed from some deep place he wouldn't acknowledge. She hadn't reached him there. No one had.

When Serena emerged from the bathroom, dressed in a voluminous terrycloth robe, she still felt raw. The bedroom was empty, and a lurch of something awfully like disappointment went through her belly to think that Luca had left.

And then she cursed herself. Hadn't she told him to *'leave me alone'*? Why on earth would he want to have anything to do with a physically and emotionally wounded woman when there had to be any number of willing women who would give him all the satisfaction he might crave without the post-coital angst?

Still…it hurt in a way that it shouldn't.

Serena belted the robe tightly around her waist and, feeling restless, went out to the living area. Her hair lay in a damp tangle down her back.

But when she looked out through the glass doors she saw him. He hadn't left. Her heart stopped as something very warm and treacherous filled her chest.

As she came closer to the open doors she could see that he'd pulled on soft faded jeans. His back was broad and smooth, his hair ruffled. From her hands or the breeze? Serena hovered at the door, on the threshold.

And then Luca said over his shoulder, 'You should come and see the view—it's pretty spectacular.'

Serena came out and stood not far from Luca, putting her hands on the railing. The view was indeed exquisite. Rio was lit up with a thousand lights, the Sugar Loaf in the distance, and the beaches just out of sight. It was magical. Other-worldly.

'I've never seen anything like this,' she breathed, curiously soothed by Luca's muted reaction to her re-appearance.

He said lightly now, 'I find that hard to believe.'

Serena's hands tightened on the railing. 'It's true. Before...I wouldn't have noticed.'

She could sense him turning towards her and her skin warmed. Just like that. From his attention. She glanced at him and his face looked stark in the moon-light.

'Did I hurt you? You were with me all the way and then...you weren't.'

'*No!*' Serena blurted out, horrified that he would think that. 'No,' she said again, quieter, and looked back at the view. 'Nothing like that.'

'Then...what?'

Why wouldn't he let it go? Serena wasn't used to men who gave any consideration to how much she'd enjoyed sex—they'd usually been happy just to say they'd *had* her. The wild child.

Luca's voice broke in again. 'You've already come in my arms, so I know what it feels like, but you shut down.'

Serena got hot, recalling the strength of her orgasm when he'd been touching her in the jungle... But that had been different... He hadn't been *inside her*.

And she hadn't been falling for him.

The realisation hit her now, as if she'd been blocking it out. She *was* falling for him—tumbling, in fact. No wonder her body had shut down. It had known before she did. She'd been right to fear his total possession.

She looked at him, shocked, terrified it might be written over her head in neon lights. But he was just raising a brow, waiting for an answer. Oblivious.

Her mind whirling with this new and fragile knowledge, she whispered, 'I told you…it's been a while.'

'What's "a while"?'

Serena stared at him, wanting him to let it go. 'Years—okay? A long time.'

Something in his eyes flashed. 'You haven't had any lovers since you left Italy?'

She shook her head, avoiding his eye again, and said tightly, 'No—and not for a while before that.'

God, this was excruciating!

'The truth is I've never really enjoyed sex. My reputation for promiscuity and sexual prowess was largely based on the stories of men who'd been turned down. I'm afraid I'm not half as debauched as you might think…a lot of talk and not a lot of action.'

Luca was quiet for a long time, and then he said, 'I could tell you weren't that experienced. But you were touted as one of Europe's most licentious socialites and you didn't do much to defend yourself.'

She sent him a dark glance. 'As if anyone would have believed me.' She looked out over the view and felt somehow removed, suspended in space. 'Do you know how I learned to French kiss?'

She could sense Luca going still. 'How?'

Serena smiled but it was bitter, hard. 'One of my father's friends. At a party. He came into my room.'

She let out a shocked gasp when Luca grabbed her

shoulders and pulled her around to face him. His face was stark, pale. His reaction took her aback.

'Did he touch you? Did he—?'

Serena shook her head quickly. '*No*. No. My sister Siena was there…we shared a room. She woke up and got into bed beside me and the man left. After that we made sure to lock our door every night.'

Luca's hands were still gripping her shoulders. '*Deus*…Serena.'

He let her go and ran a hand through his hair, looking at her as if she was a stranger. On some deep level Serena welcomed it. The other thing was too scary. Luca looking at her with something approximating gentleness…

She saw a lounger nearby and went over and sat down, pulling her knees up to her chest. Luca stood with his back to the railing, hands in his pockets. Tense.

As if the words were being wrung out of him, he finally said, 'It's not adding up. *You're* not adding up.'

'What's not adding up?' Serena asked quietly, her heart palpitating at Luca's intent look.

'You've had nothing but opportunities to be difficult since you got here and you haven't been. No one can act that well. A child who is medicated for being difficult, wilful…who grows into a wild teenager hell-bent on causing controversy wherever she goes…that's not you.'

Serena's heart beat fast. She felt light-headed. Faintly she said, 'It *was* me.'

Luca was grim. '*Was?* No one changes that easily, or that swiftly.'

He came over and pulled a chair close, sat down. Serena knew her eyes had gone wide. She felt as if she were standing on the edge of a precipice, teetering, about to fall.

'I want to know, Serena… Why were you put on medication so young?'

'I told you…after my mother died—'

Luca shook his head. 'There has to be more to it than that.'

Serena just looked at him. No one had ever been interested in knowing her secrets before. In rehab the professionals had been paid to delve deep, and she'd let them in the interests of getting better.

Luca was pushing her and pushing her—and for what? As if he'd welcome her darkest secrets…

The desire to be vulnerable and allow herself to confide in him in a way she'd never done before made her scared. It was too much, coming on the heels of what had just happened. Realising she was falling in love with him when he was only interested in bedding her. She'd been at pains to let Luca know that this was the real her, and yet she knew well it wasn't. There was a lot more to her. And she couldn't let it out. She felt too fragile.

Acting on a blind instinct to protect herself, Serena stood up abruptly, making Luca tip his head back.

Coldly she said, 'There's nothing more to it—and I thought men didn't like post-coital post-mortems. If we're done here for the evening I'd like to go to bed. I'm tired.'

She went to walk around Luca, her heart hammering, but he grabbed her wrist, stopping her in her tracks. He stood up slowly, eyes narrowed on her.

'What the hell…? *If we're done here for the evening?* What's *that* supposed to mean?'

Serena shrugged and tried to affect as bored a demeanour as possible. 'We've been to the function, we've slept together…' She forced herself to look at him and mocked, 'What more do you want? For me to tuck you in and read you a story?'

Luca's face flushed. He let her wrist go as if it burnt him. He seemed to increase in size in front of her, but instead of intimidating her it only made her more aware of him. He bristled.

'No, sweetheart, I don't want you to tuck me in and read me a story. I want you in my bed at my convenience for as long as I want you.'

He was hard and cruel. And more remote than she could remember ever seeing him. Something inside her curled up tight. But still that instinct to drive him away from seeing too much made her say nonchalantly, 'Well, if it's all the same to you, I'd appreciate spending the rest of the night on my own.'

Liar, her body whispered. Even now between her legs she was getting damp with the desire to feel him surge deep inside her.

So that she could shut down all over again? More humiliation? No, she was doing the right thing.

He came close…close enough to make sweat break out over Serena's skin… If he touched her he'd know how false she was being.

But he stopped just inches away and said, 'We both know that I could have you flat on your back and begging me for release in minutes…a release that you *will* give me next time, Serena.'

He stepped back and Serena felt disorientated. He thought she'd *wilfully* kept herself from being pleasured just to thwart him in some way?

He swept her up and down with a scathing glance. 'But right now I find that my desire has waned.'

He turned and strode back into the apartment and Serena started to shake in reaction. Everything in her wanted to call out to him.

But wasn't this what she wanted? To push him back? The shackles of her past had never felt so burdensome as they did right then. She recognised that they were protecting her, but also imprisoning her.

She could imagine Luca getting changed, walking out through the door, and her gut seized in rejection. Luca was the only person she'd come close to telling everything. She could remember the look on his face just before she'd turned cold. He'd been *concerned*. Until she'd convinced him that she had nothing to say except that she wanted him to leave.

And why wouldn't he leave? He was proud enough to take her at face value. She knew how quickly he damned people—after all he'd damned her for long enough... But that had been changing.

A sense of urgency gripped her—so what if he *did* just want her in his bed? Suddenly Serena knew that in spite of how terrified it made her feel, she desperately wanted to lean on Luca's inherent strength and face these last demons that haunted her still. She was sick of letting her past define her, of being afraid to get too close to anyone in case they saw inside her.

After all, what was the worst that could happen? Luca couldn't look at her any more coldly than he just had. And if he didn't believe her...? Then at least she would have been totally honest.

She heard a movement and saw Luca stride towards the front door, dressed now in black trousers and a black top.

He looked utterly intimidating, but Serena gathered all of her courage, stepped into the apartment again and said, 'Wait, Luca, please. Don't go.'

CHAPTER NINE

Luca stopped at the door, his hand on the knob. Had he even heard that? Or was it his imagination conjuring up what he wanted to hear from a siren who had him so twisted inside out that he barely knew which way was up any more?

He didn't turn around and forced out a drawl. 'What is it, *minha beleza?* You're ready to come this time?'

He felt dark inside, constricted. He'd really thought he'd seen something incredibly vulnerable in Serena— he'd finally believed that she truly was exactly as she seemed—and then…*wham!* She couldn't have made more of a fool of him if she'd professed undying love and he'd believed her.

There was no sound behind him and he whirled around, anger like a molten surge within him. When he saw the pallor of Serena's cheeks and how huge and bruised her eyes looked he pushed down the concern that rose up to mock him and said scathingly, 'Nice try, *namorada*, but I'm not falling for whatever part you want to play now. Frankly, I prefer a little consistency in my lovers.'

Luca went to turn and leave again, but Serena moved forward jerkily. 'Please, just wait—hear me out.'

He sighed deeply, hating the ball of darkness in his gut. The darkness that whispered to him to run fast and far away from this woman.

He turned around and crossed his arms, arching a brow. 'Well?'

Serena swallowed. Her hair was like a white-gold curtain over her shoulders, touching the swells of her breasts under the robe. Breasts that Luca could taste on his tongue even now.

Incensed that she was catching him like this, and yet still he couldn't walk away, he strode past her over to his drinks cabinet and delivered curtly, 'Spit it out, will you?'

He poured himself a glass of whisky and downed it in one. Hating that she'd even made him feel he needed the sustenance. His hand gripped the glass. He wouldn't look at her again.

'Serena, so help me—'

'You were pushing me to talk…and I didn't want to. So I pretended just now…pretended that I wanted to be alone. I didn't mean what I said, Luca.'

Luca went very still. An inner voice mocked him. *She's still playing you.* But he recalled the way she'd looked so hunted…just before something had come over her expression and she'd morphed into the ice queen in front of his eyes.

Slowly he put the glass down and turned around. Serena looked shaken. Pale. Yet determined.

'I'm sorry.'

Her voice was husky and it touched on his skin like a caress he wanted to rail against.

He folded his arms. 'Sorry for what?'

She bit her lip. 'I wanted you to think that I'd had enough so you'd leave, but that's not true.'

'Tell me something I *don't* know,' Luca drawled, and saw how she went even paler.

He cursed out loud and went over to her, taking her by the arm and leading her to a couch to sit down.

'Serena, so help me God, if this is just some elaborate—'

'It's not!' she cried, her hands gripped together in her lap. 'It's not,' she said again. 'You were just asking me all these things and I felt threatened… I've never told anyone what happened. I've always been too ashamed and guilty that I didn't do something to stop it. And for a long time I doubted that it had even happened…'

Luca knew now that this was no act. Serena was retreating, her mind far away. Instinctively he reached out and took her hands, wrapping them in his. She looked at him and his chest got tight. *Damn her.*

'What happened?'

Her hands were cold in his and her eyes had never looked bigger or bluer.

'I saw my father kill my mother when I was five years old.'

Luca's mouth opened and closed. 'You *what*?'

Serena couldn't seem to take her eyes off Luca, as if he was anchoring her to something. Her throat felt dry.

'When I was five I heard my parents arguing…nothing new…they argued all the time. I sneaked downstairs to the study. When I looked in through the crack of the door I could see my mother crying. I couldn't understand what they were arguing about, although in hindsight I know it was most likely to do with my father's affairs.'

Luca was grim. 'What happened?' he asked again.

'My father backhanded my mother across the face and she fell… She hit her head on the corner of his desk.'

Serena went inward.

'All I can remember is the pool of blood growing around her head on the rug and how dark it was. And how white she was. I must have made a sound, or something. The next thing I remember is my father dragging me back upstairs. I was crying for my mother…hysterical. My father hit me across the face…I remember one of my baby teeth was loose and it fell out… A doctor arrived. He gave me an injection. I can still remember the pain in my arm… The funeral…everything after that… was blurry. Siena was only three. But I can remember the doctor coming a lot. And once the police came. But I couldn't speak to them. I wanted to tell them what I'd seen but I'd been given something that made me sleepy. It didn't seem important any more.'

Her voice turned bitter.

'He got it covered up, of course, and no one ever accused him of her death. That's when it started. By the time I was twelve my father and his doctor were feeding my medication habit. They said I had ADHD—that I was difficult to control. Wilful. That it was for my own good. Then my father started saying things like *bi-polar*. He was constantly perpetuating a myth of mental uncertainty around me—even to my sister, who always believed that I tried to take my own life.'

'Did you?' Luca's voice was sharp.

Serena shook her head. 'No. But even though I denied it my sister was programmed by then to believe in my instability just like everyone else. My father even made a pretence of not allowing me to take drugs for the condition—while he was maintaining a steady supply to me through the doctor on his payroll.'

Luca shook his head. 'But why didn't you leave when you could?'

Serena pushed down the guilt. She had to start forgiving herself.

'I couldn't see a way out. By the time I was sixteen I was living the script my father had written for me years before.'

She reeled off the headlines of the time.

'I was a *wild child. Impossible to tame. Out of control.* And I was addicted to prescription drugs... Siena was innocent. The good girl. Even now Siena still retains an innocence I never had. My father played us off against each other. If Siena stepped out of line I got the punishment...never her. She was being groomed as the perfect heiress. I was being groomed as the car crash happening in slow motion.'

Luca's hands had tightened over hers and it was only then that Serena realised how icy she'd gone.

'Why haven't you ever gone to the police about your mother's death?'

Shame pricked Serena. 'Who would have believed disgraceful, unstable Serena DePiero? It felt hopeless. *I* felt hopeless. And in a way I had begun to doubt myself too...had it really happened? Maybe I was dreaming it up? Maybe I *was* just some vacuous socialite hooked on meds?'

Luca was shaking his head and Serena instantly went colder. She'd been a fool to divulge so much. She pulled her hands back.

'You don't believe me.'

Luca's gaze narrowed and his mouth thinned. 'Oh, I

believe you, all right. It just about makes sense. And I met your father—he was a cold bastard.' He shook his head. 'He turned you into an addict, Serena.'

Something fragile and treacherous unfurled inside Serena. *Acceptance.*

She said huskily, 'I'm sorry about before. I didn't want to tell you everything.'

'So what changed?'

Serena felt as if she was being backed into a corner again, but this time she fought the urge to escape or to push him away. 'You deserved to know the truth, and I was being less than honest.'

'Less than honest about what?'

He was going to make her say it.

Serena was captivated by Luca's gaze. Time seemed to have slowed to a throbbing heartbeat between them. In the same moment she was aware of a giddy rush through her body—a sense of weightlessness. She'd told someone her innermost secrets and the world hadn't crashed around her.

Serena's belly swooped and she took a leap into the void. 'I didn't want to spend the rest of the night alone. It was just an excuse.'

Luca looked at her and something in his eyes darkened. *Desire.* He cupped her face in his hands and slanted his mouth over hers in a kiss so light that it broke Serena apart more than the most passionate kisses they'd exchanged.

When he pulled back she kept him close and whispered shakily, 'Will you stay, Luca?'

She suddenly needed him desperately—needed a way to feel rooted when she might float off altogether and lose touch with the earth.

Luca kissed her mouth again and said throatily, 'Yes.'

He stood and pulled Serena up with him, and then he bent and scooped her into his arms as if she weighed no more than a feather. Her arms moved around his neck but she couldn't resist trailing her fingers along his jaw, and then reaching up to press a kiss against the pulse she could see beating under his bronzed skin.

His chest swelled against her breasts and her whole body pulsed with heat and awareness.

He put her down gently by the rumpled bed, where the scent of their bodies lingered in the air, sultry... Even though they'd already made love Serena was trembling as if they hadn't even touched for the first time.

They came together in a kiss of mutual combustion.

There was no time for Serena to worry about her body letting her down again because she was too feverish for Luca—hands spreading out over his bare chest, nails grazing his nipples, causing him to curse softly. Her hands moved to his trousers, and she unzipped them, freeing his erection. She took him in her hand, relishing the steely strength.

Luca's hands were busy too, opening the belt of the robe and sliding it over her shoulders. Serena looked up at him and took her hands away from his body so that the robe could fall to the floor.

His gaze devoured her...hot. Dark colour slashed his cheeks as he tugged his trousers down and off completely, kicking them aside.

He pushed her gently onto the bed. Serena was shocked at how fast her heart was racing, how ragged her breath was.

Gutturally he said, 'I want to take this slow—not like before.'

But Serena was desperate to feel him again. She was ready. She shook her head and whispered, 'I don't want slow. I want *you*.'

He caught her look and said rawly, 'Are you sure?'

She nodded again, and saw his jaw clench as if he was giving up some thin shred of control. He reached for protection and she watched him smooth it onto his erection, an almost feral look on his face.

Serena's sex pulsed with need. She lifted her arms and beckoned him, spreading her legs in a mute appeal.

His eyes flashed and he muttered something indistinct. He leant down to place his hand on her sex, cupping its heat. Serena found his wide shoulders and gripped him, biting her lip.

He spread his fingers and explored her secret folds, releasing the slick heat of her arousal.

His voice was rough. 'You're so ready for me.'

'Please…' said Serena huskily. 'I want you, Luca.'

Every cell in her body felt engorged with blood as he came down over her, pressing her into the bed, his body hard next to her softness. Crushing it deliciously.

He bent his head and took one pebbled nipple into his mouth, his teeth capturing it for a stinging second before letting go to soothe it with his tongue. This teasing was almost unbearable.

Serena was about to sob out another plea when he pushed his thick length inside her. Her eyes widened and she sucked in a breath as he pushed in, relentless, until he was buried inside her.

'You're so tight…like a vice.' He pressed a kiss to her mouth, hot and musky. 'Relax, *preciosa*…'

The endearment did something to Serena. She felt her body softening around him. He slid even deeper and a look of deep carnal satisfaction crossed his face, making something exult inside her. A sense of her own innately feminine power.

Her nipples scraped against his hair-roughened chest with a delicious friction as Luca started to move in and out, each powerful glide of his body reaching deeper inside Serena to a place she'd locked away long ago. She couldn't take her eyes off him. It was as if he was holding her within his gaze, keeping her rooted in the inexorable building of pleasure.

He reached around to her thigh and brought it up over his hip, his hand smoothing her flesh, then gripping it as his movements became harder, more powerful. That hand crept up and cupped her bottom, kneading, angling her hips, so that he touched some part of her that made her gasp out loud as a tremor of pleasure rocked through her pelvis.

Unconsciously Serena tilted her hips more and Luca moaned deeply. His thrusts became faster and Serena could feel the tight coil of tension inside her, tightening and tightening unbearably, to a point of almost pain.

She was incoherent, only able to stay anchored by looking into Luca's eyes. When she closed hers briefly he commanded roughly, 'Look at me, Serena.'

She did. And something broke apart deep inside her.

Her whole body tautened against his, nerves stretched to screaming point. Luca moved his hand between them, his fingers finding the engorged centre of her desire, and he touched her with a precision that left her nowhere to hide or hang on to. She imploded. Her control was shattered—the control she'd clung to all her life. Since her world had fallen apart as a child, when being *out* of control had become her control.

In one instant it was decimated, and Serena soared high on a wave of bliss that was spectacular. The definition of an orgasm being a *petit mort*, a small death, had never felt so apt. She knew that a part of her had just died and something else incredibly fragile and nebulous was taking its place.

She floated back down to reality, aware of her body milking Luca's own release as he shuddered and buried his head in her shoulder, his body embedded deep within hers. Her legs wrapped around him, and the pulsations of their mutual climaxes took long minutes to die away.

Luca was in the kitchen the following morning, making breakfast, before he realised that he'd never in his life made breakfast for a lover. In general he liked being in a situation where he could extricate himself rather than have to deal with the aftermath and unwelcome romantic projections.

But here he was, cooking breakfast for Serena without half a second's hesitation or any desire to put as much space between them as possible. His head was still fuzzy from an overload of sensual pleasure and the revelations she'd made.

He couldn't help thinking of her: a little girl, traumatised by the violent death of her mother, with a sadistic and mercurial father who tried to discredit her as soon as he could. Somehow it wasn't that fantastical to believe her father capable of such things.

He thought back to that night when he'd watched Siena come to bail Serena out of jail. The way she had tended to Serena like a mother to her cub...the way Serena had leant on her as if it was a familiar pattern.

Both had been manipulated by their father's machinations. Both had been acting out their parts. The good girl and the bad girl.

It all made a sick kind of sense now, because Luca knew he hadn't imagined the vulnerability he'd sensed about her that night he'd first met her…

A sound from behind him made him tense and he turned around to see Serena, tousle-haired and dressed in the robe, standing in the doorway. She looked hesitant, shy, and Luca was falling, losing his grip. Everything he thought he'd known about her…*wasn't*.

His hands gripped the bowl he was using to whisk eggs. 'Hungry?'

'Starving.'

Serena's voice was husky, and it fired up Luca's blood, reminding him of how she'd shouted out his name in the throes of passion just short hours before. How she'd begged and pleaded with him. How she'd felt around him.

Deus.

Serena came into the kitchen feeling ridiculously shy. Luca looked stern, intense.

'I didn't know you cooked.'

Luca grimaced in a half-smile, some of the intensity in his expression diminishing slightly as he continued whisking. 'I don't…I have a very limited repertoire and scrambled eggs is about as haute cuisine as it gets.'

Serena sat up on a stool by the island and tried not to let herself melt too much at seeing Luca in such a domestic setting in worn jeans and a T-shirt, his hair mussed up and a dark growth of stubble on his jaw.

'Where did you learn?'

He was taking thin strips of bacon now, and placing them under a hot grill. He didn't look at her. 'When my mother left, my father let the housekeeper go; he always felt it was an unnecessary expense.'

Serena felt indignation rise. 'But how did you cope? Did your father cook?'

Luca shook his head. 'I was at boarding school outside Rio for most of the time, so it was only the holidays when I had to fend for myself.' His mouth twisted. 'One of my father's many mistresses took pity on me when she found me eating dry cereal. She taught me some basics. I liked her—she was one of the nicer ones—but she left.'

More sharply than she'd intended, Serena said, 'She wasn't the one who seduced you?'

Luca looked at her, a small smile playing around his hard mouth. 'No.'

Embarrassed by the surge of jealousy, Serena said, 'Your father never married again?'

'No.'

Luca poured some delicious-smelling coffee out of a pot into big mugs, handing her one. Serena bent her head to smell deeply.

'He learnt his lesson after my mother walked away with a small fortune. She'd come from money in Italy, but by then it was almost all gone.'

Serena thought of his parents not even caring which boy went with who and felt sad. She remarked almost to herself, 'I can't imagine how I would have coped if Siena and I had been separated.'

Luca put a plate full of fluffy scrambled eggs and crispy bacon in front of Serena. He looked at her as he settled on his own stool. 'You're close, aren't you?'

Serena nodded, emotional for a second at the thought of her sister and her family. 'Yes, she saved me.'

Luca's gaze sharpened. 'It sounds to me like you saved yourself, as soon as you could.'

Serena shrugged minutely, embarrassed again under Luca's regard. 'I guess I did.' She swallowed some of the delicious food and asked curiously, 'Is your twin brother like you? Determined to right the wrongs of the world?'

Luca sighed heavily. 'Max is…complicated. He resented me for a long time because my father insisted on leaving everything to me—even though I tried to give him half when our father died. He was too proud to take it.'

Serena shook her head in disbelief, and was more than touched to know that Luca had been generous enough to do that.

'He had a tougher time than me—our mother was completely unstable, lurching from rich man to rich man in a bid to feather her nest, and in and out of rehab. Max went from being enrolled in an exclusive Swiss boarding school to living on the streets in Rome…'

Serena's eyes widened.

'He pulled himself out of the gutter with little or no help; he wouldn't accept any from me and he certainly wouldn't take it from my father. It was only years later, when he'd made his first million, that we could meet on common ground.'

Serena put down her knife and fork. Luca had shown signs of such intransigence and an inability to forgive when she'd first come to Rio, but now she was seeing far deeper into the man and realising he'd had just as much of a complicated background as she had in many respects. And yet he'd emerged without being tainted by the corruption of his father, or by the vagaries of his mother—vagaries that she understood far too well.

For the first time Serena had to concede that perhaps she hadn't done too badly, considering how easy it would have been to insist on living in a fog, not dealing with reality.

Luca was looking at her with an eyebrow raised. He was waiting for an answer to a question she hadn't heard. She blushed. 'Sorry. I was a million miles away.'

'You said when you first got here that you wanted to see Rio?'

Serena nodded, not sure where this was going or what might happen after last night.

'Well…'

Luca was exhibiting a tiny glimmer of a lack of his usual arrogance and it set Serena's heart beating fast.

'It's the weekend. I'd like to show you Rio.'

The bottom seemed to drop out of Serena's stomach. She felt ridiculously shy again. Something bubbled up inside her—lightness. *Happiness.* It was alien enough to take her by surprise.

'Okay, I'd like that.'

CHAPTER TEN

'HAD ENOUGH YET?'

Serena mumbled something indistinct. This was paradise. Lying on Ipanema Beach as the fading rays of the sun baked her skin and body in delicious heat. There was a low hum of conversation from nearby, the beautiful sing-song cadence of Portuguese, people were laughing, sighing, talking. The surf of the sea was crashing against the shore.

And then she felt Luca's mouth on hers and her whole body orientated itself towards his. She opened her eyes with an effort to find him looking down at her. Her heart flip-flopped. She smiled.

'Can we stay for the sunset?'

Luca was trying to hang on to some semblance of normality when the day that had just passed had veered out of *normal* for him on so many levels it was scary.

'Sure,' he said, with an easiness belying his trepidation. Serena's open smile was doing little to restore any sense of equilibrium.

One day spent walking around Rio and then a couple of hours on the beach was all it had taken to touch her skin with a luminous golden glow. Her hair looked blonder, almost white, her blue eyes were standing out even more starkly.

That morning they had taken the train up through the forest to the Cristo Redentor on Corcovado and Serena had been captivated by every tiny thing. Standing at the railing, looking down over the breathtaking panorama of Rio, she'd turned to him and asked, with a look of gleaming excitement that had reminded him of a child, 'Can we go to the beach later?'

Luca's insides had tightened ominously. She didn't want to go shopping. She wanted to see Rio. Genuinely.

Before they'd hit the beach they'd eaten lunch at a favourite café of Luca's. At one point he'd sat back and asked, with an increasing sense of defeat, 'Your family really aren't funding you...are they?'

Immediate affront had lit up those piercing eyes. Luca wouldn't have believed it before. But he did now, and it had made something feel dark and heavy inside him.

'Of course not.' She'd flushed then, guiltily, and admitted with clear reluctance, 'My sister and her husband paid for an apartment for me in Athens...when I was ready to move on. But I'm going to pay them back as soon as I've made enough money.'

Darkness had twisted inside Luca. People got handouts all the time from family, yet she clearly hated to admit it. And this was a woman who had had everything...a vast fortune to inherit...only to lose it all.

She'd flushed self-consciously when she'd caught him looking at her cleared plate of *feijoãda*, a famous Brazilian stew made with black beans and pork. 'My sister is the same. It's a reaction to the tiny portions of food we were allowed to eat by our father, growing up.'

Her revelation had hit him hard again. The sheer abuse her father had subjected her to. Anger still simmered in his belly. Luca had felt compelled to reach out and take her hand, entwining his fingers with hers—something that had felt far too easy and necessary.

'Believe me, it's refreshing to see a woman enjoy her food.'

Her hand had tensed in his and she'd said, far too lightly, while avoiding his eyes, 'I'm sure the women you know are far more restrained.'

Was she jealous? The suspicion had caught at Luca somewhere deeply masculine. And that deeply masculine part of him had been triggered again when he'd insisted on buying her a bikini so she could swim at the beach, as they hadn't been prepared.

He took her in now, as she lay beside him, the three tiny black triangles doing little to help keep his libido in check. He was just glad that the board shorts he'd bought to swim in were roomy enough to disguise his rampant response.

As if aware of his scrutiny Serena fidgeted, trying to pull the bikini over her breasts more—which only made some of the voluptuous flesh swell out at the other side.

Luca bit back a groan.

She'd hissed at him in the shop, 'I'm not wearing that—it's indecent!'

Luca had drawled wryly, 'Believe me, when you see what most women wear on the beaches here you'll feel overdressed.'

And when they'd hit the sand Serena's reaction had been priceless. Mouth open, eyes popping out of her head, she'd watched the undeniably sensual parade of beautiful bodies up and down the beach.

Luca hadn't been unaware of the blatant interest her pale blonde beauty had attracted, and had stared down numerous men.

The sun was setting now, and people were starting to cheer and clap as it spread out in a red ball of fire over the horizon, just to the left of one of Rio's craggy peaks.

Serena sat up and drew her legs to her chest, wrapping her arms around them. She smiled at Luca, before taking in the stunning sunset and clapping herself. 'I love how they do that.'

Her pleasure in something so simple mocked his deeply rooted cynicism. And then Luca realised then that he was enjoying this too, but it had been a long time since he'd taken the time to appreciate it. Even when he'd been younger he'd been so driven to try and counteract his father's corrupt legacy that he'd rarely taken any time out for himself. He'd fallen into a pattern of choosing willing women who were happy with no-strings-attached sex to alleviate any frustration.

He'd never relaxed like this in a typical *carioca* way, with a beautiful woman.

The sun had set and she looked at him now, and all he could see was the damp golden hair trailing over her shoulders, close to the full thrust of her breasts. Her mouth, like a crushed rose petal, was begging to be tasted. And those wide eyes were looking at him with a wariness that only fired his libido even more.

He said roughly, 'Let's get out of here.'

Serena couldn't mistake the carnal intent in Luca's eyes. He'd been looking at her all day as if he'd never seen her before. And today…today had been like a dream.

Her skin felt tight from the sun and sea, and she

didn't know if it was just Luca's unique effect on her, or the result of watching the Rio natives embrace their sensuality and sexuality all afternoon, but right now she trembled with the sexual need that pulsed through her very core and blood.

'Yes,' she said.

She stood up, and Luca stood too, handing her the sundress she'd put on that morning.

They walked the short distance back to Luca's car and when he took her hand in his, Serena's fingers tightened around his reflexively. He wore an open shirt over his chest, still in his shorts, and her heart clenched because he looked so much younger and more carefree than the stern, intimidating man she'd met again the day she'd arrived in Rio.

When they began winding up through the hills, away from the beaches, Serena asked, 'Where is this?'

Luca glanced at her. 'We're going to my home in Alto Gavea. It's closer.'

Serena's heart beat fast. *His home.*

The rest of the drive was in silence, as if words were superfluous and might not even penetrate the thick sensual tension between them.

This part of Rio was encased in forest, reminding Serena of the rainforest with a sharp poignancy. And Luca's home took her breath away when he turned in to a long secluded drive behind fortified gates.

It was an old colonial house, two-storey, white, with terracotta slates on the roof, and it was set, literally, in the middle of the lush Tijuca Forest.

He pulled the car to a stop and looked at her for a long moment. They were suspended in time, with no sounds except for the calls of some birds.

Then he broke the spell and got out of the car, help-ing Serena out of the low-slung seat. She let out a small squeal of surprise when he scooped her up into his arms and navigated opening the front door with commend-able dexterity.

He took the stairs two at a time and strode into a massive bedroom. Serena only had time to take in an impression of a house that was cool and understated. In his room, the open shutters framed a view showcas-ing the illuminated Christ the Redeemer statue in the far distance on its hill overlooking Rio.

Everything became a little dream-like after that, and Serena knew that on some level she was shying away from analysing the significance of the day that had passed.

Luca put her down, only to disappear into a bath-room, where she heard the sound of a shower running. When he emerged he was taking off his clothes until he stood before her naked, unashamedly masculine and proud.

'Come here.'

She obeyed without question. When she stood be-fore him he reached down for the hem of her dress and pulled it up and off. Then he turned her around and undid her flimsy bikini top so that it fell to the floor.

He turned her back and hooked his fingers into the bottoms, and pulled them down until she could step out of them at her feet. In that moment, naked, she'd never felt more womanly or more whole. Or more free of the shadows that had dogged her for as long as she could remember. They weren't gone completely, but it was enough for now.

He took her hand and led her into the bathroom,

which was fogged with steam that curled over their sticky, sandy bodies. Standing under the hot spray, Serena lifted her face and Luca covered her mouth with his, his huge body making the space tiny.

When he took his mouth off hers she opened her eyes to see his hot gaze devouring her. And just like that she was ready, her body ripening and moistening for him, ravenous at the sight of Luca's gleaming wet and aroused body. He lifted her and instructed her to put her legs around him—then groaned and stopped.

She looked at him, breathless with anticipation. 'What's wrong?'

'No protection, *preciosa*. We need to move.'

Serena was dazed as he carried her out of the shower, her legs still wrapped around his waist. She could see the pain on his face at the interruption but she was glad… She'd been too far gone to think about protection herself.

He put her down on the bed and reached for a condom from his cabinet, ripping the foil and sheathing himself with big, capable hands. Serena felt completely wanton as she watched this display of masculine virility.

And then he was coming back down over her, pushing her legs apart, settling between them, asking huskily, 'Okay?'

She nodded, her chest tightening ominously, and then Luca was thrusting in so deep her back arched and her legs went around his waist. It was fast and furious, his gaze holding hers, not letting her look away.

Bliss broke over her after mere minutes. She was so primed—as if now it was the easiest thing in the world and not something that had been torturously elusive when they'd first made love.

Serena bit into Luca's shoulder as powerful spasms racked her body just as he reached his own climax, his body thrusting rhythmically against hers until he was spent. He collapsed over her and she tightened her arms and legs around him, loving the feel of him pressing her into the bed, his body still big inside hers.

Eventually he withdrew, and Serena winced as her muscles protested. Luca collapsed on his back beside her, his breathing as uneven as hers. She looked at him to find him watching her with a small enigmatic smile playing around his mouth.

He came up on one arm and touched his fingers to her jaw. 'You make me lose my mind every time...' he admitted gruffly.

Serena looked at him. Somehow his confession wasn't as comforting as she'd thought it might be. It left her with a definite sense that Luca did not welcome such a revelation.

And then he was kissing her again, wiping everything from her mind, and she welcomed it weakly. She was far too afraid to face the suspicion that she had fallen in love with this man and there was no going back.

Three days later

'Miss DePiero? Senhor Fonseca said to let you know that he's been unavoidably detained and you should eat without him.'

'Okay, thank you.' Serena put down the kitchen phone extension and looked at the chicken stew she'd made, bubbling on the state-of-the-art cooker. *Unavoidably detained*. What was that code for?

Crazy to feel so disappointed, but she did. She'd spent her lunch hour buying ingredients, and as soon as she'd finished work at the charity office she'd rushed back to start cooking.

And now she felt ridiculous—because wasn't this such a cliché? The little woman at home, cooking dinner for her man and getting all bent out of shape because it was spoiled?

Mortified at the thought of what Luca's reaction would have been to see this attempt at creating some kind of domestic idyll, and losing any appetite herself, Serena took the chicken stew off the cooker. When it had cooled sufficiently she resisted the urge to throw it away and put it into a bowl to store in the fridge.

Feeling antsy, she headed outside to the terrace. The stunning view soothed her in a way that Athens had never done, even though she now called it home.

'Maledire,' she cursed softly in Italian. And then she cursed Luca, for making her fall for him.

The weekend had been…*amazing.* She remembered Luca kissing the tattoo on her shoulder. He'd murmured to her, 'You know the swallow represents resurrection?'

Serena had nodded her head, feeling absurdly emotional that he *got it.*

When they'd woken late on Sunday Luca had told her that he had to visit a local *favela* and she'd asked to go with him. She had seen first-hand his commitment to his own city. The amazing Fonseca Community Centre that provided literacy classes, language classes, business classes and a crèche so that everyone in the community could learn.

When she'd gone wandering, left alone briefly, she'd found Luca in the middle of a ring of men, doing *capoeira*, a Brazilian form of martial arts. He'd been stripped to the waist, his torso gleaming with exertion, making graceful and unbelievably agile movements to the beat of a drum played by a young boy.

She hadn't been the only woman ogling his spectacular form. By the time he'd finished, a gaggle of women and girls had been giggling and blushing. But a trickle of foreboding had skated over her skin... That had been the moment when he'd caught her eye and she'd seen something indecipherable cross his face. By the time he'd caught up with her again there had been something different about him. He'd shut down.

He'd brought her back here, to this apartment, and even though he'd stayed the night and made love to her, something had been off. When she'd woken he'd been gone, and she hadn't seen him again until late that evening, when he'd arrived and, with an almost feral look on his face, had kissed her so passionately that all tendrils of concern had fled, to be replaced with heat, distracting her from the fact that he clearly hadn't been interested in anything else.

The truth was that every moment she spent with Luca was ripping her apart internally. Especially when he looked at her as if she were some kind of unexploded device, yet kissed her as if his life depended on it. Clearly he was conflicted about her. He'd admitted that it was hard for him to come to terms with the fact that she wasn't what he'd believed her to be. And Serena had the gut-wrenching feeling that Luca would have almost preferred it if she *had* been the debauched, spoilt princess he'd expected.

She had to face the fact that her confession, while

liberating for her, had not proved to be so cataclysmic for Luca.

And of *course* it wouldn't have been, Serena chided herself. For Luca this was just…an affair. A slaking of desire. The fact that it had brought about her own personal epiphany was all Serena would have to comfort her when it was over, and that would have to be enough.

When Luca walked into the apartment it was after midnight. He felt guilty. He knew Serena had been making dinner because she'd told him earlier, when he'd seen her on a visit to the charity offices. It was a visit that had had his employees looking at him in surprise, because he usually conducted meetings in his own office and had little cause to visit them.

The apartment was silent, but he could smell the faint scent of something delicious in the air. When he went into the kitchen it was pristine, but he opened the fridge and saw the earthenware bowl containing dinner. The thought that perhaps she hadn't eaten because he hadn't been there made him feel guiltier. He hadn't even known that Serena could cook until she'd told him she'd taken lessons in Athens.

And he hadn't known how deeply enmeshed he was becoming with her until he'd looked at her in the *favela* and the enormity of it all had hit him. It had taken seeing her against that dusty backdrop—Serena DePiero, ex-socialite and wild child, looking as comfortable in the incongruous surroundings as if she'd been born into them like a native. In spite of the white-blonde beauty that had set her apart. He'd certainly been aware of the men looking at her, and the same black emotion that had gripped him at the beach had caught him again.

Jealousy. For the first time.

It was in that moment that a very belated sense of exposure had come over him and made him pull back from a dangerous brink. Luca knew better than anyone how fickle people were—how you couldn't trust that they wouldn't just pull your world out from under your feet within seconds.

His own parents had done it to him and his brother—setting them on different paths of fate almost as idly as if they were Greek gods, playing with hapless mortals. For years he'd had nightmares about his parents pulling them limb from limb, until their body parts were so mixed up that they didn't even know who was who any more.

Serena was getting too close—under his skin. Everything kept coming back to how badly he'd misjudged her—and never more so than now. He'd just had a conversation with his brother, who was in Rio on business.

And yet as he stood in the doorway of her bedroom now and saw the shape of her under the covers, the bright splash of white-blonde hair, he was taking off his clothes before he even realised what he was doing, sliding in behind her, wrapping himself around her and trying desperately to ignore the way his soul felt inexplicably soothed.

Even as she woke and turned towards him, her seeking sleepy mouth finding his, Luca was steeling himself inside—because this would all be over as soon as she knew what his brother had just told him. Because then everything that had bound them from the past would be gone.

But just…not yet.

When Serena woke in the dawn light, the bed was empty. But the hum in her body and the pleasurable

ache between her legs told her she hadn't dreamt that
Luca had come into her bed last night. Or dreamt the
mindless passion he'd driven her to, taking her over the
edge again and again, until she'd been spent, exhausted,
begging for mercy.

It was as if Luca had been driven by something desperate.

She blinked, slowly coming awake. And even though
her body was sated and lethargic from passion, her heart
was heavy. She loved Luca, and she knew with cold certainty that he didn't love her. But he wanted her.

His love was his commitment to the environment,
to making the world a better place in whatever small
way he could, born from his zeal not to be like his pre-
decessors—a zeal she could empathise with.

And Serena knew that she wouldn't be able to continue falling deeper and deeper without recognising
that the heartbreak would be so much worse when she
walked away.

It was only when she sighed deeply and moved her
head that she felt something, and looked to see a note
on the pillow beside her.

She reached for the thick paper and opened it to read:

Please meet me in my office when you wake. L.

A definite shiver of foreboding tightened Serena's
skin. No wonder there had been something desperate
in Luca's lovemaking last night. This was it. He was
going to tell her it was over. The signs had been there
for the last few days, since the *favela*.

Anger lanced her. To think that he would just send
her away so summarily after sating his desire, which

was obviously on the wane, and after she'd enjoyed working in the charity office so much. But, as much as she'd come to love Rio de Janeiro, she didn't relish the thought of being in such close proximity to him in the future—seeing him get on with his life, take another lover.

She wasn't going to let him discard her completely, though; no matter what had happened between them personally he owed her a job. In any event, she knew now that she had to go home. So, while Luca might be preparing to let her go, Serena told herself stoutly that she was ready.

It was only when she noticed her hands trembling in the shower that she had to admit her anger was stemming from a place of deep fear that she was about to feel pain such as she'd never felt before—not even when she'd been at her lowest ebb, trapped by her addictions. Before, she'd anaesthetised herself against the pain. Now she would have nothing to cling on to, and she wasn't sure how ready she was to cope with that.

CHAPTER ELEVEN

WHEN SERENA KNOCKED on Luca's office door about an hour later she felt composed, dressed in plain trousers and a silk shirt. Hair tied back. It had been a mere two weeks since she'd come here for the first time, but she was a different person.

Damn him.

His assistant opened the door and ushered her in, and it took a second after the girl had left for Serena to realise that there was another man in the room. He was standing on the other side of Luca's desk, and Luca stood up now from his high-backed chair.

'Serena—come in.'

Her heart lurched. So formal. For a crazy moment Serena wondered if the other man was a solicitor, so that Luca could get out of the contract?

When she came closer, though, she saw a resemblance between the two men, even though this man had tawny eyes and dark blond messy hair. They were almost identical in size and build. The stranger was as arrestingly gorgeous as Luca, but in a more traditional way—in spite of the scar she could see running from his temple to his jaw. He oozed danger, even though he looked as if he might have stepped from the pages of Italian *Vogue* in an immaculate dark suit.

She sensed a subtle tension in the air, and had just realised herself who he was when Luca said, 'This is my brother—Max Fonseca Roselli.'

She came forward and took the hand offered to her, suffering none of the physical reaction Luca caused within her with only a look. Even so, she saw the unmistakably appreciative gleam in his unusual golden-green eyes and could well imagine that he must leave a trail of bleeding hearts wherever he went. He had that same indomitable arrogance that Luca wore so well.

'Nice to meet you.'

His hand squeezed hers. 'You too.'

Serena pulled away, getting hot, sensing Luca's intense focus on them and Max's desire to needle his brother. When she looked at Luca, though, he gave nothing away and she cursed herself. Of *course* he wouldn't be proprietorial or jealous.

Luca indicated for them to sit down and said heavily, 'Max has some news for you…and me. I thought I owed it to you to let him tell you face to face.'

Now Serena was nervous, and she looked from him to Max and back. 'What is it?'

Luca explained. 'I asked Max to look into what happened at the club that night—to do some digging.'

Before she could properly assimilate that information, Max drawled in a deep voice, 'My brother knows I have some…less than legitimate connections.'

Serena looked at him and her heart went out to both of them for what they'd been through as children. The way their parents had all but rolled the dice to decide their fate.

Huskily she admitted, 'I… Luca told me what happened.'

Max's eyes flared and he shot his brother a scowl.

Luca said warningly, 'This isn't about *us*.'

For a second Serena could have laughed. They might not be identical, but right then she could see how similar they were—and they probably didn't even know it themselves.

Max looked back to her. 'I did some digging and discovered who did plant the drugs on Luca that night. He was a small-time dealer and in the crush he spotted you together. He knew that if he could plant the drugs on you or Luca no one would ever dispute that you had been involved.'

Shame lanced Serena to be reminded that everyone knew of her exploits and how tarnished her reputation was, even as her heart beat fast and she wondered why Luca had asked his brother to do this.

Max continued. 'He's actually in jail at the moment on another charge, and he's been bragging to anyone who will listen about how he set you and Luca up— it would appear that he couldn't bear to keep such a coup to himself. He's been charged with the offence and hasn't a leg to stand on because he's confessed to so many witnesses.'

For a moment the relief was so enormous that Serena felt dizzy, even though she was sitting down. She looked at Luca, whose face was stern. 'You can clear your name.'

He nodded, but he didn't look happy about it. He looked grim.

Max stood up, rising with athletic grace. 'My flight leaves in a couple of hours. I have to go.'

Serena stood up too. 'Thank you so much. This means…a lot.'

Max inclined his head before sending an enigmatic look to his brother. 'I'll be in touch.'

Luca nodded. They didn't embrace or shake hands before Max left, striding out with that same confident grace as his brother.

When he was gone, Serena sank down onto the chair, her head in a spin. She looked at Luca, barely taking in that he looked a little pale, his face all lean lines. 'How…? Why did you ask him to do this?'

He sighed heavily. 'Because I owed it to you to find out the truth. After all, you've been nothing but honest with me. The fact is that I think I suspected you were innocent in the jungle. This just proves that you were as much a victim as I was. You deserve to have your life back, Serena. And you deserve to have the slate cleared too. My lawyers and my PR team will make sure this is in all the papers.'

Serena felt an almost overwhelming surge of emotion to think that Luca was going out of his way to clear her name too. Perhaps now people wouldn't always associate her with feckless debauchery.

Treacherously, this made her hope for too much, even when *The End* was written into every tense line of Luca's body. Clearly he just wanted to move on now.

It made her want to push him away again, for making her feel too much. For making her fall in love. *Damn him*.

'And if Max hadn't found the culprit so easily? Would you have believed me anyway?'

Luca stood up and paced behind his desk, his white shirt pulled across his chest, trousers hugging slim hips. Just like that, heat flared in Serena's solar plexus.

He stopped and looked at her. 'Yes.'

Serena cursed herself for pushing him. She hated

herself for the doubt, for thinking that he was lying. And then she had to concede that Luca *didn't* lie. He was too moral. Too damn good.

She stood up again, her legs wobbly. 'Well, thank you for finding out.'

Luca looked at her for a long moment, and then he said, 'Serena—'

She put up her hand, because she couldn't bear for him to say it. 'Wait. I have something I need to tell you first.'

His mouth closed and he folded his arms across his chest. Serena knew she couldn't be anything else other than completely honest. She had been through too much soul-searching to ever want to hide away from pain again. She might never see him again. The urge to tell him how she felt was rising like an unstoppable wave.

'I've fallen in love with you, Luca.'

He looked at her, and as she watched, the colour leached from his face. She broke apart inside, but was determined not to show it.

'I know it's the last thing you want to hear. We were only ever about...' she stalled '...not *that*...and I know it's over.'

She gestured with a hand to where Max had been sitting.

'After this...we owe each other nothing. And I'm sorry again that your association with me made things bad for you.'

Luca unfolded his arms and slashed a hand in the air, looking angry. 'You don't have to apologise—if I hadn't been so caught up in blaming you, I would have ensured a proper investigation was carried out years ago. You had to suffer the stigma of those accusations too.'

Serena smiled bitterly. 'I was used to it, though. I had no reputation to defend.'

'No—your father took care of that.'

Responsibility weighed heavily on her shoulders. 'I have to go home… I have to tell people about my father—see that he's brought to justice finally.'

'If there's anything you need help with, please let me know.'

Her heart twisted. So polite. So courteous. A million miles from their first meeting in this office. And even though she knew her own family would be there to back her up, she felt an awful quiver of vulnerability—because, really, the only person she wanted by her side the day she faced her father again was Luca.

But that scenario was not to be part of her future.

She hitched up her chin and tried to block out the fact that she'd told Luca she loved him and had received no similar declaration in return. That fantasy belonged deep where she harboured dreams of the kind of fulfilment and happiness she saw her sister experiencing with her family. But at least she could take one good thing with her.

'Are you still going to give me a job?'

'Of course—wherever you want,' Luca said quickly, making another piece of Serena's heart shatter. He was obviously *that* eager to see her go.

'I'd like to go back to Athens today.'

Luca said tightly, 'Laura will arrange it for you.'

'Thank you.'

So clipped, so polite.

Before anger could rise at Luca's non-reaction to her baring her soul to him, she turned to leave.

She was at the door before she heard a broken-sounding, 'Serena…'

Heart thumping, hope spiralling, Serena turned around. Luca looked tortured.

But he said only two words. 'I'm sorry.'

Her heart sank like a stone. She knew he didn't love her, but she marvelled that the human spirit was such an irrepressibly optimistic thing even in the face of certain disappointment.

She forced a smile. 'Don't be. You've given me the gift of discovering how strong I am.'

You've given me the gift of discovering how strong I am.

Luca was stuck in a state of paralysis for so long after Serena left that he had to blink and focus to realise that Laura was in his office and speaking to him, looking worried.

'Senhor Fonseca? Are you all right?'

And as if he'd been holding something at bay, it ripped through him then, stunning and painful in its intensity, like warmth seeping into frozen limbs. Burning.

'No,' he issued curtly, going over to his drinks cabinet and helping himself to a shot of whisky.

When he turned around, Laura's eyes were huge and she was pale. And Luca knew he was coming apart at the seams.

He forced himself not to snarl at the girl, but the pain inside him was almost crippling. 'What is it?'

Laura stuttered, making him feel even worse. 'It's—it's Miss DePiero. I just thought you'd want to know she's on her way to the airport. She's booked first class on a flight to Athens this afternoon.'

'Thank you,' Luca bit out. 'I'm going to be unavailable for the rest of the day. Please cancel all my appointments. Go home early if you want.'

Laura blinked and said faintly, 'Yes, sir.' And then backed away as if he might explode.

He waited until Laura had left and then left himself, knowing nothing more than that he needed to get out—get away. Because he felt like a wounded animal that might lash out and cause serious harm.

He was aware of one or two people approaching him as he walked out of the building, but they quickly diverted when they saw his face. He walked and walked without even knowing where he was going until he realised he was at Ipanema Beach. Where he'd taken Serena just a few days ago.

The scene was the same, even during the week. The beautiful bodies. The amorous couples. The crashing waves. But it mocked him now, for feeling so carefree that day. For believing for a moment that he could be like those people. That he could *feel* like them.

Anger rose up as he ripped off his tie and jacket, dropping them on a bench and sitting down. That was the problem. He knew he couldn't feel. The ability had been cut out of him the day he and his brother had been torn apart.

As young boys they'd been close enough to have a special language that only they understood. It had used to drive their father crazy. And Luca could remember that they'd sensed something was happening that day when their parents had brought them into their father's study.

Luca's mother had bent down to his level and said, with the scent of alcohol on her breath, 'Luca, darling,

I love you so much I want to take you to Italy with me. Will you come?'

He'd looked at Max, standing near his father. Luca had known that Max loved their mother—he had too—but he didn't like it when she came home drunk and falling down. He and Max would fight about it—Max hating it if Luca said anything critical, which he was more liable to do.

He'd looked back at his mother, confused. 'But what about Max? Don't you love him too?'

She'd been impatient. 'Of course I do. But Max will stay here with your father.'

Panic had clutched at his insides, making him feel for a moment as if his bowels might drop out of his body. 'For ever?'

She'd nodded and said, slurring slightly, 'Yes, *caro*, for ever. We don't need them, do we?'

Luca had heard a noise and looked to see Max, ashen, eyes glimmering with tears. 'Mamma...?'

She'd made an irritated sound and said something in rapid Italian, taking Luca by the hand forcibly, as if to drag him out. Luca had felt as if he was in some kind of nightmare. Max had started crying in earnest and had run to their mother, clutching at her waist. That was when Luca had felt some kind of icy calm come over him—as if Max was acting out how he felt deep inside, but he couldn't let it out. It was too huge.

His mother had issued another stream of Italian and let Luca go, shoving him towards his father, prising Max off her and saying angrily, '*Bastante!* Stop snivelling. I'll take you with me instead. After all,' she'd said snidely over Max's hiccups, 'your father doesn't care *who* he gets...'

The black memory faded. His mother had told him she loved him and then minutes later she'd demonstrated how empty her words were. Swapping one brother for the other as if choosing objects in a shop.

Serena had told him she loved him.

As soon as she'd said the words, Luca had been transported back to that room, closing in on himself, waiting for the moment when she'd turn around and show him that she didn't mean it. Not really. She was only saying it because that was what women did, wasn't it? They had no idea of the devastation they could cause when the emptiness of their words was revealed.

But she hadn't looked blasé. Nor as if she hadn't meant it. She'd been pale. Her blue eyes had looked wounded when he'd said, 'I'm sorry.'

He thought of her words: *You've made me see how strong I am.*

Luca felt disgusted. And how strong was *he*? Had he ever gone toe-to-toe with his own demons? No, because he'd told himself building up trust in the Fonseca name again was more important.

He heard a sound and looked up to see a plane lifting into the sky from the airport. He knew it couldn't be her plane, but he had a sudden image of her on it, leaving, and panic gripped him so acutely that he almost called out.

It was as clear as day to him now—what lay between him and his brother. He should have ranted and railed that day when their parents had so cruelly split them up. He should have let it out—not buried it so deep that he'd behaved like a robot since then, afraid to feel anything. Afraid to face the guilt of knowing that he could have done more to protect them both.

If he'd let out the depth of his anger and pain, as Max had, then maybe they wouldn't have been split apart. Two halves of a whole, torn asunder. Maybe their parents would have been forced to acknowledge the shallow depths of their actions, their intent of scoring points off each other.

It all bubbled up now—and also the sick realisation that he was letting it happen all over again. That while he'd had an excuse of sorts before, because he'd only been a child, he was an adult now—and if he couldn't shout and scream for what he wanted then he and Max had been pawns for nothing.

And, worse, he'd face a life devoid of any meaning or any prospect of happiness. Happiness had never concerned him before now. He'd been content to focus on loftier concerns, telling himself it was enough. And it wasn't. Not any more.

Serena stood in line for the gate in the first-class lounge. She was grateful for it, because there was enough space there for her to feel numb and not to have to deal with a crush of people around her.

She couldn't let herself think of Luca, even though her circling thoughts kept coming back to him and that stark look on his face. *I'm sorry*.

She was sorry too. Now she knew how he'd felt when he'd told her that he wished he'd never set eyes on her.

She wanted to feel that way too—she actively encouraged it to come up. But it wouldn't. Because she couldn't regret knowing him. Or loving him. Even if he couldn't love her back.

For a wild moment Serena thought of turning around and going back, telling him she'd settle for whatever he could give her... And then she saw herself in a few years...months...? Her soul shrivelled up from not being loved in return.

The man ahead of her moved forward and the airline steward was reaching for her boarding pass.

She was about to take it back and go through when she heard a sort of commotion, and then a familiar voice shouting, 'I need to see her!'

She whirled around to see Luca being restrained by two staff members a few feet away, dishevelled and wild-looking in shirt and trousers.

'What are you *doing*?' she gasped in shock, stepping out of the way so that people could continue boarding.

She wouldn't let her heart beat fast. She couldn't. It didn't mean anything.

His eyes were fierce. 'Please don't go. I need you to stay.'

A feeling of euphoria mixed with pain surged through her. 'Why do you want me to stay, Luca?'

The men holding him kept a tight grip. Luca didn't even seem to notice, though. He looked feverish, as if he was burning up.

His voice was rough with emotion. 'When you told me you loved me...I couldn't believe it. I was too afraid to believe. My mother said that to me right before she swapped me for my brother...as if we were nothing.'

Serena's belly clenched. 'Oh, Luca...' She looked at the security men, beseeching, 'Please let him go.'

They finally did, but stayed close by, ready to move in again. Serena didn't care. She was oblivious.

He took her hand and held it to his chest, dragging her closer. She could feel his heart thudding against his chest.

'You say you love me…but a part of me can't trust it…can't believe it. I'm terrified that you'll turn around one day and walk away—confirm all my twisted suspicions that when people say they love you, they'll annihilate you anyway.'

Serena felt an incredible welling of love and reached out her other hand to touch Luca's face. She knew he was scared.

'Do you love me?'

After a long moment—long enough for her to see how hard this was for him to admit—he said, 'The thought of you leaving, of life without you…is more than I can bear. If that's love then, yes, I love you more than I've loved anyone else.'

Serena's heart overflowed. 'Are you willing to let me prove how much I love you?'

Luca nodded. 'The pain of letting you go is worse than the pain of facing my own pathetic fears. You've humbled me with your strength and grace.'

She shook her head, tears making her vision blurry. 'They're not pathetic fears, Luca. I'm just as scared as you are.'

He smiled, and it was shaky, all that arrogant bravado replaced by raw emotion. He joked, 'You? Scared? Not possible. You're the bravest person I know. And I have no intention of ever letting you out of my sight again.'

Serena smiled and fought back tears as Luca pulled her in to him and covered her mouth with his, kissing her with unrestrained passion.

When they separated, the crowd around them clapped and cheered. Giddy, Serena blushed and ducked her head against Luca's neck.

He looked at her. 'Will you come home with me?'

Home. Her own place—with him.

The ferocity and speed with which they'd found each other terrified her for a moment. *Could she trust it?* But she saw everything she felt mirrored in Luca's eyes, and she reached out and snatched the dream before it could disappear.

'Yes.'

The next day when Serena woke up she pulled on a big T-shirt and went looking for Luca in his house in Alto Gavea. She still felt a little dizzy from everything that had happened. She and Luca had come back here from the airport, and after making love they'd talked until dawn had broken. He'd promised to go to Athens with her to start the lengthy process of telling her family everything and pursuing her father.

She heard a noise as she passed his study and went in to see him sitting behind his desk in only jeans. Stubbled jaw. He looked up and smiled, and Serena couldn't help smiling back goofily.

He held out a hand. 'Come here.'

She went over and let him catch her, pulling her onto his lap. After some breathless kisses she moved back. 'What are you doing?'

A glint of something came into his eyes and he said, 'Catching up on local news.'

He indicated with his head to the computer and Serena turned to look. When she realised what she was seeing, she tensed in his arms. The internet was filled with photos of them kissing passionately in the airport—obviously taken by people's mobile phones. One headline screamed: *Has Fonseca tamed wild-child DePiero at last*? Another one: *Fonseca and DePiero rekindle their scandalous romance!*

She felt sick and turned to Luca, who was watching her carefully. 'I'm sorry. This is exactly what you were afraid of.'

But he just shrugged, eyes bright and clear. No shadows. 'I couldn't care less what they say. And they have it wrong—you tamed *me*.'

Serena let the past fall away and caressed Luca's jaw, love rising to make her throat tight. 'I love you just as you are.'

Luca said gruffly, 'I want to take you to every beach in South America to watch the sunset—starting with the ones here in Rio.'

Serena felt breathless. 'That could take some time.'

Luca kissed her and said, 'At least a lifetime, I'm hoping.'

He deliberately lifted up her left hand then, and pressed a kiss to her ring finger, a question in his eyes and a new tension in his body. Serena's heart ached that he might still doubt her love.

She nodded her head and said simply, 'Yes. The answer will always be yes, my love.'

Three years later.

The wide-eyed American reporter was standing in front of Rome's supreme court and saying breathlessly, 'This is the trial of the decade—if not the century. Lorenzo DePiero has finally been judged and condemned for his brutality and corruption, but no one could have foreseen the extent to which his own children and his wife suffered. His landmark sentencing will almost certainly guarantee that he lives out the rest of his days in jail.'

The press were still stunned to have discovered that the privileged life they'd assumed the DePiero heiresses to have lived had all been a lie.

Behind the reporter there was a flurry of activity as people streamed out of the majestic building. First was Rocco De Marco, the illegitimate son of Lorenzo De-Piero, with his petite red-haired wife Gracie. Quickly on their heels were Siena Xenakis and her husband Andreas.

But the press waited with hushed reverence for the person they wanted to see most: Serena Fonseca. She had taken the stand for four long days in a row and had listed a litany of charges against her father. Not least of which had been the manslaughter of his wife, their mother, witnessed by her when she was just five years old.

If anyone had been in doubt about the reliability of a witness who had been only five at the time, the further evidence of her father's systematic bullying and collusion with a corrupt doctor to get her hooked on medication had killed those doubts.

Her composed beauty had been all the more poignant for the fact that she hadn't let her very advanced pregnancy stop her from taking on such an arduous task: facing down her father every day. But then, everyone agreed that the constant presence by her side of her husband, Luca Fonseca, had undoubtedly given her strength.

They finally emerged now—a striking couple. Luca Fonseca had an arm curved protectively around his wife and the press captured their visible smiles of relief.

Lawyers for the respective parties gave statements as the family got into their various vehicles and were whisked away with a police escort to a secret location, where they were all due to celebrate and unwind after the previous taxing months.

Luca looked at Serena in the back of the Land Rover, their hands entwined. He lifted them up and pressed a kiss to her knuckles. 'Okay?'

Serena smiled. She felt as if a weight had finally been lifted off her shoulders for the first time in her life. She nodded. 'Tired…but happy it's finally done and over.'

Luca pressed a long, lingering kiss to her mouth, but when he pulled back, Serena frowned and looked down. Immediately concerned, Luca said, 'What is it?'

Serena looked at him, a dawning expression of shock and wonder on her face. 'My waters have just broken… all over the back seat.'

The driver's eyes widened in the rearview mirror and he discreetly took out a mobile phone to make a call.

Serena giggled at the comic look of shock and pure fear on Luca's face. He'd been on high alert for weeks now, overreacting to every twinge Serena felt. And then it hit her—along with a very definite cramping of pain.

Her hand tightened on his. 'Oh, my God, we're in labour.'

Luca went into overdrive, instructing the driver to go to the nearest hospital.

Their police escort was already peeling away from the rest of the convoy and the driver reassured him in Italian, 'I'm on it—we'll be there in ten minutes.'

Luca sat back, heart pumping with adrenalin, a huge ball of love and emotion making his chest full. He drank in his beloved wife, her beautiful face, and those eyes that never failed to suck him in and make him feel as if he were drowning.

'I love you,' he whispered huskily, the words flowing easily from his heart.

'I love you too.'

Serena smiled, but it was wobbly. He could see the emotion in her eyes mirrored his own. He spread his hand over her distended belly, hard with their child who was now starting the journey to meet them.

His wife, his family...*his life*. He was enriched beyond anything he might have believed possible.

And eight hours later, when he held his newborn baby daughter in his arms, her tiny face scrunched up and more beautiful than anything he'd ever seen in his life—after his wife—Luca knew that trusting in love was the most amazing revelation of all.

* * * * *

WHO'S AFRAID OF THE BIG BAD BOSS?

NINA HARRINGTON

CHAPTER ONE

SCOTT ELSTROM LOOKED out across the sea ice and squinted as the Alaskan sun rose over the horizon and made the light covering of snow suddenly turn brilliantly white.

It was so beautiful that for a moment he forgave the brutal biting wind that came with crossing the frozen sea. There was no cover for himself or his team of nine sled dogs and he could feel his cheeks burning with frostbite under the mask covering his face.

Reaching up with gloved hands, Scott turned off his head torch to save the batteries and, stepping off the sled, he ran a hundred paces on the thick plate of ice to get some warmth into his body and then jumped back onto the sled, much to the amusement of the dogs. The lead dog, Dallas, actually looked back and seemed to grin at him.

The dogs loved this weather: bright sunshine and a clear trail ahead across the sound to the base camp on the other side of the bay.

The fact that they had only crossed this stretch of sea ice once before didn't matter. They were happy just to be out and doing what they did best. *Running.*

He had been out with his dogs for thirteen days, taking mapping and geo readings at each of the twenty stations the ecological survey company had established. Sometimes that meant staying in a small town along the way but often the station was a simple wooden house or shack where he would be alone with his dogs, checking their feet and feeding them. He loved this way of life and the gentle routine that they had settled into.

Out here in the silence he felt a kinship with all of the explorers who had used Elstrom maps in the past to find a route to new worlds as well as to hunt and fish.

Now that routine was shattered. The message from his sister, Freya, had been short and to the point.

Their father was in hospital. He had suffered another stroke and, although it was a small one and the doctors said that he should make a good recovery, his father wanted to talk to him. Urgently. *Come home, Scott. We need you here.*

Scott rolled his shoulders and fought back a sense of guilt at his resentment at having to go back to what passed for civilization a week earlier than he had planned.

They needed him. *Well, that was new!*

It had been two years since his father had handed over the management of their family business to his stepbrother, Travis. And look how well that decision had turned out! Now Travis was long gone and his father had been fighting for months to save what was left of Elstrom Mapping.

For their father to even admit that he needed Scott was astonishing.

That was why Scott had taken the decision to cross the open water instead of travelling inland and taking the slower route through the frozen forest and rivers to the station where he would find a snow machine and a lift to the local airstrip.

There was no other choice. He had to cross the frozen sea ice to get to the base camp to the airbase in time to catch the weekly cargo plane—it would take too long any other way.

But crossing open salt water ice was a serious commitment. The sea froze in huge cracked and floating plates which moved and heaved under the sled, making progress slow and dangerous. The ice was always unstable and never more so in the unusually mild Alaskan February.

Scott looked over the sled and, to his horror, he could see the ice ridges flexing and cracking. A giant piece of ice had broken away and was floating out to sea. He was driving across the frozen-over thinner layer.

One crack in a weak spot and the weight of the sled would drag him and the whole dog team underwater to their deaths, never to be found again.

There was a low grunt from his lead dog, Dallas, as she picked up a scent and set off at a steady pace onto the thicker ice, the other eight dogs behind her panting and settling into a trot from months of training and working together. They would run all day if he asked them, without complaint.

The blinding sunlight made Scott squint and glance sideways towards the open water of the sea.

For the last twenty-four hours he had been travelling and had barely dozed in the wooden trappers' cabin for the the four or five hours while the dogs rested. Now, as the sun rose higher and warmed his skin, and the dogs moved steadily forwards, his mind drifted seawards.

The only sound was from the movement of the sled on the ice and the comforting panting noises of nine dogs moving as a team.

Beautiful. Unique. *Mesmerising*.

This was his life now. Not central London and everything that went with it.

He had waved goodbye to that world two years ago and would quite happily not see it again unless he had to. The technology he was using for his mapping and surveying meant that he could talk to his sister and his father, if he chose to, most days and at least once a week.

Of course Freya had tried to persuade him to come home for Christmas but what had been the point?

His quiet academic father had never understood how his son preferred adventure sports and a hard outdoor life to the quiet study of the maps and charts that had made Elstrom Mapping a familiar name around the world.

The only common thing holding them together had been the mapping company, and when his father had decided that Travis could be trusted to lead the company that link had been swept away, leaving nothing but regrets and harsh words behind.

The weather had closed in during December and made travel impossible for anyone at the research station, so he had a perfectly valid and very convenient excuse to stay in Alaska.

Way too convenient an excuse according to his sister, who'd ended up coping on her own for the holidays, being bounced between divorced parents who had drifted away from one another for years before their mother finally gave up trying to make a family with a father who was never home. Freya had spent New Year's with their quite happily settled mother and her new boyfriend—a lawyer with a fine selection of colourful bow ties.

Scott chuckled to himself deep in the back of his throat. Freya would make him suffer for that one. He looked up and was just about to check his GPS position when his world shifted.

He felt the sled shudder and slip underneath him.

They had hit a weak spot in the ice.

Instantly every cell in his body leapt to attention, adrenaline surging through his veins.

While he had been thinking about London firesides, Dallas had slowed down, her tail high and in the shape of a question mark instead of hanging straight down. And her paws were dancing.

Scott's heart almost stopped.

He couldn't swim in five layers of thermal clothing and, even if he could, the water was so cold he wouldn't last more than a few minutes. He would go down with the sled and the dogs.

The dogs would die because his father had given up the fight.

No way. Not while he still had breath in his body.

Scott snatched up the solid grab rope and dropped off the back of the sled onto his stomach, his legs spread wide so his body weight would be spread over the thin ice. 'Dallas. Gee right. Gee right. Dallas.'

Dallas knew that this was the instruction to turn right to safety and she tugged and tugged as the team fought her, the other eight dogs desperate to run hard and straight. But she did it and after a few terrifying minutes Scott felt a ridge of hard ice under his stomach and they were back on the older solid pan ice.

The broken shards of ice ripped his right glove to shreds and his fingers instantly turned numb and blue. Frostbite. But he managed to haul himself back onto the sled and the dogs sped on to safety as the shapes of the cabins on the other side of the bay grew clearer in the growing early morning light.

He was going to make it home in time to hear what his father had to say after all.

But one thing was for sure. This was his chance to prove to his father that he was a better man than Travis could ever be. And nothing was going to stand in his way and stop him from making that happen. Not this time.

* * *

'So let me get this straight. Those G-strings are edible?'

Toni pulled away the wrapping paper from the pink and black gift box that her sister Amy had given her and started reading the instructions on the back.

'Of course.' Amy shrugged and flicked the fluffy feather end of her pink whip against the packing. 'Why else would you want to wear something that uncomfortable?'

'I have just had a vision of what happens when those candy pieces come adrift and where they might end up in my lady parts. Amy, I love you and you are my only sister but I may save modelling this particular birthday pressie for another day.'

Amy giggled and shook her head. 'Those knickers are not for us to ogle at. Save it for that hunky boyfriend you're going to meet.' She knocked her on the head with the feather whip again. 'Very soon.'

'Well, in that case I might as well put the box in the freezer right now and stick to eating supermarket chocolate bars.'

Amy sighed out loud and collapsed down on the arm of the dining chair next to Toni. 'Now don't be like that. It has been a whole year since you got rid of that skanky Peter and what did we agree? He was totally not worthy of your luscious magnificence. Right? Of course right. This is a new year and a new you, remember?'

Toni smiled and hugged the present to her new burgundy satin bra. 'When did you get to be so clever? I'm going to miss having you around. You know that, don't you?'

'Of course. That's why I've loaded up all these fancy gizmos on my tech so that we can talk every week!'

Amy wrapped one arm around Toni's bare shoulders

and rocked from side to side. 'It's only a few months and I'll be right back in time to start university in September.' Then she slid back and sniffed once. 'And, for the record, I'll miss you too but I'll work hard to block out my pain by having the best gap year trip this world has to offer.'

Then she pointed the whip at Toni. 'All thanks to the lovely Christmas present from my darling sister.' She nodded over her shoulder. 'The gals still cannot believe that you bought me a round-the-world plane ticket. Magic!'

'How else could I get you out of the house long enough to get the plumbing fixed?' Toni grinned. 'You're welcome. But you do remember that there's one condition. You have to enjoy yourself and not spend the whole time digging up bits of ancient Peru.'

'I can guarantee it. Oh! Looks like I'm getting the signal. I think more birthday cake might be almost ready. Be back soon.'

And with that Amy got to her feet and sashayed off as though she always wore a black laced-up pink and cream frilly basque and feather-trimmed mules around the house.

Toni sat back in her hard wooden chair and swayed a little from side to side as her whole crew of pals and colleagues from the media company where she worked joined in a very loud and very out of tune version of an old hit song about an uptown girl which was playing at full volume in her honour.

There was cheap Prosecco and white wine spillages and pizza and cheesy biscuit breadcrumbs all over the tablecloth, and probably the new plum lingerie that Amy had squeezed her into as the star of her Birthday Goddess sexy party special. At some point she had lost her shoe under the table when she sat down after all the toasts had been made.

Then Amy had presented her with a crown she had

made from gold paper and wire and insisted that she wear it as a party princess. At a jaunty angle, of course.

Worse. Her make-up was probably a wreck after a brief but intense crying jag when Amy had said some incredibly sweet things about how lucky she was to have her as her sister and that leaving home for the first time was not going to change a thing.

The waterworks had started again when Amy gave her a bound book of their mother's sketches of them as children and told her how proud their late parents would have been of her and what she had achieved, which had everyone in the room reaching for the tissues, paper napkins or, in more than one case, the corner of the tablecloth. There was not a dry eye in the house. Even Amy the Strong 'accidentally' dropped her napkin on the floor and had to drop out of sight for a couple of minutes to find it.

Good thing that the birthday chocolate iced cupcakes had arrived just in time to prevent a meltdown of nuclear proportions.

Toni glanced up across the tables and clusters of women spread out around the room. It didn't matter that she looked a mess and that her guests were in great danger of trashing the dining and living room of a house she was borrowing from Freya Elstrom. Not to her friends, who had come out on a cold February evening to help her celebrate her birthday.

Amy had a lot to answer for. She had told Amy for weeks that she did not want a birthday party. It would only remind her of what had happened on her last birthday, when she had found her so-called boyfriend in the shower with the Brazilian lingerie model who turned out to be his real full-time girlfriend.

The one he had so conveniently forgotten to mention

during the previous few weeks when he had been dating her.

That had not been one of her life's finer moments.

Especially since she had already stripped off and was ready to make sure that Peter was washed in all of his important places.

Hence this surprise party. Toni's latest project had been staging professional studio photo sessions on the explosion in demand for sex toys and bedroom accessories and daring lingerie among women of all ages. Young and old.

When Toni had mentioned it was her birthday in a few days *and* the first anniversary of breaking up with her cheating boyfriend then the girls had insisted that they hold a party for her to mark the occasion while Amy was still in London. Complete with the full range of accessories which had been used on the show. Amy thought this was a great idea and had arranged the whole thing while Toni was at work.

These were her real friends. Her real family. Girls from the local school she had known all of her life, who had left their husbands and boyfriends at home for one evening to share her birthday party, pals from her work, students from Amy's school. All loud, boisterous and having fun. And that was precisely how she liked it. No false pretenses here. Real people who shared her life each and every day.

She was so lucky to have them.

And she was officially on holiday for two weeks. Now that was worth celebrating. Even if she would be spending most of the time painting the company portrait of a very serious-looking businessman. According to his daughter Freya, Dr Lars Elstrom was a quiet academic used to desk work and she had talked him into sitting for his portrait while he was in the office researching some work for a client.

But there was a problem. The painting had to be painted in a specific two-week window in February before her father went back to Italy for the spring. Could she do it?

Piece of cake.

Especially when the cake came decorated with half the fee for the commission in advance.

Thank you, Freya, and thank you, Dr Lars Elstrom.

That fee had bought Amy's round-the-world plane ticket *and* was paying to have the boiler replaced in her little house. Hot water! Central heating she could rely on! Bliss. Apparently any tenant thinking of renting her house would expect plumbing that worked. Amazing. Some people had no appreciation of character properties.

Toni glanced out of the dining room window at the flurries of February snow which were forecast to be with them for a few days to come. Not the weather to be modelling fancy lingerie in her freezing terraced house. It might only be thirty minutes away on foot but it might as well be in another world. *Brr.*

No. Much better to do it here in this nice warm house.

Freya had a lovely home and Toni was going to enjoy living here for the next two weeks rent-free. And with all of the hot water she could use.

She loved patrons who believed in carrying on old traditions! Especially when that tradition meant that the CEO of the company always had their portrait painted by a Baldoni. And since she was the last in the line... Result!

A warm glow of happiness and contentment spread from deep inside her like a furnace that pumped the heat from her heart to the very ends of her fingertips. She had not felt so safe and secure for years. Protected. And cared for and part of a very special community of friends who looked out for one another.

She grinned across at Amy's best friend, Lucy, who

was demonstrating the finer points of how to tie a sarong. They had known one another since they were at primary school together just a few streets away. It was hard to imagine that Amy, Lucy and the other girls parading up and down in various stages of undress would be flying out tomorrow, all ready for trekking through rough terrain in South America.

It was actually happening. Her baby sister was going around the world with her best friends. One month travelling. Four months on an archaeological dig in Peru then another month relaxing. Six months. Three girls. Three boys. All great teenagers she had known for years. But six months? The longest they had lived apart since their parents died was over a year ago, when she'd worked in Paris for five weeks but came home most weekends.

They might have had the training and they all spoke excellent Spanish but the hard reality of what they would be facing made her shudder.

But no sniffles allowed. Time to start living a bit. Right? That was what they'd agreed at some mad hour on New Year's Day. A new start for both of them. Pity that Amy was insisting that a new boyfriend was part of the package.

Maybe turning twenty-seven was not so bad after all when she had friends like these in her life. So what if she didn't have a mega career as a fine artist? She had something much better.

And somehow she knew that her father would understand that trying to scrape a living as a portrait painter had never been the life she wanted and never would be. That had been her father's dearest wish, but it wasn't hers. No. This portrait for Freya Elstrom would be the last. No more commissions as the last of the Baldoni family. It was time to say goodbye to foolish ideas like that and start focusing totally on her photography career.

Amy sashayed forward with a plate with a cupcake on and leant sideways and rested her head on Toni's shoulder. 'I stashed two of the red velvet specials, which I happen to know are your favourite, in the washing machine.'

'Clever!' Toni replied and popped a little finger loaded with creamy chocolate icing into her mouth and groaned in delight. 'Delish. And have I said thank you yet again for arranging all of this? It's amazing and I love it.'

Amy laughed out loud and gave her a one-armed hug. 'Several times. It's the wine, you know. Causes short-term memory loss in older women.'

Then Amy started rubbing her hands together and mumbling under her breath. 'Now. Back to the important stuff. What totally outrageous thing have you decided to do while I'm away? Remember the rules—it has to be spontaneous, the opposite of what you would normally do, and fun! Points will be awarded for the most ingenious solution!'

'Dance on the table? Toni suggested then shook her head and waved her arms around. 'No. Forget that one. The table legs wouldn't cope with my current body weight and this food is too good to waste. Something outrageous. Um…'

Then she looked over Amy's shoulder back towards the door leading to the hallway and her breath caught in her throat.

Standing not ten feet away from her was one of the most remarkable-looking men that she had seen in her life.

She was five foot nine so he had to be at least six foot two, from his heavy working boots and quilted jacket to the black cap pulled low over long, crazily curled dirty blond hair.

Slim hips. Broad shoulders. Long legs.

Her gaze tracked up his body before the sensible part of her brain clicked in to stop it.

'Oh, Amy—' she breathed in a low hiss of appreciation '—I owe you big time.'

'This is so true! But what particular thing have I done now?' Amy replied between mouthfuls of cake.

'You didn't tell me that you hired a lumberjack male stripper.'

'Who? What?' Amy looked up and whirled her head around like a meerkat before it froze in the same direction Toni was focusing on.

'Oh. I see what you mean,' she said with a cough and started taking photographs with the small digital camera that Toni carried with her everywhere.

'I have no idea who that is and he is nothing to do with me, but what are you waiting for? Go and find out who he belongs to and if he's available—nab him for yourself before any of the other gals do.'

And with that Amy pranced off towards her friends in her frilly lace-trimmed corset, which was going to be of zero value on an archaeological excavation in the Andes.

Leaning against the door frame, the mystery man didn't move an inch. The very tall, very rugged, very cold-looking mystery man.

He was a fashion stylist's idea of what would pass for an Indiana Jones style adventurer—after the action. In fact she would go so far as to say that he was quite scruffy.

Conscious that she was standing there ogling his long denim-clad legs, Toni's gaze ratcheted up to his face just as he glanced in her direction. Blue eyes gazed at her so intently from under heavy dark blond eyebrows that she almost blushed under the fierce heat of that focus.

With cheekbones that sharp he could have passed for a male model if it was not for the heavy, definitely non-designer dirty blond and grey beard and the blue strapping that was bandaged around his right hand. His clothing was practical. Stained and well used. If this was a costume then it was entirely authentic!

He had not said one word to anyone but in those eyes and on that powerful face she recognised something very special. Confidence oozed out of every pore of this man's body. He knew exactly who he was and what he wanted and what he was doing there.

That must be nice!

The way he simply leant against the door frame enjoying the view, as though he walked into a lingerie party every day of the week, screamed someone who was so totally comfortable in his own skin that it was sickening.

While she was dressed in a tiny purple satin push-up bra and matching shorts.

Oh, what? Not funny. So not funny.

Toni grabbed her kimono from the back of the sofa and pushed her arms into the sleeves faster than she'd thought possible!

Okay, some of these girls were used to wearing lingerie in front of the camera for a living, but she wasn't. She didn't like the idea that some stranger was standing there getting a good eyeful of a catwalk show.

Wait a minute. What the hell was he doing here? And who had invited him? Freya never said anything about having a boyfriend.

Perhaps he was just passing and someone left the door open!

'Man alert!' Toni cupped her hands around her mouth and yelled, 'Unaccompanied male in the room, girls!'

The screaming and squealing had to be heard to be believed.

Utter chaos erupted on all sides as the girls scattered to the wind, mostly upstairs to the bedrooms from the sound of it.

Righty. Time to sort this out.

Toni narrowed her eyes and pulled the edges of her kimono tighter together.

She tried to stomp over to the hulk but it was a tad tricky in feather mules so she ended up mincing across the room instead. Head high, chin forward.

And those blue eyes focused on every tiny step she took.

She cleared her throat and looked him straight in the eye.

'Okay. You look like the kind of guy who likes straight talk. I'm Antonia Baldoni, house guest of Freya Elstrom. This—' and she waved one hand towards the abandoned articles and some very odd bedroom toys '—is my birthday party. And you are?'

He moved slightly away from the wall to an almost upright position so that when he spoke the sound came from several inches above her head.

'Tired. Hungry. Surprised. And delighted to make your acquaintance, Antonia Baldoni. House guest.' He rolled back his shoulders and exhaled very slowly through his nose. 'Strange. I've just come from Freya and she never mentioned anything about a house guest.'

There was a definite squeak and a giggle from behind Toni's back and one side of this man's mouth twitched just once before he breathed, 'Make that house guests. And just when I thought this day could not get any more bizarre.'

'You've just seen Freya?' Toni looked at him with her

eyes narrowed and her head tilted to one side. 'Really? You have to forgive me, but I find that a little hard to believe. Freya was invited to my party tonight but sent her apologies from Italy. So. Perhaps it's time for you to start talking before I throw you out. Let's start with the big ones. Where exactly did you say you met Freya? And what are you doing here? And who are you?'

A low thundering sigh rumbled low in this big man's chest and Toni stepped back as he slung his body forward as though it was taking a huge effort and strode past her into the kitchen, looking around as he did so from side to side, leaving an aroma in his wake which made her waft the air with one hand.

'Hey. Wait a minute. I didn't invite you in,' Toni said and shuffled after him in her mules.

'You don't have to,' the blond said and pointed to a framed photo on the wall between the cabinets. It was one of a collection of what looked like holiday snaps which Toni had not had time to admire. Until now.

By going up on tiptoe Toni could get a better look at what seemed to be a family photo of people gathered around a dinner table. She recognised Freya and an older man who looked so much like her that he had to be her father, Lars Elstrom. And standing behind them, grinning for the camera, was a tall handsome blond man with broad shoulders and blue eyes the same colour as…

She whipped around, blinked at the man standing with his arms folded and then back to the photo.

Her shoulders dropped. He nodded very slowly up and down. Once.

'Scott Elstrom. Freya's brother. And I live here.'

Then he sniffed and gestured with his head towards the worktop. 'Is anyone going to eat that pizza?'

Toni stared at the photograph and then glanced up at the serious expression on his face before returning back to the framed snapshot of the man, scowling at her at some sort of winter sporting event.

It was definitely him. No mistaking the dirty blond hair and physique.

It was definitely on Freya's kitchen wall.

And, just like that, the effects of two hours of wine-drinking and general merriment popped like an over-stretched balloon and what was left of the rational part of her brain kicked right back in.

Not a male stripper.

Not a birthday present in the shape of a hunky lumberjack.

He was Freya Elstrom's brother.

Nightmare!

Toni closed her eyes and pinched the top of her nose. She gestured back towards the party, which had magically returned to full swing inside the dining room, with the flat of her hand. 'As you can see, this is my birthday party. And I'm rather occupied at present.'

His slightly bloodshot blue eyes locked onto hers. 'I'm not going anywhere.'

At this distance all she could focus on were the thin pale tan lines radiating out from the corners of his eyes and the dark stubble and grey-blond beard above that full, sensuous upper lip.

But there was nothing polished about this man. Far from it. His cheeks looked more sunburnt than tanned and his jacket and trousers were designed for hard use and had seen it. Unshaven. Unkempt.

Inhaling was a mistake. He smelt of leather and travel and acrid sweat mixed with wet dog in a combination which perfume manufacturers could bottle as instant girl-repellent.

Smelly did not quite cover it. This man was seriously in need of a long soak and a shave and several cans of deodorant.

Then the right side of his mouth turned up into what was probably meant to be a reassuring smile.

And every sensory switch inside her body turned on to maximum power.

Just like that. Completely out of the blue and totally, totally not what she wanted to happen. *Especially not now.*

Speech was impossible and for what seemed like minutes, but was probably only seconds, they both stood there in silence. Breathing in air which positively crackled with electricity. Neither of them willing to shift an inch.

It was almost a relief when someone's mobile phone started ringing. The ringtone was the theme song for a popular Italian coffee shop. Amy had been playing with it earlier that day; she loved coffee and wasn't sure when she would see her next cappuccino.

'I think it's yours.' He blinked, breaking the connection, stepping back and folding his arms.

Toni turned away and sucked in some air because apparently she had stopped breathing. She reached into the tiny evening bag she had left on the kitchen worktop and found the phone in the inside pocket, flipping open the tiny, silver, high-tech unit as a familiar voice hissed down the line.

'Sorry to interrupt, but are you coming back in?' Amy whispered. 'Lucy is just about to light the candles on the birthday cake and we're frightened of the fire risk. You can bring the hunk with you if you'd like to help.'

'Be right there,' she replied and closed the phone.

Sucking in a long breath, Toni lifted her head and stared

into the face of one of the strangest-looking men she had ever met in her life.

Hell. Who was she kidding? He was smelly, bandaged and glaring at her. And totally gorgeous.

'Stay right where you are. Help yourself to the pizza. I'll be back soon and we can sort all of this out.'

CHAPTER TWO

HUSTLING A GAGGLE of still giggling party girls into their clothes proved more difficult than Toni had imagined, especially when their unexpected male guest was trapped in the kitchen and they were all desperate to take another peek before they left.

In the end Amy came to her rescue with the vague excuse that it was getting late and some of them had an early plane to catch. The next ten minutes were a mad rush of tidying up, distributing the bedroom toys and assorted lingerie items into party bags and arguments about whether they should break into the kitchen to rescue the chocolate brownies they had saved for the coffee.

It was almost a relief when she finally kissed Amy goodnight with promises that she would call if there was any trouble, and finally waved the girls goodbye from the doorstep.

Toni dropped her head back against the heavy door and gazed down the hallway towards the kitchen.

Trouble was waiting for her behind that innocent white-painted door. She just didn't know how much.

Swallowing down a huge lump of apprehension, Toni inhaled a couple of short, sharp breaths. Perhaps she shouldn't have downed all of those mystery cocktails Lucy had concocted followed by the champagne and wine.

Probably.

Blinking hard, she pushed away from the front door with the flat of both hands. Time to find out what Scott Elstrom was doing back in town.

Casually pushing the door open, Toni sauntered into the kitchen with as much aplomb as she could muster.

Scott was sitting on a bar stool with his back against the kitchen wall and an empty plate in front of him.

He had stripped off his outer coat and hung it from a hook near the back door that Toni had not even noticed before. *Um.* Maybe he had been here before?

'How was the pizza?' she asked in a sing-song voice as she took in the heavy grey and blond beard and dark blond hair. 'If you fancy dessert, why don't you help yourself to the chocolate willy lollipops? There are several flavours and they are anatomically correct.'

He scowled at them and coughed. 'That's good to know but I'll pass.' Then he nodded to the brownie pan. 'Those look good.'

Toni clutched the tray and slid it across the worktop out of his reach. 'My finest recipe. Which my birthday party guests would have enjoyed if the party had not been broken up so early by an unexpected guest. These brownies are staying over here until I have a few more answers.'

'I didn't ask you to send the girls home. As for unexpected—' he raised his bandaged right hand in the air '—no clue you were going to be here. No apologies. No excuses. And those brownies do smell good.'

'No brownie until I know who you really are,' she replied with a shake of her head and folded her arms. 'That's only one photo. You could be some distant freeloading relative who Freya doesn't want sleeping in her spare room. Or some ex-boyfriend. Or something.'

Without saying another word, he lifted a smartphone

out of a side pocket on the leg of his cargo trousers, placed it on the breakfast bar and started tapping away. Toni couldn't help but notice that his body might be on the sinewy side but his fingers were long and slender.

'Hiya. Yes, I got here. How are things? Really? He's already asking for pen and paper? Unbelievable…yes, I know.' Then he shot her a glance. 'By the way, I've just met your house-sitter. She gave me pizza and is ready to call the police to get rid of the crazy vagrant who thinks he lives here. Now don't be like that. Calm down. You've had a few other things on your mind these past few days. Take a deep breath. That's better. Inhale slowly. It's all under control. Now, why don't you have a word with your pal while I eat her brownies, okay? Okay.'

Toni could only watch, stunned, as this tall man in a check shirt turned around on the bar stool and calmly stretched out his hand towards her. 'It's for you. My sister would like a word.'

Five minutes later Toni collapsed down on the bar stool opposite Scott in a complete daze.

'I am so sorry. We had no idea or we would never have organised a birthday party while your dad is in the hospital. Wow. That is so inappropriate I don't know where to start.'

She reached into the brownie tin and cut an enormous cube and started nibbling at it to try and calm her nerves.

'We had absolutely no clue. Because I would definitely have cancelled if Freya had let me know. Seriously. I would. This is awful. I feel so embarrassed. Mortified, really. That is all so inappropriate. Please let me apologise again and…'

Scott held up one hand. 'I get it. You didn't know. It's your birthday. So you organised a party and enjoyed yourself. No problem.'

'Actually, my birthday isn't until Thursday but my sister Amy is leaving on a gap year trip tomorrow and she wanted to help me celebrate before she left so she arranged this surprise party and all my friends from the company turned up and… I am babbling. Because I am mega embarrassed.'

'That would be true. About the babbling.'

Toni took another nibble of brownie before daring to glance up at this man who was just sitting there in silence, dominating the space.

'So you are not a male stripper. Sorry about that little confusion. It was a ladies only night so any man had to have a very good reason for being there. And, seeing as none of the girls claimed you…I might have jumped to the wrong conclusion.'

His mouth opened slightly as though he was about to reply, then he reconsidered and closed it again. A rough-skinned hand rasped over his beard and he glanced quickly over his clothing as his voice rasped low in his throat. 'You thought that I was a male stripper? What kind of stripper turns up dressed like this?'

She winced and closed one eye and pretended to duck slightly.

'Scruffy lumberjack. Check shirt. Beard. Very popular with the city girls who like a—' she coughed quickly '—less refined country look.'

Then she blinked. 'The oiled chest and man string are a bit old-fashioned these days. The hunky bit of rough… oh, I didn't mean to say…imply that you're rough or anything, but…'

'Maybe you ought to stop talking now. I am not the oiled chest type even on a good day and this has not been one of them.'

'Oh. Yes. Right. Good. Or not good, depending on how bad your day has been. If you know what I mean.'

'How bad has it been? Let me see.'

His dark blond eyebrows squeezed tight together and he pinched his forehead with a thumb and middle finger.

'Almost lost a hand to frostbite. A pig of a snow machine to an air base. Cargo plane from Alaska to Iceland, scheduled flight to Rome, where I had to pay first class to get a seat, four hours at a hospital trying to work out what the hell was happening then a flight back to London. And don't get me started with how long it took me to get from the airport to the hospital and back again.'

He lifted his chin and dropped his hand away.

'So, overall, I'm not too happy about being here right now. I think that would sum it up.'

Toni blew out fast through narrowed lips. 'Alaska? In February? Frostbite? Well, that explains a lot.'

Then she slipped off the breakfast bar stool and flicked out both of her hands. 'Righty. What would you like? Coffee or tea? And I can easily reheat these brownies for you. Oh—you've already eaten the last of them. No problem, there are plenty more in the freezer. It will only take twenty minutes tops.'

He replied by easing his weight off the bar stool and rolling back his shoulders, making his chest pop.

'Thanks for the offer, but it's late and my body clock is deep-fried. Nice to meet you and thanks for the unexpected entertainment but I'm heading to bed. If you're here in the morning we might try to have a conversation which isn't in code. But right now I am way too tired to talk about the why and how.'

Then he looked up at her and asked, 'The bedroom with the blue door—I usually keep it locked. Anyone sleeping in there?'

'Oh, no. Still locked. Freya said it was private.'

And, with a quick nod in her direction, Toni watched him sling the huge duffel bag over one shoulder with a grunt and a wince. The weight of it meant that he had to lean forward from the waist but he shifted the load a few times before striding into the hallway and to the staircase which led to the bedrooms.

It took a few seconds for her champagne and wine-fuddled brain to connect with what was going on.

Her commission! Oh, no!

'Wait a minute. One last question. I'm supposed to stay with Freya for another week and work with her father at the Elstrom office. Do I need to reschedule? I mean…when will your father be back in London?'

His steps slowed and with one movement he lowered the duffel on to the hall carpet. There was something in the way his shoulders were braced tight that made Toni feel the heat of his gaze even before he looked sideways at her.

Her body locked into a half-in-the-hallway-half-in-the-kitchen position. She simply couldn't move. It was as if her feet were reluctant to leave the relative safety of the kitchen, just in case.

'News flash. I'm back. Freya's in Italy. Dad won't be coming back any time soon. As of today, he has officially retired. Goodbye Elstrom Mapping. Hello Italy.'

Then he gave a twitch. 'Sorry. But it looks like you're out of a job.'

His gaze scanned her scantily clad body from the toes sticking out from the feathery mules to the top of her gold paper crown and lingering at all of the right places on the way up.

The start of a lazy lopsided smile warmed his mouth. 'No rush to get packed tonight. Tomorrow will do. Good-night.'

* * *

Goodnight? Out of a job? What?

Any lingering after-effects of the party had gone in a flash.

Before Scott could start up the stairs, Toni dashed in front of him and stood on the bottom step so that they were at more or less the same height.

To his credit, Scott Elstrom didn't even flinch but braced himself, legs apart, and stared at her as she crossed her arms and stared him out.

'Oh, no, you don't. I signed a contract with Freya Elstrom to paint a portrait of the CEO of Elstrom Mapping. She was the one who got in contact with me. Begging me to do the work. I've dropped everything to be here.'

There was a deep low sigh from the man standing only inches in front of her and he shifted his gaze from her face to the wall for a few seconds.

'What was your surname again?'

'Baldoni. Ah, I can see that you recognise it. The Baldoni family have painted the last four generations of Elstrom chairmen. Freya called me just after Christmas to set it up for her father. Apparently he had been thinking about it for a while and finally just decided to go ahead with his portrait. This is the earliest I could do it, which makes me feel sick.'

'Christmas. Right. So she asked you to paint his portrait after the holidays. No wonder she wanted me there.'

'Actually, she was more concerned that it was a Baldoni than which member of my family it was. Apparently your father is a stickler for tradition.'

'You might say that,' he murmured and ran his hand back through his dirty blond, very scraggy hair. 'He would want the same artist if he could do it.'

'Tricky, since my grandfather is long gone. But if Mr

Elstrom is ill,' she murmured to herself, and then realised that Scott was still listening, 'of course I can reschedule the sitting. That's not a problem. When your father is better, Freya can let me know. I have some photos that she sent me and I'm sure I can come up with something he will be pleased with... Why are you shaking your head? Is there something else?'

'My father is retired, Miss Baldoni. As of this afternoon, I am the new head of Elstrom Mapping.'

His eyebrows squeezed closer together but his gaze focused laser-sharp on her face.

'And the last thing I need is my portrait painted.'

Scott stood back and watched the fiery brunette with the lovely brown eyes stomp past him up the staircase towards the guest bedroom before picking up his over-heavy duffel.

Toni Baldoni probably had no idea how much he enjoyed following her up the stairs. One slow step at a time.

The last time he had shared this house with girls wearing nothing but lingerie had been on Freya's university graduation party, when he had dared to turn up an hour early and walked in on way too many over-excited girls high on champagne and life, all fighting for the hair straighteners and his attention. They had even taken over his en suite bathroom to cope with the party preparations.

Strange. He hadn't thought about that in a long time.

An unexpected quiver of a laugh surprised him as this brunette stomped in her ridiculous shoes down the landing and her light gown wafted up, giving him a delightful flash of creamy thigh.

Eyes flashing, she instantly flung a glance at him over one shoulder and tugged down her gown, shot into the guest room and shut the door very firmly behind her.

Shaking his head and blinking to stay awake, Scott

found the key, turned it in the lock and stepped inside the same bedroom that he had claimed the very first day he had arrived with Freya and his mother. This clean and uncluttered modern town house had seemed like another world from the dark, creaky old Victorian stone villa that was the family home they had shared with their father.

Sheer force of habit made him drop his duffel bag next to the bed and unlock and fling open the double windows to let some air into the overheated and stuffy room.

He didn't need the heat.

He just wanted sleep and quiet to process the events of the day.

Freya had known that he wasn't planning to come back any time soon and not that much had changed in the two years since he had last slept here.

It looked like the same bed, wardrobe and furnishings that he remembered.

But there was something new. Perched on the window ledge was a silver-framed photograph of a stunningly pretty slim blonde in a flimsy summer dress with legs that went on for ever.

Alexa.

Scott picked up the frame and glanced at it for a second before stashing it in the drawer of the bedside cabinet.

He had taken the photograph that first summer holiday they spent together walking in Switzerland. They were both single, in their twenties and had the whole world ahead of them.

In his eyes Alexa was the perfect woman for him. As a teenager he had watched his very different parents drift apart over the years and lead separate lives until the only thing they had in common was Freya and himself.

He wouldn't make that mistake.

Alexa was clever, stunningly pretty and, best of all,

a total sports fanatic like himself. They used to talk for hours about the things they both loved, laughing over tall tales from all of the exotic places that they had visited. They had been inseparable.

Heady with the mountain air, they had fallen in love. Over the next twelve months, they were so caught up in their engagement and the whirlwind of a top London wedding that he didn't have time to stop and consider what married life was going to be like.

It was hard to believe that it could have ended so badly.

If Freya thought that being reminded of happier times with Alexa would help him to get over his cheating ex-wife then she didn't understand.

There were some things a sunny disposition couldn't fix.

Sometimes betrayal went too deep, like a bullet to the chest which lay too close to vital organs to be removed. Always there. Always catching you out when you least expected it.

A flash of memory surged through his brain, hot and wild. He could almost see Alexa reclining on this same bed, with a look of love in her eyes, beckoning him to join her. Her long straight blonde hair that he used to adore spread out across the pillow, warm, soft and inviting.

The frostbite in his fingers was nothing compared to this type of deep-seated pain.

Scott's fingers tightened around the edge of the window frame as he looked out into the night sky, which in London was never going to be truly dark or clear.

Closing his eyes for a second, he gave way to the surge of anger and disappointment that he had buried deep inside himself since the moment he had walked into that hospital room in Rome.

It had been one of the most humbling experiences of

his life. It was astonishing to see his father looking so low and depressed. Lars Elstrom had given up. Stopped trying. Beaten down by the events of the past few years to the point where he didn't even see any point in keeping the company as a viable concern.

His speech was slurred slightly and he was going to have problems with the left side of his body for a long while, but his mind was still alive and sharp.

Suddenly the real reason why Freya had pleaded with him to come home for Christmas was only too apparent.

Elstrom Mapping was finished. Over. After two hundred years of creating maps and sea charts, the company was dead in the water.

A dinosaur.

That was the exact word that his father had managed to say to describe the family business that he had devoted his life to. An extinct creature which no longer had a place in the modern world.

His father had given up in every way possible.

How could this have happened so quickly? Two years ago, the business was not only healthy but thriving and he had almost managed to convince his father that modern technology was the best way forward. There had been plans. A budget. They had actually laughed that Elstrom would last another two hundred years.

But, of course, that was before he'd walked out on the company, leaving his stepbrother in charge.

Travis had taken over and destroyed Elstrom Mapping from the inside out. And his father had let it happen without a fight rather than admit that he had made a horrible mistake.

Now he wanted Scott to finish the job that he had started. Would he do it? Would he take over the company and be the final Elstrom at the helm? Even if it was for a short time, it would please him to think that Elstrom Mapping was still in the family.

What choice did he have? Of course he had to say yes.

He loved his sister and admired her more than he could say but there was only one thing that photograph screamed out to him and it had nothing to do with happy memories.

It was failure.

He had failed. Their marriage had failed and Alexa had betrayed him in the worst way possible. The last thing he needed today was a reminder of his past.

Just the opposite. He was going to need every scrap of positive energy he possessed if he had any hope of making good on the promise he had made to his father that afternoon. And a whole lot more.

Nothing was going to stand in his way.

He was going to have to pick up the pieces and prove that he could do what Travis couldn't. Save Elstrom from going to the wall.

Elstrom Mapping was his. And it was not going to fail.

CHAPTER THREE

'So COME ON. Spill. What happened last night with you and the scruffy rich lumberjack?'

'Nothing happened,' Toni replied with a light casual lilt.

There was a roar of boos and hisses from around the chaos of the breakfast table in the tiny apartment Lucy shared with her flatmates and, for the last few days, her pal Amy Baldoni. Usually it was clean and organised. But this morning there were three girls crammed into the small kitchen diner with all of the kit they needed for their six months gap year expedition parked in the hallway. And they were eating as though it was the last decent breakfast they would have for ages. This was probably not far from the truth.

'Come on, Antonia—' Lucy grinned '—we know that guilty look.'

'Guilty? *Moi?*' Toni replied and pressed her right hand to her bosom in the most elegant ladylike manner.

'Who's guilty?' Amy laughed as she waltzed in with her huge rucksack slung over one shoulder.

'The girls are accusing me of holding out on the tantalising news about Scott Elstrom, that's all,' Toni replied and pressed her lips together tightly.

'Aha. Busted. You are looking remarkably perky for a twenty-seven-year-old lady who partied late into the night,'

Amy replied and set her rucksack in a corner before taking her place at the table, loading her plate with toast and marmalade and ham and cheese croissants. 'Go on, then,' Amy said before biting into the toast. 'Out with it.'

'We did have a small interlude after you all left,' Toni replied in a totally casual voice. 'The man was jet-lagged, ate all the pizza and most of the pan of brownies. And no—' she pointed to Lucy, who was just about to say something rude between eating because she always did '—I did not ask him to warm my toes for me or any other parts.'

'Why not?' Amy asked between chewing. 'You promised that this year was going to be different. Now that creepy Peter is out on his ear, you're young, free and single. All ready for a new date to be installed by the summer. That was what we agreed, wasn't it?'

'Was that at the New Year's party?' Lucy blinked. 'I don't remember much after that third cocktail. Or was it the fifth?'

'New Year resolutions definitely have an expiry date.' Toni laughed then caught the look that Amy was giving her. 'Okay, I did sort of say that this year was going to be the start of new exciting things. New job. Lots more travel. New central heating boiler! Redecorating! Those things can be exciting too. So you can stop booing. A new boyfriend is an optional extra.'

'Six months, darling sister,' Amy replied, pointing her toast at her. 'You said that you would be fixed up in six months. I have an excellent memory for facts and dates!'

'Anyhow, when I surfaced an hour ago his bedroom door was open, his breakfast dishes were washed and draining in the kitchen and the house was in silence. The man had obviously gone to work on a Sunday. Either that or the sight of so many lovely ladies in their lingerie last night was more than he could stand and he took off back to Alaska.'

'Alaska,' Lucy sighed. 'That's on my list.' Then she sniffed. 'But not this trip. Way too cold. Bring on the sun. Oh. Speaking of which. We have twenty minutes until the boys get here.' And with that she slurped her coffee and scraped back her chair.

'Packing. That would be good. Be back soon. Amy, have you seen my hair straighteners?'

Toni got to her feet and started clearing away the breakfast plates as Amy chuckled into her tea and toast.

'Hair straighteners? I think Lucy may be in for a bit of a disappointment when she gets to the campsite.' Amy waved her hand from side to side and rocked her shoulders. 'Apparently the electricity generators can be a bit temperamental.'

Then she looked up at Toni and grinned. 'Don't look so worried. I've packed a tool kit with a full set of screwdrivers into my suitcase. We shall—' and she waved her butter knife in the air '—have power. So fear not, darling sister, the magical sat phone will be charged at regular intervals. How else am I going to be able to keep tabs on this amazing love life you promised to throw yourself into? I can see our house being turned into a real little love nest now that you've cleared out the lodger. Cool!'

Then she tucked into the marmalade with great gusto.

'You are incorrigible!' Toni replied with a grin and flicked the tea towel towards Amy. '*Love nest?* Where did you hear that expression? You know that it's totally going to be the other way around! The boys will be falling over themselves when they take a look at you! Try not to break all of their hearts.'

'Can't promise a thing.' Amy smirked and then startled Toni by wrapping her arms around her and giving her a big squishy hug. 'I'm going to miss you but you understand why I don't want you at the airport making a mushy scene, don't you?' Then, before Toni could answer, she stepped back and dropped her plate and cutlery into the sink. 'Thanks for doing the washing-up! I should probably get dressed.'

And, with a wide-armed stretch, Amy walked slowly back to the bedroom where, from the sound of it, Lucy and two of her flatmates were already arguing about what to take in their hand luggage.

Madness. Total madness.

But she waited until Amy was out of sight before pulling out a tissue and blowing her nose. *Stupid girl.* She had known this day was coming since Christmas and she had promised Amy that she would not get all gooey...but look at the state that she was in!

Of course she understood. That was why she was here now instead of weeping buckets at the departure gate. But it didn't make it any easier.

It helped if she imagined it was Scott Elstrom's face at the bottom of the washing-up bowl.

This was entirely his fault!

Her brain had been spinning most of the night, working through the options, over and over again, weighing up the pros and cons, and the more she thought about it, the more obvious the answer had become.

She had to convince Scott that he should sit for a portrait in place of his father.

He was the new head of the company, after all. It was his duty to go ahead with the project that Freya had already paid half in advance. Wasn't it?

But there was something else which kept whirling around inside her head every time she'd punched her feather pillow to try and find a comfy spot.

Freya had come running to her to ask for help. It had to be a Baldoni. No one else would do!

Surely that had to give her some bargaining power?

Toni scrubbed extra hard on the frying pan. Now all she had to do was pluck up enough courage to insist on it the next time she saw Scott.

Toni's hands closed around the cool edge of the sink and she closed her eyes for a few seconds.

She didn't have any choice. That portrait had to be finished, one way or another.

She needed the rest of the money to pay for Amy's university fees in the autumn.

Girlish laughter broke through her thoughts and Toni smiled as she stacked the cups and plates.

Amy was right.

This *was* her chance to make a new start and claim her life.

The little girl who she'd promised to take care of the morning their parents died was a young woman now with her own life.

Amy was amazing and was going to go far in life. She knew exactly what she wanted and how she was going to get it. It had been Amy's idea to talk to the university professors who were going to be teaching her and find out what kind of expedition would suit the coursework. Thinking ahead. Planning her future.

She had taught her sister well.

They had watched the dawn come up together in the garden of their little family house early on New Year's morning and made promises to one another that could not be broken.

In three months' time both of their lives would be completely different. Amy would be in Peru and working hard. And she would have finished this portrait, cleared out the clutter from their little house and redecorated every room. All ready for their cute London house to be rented out for the next three years while Amy was at university.

This was her chance to take her photography career to the next level and she was ready to grab it with both hands and do what it took to learn from the best. Travel. Live a little. Maybe even find the time to enjoy herself.

It was scary to think of the transformation that was going to take place but it was make the change now or stay locked in the same groove forever.

She chose now.

By the time she was thirty, her plan was to have the Antonia Baldoni photographic studio up and running. No more working for someone else. No more being taken for granted. No more being used by other people.

Three more years' experience and training and she would be ready to start out on her own.

Starting with this portrait.

This was not the time to let one man who refused to have his portrait painted get in the way of Amy's education.

Scott Elstrom was not going to escape that easily. And if she had to become a total pest to make that happen? Then so be it.

Because the new and improved version of Antonia Baldoni had decided to make some changes in her life and it all kicked off today.

Look out, world. Here I come. *Bring it on.*

Scott strode down the busy London pavement in the light morning sleet, wincing in pain.

His senses were assaulted by a cacophony of noise which seemed to come from every direction. Cars, buses, taxi cabs and motorcyclists. And people. So many people all crushed together. Jostling and pushing and manoeuvring around one another.

What were they all doing here at this time on a Sunday morning? Strange. He had forgotten what the barrage of noise and bustle of city life was like. Right now, his life in Alaska seemed like a distant dream. A fantasy of calm and quiet and beauty and…

He jumped out of the way as a cycle courier flashed across the path in front of him at high speed with only inches to spare. The light sleet mixed with loose snow that had been falling most of the night had made the pavements treacherous for cyclists.

Control. In Alaska he was in control of where and what and how he lived his life. The climate and the harsh conditions were all part of the job. He respected that. But here? Here, he had to battle very different challenges.

And every one of them was just as tough as climbing a mountain range or crossing sea ice.

But that was what he was here for.

He had promised his father and sister that he would give the family business six months of his life and stay in London until early September.

Six long and arduous months which right at that moment felt like an eternity of living in the city.

It was Freya who'd filled Scott in on the details when they had taken off to the hospital café to leave their father to rest.

The plan was to sell the building to property developers, who would give them a serious amount of money to build apartments in such a prestigious address. Any remaining charts and maps would be snapped up by collectors and specialist museums. With the money from the sales there would enough to pay off the debts and have some left over for their father's retirement.

Because otherwise? Otherwise, things were going down so fast that it would mean bankruptcy and their father couldn't tolerate the idea of not paying his bills to the suppliers who had been so loyal for the past few years.

Last resort? They had an amazing offer from a marketing company who wanted to create tacky mapping merchandise using the Elstrom company name.

Freya had been quite shocked at his expletive-laden reply to that suggestion and had to ask him to lower his voice.

No way. He was not going to see two hundred years of his family heritage handed over as a prestige symbol on cheap magnifying glasses and plastic rulers.

Little wonder that Freya had telephoned him to ask him to come home. His baby sister certainly knew what buttons to press to bring on even more guilt.

Lars Elstrom had just handed him the keys to the shop. He would be damned if he was going to be the one turning the lights out on the day they closed for good.

But it was more than that and he knew it.

It had been his decision to walk away and leave the company two years ago when things went off the rails in his life. He could have fought his father's decision to appoint Travis to run the company through hard evidence and facts.

Instead, he had forced his father to choose between his apparently charming and talented and inspirational new stepson, Travis, and the angry man who Scott had become.

And that one decision had cost the company.

And now the stepson was long gone, the money had run out and suddenly his father needed him to step in and help the company with as much peace and dignity as he could.

How ironic was that?

But one thing was not so clear. Had he come back in

time to save Elstrom Mapping? Because that was precisely what he intended to do. Or go down trying.

It was going to take all of his strength and ingenuity to survive the next six months.

Just as he had survived when his world was destroyed two years ago. Taking things one day at a time.

Starting right now.

Head back, chin up, Scott stopped outside the antique facade of Elstrom Mapping and glanced up at the old three-storey building which had been his playground and school as a boy, his centre in the middle of his parents' divorce and then his chance to get close to his father again when he came to work here.

It had been two years since he had stood outside this door and waved goodbye to Freya as casually as if he were heading to the pub instead of a series of long arduous flights to a remote environmental survey base in Alaska.

It felt a lot longer.

Freya had organised a very casual meal out for the family before he took off and he had been a bear the whole evening. Bad-tempered and sullen and quiet. He couldn't even recall why. Probably some snide remark his father had made about how much the business needed him to bring some new orders—with Travis managing the company they could use someone experienced to work with clients on operational mapping projects in the field.

Scott could see that now in hindsight but he had been blind to just how overwhelmed his father had been at the time by everything that had happened.

Two stubborn men. As different as possible from one another. It was hard to believe that they were even related.

They were from different planets which only collided in astrological time zones.

Neither of them ready to admit that the other person might need help.

Neither of them willing to talk about the real problem that was never going away.

No way was his father going to lower himself to plead with Scott to give up a paying job and a contract he had signed to come back to London and dig Elstrom out of a large hole which had nothing to do with him and everything to do with his own bad judgement.

Scott clenched his fingers tight around the elaborate key set that Freya had passed him and braced his jaw as he turned the three keys, one after the other.

His feet hesitated for just a fraction of a second before he brushed the fear away.

Time to find out just how bad things had become. Because, for better or worse, he was in charge of Elstrom Mapping now and things were going to have to change. And fast.

Two hours later, Toni stepped down from the red London bus and darted under the shelter of the nearest shop doorway. The February rain had swept in and was pounding on the fabric awning above her head and bouncing off the pavement of the narrow street in this smart part of the city.

Her gaze skipped between the pedestrians scurrying for cover until it settled on the elegant three-storey stone building across the street.

What was she doing here? She was a commercial photographer and wannabe studio business owner.

Toni closed her eyes and wallowed in ten seconds of self-pity and shame before shaking herself out of it. This had been her decision. Nobody had forced her to take Freya Elstrom's offer when she'd called. But Freya had kept going on about how important it was to her father that

a Baldoni had to paint the last of the Elstroms. It meant a
lot to him and he was willing to pay her a special bonus
if she could drop everything and work on the portrait in
the next few months.

Now she knew the reason for the sudden urge to have
his portrait painted was nothing to do with artistic appreciation and a lot more to do with the fact that the poor
man was ill.

The last of the Elstrom family. A shiver ran across Toni's
shoulders. She didn't like the sound of that.

Like it or not, she and Amy were the last of the Baldoni
dynasty. Her father had been an only child and the only
male cousins were far more interested in IT than fine arts.

Perhaps she had more in common with Scott Elstrom
than she was prepared to admit?

Now all she had to do was convince him that the best
thing for the business was to have his portrait painted. She
couldn't return the fee. The money had already been spent
on Amy's round-the-world plane ticket. And she needed
the rest of the fee to help her through university.

So Scott had better get used to the idea.

Being immortalised in oil and acrylics was quite pain-
less really.

Oh, yes. A man who chose to work in Alaska in the
middle of winter was really going to go for that idea.

Now that did give her the shivers. That and the rivulet
of rain water spilling out from the awning.

She was doomed!

Toni dropped her shoulders and shoved her free hand
into the pocket of the practical but not very elegant all-
weather coat she used for outdoor photo shoots.

The things she did for her sister!

Two weeks. She had two weeks' holiday to sketch the

portrait and work in at least two full sittings before heading back to work. She could finish the portrait at home over the next few weekends and collect the rest of her fee. With a bit of luck, there might be a little left over from paying Amy's university fees to squeeze in a quick holiday somewhere warm and sunny.

Now that—she shivered in the icy wind—would be nice.

Exhaling slowly, Toni glanced from side to side to find a gap in the stream of people who had their heads down, their umbrellas braced forward against the driving sleet and rain and oblivious to anyone who might walk in their way.

Seizing on a momentary lull, Toni dashed out onto the road in the stationary rush hour traffic. She had almost made it when she had to dive sideways to dodge a bicycle courier and planted her right foot into a deep puddle. Dirty cold water splashed up into her smart high heeled ankle boots and trickled down inside, making her gasp with shock.

Hissing under her breath, Toni stepped up onto the kerb and inside the porch.

A brass plaque set into the old stone read: 'Elstrom and Sons. Map-makers' in the most stunning cursive script.

Blowing out hard, Toni rolled back her shoulders and tried to think positive thoughts. A flutter of nervous apprehension winged across her stomach.

This was so ridiculous.

She was here to paint Scott's portrait. That was all. The small fact that he did not actually want his portrait painting was not important.

Much. She peered through the tiny squares of thick old glass set into the door but couldn't see a thing—no lights or movement.

She ran her hands down the front of her raincoat and lifted her chin, stretched her hand out and rang the doorbell.

Instantly a low buzzing sound came from the door and a green light flashed.

Oh. Right. Security door. Well, that made sense.

She turned the handle, pushed the door a little and stepped inside.

Water dripping from every part of her, Toni shook the rain from her hair and instantly inhaled the glorious deep, rich aroma of antique wood, polished leather and that certain delicious muskiness that came from old manuscripts and bound books.

Laughing and half choking in the slightly dusty air, a sudden smile caught her unexpectedly.

Strange, Toni thought. That smell. It was so distinctive. She inhaled deeply and instantly recognized it. Of course. Her mother used to have a tin of beeswax and linseed oil mixed with lavender under the sink and brought it out whenever she dusted her father's studio, which wasn't often, considering how rarely any flat surface remained uncluttered with paperwork and art exhibition catalogues and letters and, occasionally, bills.

She hadn't thought about that polish for years. Perhaps she should make some up when she got back to the house to protect the furniture against the ravages of a new tenant?

The door buzzed behind her, demanding to be closed, breaking the spell.

Then she stood, frozen and blinking, trying to take in what she was looking at.

It was like stepping back in time. Light streamed into the space from long, narrow stained glass window panels at the other side of the room that seemed to lead into a corridor. But in front of her, on either side, the walls were covered in rows of square wooden panels probably not wider than her arm above a tough-looking, very weathered wooden floor.

No carpet or textiles. Just hardwood panelling.

Cupboards and cabinets were lined up to her left and at head height along each wall were sea charts and maps in heavy gilt frames.

Well, that explained the security door!

The last time she had seen anything like this was at a stately home which had not been touched for hundreds of years. The financial demands of keeping the place going had finally caught up with the family and they had very reluctantly opened their home as a film set for historical dramas. The media company she worked for had been there for months, filming what they needed.

But this room? This was more like a museum.

Toni strolled over to a stunning wide table decorated in marquetry which stretched the full length of one wall. It was covered with scrolls, brightly coloured documents inside plastic sheets and an assortment of what looked, to her uneducated eyes, like antique survey equipment and sextants.

She was so engrossed in admiring the stunning elaborate engraving on the handle of a brass magnifying glass that it took a blast of cold air on her neck to snap her back into the real world. Toni whirled around in surprise and inhaled sharply.

Little wonder. A towering dark blond-haired man filled the entrance to the corridor, blocking out the light. He was wearing a navy blue round-necked light sweater with the sleeves rolled up, oblivious to the cold and wet outside.

His deeply tanned face was glowing from the rain and wind and he ran the fingers of his right hand back through his long damp hair from forehead to neck in a single natural motion. That simple movement only made his paler heavy eyebrows and pepper-and-salt moustache and beard even more pronounced.

Last night at the town house, his eyes had seemed dark and cloudy. But here Toni realised just how wrong she had been.

Despite the lack of a comfortable bed, the exhaustion had faded to a slight crease between those eyebrows, drawing her gaze to eyes the colour of a Mediterranean sea.

His square jaw was so taut it might have been sculpted. But it was his mouth that knocked the air out of her lungs, and had her clinging on to the edge of the table for support.

Plump lips smiled wide above his light beard, so that the bow was sharp between the smile lines.

His button-fly denims sat low on his slim hips but there was no mistaking that he was pure muscle beneath those tight trousers. Because, as he stood there for a second, his hands thrust deep into his trouser pockets, looking from table to table, scanning the horizon that was the confines of the shop, every movement he made seemed magnified.

The entire room seemed to shrink around him.

How did he do that? How did he just waltz in and master the room as though he was in command of the space and everyone in it?

This man was outdoors taken to the next level. No wonder he worked in Alaska. She could certainly imagine him standing at the helm of some ice-breaker, head high, legs braced. The master of his universe.

The hair on the back of her neck prickled with recognition.

Instead of giving her the up and down once-over, his gaze locked on to her face and stayed there, unmoving for a few seconds, before the corner of his mouth slid into a lazy smile.

The corners of those amazing eyes crinkled slightly and the warmth of that smile seemed to heat the air between them. And, at that moment, this smile was for her. And her heart leapt. More than a little. But just enough to recognize that the blush of heat racing through her neck and face were not due to the extra-warm coat and scarf that she was wearing.

In that instant Toni knew what it felt like to be the most important and most beautiful person in the room. Heart thumping. Brain spinning. An odd and unfamiliar tension hummed down her veins. Every cell of her suddenly alive and tuned into the vibrations emanating from his body.

Suddenly she wanted to preen and flick her hair and roll her shoulders back so that she could stick her chest out.

It was as if she had been dusted with instant lust powder.

Standing a little straighter, Toni quickly focused her gaze on the engraving on the glass that she was still holding, trying to find something to do with her hands, only too aware that he was still watching her.

She could practically feel the heat of that laser beam gaze burning a hole through her forehead and was surprised that there was no smell of smoke or a scorch mark on the wall behind her.

'Miss Baldoni. I'm surprised to see you here at this time on a Sunday morning. I thought that you might be enjoying a lie-in. I do hope that I didn't wake you up on my way out this morning. It was very early.'

'I didn't hear a thing, Mr Elstrom. As for my being here?' Toni very carefully put down the glass and lifted her chin. 'As I explained last night, I have a contract to paint the head of Elstrom Mapping. No matter whom that may be.' She braved a small smile. 'I am so looking forward to painting your portrait. Perhaps we can get started with some photographs? Show me your best pose. I dare you!'

CHAPTER FOUR

SCOTT'S REPLY WAS to rest his hands, splayed out, on the table, his left hand loose and relaxed, the right bandaged around the fingers. He leaned the top half of his long wide frame towards her from the hips so that she had to fight the urge to lean back against the display table and protect her space.

She liked hands, always had. It was usually one of the first things she noticed about a person. She could tell from the way he protected his bandaged fingers that he must be in pain. His left hand had long slender fingers with clean short nails. The knuckles were scarred and bruised as though they had been bashed at regular intervals and the veins on the back of his hand stood out in prominent raised rivers. Sinewy. Powerful.

They were clever, fast, working hands.

No manicures for Scott Elstrom.

The neck of his top stretched open and revealed a hint of deeply tanned skin around the neckline and more than a few dark blond chest hairs.

At this distance, she could have reached out and touched the curved flicks of thick blond slicked-back hair that had fallen over one side of his temple, but she had the idea that he would like that far too much so she simply lifted her chin and inhaled a long calming breath through her nose.

Big mistake.

Instead of a background aroma of leather and lavender and old books, she was overwhelmed with the scent of gentle rain on freshly cut grass blended with lime zest which was tangy and fresh against the sweetness of the air.

He had certainly made good use of the bath at Freya's!

He smelt wonderful. Expensive, distinctive and on a scale of one to ten on the testosterone level she would give him a twelve. From the sun-bleached hair on his arms and the way the muscles in his neck flexed when he moved, to the know-it-all confidence in the smile he was giving her at that moment, he was off the scale.

He was about as different from Peter as it was possible to be—on the surface.

He was a fashion photographer's dream. She knew several professionals who would have signed him on the spot if they had seen him like this. And somehow she had to paint his portrait! Wow! *Thank you, Freya.*

So what if she was attracted to him? It was only natural.

Until now, she had believed that she was immune to such charms. After all, she had been exposed to this type of infection many times before and just about survived. Working in studio photography exposed her to egos the size of small planets most days of the week, girls and boys.

But this man was a carrier for a super-powerful version of charm that no amount of previous experience had a chance of fighting off.

For a moment her heart went out to him.

He had travelled thousands of miles to come back to take over a family business with frostbitten fingers. The last thing he needed was a pest like her turning up to annoy him.

Then his gaze shot to her face. It was fierce and intense, and for one microsecond she had an insight into the power and strength of this man who could freeze her to ice with just one glance.

She might have guessed. He probably expected everyone to jump when he clicked his fingers and not complain in the process.

'There seems to be a misunderstanding, Miss Baldoni. I thought that I made it clear last night that the situation has changed. And I have no plans to have my portrait painted by you or anyone else for that matter.'

His voice came from the depths of his chest and was no doubt intended to intimidate lesser mortals who got in his way.

Not this time! She was way too used to dealing with the divas of the media world to let a feeble excuse like logic stop her from getting her way.

She needed this commission!

'Oh, I understand what you're telling me perfectly, Mr Elstrom. Plans do have a nasty habit of changing on us without warning, don't they? It's most inconvenient.'

Rubbing her hands together in delight, Toni dived into her capacious shoulder bag and pulled out her digital camera. 'My motto? Let's look at this as an opportunity. In fact, I was just telling Freya this morning that I have a wonderful feeling that this project is going to be something extra special.'

His nose wrinkled and a sound close to a low, deep grunt escaped his lips. 'You spoke to Freya?'

'Well, of course I had to clarify my position. Seeing as she has already paid me half my fee. And guess what? Your father is *so* looking forward to seeing your final portrait! He can hardly wait to see it join the others in your boardroom.'

Then she grinned, fluttered her eyelashes at him, raised

the camera to her eyes and fired off a flash photograph of his stunned face before he could say a word.

'Excellent. Now, shall we peek at the gallery?'

'The gallery?' he asked with a less than happy expression on his face, eyebrows high.

'The Baldoni collection, of course. I would love to see my father's work again. And you can talk to me about the Elstrom family history at the same time. What fun!'

His lips formed the word 'fun'—at least she thought that the word was fun—and he made that low groaning sound again.

'Only if you promise not to even try to take my photograph again.'

'No photographs? That's going to make it tricky.'

'Camera-shy,' he murmured.

'Okay—' she winced '—that's a first but I can handle that. It will mean more work but I can run a few sketches and make notes on your ideas.'

'No ideas. You're on your own, Miss Baldoni. But if you want to see the other portraits before you go, the boardroom is on the first floor.' He nodded to the narrow polished wooden staircase at the other end of the reception area. 'After you.'

'What a wonderful table,' Toni said as she strolled into a long narrow room with wood-panelled walls which was dominated by a stunning table which ran almost the full length of the room. The surface of the table was decorated by inlaid pictures crafted from fine marquetry and gold bands which had been inserted into the golden wood.

She ran her fingers along the wood, which was worn down by wear and slightly rough under her fingertips, and then strolled over to the four large windows which ran from waist to head height. 'Is this stained glass original?'

'The whole building was bomb-damaged during the war so some of the glass was replaced with replicas.'

'It's lovely work.'

Then, with one deep breath, she swung around and, with her back to the windows, plunged her hands deep into the pockets of her coat to try and get some warmth.

Facing her was a collection of some of the most stunning and unusual portraits that she had ever seen.

Looking from left to right, it was immediately clear that the oldest full length paintings were on the wall directly facing the chair at the head of the table. She dashed across the room so that she could take a closer look, moving from picture to picture, nodding and smiling in appreciation of the remarkable workmanship. And chatting to herself as she went.

'Now that older gent with the sea charts and sextant—that has to be of the seafaring Elstrom shipping clan. All beards and rough and tough dangerous sea crossings. But this one.' She paused and tapped her lower lip and tilted her head to one side. 'This Elstrom looks more studious. Was he a scientist?'

She turned around to ask Scott but he was standing at the other end of the room, close to the door, with his gaze totally focused on the centre of the table. Deep in thought and totally oblivious to her and what she had been asking.

Toni had staged photo shoots long enough to recognize that something was very wrong with the man she was looking at.

His shoulders were braced hard, his jaw was locked tight shut and those eyes were not blue at all but had turned as grey and steely as the ocean waves on the portraits she had just been looking at. Dark. Stormy. And troubled.

Everything about Scott's body language screamed out to her that he took absolutely no pleasure in being in this room.

Well, that made sense. The last twenty-four hours must have been quite a roller coaster. His father was ill and he'd had a terrible journey from Alaska to take over a job when he wasn't expecting it. She would be totally wrecked! Maybe she should be a little more forgiving? Her journey this morning had been a short ride on a heated bus.

She quickly glanced away and pretended to move to the next portrait and then the next until she came to an Elstrom in a business suit and a painting style that was totally familiar to her. Instinct and a slight rustle of papers behind her back told her that Scott had moved.

'Ah. Look at that classic pose,' she called out in a cheery voice. 'Your grandfather must have been a wonderful chairman of the board. So dominant. My grandfather really did capture something about him. There is real spirit behind those eyes.'

Toni glanced across at Scott but he seemed more interested in scanning through a bundle of mail he had brought with him from the reception area.

'But we can be more creative if you want,' she suggested and stepped closer to him. 'Maybe even take it out of doors and have more of an action shot. Sailing could work. Or mountaineering? Just pass me some action shots and let me work my magic. All good control metaphors.'

'Control metaphors,' he repeated. 'That sounds good. Do you do this a lot?'

Suddenly Toni's patience ran out. 'My CV is with Freya and your father sounded very keen on me painting something worthy of hanging on these walls next to your family. Is there a problem I don't know about here? Or is the problem with me? Because, for the record, I don't normally spend my evenings modelling lingerie.'

That got his attention and the mail hit the table.

'For the record. My decision to cancel your contract

has nothing to do with what happened last night. You have every right to hold a birthday party if you choose.'

'Cancel? Oh, no...' She coughed and shook her head. 'Freya told me that this was a top priority job. I turned work away to come here to do this. You don't cancel at this short notice. I won't allow it.'

Then she whirled around and waved her arm towards the paintings.

'This is your family! My grandfather started the tradition of painting portraits of every head of the Elstroms, starting with your great-grandfather right down to that one of your uncle, which my dad worked on when I was a girl. And now it's my turn. Tradition. I like that idea just fine. You are carrying on the family tradition and so am I. So you're having your portrait painted whether you like it or not.'

She blinked and grinned but his reaction was to close his eyes for a second and cross his arms.

'Then let me explain again. It's very simple. I have absolutely no intention of having a painting of my face hanging on that wall and I certainly do not have the time to sit around while you sketch my wrinkles. As far as I'm concerned, you can take your fee and go home right now. Think of it as a bonus.'

'Are you serious?' she choked. 'You dragged me all the way out here to the centre of London to do the work and now you've changed your mind? Is that what you're telling me?'

'I haven't changed my mind. This was never my idea in the first place. The first thing I knew about it was when you told me last night. My sister made the arrangements, not me.'

'I have a signed contract,' Toni replied, crossing her arms to match his, her eyebrows high.

'I can cancel it and you can keep your fee. Go home with my blessing.'

'Just like that?' she gasped.

'Just like that. You will have your fee in the bank today. I'm sorry for wasting your time. Do we have a deal, Miss Baldoni?'

He held out his hand and she took it. And held it and kept on holding it until he looked down and frowned and tried to pull it away.

'What are you doing?'

'My job. Part of creating a portrait is making a connection with the sitter so you can capture something unique about them. I always start with the hands. Or, in your case, one hand. I like hands and yours is spectacular.'

She gave a quick nod. 'You like being outdoors and working for a living in hard environments. Alaska makes sense now. Yes. I can do something with that. And it explains why you're so grumpy here in the office.'

'I am not grumpy,' he said and pulled his hand back. 'Did you hear what I said? You're going to have your fee. So feel free to go and do one of those jobs that you passed over to come here.'

'Grumpy. Here is how it works. I sign a contract and I deliver the goods. No arguments, no discussion; that is what's going to happen.'

He glared at her and did the eyebrow thing again. 'Are you always so stubborn?'

'Frequently. Especially with uncooperative subjects like you. So you may as well get used to the idea, because I am painting you. Even if I have to do it from memory and press clippings. That's the way it works.'

She stepped back and made a square with the thumb and forefingers of both hands. 'Oh. Would you mind doing that look again? Scowl a little more to one side. That's super. I was looking for a scary image for Halloween.'

'Double the fee if you leave now.'

That stopped her and she clasped hold of one of the boardroom's carved wooden chairs.

'What? No. I gave Freya my word that I would do the very best work that I could. Promises mean something in my family. If I give my word that I will do something I will do it. End of story.'

'Is it? Let me guess. I know a few things about families too. Something tells me that you're desperate to prove to your father, the famous portrait painter, that you're his equal.'

He leant back against the wooden panels with a smug expression on his face. 'Am I right?'

The words hit Toni like a slap across the face and she reeled back in a reflex action which had her gasping for breath.

Suddenly it all became too much. Lack of sleep, the sadness of waving Amy goodbye as she drove away in a taxi, and then the harshness of this man all combined together in one mighty wave which washed over her, leaving her exhausted.

Toni whirled around sideways to look at the portrait that her father had painted. There was no way that she was going to let Scott see how close she was to bursting into tears.

It was several minutes before she was ready to reply in a hoarse whisper. 'Whose family are we talking about? Yours or mine? Because I'm sorry to disappoint you, Mr Elstrom, but this time you're wrong. My father passed away several years ago. The only person I have to prove anything to is myself.'

There was a sharp intake of breath followed by a long slow sigh. 'My apologies. I didn't know.'

Toni replied with a sharp nod. 'There is no reason why you should know. But, you see, I really am the last of the Baldoni artists and your father wants a Baldoni hanging on this wall. Which means. Me.'

Toni half turned from the waist and risked glancing at Scott, who was looking at her with something close to respect in his eyes.

She stood in silence for a moment and then her shoulders dropped. 'Freya has already paid me half my fee for the portrait. I don't want to give that money back.' Then she shrugged. 'In fact I have already spent it on something important—but that doesn't matter.'

She lifted her chin but carried on in a softer voice. 'What does matter is that I want to deliver this portrait. I can work on your likeness from photos and sketches. But it makes a big difference if I can get my client to sit down and be fairly still for a while. I can see that might be a problem. So tell me how we can work together to make this happen.'

Scott waved an arm around in a circle.

'I cannot give you that time. Look around you, Miss Baldoni. I have just been made the head of a company which no longer exists. My father decided to close the business a month ago and make the few remaining staff redundant.'

His fingers clasped around the back rung of a chair.

'It's going to take me months to sort out the financial situation and come up with some sort of rescue package before this building is sold to developers. Apparently, they could make at least six luxury apartments out of this three-storey building.'

'Apartments? Oh, no. That's terrible. Are they allowed to do that? Seriously?'

'Oh, yes. Specialist builders can prop up the creaky outside walls and make the structure safe and strong but it will mean gutting the inside and starting again. Two hundred years of history is about to be wiped away as if it never happened.'

'I see. Well, that explains something I'd been wondering about,' Toni replied in a low voice, almost mumbling to herself before she looked up into Scott's face to find him looking quizzically at her.

'From what Freya told me, your father has been working here most of his life and took over about twenty years ago—that must be from your uncle. Yes? But he didn't have his portrait painted. Even though he is obviously very traditional. It makes sense now. This was going to be his last chance to be painted as the head of Elstrom Mapping before the company closed. He wanted the last portrait on the wall on the day the building was sold.'

She pushed her hands deep into her pockets. 'That's sad,' she sniffed.

'Sad but true. Because you're right.'

He stepped in front of the portrait painted by Toni's father and they stood side by side and stared up at the young, vibrant blond-haired man whose essence had been captured in oil paint on canvas.

'My uncle Neil was the action businessman—the dynamic and charming star who was a natural athlete and medal-winning explorer. He excelled in public speaking, making presentations and was dazzling to the media. While my father...?'

Scott pushed his hands into his trouser pockets.

'My father worked out as a boy that he was never going to compete with his older brother Neil. He preferred to stay in the background and let his brother take the lime-light. So they sat down and worked it out between them. My father would stay here in the office and do the meticulous work behind the scenes while my uncle Neil travelled the world using Elstrom maps and bringing in more orders than they could cope with. It was win/win. Until my uncle was killed in an avalanche in the Himalayas. And the whole thing fell apart.'

'Now it's my turn to be sorry. He looks like a remarkable man.'

'He was extraordinary. And that was part of the problem. Do you know why my father never contacted the Baldoni family? Because he never once felt that he was the man in charge. I was about twelve when my uncle had the accident and as far as my dad was concerned I was the man who was destined to take my uncle's place. My uncle had never married or settled down anywhere long enough to have a family, although he was never short of female company. Which meant one thing. I was the heir. The man who was going to be the next head of Elstrom Mapping. My father told me on my eighteenth birthday that all he'd been doing was keeping my seat warm for me.'

'Wait. Are you telling me that he never wanted his portrait painted?'

'Never. It was going to be my portrait hanging on the wall next to my uncle. Not my dad. Me.'

'Wow. So why…?'

'He finally accepted this Christmas that it was never going to happen.'

'I don't understand.'

'Oh, it's quite simple. I walked out of this building two years ago and made it perfectly clear that I had absolutely no intention of ever coming back. That was it. Unless Freya suddenly developed a burning fascination for sea charts, the Elstrom line ended with my dad. I was out and was out for good.'

Scott nodded to the wall and as he spoke every word seemed to come from a deep, dark place. 'It has taken two years for him to finally get that fact into his head and admit defeat. Lars Elstrom truly would be the last head of Elstrom Mapping. There was no way he was going to get me to come back and run the business. No way at all.'

Then he turned around to face her and leant back against the table. Head high. Eyes narrow and all business.

'Do you get the picture now, Miss Baldoni?'

CHAPTER FIVE

TONI SAT BACK in one of the boardroom chairs and tried to take in what Scott had just told her.

Scott Elstrom didn't want to be here one little bit. In fact he had made it clear to his family that he had no intention of ever coming back to run the business.

No wonder he was grumpy!

She knew what it was like to be dragged out of your normal life by a situation out of your control.

When her parents died in the train crash she had been left utterly alone at eighteen with a ten-year-old sister to bring up.

Scott was lucky. He still had his parents and a sister who cared about him. He could pull this off. *If he wanted to.*

'But you're back to stay now. Aren't you?' she asked cautiously.

'I promised my father that I would give him six months.' Scott's voice was flat and cold but at least he had stopped scowling at her.

Toni pushed off from the chair and flipped both hands into the air with a big grin on her face.

'Then everything has changed. Your face should be right up here on this wall next to your uncle. Six weeks or six months—it doesn't make the slightest bit of difference to me. You're the latest CEO of Elstrom Mapping and it's my job to paint your portrait.'

Then she rubbed her hands together. 'Any chance of a coffee before we get started on the sketches? It's a bit nippy in here.'

Scott didn't move an inch. 'You really aren't going to let this go, are you?'

'Nope—' she grinned '—I have every intention of sticking around and taking your photograph and generally making a nuisance of myself until I have all the material I need to work my magic. It's so important to get to know the client as much as possible. So, you see, there is no way that you're going to get rid of me.'

He stepped forward, totally invading her space until she could see every hair of his grey and blond beard and practically feel his breath on her cheeks.

His skin was red and chapped and his hair needed cutting but somehow Scott Elstrom rocked that master-of-all-he-surveyed look better than any stylist she knew could have pulled off.

Any lesser mortal would have backed off. *Not her.*

'I could pick you up one-handed and carry you outside. You know that, don't you?'

'Absolutely.' She smiled, reached out with her right hand and squeezed his rock-hard biceps, sighing in appreciation, and then her gaze locked on to his eyes. 'But then I would have to set up my paints on the pavement outside your front door and call on all of my media friends to interview me. Just think of the TV crews and reporters who would be hassling you day and night. Wouldn't that be a nice treat?'

'Stalker,' he replied in a low, deep voice which seemed to echo around inside her head and come out of her ears.

'Grumpy.' She blinked then instantly refocused on those startling blue eyes which seemed locked onto hers.

Time expanded. All she could hear was the sound of their breathing and the chiming of a very old clock somewhere in the building.

Oh. And the burning of the air between them as if it was ignited by the fierce electricity that sparked in the few inches that separated them.

She had heard that ozone was addictive and maybe they were right because the air she was breathing now was so thick with pheromones and testosterone she could have sliced it and served it with tea.

It was almost a relief when Scott stepped back. But, to her astonishment, he grabbed her hand with his long strong fingers and started marching towards the door.

Was this it? Was he calling her bluff and throwing her out on to the street?

'Come with me,' he growled. 'I want you to see for yourself why there is no time to spend hours of my life sitting for a portrait.'

It was an office of sorts. But it was totally unlike anywhere she had ever seen.

Every flat or even vaguely flat surface was covered with stacks of paper. All sizes—plain, decorated, scraps of what looked like paper napkins covered in handwriting, envelopes of every description.

Tables, chairs and bookcases were all crammed full of sheets of yellowing paper with the overspill stacked in vague piles on a faded threadbare carpet.

There was a rounded shape in front of the window which might be a sofa because she could see curved wooden feet at either end but, instead of cushions, there were scrolls tied with string and ribbon, about twenty cardboard tubes standing on end and box after box of padded envelopes with exotic bright stamps on the outside.

Floor-to-ceiling bookcases with glass doors lined each wall and Toni could just see through the thick layers of dust that they were crammed to bursting with double-stacked papers and books of all sizes and bindings.

At some point a stack of thin booklets had been knocked off the desk and lay scattered on the floor where they could easily be stepped on.

Scott released her hand with a flick and Toni gingerly stepped forward and picked up one of the booklets.

It was a catalogue promoting *Elstrom Rare Documents Restoration Services*, dated 1958. The original cover must have been a deep blood-red but the colour had faded until it was a faint spotty pink. The letters were blurred and indistinct, the paper inside yellow and fragile.

Replacing the booklet on top of another like it on the desk, Toni looked around at the chaos and swallowed down a lump of cold concern.

'Have you been burgled?'

'Burgled? No.' He laughed. 'This is my dad's private office. Sorry. *Was* my dad's office. Mine now. And it has been like this ever since I can remember.'

'You're kidding me. Seriously? He ran the company from this room?'

'He knows where everything is. Every invoice, every receipt, and every letter he has ever written or received is in this room. You're looking at forty years of his accumulated paperwork plus everything he inherited from my uncle, who had this office before he did.'

'Wow. It's really quite remarkable. Do you mind if I take some photographs?'

'Of what?'

'This room. I had no idea that places like this exist any more.'

'They don't—' he coughed '—not if they want to run as a business. Somewhere in that heap of unopened mail are bills which need to be paid so that the telephones and lights still work. Somewhere. I've been here two hours and I've hardly touched the surface.'

Toni whistled out loud as she took several pictures with her digital camera.

'Good luck with that little challenge.'

Then she snuggled deeper inside her padded coat and looked from side to side. 'I wouldn't even know where to start,' she whispered. 'And this office is freezing; any chance you could turn the heating on—' she cupped her hands and rubbed her palms together '—or is that bad for the documents?'

'Leather and paper like the humidity. It keeps them soft. As for the heating? The temperature seems fine to me, but I haven't had time to check the boiler and the electrics. A building this old has its quirks.'

Toni peeked around Scott and nodded towards the desk.

'How can you not feel cold? I'm standing here shivering.'

He frowned. 'Your hand did feel cool.'

'It's a cold day. By London standards, anyway. Is there a tea room? Kettle? Cups? Anything?'

'Yes. But here's a suggestion.'

Scott grabbed a light padded jacket from the back of a chair stacked with unopened packages. 'Before I set out on a survey I always check that I have the equipment and essential supplies that I need. Food and drink are up there on the top five. As it happens, there are a few things about the city that I do miss when I'm working in the field.'

'Soap and hot water?'

'No. Although those things can be few and far between. But right now I was thinking about real coffee made from ground coffee beans. And something laden with fat and sugar to help me get through this jet lag.'

'Well, I know the local terrain fairly well. Willing to risk having a local guide?'

'Let's get out of here.'

'Two-shot Americano,' they both said at the same time as the barista took their order and then jumped back at the sound of each other's voice.

'Seriously?' He turned and peered at her, arms folded. 'I would have thought that some elegant green tea would be a more suitable hot beverage for a portrait painter. All elegance and refinement and artistic expression.'

Toni snorted out loud. 'Ah, you're back to the stereotypes again. I think it's my solemn duty to flip that illusion and pronto.'

She pressed her right forefinger to her chest. 'A two shot Americano is perfect for a part-time portrait painter who has a day job as a commercial photographer. You get the instant hit from the caffeine but it's not quite enough to bring on a bad case of the jitters. And, believe me, there are some days I'm run so ragged that one coffee has to keep me going for a long time.'

'Aha. So you don't paint portraits full-time. Interesting. Well, that explains a few things.'

'Really. Such as? Please carry on. I would hate for you to keep all of that valuable insight to yourself. What gave the game away?'

To her astonishment, Scott reached across the table and picked up her hand and looked at it, fascinated. Then turned it over and brought it up to his lips.

That simple movement was bad enough, but Toni wasn't

prepared for the rush of heat she got from the touch of his full lips on the sensitive skin at the centre of her palm which had nothing to do with the fact that she had chosen a table right next to the radiator.

It was so unexpected that she took a second before re-flex action kicked in and she tried to slide her hand back. No luck. It was locked solidly in his grip of iron.

'What are you doing?' she muttered between locked teeth. 'Stop that right now. People. Are. Looking. At us.'

She smiled over to a group of girls who were giggling at her on another table while she tried to tug her hand away without making it look too obvious.

'Answering your question. So stop struggling. You see, I like hands too. And yours tell me so much about you. No paint under the fingernails or ink or charcoal ground into your palms.'

He pressed his lips to her knuckles and then lowered her hand to the table. 'Your skin smells of shower gel. Not linseed oil or acrylics and it is certainly not used to out-side work. A studio photographer. Now, that makes sense.'

'How very observant. I like to think I am creating portraits of a different sort. But—' she took a sip of the scalding-hot fragrant coffee '—you have a point. My first sketches can be taken from a photograph rather than a live sitting straight onto the canvas. That's the way I work. I think about how I want the sitter to look in the final piece. Not always easy.'

He coughed just once and picked up his drink when one of the waitresses nudged him accidentally and the hot coffee splashed on to his bandaged hand, which was resting on the table.

'I'm so sorry. Are you okay?'

'No harm done,' Scott reassured the young girl.

Toni waited until she was gone before looking up at

Scott over the top of her cup. 'Do you mind if I ask—how did you hurt yourself?'

'For a girl, of course! Why else would a man throw himself on to frozen sea ice and let his fingers go anywhere near ice water?'

'Wow. Sea ice. That's astonishing. Scary. Wild. And a bit mad'.

'It's my life. And Dallas does have the most amazing blue eyes.'

'Well, she must have to make you go to those sorts of lengths. Is she okay now? Your Dallas?'

'My Dallas is having the time of her life being pampered and well fed by a whole survey team of boys. Probably not missing me one bit.'

'Not missing you? After what you did for her! That's a bit ungrateful.'

'Probably. Doesn't stop me from missing her. She's been a good friend.'

'Well, in that case the lady is forgiven. Good friends are hard to find. And I hope you finish your business here soon so that you can get back to her charms.'

'I'll drink to that. To Dallas. See you in six months, girl.'

Six months. *Interesting.*

Toni lifted her cup of steaming coffee. 'Six months—is that how long you have to turn the business around?'

'Less. That's how long I have committed to. Different thing.'

'Any ideas about what you're going to do?' Toni asked over the top of her coffee. 'I mean, apart from finding a new office to work from. Because, I have to tell you, I did not see any sign of modern technology just now and I think you might need a few more things besides paper and pens.'

'Maybe. I'm a scientist. And don't look at me like that.

It might be hard to believe. But it's true. Before I make a decision I like to know the facts.'

Scott put down his coffee and nodded back towards the Elstrom building, just down the street. When he spoke it sounded to Toni as though he was simply speaking his thoughts out loud rather than having a conversation. 'Top of the list is to create some operating income. If things are as bad as Freya thinks they are, it could be a shock at the bank tomorrow. Right now, I have no clue about what has happened to our archive of valuable documents— instruments, maps, sea charts going back almost two hundred years. There has to be something left.'

He shrugged and took a long drink before going on. 'I need to make an inventory of the entire stock. Once I know what I have left, I can start work. Sell some items to specialist dealers. Loan others to museums for a fee. That should give me enough time to put together a long-term plan. But I need to work fast. Clear the office. Make space to work. Then I need to create a brilliant sales catalogue in weeks, not months, and…'

Scott's voice faded away and his eyes narrowed and focused on Toni so intently that she glanced around the room before putting her coffee down.

'What? What have I done now?'

'It's not what you *have* done, Miss Baldoni. It's what you are *going* to do.'

He stretched both arms flat on the small table and leant forwards from the waist until he was close enough for her to touch him. 'I need someone who can photograph my stock and create a sales catalogue. Someone with experience as a studio photographer would be absolutely perfect. What do you say?'

Toni gulped down some coffee so fast that she almost choked.

'What do I say?' she replied, blinking. 'I say that Freya paid me to paint your portrait, not work as your commercial photographer.'

Scott slid backwards but his attention was still completely focused on her.

'You wanted to stick around and make character studies. I'm giving you the chance to do that. For the next seven days you can photograph anything you like, including me. On one condition. You help me out with the business side at the same time. Do we have a deal?'

He stretched out his hand across the table and tilted his head slightly to one side.

Toni took a breath, her heart pounding and her mind racing.

Seven days? He was offering her seven days to take the photographs and make the sketches she needed to paint him. And something else. Something even more important. The chance to get to know him a little more.

It was the one thing that had been drummed into her from the very start of her training with her father. To be a real painter, she had to capture the essence of the sitter in paint on the canvas. That was the extra-special quality of a Baldoni portrait. Without that? She might as well just take his photograph and be done with it.

Scott coughed low in his throat and she looked up into eyes which she knew she could paint in a heartbeat. But the rest of him? Somehow, she got the feeling that she had only just touched the surface of the real Scott Elstrom.

So why was she hesitating?

A muscle twitched at the corner of his mouth and her heart rate sped up just enough to answer that question perfectly.

She had known Scott less than a day and she was already far more attracted to him than she had any right to be.

The last time she had worked alone with an attractive man on a project had been the few weeks she'd spent on assignment with Peter. She had fallen and fallen fast and look how well that had turned out. He had lied to her, betrayed her and broken her heart.

Could she trust herself to be more careful with Scott? *But what choice did she have?* She needed this work.

Toni looked into his face, then at his hand, and then back to his face again before sighing out loud and placing her hand in his. It was like being crushed in a vice.

'Fingers! I need the fingers!'

Shaking the blood back into her crushed fingers, she exhaled slowly. 'Well, Mr Scott Elstrom. What have I just let myself in for?'

His reply was an evil chuckle that would have been perfect for a horror movie. 'You saw my dad's office, Antonia. Wait until you see the archive. The Elstrom family take hoarding very seriously.'

A shudder ran across Toni's shoulders. More hoarding! Oh, no. She was an expert on the topic. She had a whole house of her own clutter to clear.

'Come on, girl. Let's make this happen. And on the way I want to hear how you plan to make those dusty old maps of mine look a million dollars. Shall we?'

And with one tiny nod he stepped back and gestured towards the exit. She peered at it for a fraction of a second before rolling her eyes and waving towards the counter. 'Could we have the same again, please? And make that four jam doughnuts this time. I think I'm going to need them.'

CHAPTER SIX

IT WAS ALMOST eight on the Sunday evening when Scott eventually turned the key and staggered into the hallway of Freya's house.

What a day! He would cheerfully take a hard day in the field any time compared to the chaos that was Elstrom Mapping.

The financial situation was not just bad—it was shocking.

His father really had given up. It was obvious from the few decent bank records that he had managed to find, that several valuable items had already been sold to specialist museums so that the loyal skilled staff could have the generous redundancy packages that they deserved.

Damn right. The small team at Elstrom had been the best in the business. Most of them were well beyond retirement age and simply loved working in the old place. The others had been given excellent references and were already working elsewhere.

But the really shocking thing was that all of this had happened over the autumn. A quick call to Freya confirmed what he had started to suspect. That piece of silvery tinsel paper he'd found in one of the drawers was a souvenir from the very last Christmas party that Elstrom would ever hold.

It was enough to bring tears to his eyes. They had always been such amazing parties. Everyone, from corporate clients to solo adventurers and oil exploration companies, would usually be in London for Christmas and found the time to come to Elstrom Mapping to raise a glass.

It was shocking to think that he had missed such a momentous event. And, more than sad, it was tragic to imagine his father sitting in that chair on New Year's Day. Alone. In the wreckage of the business he seemed to have given up on.

That was some start to the New Year.

The only bright spark in his day had been Antonia Baldoni. The girl who had started off as just another nuisance had turned out to be the most astonishing office manager that he had ever met. Not that he was an expert in the subject, but she had worked wonders.

He had been totally sceptical when Antonia suggested clearing one heap of papers at a time and sorting them by date and subject. What difference could it make?

How wrong could he be? In a few hours that bustling brunette bundle of energy and purpose had cleared everything from the huge partners' desk using a battered old tea tray she'd found in the kitchen, giving him space to work.

He had peeked into the boardroom when his back became too stiff to sit any longer and found her sorting every sheet into neat stacks on the boardroom table. And the stacks made sense! She had even found some empty boxes and loaded up the old brochures and pamphlets in case he wanted them for inspiration about future projects.

A single in tray from one of the mapping rooms held everything that needed attention and all of the unopened mail.

He had taken one look at the pile and the fact that Antonia was wearing her hat, coat and gloves to work in and decided that his first executive decision was to try and get the heating working in at least the first floor of the building before she froze.

It had taken him almost an hour to coax the ancient gas boiler down in the freezing dark basement back into life. At least that hadn't changed. It was as temperamental as ever and the tangle of electrical wiring looked as though a toddler had been at play but he could be as stubborn as Antonia when he wanted to be. Any gas engineer would probably condemn the old kit, but right now? That was what they had to work with. And by six she had taken off her hat and coat. So he had achieved something positive today. Maybe tomorrow she could work without the gloves?

Good news was in short supply. He would take what he could.

Starting with Antonia Baldoni.

Apparently he hadn't noticed how messy the house was that morning when he'd left but there was a lot of clearing up still to be done after her birthday party. So she had left the office earlier to tidy up the house.

Scott strolled into the kitchen and turned on the kettle. He could smell something delicious and savoury cooking in the oven and the room felt warm and cosy. Hanging up his coat, he lifted one arm and then the other towards the ceiling, wincing as the tense muscles complained.

Nothing that about ten hours of decent sleep wouldn't fix.

Yeah. Like that was going to happen. *Not in that bedroom.* Too many memories. The ghost of his ex-wife was right there every time he'd woken from a restless dream of falling through the ice. He didn't need a photograph to bring back her beautiful face. Just walking into that boardroom at Elstrom had been traumatic enough.

How could he tell Antonia that his last memory of that room had been finding his wife having sex with his step-brother on the boardroom table?

Not something a man forgot in a hurry. And definitely not an image he was going to share any time soon.

He closed his eyes for a second then blinked awake.

Get over it.

There was no sign of Antonia so he slowly dragged his weary body up the stairs and had only taken a few steps towards his room when the door to the large family bath-room opened.

And through a cloud of hot fragrant steam a small fig-ure emerged.

Antonia was wrapped in a white bath towel which was just large enough to cover her chest to the top of her thighs.

But it was what the towel was not covering which rocked him back on his heels and lighted a fire in his belly hotter than any gas boiler could manage.

Her spectacular arms and shoulders were slick and steamy from the bath and her face was flushed pink and absolutely gorgeous.

Problem was, she was winding a smaller towel around her head as she strolled out on to the landing, with her feet pushed into those silly fluffy slippers she had been wear-ing the night before.

This meant that her arms were lifted, stretching the towel around her chest and making it slip a little lower, then lower until it was heading for her waist.

So what if he was a boob man and proud of it?

As a gentleman, he should probably say something... but as a man? Strange how it took a few seconds before his brain took over from the other parts of his anatomy, which were waking up on their own and enjoying the view way too much.

The scent of her warm body and her sensuous movements started turning on switches which he had started to believe Alexa had turned off for good.

A hot flush of desire hit him hard and then hit him again. Apparently he still had what it took after all. That was a relief. He had started to wonder. It was hardly surprising—Antonia was absolutely stunning!

Just for a second a totally off-the-wall idea flitted through his brain.

Would she be interested in him?

A week was not long enough for anything serious but a short casual fling could be just what he needed to bring some spice back into his life. He had barely looked at another woman for the last two years but, now he was back in London, maybe it was time to find out if he was ready to share his life again.

A fling. No strings. No commitment or promises and definitely no emotional mess. Just two people enjoying one another for a casual affair.

He was certainly enjoying her right now. Thank you, Miss Baldoni!

Maybe it was time to play fair.

'Hello,' Scott said and Antonia gasped and flung herself back towards the bathroom.

'I didn't mean to startle you—' he coughed '—but…' He gestured towards the towel with his head and she immediately hoisted it higher.

'Sorry about that.' She tugged the towel a little closer to her chest. 'I don't have any hot water in my house at the moment. The plumber has the flu. Won't be back to work for another few days. And I like a bath.' Her tongue flicked out over her hot lips and every male hormone in his body pinged to attention. 'Sorry.'

'No problem.' Scott smiled and ran his hand over his

beard before saying in a casual voice, 'Stay the night if you want. You won't be disturbing me.'

'Really?' Antonia asked, her voice a high-pitched squeak.

'Sure. How about some dinner? It smells good. See you downstairs in...' Then his throat went dry as the back of the towel slipped a little, revealing a back with flawless creamy skin which was moist and warm and smelt of all of the good sweet things in his life which he'd been putting on hold since he'd divorced Alexa.

She turned slightly towards him and he noticed for the first time, in the warm ceiling lights, that Toni's eyes were not brown but a shade of copper the colour of autumn leaves. The same colour as the highlights that burnished her damp hair. And at that moment those eyes were staring very intently at him.

On another day and another time he might even have said that she was more gorgeous than merely pretty. Slender, funny and so sharp-witted that she matched him round for round.

But even the loveliest of girls had their flaws. He had learnt that from bitter experience.

Even sweet Antonia Baldoni would be hiding something from the world.

He leant closer into the light and in the harsh shadows her cheekbones were sharp angles and her chin strong and resigned. Strong. Stubborn, that was sure. But not harsh or cruel. He couldn't see that about her.

'Twenty minutes.' He grinned then waved towards her head. 'Hairdryer. Okay.'

Then he turned and almost jogged back to his room and the hot shower he wanted and the cold shower he needed.

The howling icy wind had finally eased away when Toni gave up tossing and turning from side to side and threw back the covers on the perfectly comfortable double bed in Freya's spare bedroom.

Somewhere in the house a large mechanical clock was striking every quarter hour with a musical chime but, apart from that comforting sound, the house was completely silent, as though it was a sleeping giant waiting for some magical spell to be broken.

Scott looked so exhausted and jet-lagged after dinner that he must have dropped off to sleep the minute his head hit his pillow.

The pest.

How did he expect her to sleep after walking into her coming out of the bathroom like that? She couldn't go home to have her bath—she didn't have any heating! But that didn't mean she was any less embarrassed.

To make it worse, he hadn't once mentioned seeing her half naked during one of the most awkward dinners that she had ever eaten. It was almost a relief when Scott covered a yawn with his hand and said goodnight.

She peeked out through the bedroom curtains to see that the rain had cleared, leaving a lovely clear frosty night with a bright new moon and stars. Perfect for stargazing. And, seeing that Scott was asleep…

Toni tiptoed over to the bedroom door and slowly turned the handle and peeked out through the gap. She couldn't hear any snoring or tossing but the last thing she wanted to do was wake Scott up. No repeat performances, thank you!

Slowly and quietly sneaking open the door, she stepped outside on to the landing and then crept down the staircase one stair at a time, cringing every time her slippers made the stair creak.

She could see lights from the house on the other side of the street but, apart from that, all was still calm and serene.

Toni drew back the curtains in the living room so that she could see the stars. She snuggled up on the sofa and soaked in the silence as though she were drinking the contents of a deep well of cool refreshing water. True silence like this was so rare in her life that, when it happened, she took the time to appreciate the tranquility, no matter how temporary it might be.

Especially after the roller coaster ride of the past twenty-four hours.

It was going to take a while to process everything that Scott had told her. Just when things were going so well and she'd thought this would be an easy commission and she could finally put the brushes and paints away for good.

Today had been a nightmare of such conflicting emotions. One minute she could have cheerfully taken the fee Scott was offering her...and the next?

She liked him. Heaven help her, she might even feel sorry for him.

Scott had taken on an enormous task, alone. The deal they had made could work. She knew that the longer she spent working with Scott the more she would learn about him to help her create a likeness which captured something of the real man.

But who was the real Scott Elstrom? The frostbitten lumberjack rough and tough guy who had walked into her party? Or the other Scott Elstrom who was working so tirelessly to save his heritage from the jaws of defeat and closure?

There was one thing she was certain of—everything she turned her hand to seemed to make her life more difficult instead of easier.

Even her plumber had gone down with the February flu!

The New Year had seemed so full of possibility—a white clean space just begging to be filled with activity and life and…a loud clattering sound quickly followed by a low mumble rang out from the other side of the patio doors and she practically jumped over the sofa. The sound ricocheted like a bullet around the house in the deep background silence.

Toni grabbed the sofa cushion and, holding her breath, she slowly slipped off the sofa and listened for any further signs of movement as she carefully edged her way towards the kitchen.

Perhaps she should wake up Scott?

No. Bad idea. She was embarrassed enough for one night, thank you.

There was only one thing for it—she would have to go outside and find out what was going on. And if it was a burglar, she could deal with it.

Grabbing a large wooden pepper grinder from the table with one hand, Toni carefully turned the creaking handle of the heavy doors that opened on to the patio, anxious not to make too much noise, and stepped out on to the stone patio.

The wind might have dropped but it was still freezing, with a feeling of ice in the air.

The only light was from the street lamps and local houses but, as she gingerly strolled towards the side garden in her slippers, even that background light was blocked by the house.

'Too hot? Can't blame you; it's much cooler out here.'

She practically jumped out of her skin.

There was a movement from a bench at the far end of the patio and, as her eyes became more accustomed to the low light, she saw Scott stretched out with his long legs crossed at the ankles, hands behind his head. He seemed to be fully dressed with only a light fleece jacket and she could only hope that her thin pyjamas and towelling dressing gown were not too transparent.

'Best time of the day. Here. Try this for a viewpoint. And it even has a seat.'

Scott pointed to the old wooden bench, which Toni had not even noticed on her mad dash that afternoon from the office to the kitchen. It was half hidden in a tiny arc of flowering bushes and potted plants which almost covered the surface of a small paved patio area. Completely secluded and separated from the house by a low hedge, it was a perfect private space.

'Nice spot,' Toni murmured after a few minutes to break the silence. 'Come here often?'

Scott seemed to stretch out longer and laid his head back against the wooden bench so that when he spoke it was as though his words were addressed to the sky.

'The first time I saw this garden I was fifteen years old and my parents had agreed to divorce. My mother had finally had enough of cooking meals that never got eaten because my father slept at the office and simply forgot to tell her. I can't remember a time when he ever spent more than a couple of days with us in a row. Family holidays were a joke. So out went the old Victorian museum we called home and in came this modern clean house. With heating. And lights and plumbing. It was quite a shock.'

'Tell me about it—' Toni laughed and stepped closer '—I think you just described my house.'

'Some things stayed the same.' Scott raised one arm and pointed upwards. 'The constellations didn't stomp around and cry like Freya did or collapse on the sofa exhausted every night like my poor mother. They stayed in pretty much the same place in one part of London compared to another.'

'Well—' Toni tried to keep her voice light and her heart

from exploding '—I wondered where all of those lovely diagrams came from on your maps. Scott the astronomer.'

He chuckled, his voice low, deep and resonant in the absolute stillness and silence of the night.

'Star signs were traditional on sea charts and it helps having a basic knowledge when you're out in the wild,' he replied. 'How about you? Long history of solar exploration in your family?'

'Oh, just one of my many talents,' Toni replied and was just about to make some dismissive quip when it struck her that, from the tone of his voice, he sounded different somehow. Relaxed and comfortable. At home. Unencumbered by responsibility.

So she fought back the urge to be sarcastic and strolled over towards the bench in the dark. Except her toes connected with something solid on the way.

'Ouch,' she muttered, 'what have I just banged into?'

'That would be the metal chair,' he replied with concern in his voice. 'Any damage done?'

'To my toe or your furniture?' she whispered, and then flexed her toes. 'No, I don't think so; I still have some movement. I can't speak for the other party.'

'Excellent,' he replied. 'Then please feel free to enjoy the free floor show. No charge.' Then he patted the bench next to him and Toni could have sworn that there was a certain smirk on his lips.

'Perhaps I will,' Toni said and pushed her hands into the pockets of her dressing gown as she perched on the edge of the bench and looked up into the night sky.

They both gazed skywards without speaking for a few minutes, their peace disturbed only by the sound of the traffic on the road nearby and the occasional sound of distant laughter.

She snuggled deeper into her gown. 'The sky in Alaska must be wonderful on nights like this.'

'Stunning. Have you ever seen the Northern Lights? They are the most astonishing effects. Last week I spent most of the night with the aurora as my guide.'

She shrugged and then realised that Scott probably wouldn't be able to see her. 'That makes me so jealous. I spent four days in Iceland last January and it was cloudy every single night but I still went out, just in case. My reward was a bad nosebleed and frozen eyeballs.'

Just the memory of those evenings sent a shiver down her back and she quivered and rubbed her arms.

'Feeling cold?' he asked.

'Very' she replied. 'Time for me to head back inside. Lots to do tomorrow. Oh. Make that later today.'

She heard a low grunt as Scott shuffled closer along the bench. Before she had a chance to speak, he pressed his body against the length of her side and slid his arm around her waist. A delicious glow of warmth spread across her hips and she instinctively leant sideways to enjoy the heat from his body, wrapped in his warm fleece around the front of her gown.

The whole sensation was absolutely wonderful. Solid, protective and exactly what she needed. This had been one hell of a day and she was already missing Amy so much.

'Another five minutes. We stargazers have to stick together,' Scott murmured.

He raised one arm and pointed to the bright star on the horizon below the new moon. 'On a night like this Venus and the pole star are my navigation. They get me back to base.'

'My sister is travelling in South America,' Toni replied in a low voice, thinking of Amy. 'She arrived this evening and somehow it makes me feel better to think that she is seeing the same stars as I am right now.'

'Ask me to show you a star map tomorrow.'

Toni lowered her head and watched the steam from her breath in front of her face.

'The only stars I've ever seen have been through the London haze.'

'Well, that is a shame,' Scott replied and rubbed her arms with his unbandaged hand. 'Maybe one day.'

He turned and smiled at her, and the expression on his face was so overwhelmingly full of understanding and emotion that the invisible bond that drew her to him tightened so much that it was impossible for her to resist.

Then he kissed her on the tip of her nose. And the touch of his lips was as gentle as a butterfly landing and she closed her eyes to revel in that brief moment when her skin was in contact with his.

Scott closed the tiny gap between their bodies. It seemed only natural for him to tip her chin towards him, slant his head and press his lips against hers. Softly at first, then firmer, harder, wider.

And Toni kissed him back, filling her lips and mouth with such luscious sweet warmth that any lingering resistance melted away and she moved deeper into the kiss. Eyes closed, she revelled in the sensation of falling into his mouth, their tongues touching, heads pressed together for a moment longer than she should have, before she felt Scott pull back.

His breath felt hot and fast on her neck, and Toni pressed the palms of both hands flat against the front of his fleece so that she could feel the pace of his heart beat faster to match hers as he gently lifted a strand of her hair behind one ear.

'I do have one more suggestion,' he whispered.

'Um?' Toni murmured as his fingertips slid down from her forehead to her chin in one smooth motion, as though he was unwilling to lose contact with her skin.

His fingers stilled on her chin, but she knew that his gaze was firmly locked on to her face so that when he spoke every word resonated deep into her skull. 'Why don't you stay with me tonight? I can guarantee a lot more body heat, Miss Baldoni.'

What? Her poor heart performed a crazy acrobatic dance inside her chest. The very idea was so ridiculous that it made her head spin. It was a terrible suggestion. Wasn't it? Her fingers clutched tighter to the warm, soft fleece jacket and in a moment of weakness she wondered what it would be like to skip upstairs and find out just how hot this man's body truly was.

She glared at Scott and even in the faint light she could see that he was grinning at her. As though he knew perfectly well what a temptation he was offering and was teasing her at the same time.

And he was a temptation. A serious one. She was already missing the touch of his mouth on hers and the heavy breath on her skin from the man who had the power to make her feel desirable for the first time in over a year.

Since Peter. *Peter.*

She instantly pushed Scott away with both hands flat against his chest and slid unsteadily to her feet out of the warmth of his jacket and into the cold air.

'Oh, I bet that you can. Sorry, but that is such my cue to get back to bed. My own bed. In the guest room, Mr Elstrom!'

Then, before she could change her mind, Toni stretched out and grabbed hold of the edges of his jacket and kissed him on the mouth. Hard and fast and bruising. Taking control. Calling the shots. Then she pulled away, leaving her panting for breath and maybe a lot more.

A cool breeze flitted across Toni's feet and she slipped in the flimsy mules as Scott laughed. 'Good night, Antonia.'

She half turned. 'Actually, my friends call me Toni. See you later.'

CHAPTER SEVEN

THE NARROW TERRACED house was in darkness when Toni walked up the path and turned the key in the front door. The light drizzle had turned into sleet and she was immensely grateful to step inside.

This part of Hampstead was only a few minutes away from the busy roads and the hustle and bustle of the main streets of London, but this tree-lined street seemed a world away from all of the noise and pollution.

She had waited for the bus that never came. So she had gritted her teeth and walked for thirty minutes in her smart boots, dragging her pull-along suitcase behind her rather than just stand there and wait or pay for a cab.

Waiting was for losers. Scott would never have waited—and neither would she.

She had waited for her parents to stop telling her that she was ridiculous to throw away her heritage to take up photography instead of fine art. Then waited in vain for her father to acknowledge her talent as she worked with him on his paintings, day after day, week after week until she was doing most of the work.

Slipping off her damp coat, she strolled slowly down the hallway to the kitchen, her feet dragging and her boots feeling like lead weights. Each step made the old floorboards creak and the sound echoed down the tall empty hallway, but she had become used to each familiar sound in this tiny house. Her faithful friends were the chiming of the grandfather clock in the hall and the faint whistling of the wind in the eaves.

Toni looked through the stained glass panel from the kitchen into the artist's studio where her father used to invite sitters. In summer the house was filled with coloured light and seemed a magical place, bright and positive and bursting with life.

But at that moment it was dark, wet and windy and the sleet lashed against the roof and the only light was from the streetlight outside streaming in from the glass panel over the front door.

And as she stood there in the kitchen, suddenly exhausted, Toni slid sideways on to a hard wooden chair at the kitchen table with her back against the wall as though the events of the day were too heavy to carry any longer.

What a day!

For a start, she didn't usually go around kissing men she had just met. In fact this was a first. And the fact that she had enjoyed it enormously didn't change the fact that she might just have made a huge mistake.

Scott had already left for work when she got up that morning and had been out most of the day visiting banks and suppliers bright and early on a Monday morning. In fact she had only seen him once when he'd let her into the building and passed her a set of keys and he had been all cool politeness and calm.

It was as if they had never kissed or snuggled.

So where did that leave her?

Deny it as best she could, at that moment last night when Scott pressed his lips to hers…her poor parched heart had soaked in every precious second of that glorious intimacy and physical sensation like a desert in the rain.

It frightened her just how much she needed someone in her life.

But not just anyone. She wanted to be intimate with someone she could call her friend as well as her lover. Peter had never been her friend.

Scott Elstrom was the last person she wanted to fall for. He was gorgeous and she had been more than tempted to spend the night with him. But then what? A few days of fun before she went back to work?

She had never had a one-night stand in her life and this was not the best time to start.

No. It would be better if she followed Scott's example and put last night behind them and got back to being professional colleagues who would be working together for the next few days. Side by side. She could do that.

Um. *And the garden was suddenly full of a squadron of purple piglets in pink tutus singing as they flew across the sky.*

She let her head drop back and just sat there, listening to the sound of her breathing and gentle sobs in the darkness.

Pathetic!

It wasn't the dark, or the silence.

No, it was the crushing feeling of loneliness which drove her to feel sorry for herself. She had never got used to being so lonely. Amy was the only family she had left and she was currently in the depths of South America so it was silly to want to talk to her so very badly. Amy would ring or text the minute she could. She always did.

And nobody was prouder than Toni.

What had she promised Amy? This was a New Year. A fresh start.

Stupid girl! She didn't need to be alone if she didn't want to be. She had friends. Real friends who would come around in an instant if she needed them.

Toni rolled her shoulders back and was just about to pull herself to her feet when her cellphone rang out from her bag.

Amy! She scrabbled around in her bag, terrified that she would ring off before she found her phone in the near darkness, and flicked it open, instantly creating a bright panel of light. Her shoulders slumped down in disappointment. It wasn't her sister. It was an email.

With a photo of the purple underpants she had modelled last evening at her birthday party. A small smile creased her lips and Toni blinked away her tears and sniffed. Apparently Scott had found the underwear under the sofa and it had looked vaguely familiar.

Did the item belong to her or should he put it in Freya's room?

Toni giggled at the screen, tapped out a quick reply saying that she was claiming them but gift-wrapping was not necessary, thank you, and pressed the send button before she could change her mind.

That outrageous man!

But he had made her laugh and for that she was grateful.

Grinning like mad, Toni quickly scanned the other messages from her work colleagues and pals and took a sharp intake of breath. It was a perfectly friendly and chatty email from the same team she had worked with on the documentary with Peter. Apparently Peter had just joined the company's new production team, working on ideas for a five-part series on the legacy of the Raj in India. Houses and heritage. Wasn't that exciting? Why didn't she come along to the ideas meeting? Could be fun!

She almost threw the smartphone at the wall.

Peter.

Toni pressed her hand to her mouth, and then wiped away the tears from her cheeks.

Oh, what a fool she'd been.

She'd been prepared to wait for Peter to make the first move and start dating her properly. Too busy with the project at work, he had said. The film production and editing had to be perfect—but then they could relax and spend a weekend away together and tell the other people at the media company office back in London that they were a couple. Surely she could wait a few more weeks?

She had been his guilty little secret.

Sordid. Dirty. Expendable.

She had been the temporary stand-in girl he would simply throw away when he had used her enough to do his work for him. How many times had he asked her to cover up for him when he'd felt the need to sunbathe or shop?

And once their film work was over? Then he would get back to his real girlfriend, who was working on a fashion shoot and designer shows in the Caribbean.

Peter had deceived her. Tricked her. Used her for his own advantage. Amy had never liked Peter from the start and on the one occasion they had met in person had openly declared him to be a fake.

Well, that was over now. She was done with being used by other people who lied to her. That was then and this was now.

And she had waited long enough.

Lesson learnt. No more waiting. No more putting things off until later.

Toni jumped to her feet, suddenly energised and, shoving her arms into the sleeves of an old warm fleece jacket she kept by the door, she started pacing up and down to keep warm and to help clear her head.

Houses and heritage, her armpits!

What did Peter the flea know about heritage? He could

learn a few things from Scott Elstrom, and people like him, whose life was a tribute to family heritage.

Her steps slowed. Two hundred years of heritage, in fact.

A crazy idea fluttered around inside her head.

The media company she worked for was always looking for clever and special ideas and the creative director had a passion for British heritage. He had been heading up the government think tank on traditional crafts for years.

What about traditional skills such as fine British map-making?

Diving back into her bag, Toni quickly reread the email about Peter. Yes! They were using the same brilliant location scouts who had the most amazing talent for tracking down authentic buildings and sites to film historical dramas and documentaries.

They would probably faint if they walked into Elstrom Mapping!

Yes! She could see how the right director could come up with a brilliant proposal. And of course they would have to pay Scott for the exclusive use of the building for weeks, if not months!

Before she could change her mind, Toni jogged up to her freezing-cold bedroom and quickly downloaded the photographs she had taken during the past two days on to her laptop computer. It only took a few minutes to compose a few lines of explanation and her suggestion and fire off the emails and photos to the location scouts and the creative director.

The first reply came winging back before she had time to light the fire in the living room and make her hot chocolate. Every one of the scouts was pleading for more details and begging for an appointment.

Toni sat back on the sofa in front of the fire, wrapped

in a duvet, sipping her hot chocolate and then picked up her phone.

Time to call Scott. This could be fun!

Scott carefully swung Freya's hatchback around the corner from the main street and checked the name plate high on the wall of the end house. Toni had warned him that he should look out for a quiet cul de sac close to a park with trees lining the street.

The house numbers on the terraced Victorian houses were mostly hidden behind leafy evergreens or elaborate railings but as his gaze scanned the houses he spotted a bright blue and white hand-painted sign attached to a stone gate pillar. Baldoni House. This was it. He pulled into a narrow parking spot a few metres away along the street and turned off the engine and sat in the car, gathering his thoughts.

What was he doing in Hampstead at this time on a Tuesday morning? The traffic was mad, his hand was hurting and Freya's car wasn't designed for anyone over six feet tall.

He could have walked from the office in less than twenty minutes. Instead of which, it had taken him almost an hour to negotiate the road system with no help at all from Freya's new satellite navigation system. Which, for a map-maker, was not only embarrassing but incredibly frustrating.

Shrugging into his fleece jacket, Scott stepped out of the car on to the wet tarmac, which was strewn with sodden leaves, and slowly rolled back his shoulders.

The sleet and rain had cleared during the night, leaving a fresh cold morning with plenty of broken sunshine to brighten the air.

Working outdoors had made him acutely sensitive to

even the smallest change in the weather and, as he stood and gazed past the trees into the small park area, there was something in the wind that told him that this was winter's last waning steps. No more cold weather gear. No more feet of snow to plough through. No more icy winds and frozen skin.

He missed Alaska—the space and the quiet—and he missed the work. More than he'd thought possible.

Maybe this was a mistake? All it would take was one phone call and he could be on a plane back to the real life he had left behind in a couple of hours.

Inhaling sharply, Scott looked up into the branches of the trees that lined the street and focused on the sound of the birdsong instead of the incessant hum of the heavy traffic a few minutes away. A pair of grey squirrels bounced along at the foot of a large beech tree only a few metres in front of him, seeking out nuts. Playful. Spring was in the air. He had forgotten how quickly the seasons changed in Britain.

Shaking his head, Scott turned towards the narrow terraced house. It didn't look so very different from the others from the outside. Two storeys. Red brick with tall sash windows and stone window ledges. And, to his eyes, narrow. As in very narrow.

In two strides he pushed open the black wrought metal gate and crunched his way up a brick and gravel path to a covered porch. The front door was painted in the same dark blue as the window frames and a pair of bay trees in bright painted pots provided a splash of welcome green against the dark wood.

He could hear the sound of the door knocker echo inside the house as he waited on the doorstep. And waited. So this time he knocked a little harder. Still no reply.

Strange. She must have slipped out. And he had been a

bit vague when he'd said that he'd be around in the morning to collect some extra lighting equipment.

Scott was just about to head back to the car when he spotted a flash of colour out of the corner of his eye. Stepping forward, he could just see one corner of what looked like a living room from where he was standing in the porch. One step further and he had the best seat in the theatre.

The entertainment was Toni Baldoni. She was dancing. Swaying from side to side and apparently singing along to the music being fed into her ears through the wires dangling around her neck. No wonder she hadn't heard the door knocker.

Plastic crates were stacked to one side and she seemed to be moving books from the shelves as she danced.

Hands in his trouser pockets, Scott leant his back against the wall and enjoyed the moment, suddenly content to simply watch in silence as the girl he'd come to see enjoying life on her own terms. There was a fire burning in the grate and the glow from the flames lit up one side of her face in the faint morning sunlight, turning her pale skin a golden shade of flickering shadow and light on sharp cheekbones and round full lips.

How many more variations of Toni Baldoni were there?

A bright red bandana held back her hair, focusing his attention on her face. And what a face that was! The girl who had come to Elstrom Mapping was bright and intelligent and happy to challenge him on every level. Confident in her ability and fighting her corner against all of the perfectly logical reasons he could come up with why the last thing he wanted was to sit still for hours while she painted his scraggy face.

But the girl he was looking at now was completely different. It was as if a weight had been taken from her shoulders and she was free to be herself in her own space. Her fine cheekbones glowed and a big smile creased her face, which positively beamed with warmth and happiness.

Yes. That was the difference. She looked happy. Joyous, even. High on life.

With a dress sense to match her mood.

Toni was wearing what looked to him like a flying suit, only the strangest one he had ever seen. It looked as though some toddler had melted every crayon in the box and sprayed the whole lot over a pair of workman's overalls. It was astonishing. Put that with a brunette who was dancing across the floor and the whole picture was worth taking the time to admire.

In fact he could do better than that. He could try and capture some of that happiness.

Tugging his smartphone out of his jacket pocket, Scott lifted it to his eye but the second he pressed the camera button he knew that he had made a mistake.

The flash went off. Toni immediately whirled around and came to the window to find out what was going on. And saw him. Ogling her.

The expression on her face would have broken the camera lens. *Oops.*

Then he made it worse by giving a casual wave.

Toni stood with her hands wrapped around a copy of an old encyclopaedia for several seconds, staring at Scott in disbelief, before she whirled around, tossed the book on to the sofa and lifted the ear pieces out and turned off her music system.

Her heart was thumping so hard that she was certain that it would beat out of her chest and that Scott would be able to hear it on the porch.

Oh, no. She hadn't expected him to show up this early.

She wasn't dressed for visitors and especially not him! She had planned to get showered and blow-dried and nicely dressed before he turned up to collect the lighting equipment.

Plan B.

A low groan of exasperation escaped her lips and, with a quick shake of her head, she padded out to the hallway in her stocking feet.

Catching a glance at her reflection in the hall mirror wasn't a good idea but there wasn't much she could do about that now, and he had already seen her, so...chin up, smile on. She could carry this off...couldn't she?

With her head high, Toni flung open her front door, ready to give Scott a lesson on manners.

The words caught in her throat as she gulped in a breath of air in startled shock.

She had been too busy reacting to seeing him standing there to pay attention to what he really looked like, but as the morning sunlight hit the porch she was hit by the full-on splendour that was the cleaned up version of Scott Elstrom.

He was wearing a smart cashmere jacket and dark trousers, a pale blue button-down collar shirt which only made his deep tan more pronounced and he had done something to his hair. *Washed it.*

Her stomach turned over just to look at him and her heart was doing things which were probably dangerous to her blood pressure.

She had thought that Scott was attractive when he'd first walked in on her birthday party, and he had changed his shirt yesterday at the office, but this version leaning against her porch was from another planet.

A planet of hunky handsomeness where the adult males

were all tall, blond and had neatly trimmed beards which only highlighted their square jaws and long straight noses.

His cheekbones were so taut they might have been sculpted. But it was his mouth that knocked the air out of her lungs and had her clinging on to the door frame for support. A plump lower lip smiled wide above his cleft chin, so that the bow was sharp between the smile lines. It was a mouth made for smiling.

The corners of those amazing blue eyes crinkled slightly in his deeply tanned skin and Toni realised that he had been watching her. The warmth of that smile seemed to heat the air between them. It was so full of genuine charm and delight that she knew, no matter what, this was the smile that would stay with her for a long time.

This smile was for her. And her heart leapt. More than a little. But just enough to recognize that the blush of heat racing through her neck and face were not only due to the flames that had been warming her back.

That killer smile and those blue eyes came together in one single look that could charm anything in its path and knock it senseless. There was no escape. She was hit with the full blast.

The top two buttons of his pale blue shirt gaped open as the fabric stretched over a broad chest and revealed a hint of deeply tanned skin, and more than a few dark chest hairs.

He was stunning.

Oh, no. Do not stare at his chest. Just don't.

The pounding in her chest was simply because she had been taken by surprise—that was all. Trying desperately to regain some kind of control over feelings that were so new and raw, Toni stepped forward to meet him.

Luckily he spoke first, his voice low and husky in the quiet garden as he smiled and reached out his hand. Toni felt his long cold fingers clasp around hers for only a few seconds before she released him. The calloused surfaces of his fingers rasped against her skin on the back of her hands. Gentle but firm.

'Good morning. Apologies if I startled you but I tried the front door and there was no answer.' He made a point of checking his gold wristwatch. 'And I am early. I hope that isn't a problem.'

Oh, no. No problem at all. It was perfectly normal for her to welcome clients who looked like Viking gods when she was wearing her grungiest painting overalls!

She should be annoyed. But look at the man!

Toni inhaled deeply, straightened her back and managed to find her voice at last as she smiled back at him. 'No problem at all. Please do come in out of the cold. I have a fire going in the living room and hot coffee on the table. Want to join me? Because I can't wait to hear what you think about my idea. You're going to be in the movies! Isn't that exciting?'

'You're serious, aren't you?' Scott said as he followed Toni into the house. 'You really think that TV companies will want to keep Elstrom locked in some strange hibernation so that they can use it as a film set?'

'Absolutely,' she replied. 'There are plenty of location scouts who would love to use the building as a movie set for documentaries or dramas set in wartime or 1930s Britain.' Then she winced and bared her teeth. 'No offence but it is a bit of a time warp when you walk in those doors. And you don't even have to clear the rooms because they will do all that for you. Scott? Are you listening?'

Listening? He was far too busy trying to cope with the sensory overload that was the Baldoni house. The entire living room was more like an expressionist art gallery than a family home.

Colour was piled on tones and shades of colour. The walls were covered in heavy red wallpaper with a faint gold pattern embossed in what looked to him like random patterns. Not that he could see too much of the wallpaper. There must have been at least twenty pictures on the walls, of all shapes and sizes. Portraits of people in various styles of dress, landscapes, fruit and flowers. It was all there on the walls of this tiny room, about the size of Freya's kitchen.

And then there were the fabrics. Curtains, sofa and cushions. All red, all different, all bursting with pattern and shades of crimson and gold trim.

Scott couldn't imagine a greater contrast between the cold grey February street outside and the shock of this space. It was like a rich tent in the desert. Exotic and luxuriant and bursting with interest and textures.

'Wow—' he coughed '—this is remarkable. Sorry, but my poor scientific brain is struggling to cope. I know that you come from a family of artists but I had no idea that you had to surround yourself with so many colours.'

Toni laughed and shrugged. 'My grandparents bought the place when Hampstead was famous for the artist colonies. The Baldoni family were very popular and they bought paintings from their friends and even a few clients. You know that store room at the back of the Elstrom mapping room? I have one of those upstairs to cope with the overflow.'

'There's more?'

'Oh, this is nothing. You should have seen the place before Amy and I started to declutter over the Christmas holiday. Black coffee okay?'

'Please,' Scott replied and strolled around the room,

picking up hand-painted china ornaments then peering at the stack of books that Toni had been looking at when he'd spied on her through the window.

'Doing some spring-cleaning?' he asked, glancing at her over one shoulder. Her answer was the kind of laugh that made the glass in the windows rattle.

'Cleaning? Oh, if only that was all I had to do.' Then she must have spotted the confused look on his face and she passed him a coffee with a grin.

'Amy and I have decided to rent the place out while she is away at university. I plan to do more travelling for work and she won't be here and we need the loot. One of my neighbours gave me all of the details and a couple of agencies have been around. Strange how they all say the same thing. It seems that there are a few small things I need to do before I can rent this house to anyone.'

Toni squeezed her thumb and forefinger together. 'Very small. Nothing really. Ha!'

She collapsed down on the sofa, which was covered with a dust sheet, and picked up her coffee mug and waved it towards the bookcases.

'Fix the plumbing. Put in a new bathroom. And the big one? Get rid of ninety per cent of the books and paintings and the rest of the clutter and paint the walls a beige, creamy buttermilk-type colour. Neutral. Bland. Plain. In fact the colour of the walls in Freya's kitchen. It looks great in a modern house. Here? Not so sure.'

'No alternative? Rent it to art lovers? No? Ah, then I can see the problem. There does seem to be a lot of—what did you call it?—clutter?'

'You have no idea. Elstrom was easy compared to this. Let's just say that your father wasn't the only one who didn't want to change things in a hurry.'

She sniffed and looked from side to side. 'When you've

used this room every day it comes as a bit of a shock when other people see it differently. But they're right. I need to clear the room, get rid of the paintings and wallpaper and start all over again…' Her voice faded away. 'So that is what I plan to do. A new start in a nice new bright home. All white and fresh. Oh, yes.'

'What are you going to do with it all? Some of these paintings must be valuable.'

'That's why I have a professional lighting rig. Every piece has to be photographed for the insurance and then put into storage or sold.' Toni exhaled sharply. 'Then it's going to take weeks to redecorate and work out what to do with boxes of ancient books.' She glanced up at Scott. 'Sorry. Too much to do. Not enough time. Sound familiar?'

'Very.' He grinned and hooked his arm over the back of the sofa and looked from side to side. 'Are all the rooms like this?'

'Oh, no. This is tidy. The only reason I'm working in here is the fire.' She laughed. 'No plumbing. No heating. Electric heaters are great but an open fire is bliss.'

Scott put down his mug with a clatter. 'I thought that you meant the hot water wasn't working! You should have told me! Freya's house is so hot I can hardly breathe and she hates it when I turn the thermostat down. Please. Come back and stay there until you have heating.'

Toni smiled at him. 'Now you're being kind. But this is my space and, as you can see, I have a fire and lots to do.' Then she took a breath and sat back on the sofa and brought her knees up to her chest. 'There is one thing I find curious. You keep saying Freya's house. Isn't that your home too?'

The reply stuck in Scott's throat. *It was until I got married and moved into my own place. Alexa got the apart-*

*ment in the divorce. I certainly didn't want it. Not after
she admitted taking Travis there.*

Toni must have seen the expression on his face and immediately held up one hand. 'Forget it. I am far too nosey and you are here for the lighting rig. It's all ready for us in the studio and...'

Scott rested one hand lightly on Toni's knee and looked into her face.

'When our mother moved to Paris I shared the house with Freya until I bought my own place with my fiancée. Two years ago I moved to Alaska and my former wife got the apartment as the divorce settlement. Since then Freya has kept my old bedroom in case I needed it. But home? No. It's not my home. Not any longer.'

'I am so sorry. About the divorce and about the apartment. That's hard to imagine. Amy and I have already organized a tiny studio flat we're going to call home in a few months. We need that.'

'Everyone's different. I'm on the move so much I don't need a permanent base. The only place that I have ever really called home was the massive Victorian mansion in north London that I grew up in.' He smiled across at Toni. 'It wasn't that much different from this house. Bigger rooms meant more space to clutter up. And my dad was certainly up to the challenge. Believe me, this place would fit him like a glove.'

Scott froze and took a few seconds to take in everything, from the Victorian glass lamp shades to the leather-bound books and heavy gold-framed landscapes.

'He would love it here,' Scott whispered and his two middle fingers tapped out a beat on the hard cover of a book about Victorian watercolours.

Then they stopped and he lifted his chin and stared at

Toni, who had started lifting smaller books down from the bookcase on the other side of the fireplace.

'It's a shame that we don't have an elevator at the office. My dad can't move back to his top floor studio until he has more control of his legs.'

Toni glanced at him over one shoulder. 'Oh, that is a shame. Will he move in with Freya?'

'No. He hates modern houses. That's one of the reasons why he stays in Italy. I do have an idea for somewhere he could rent…but it would all depend on you.'

Toni put down her book and turned around and sat on the edge of the sofa. 'Me? Why? Do you need a second opinion?'

Scott slid forward and rested both hands on his knees so that his whole body pointed towards her.

'Not exactly. You see, I think this little house would be perfect for my dad, and for me. I can't stay at Freya's, I know that now. Which means that I need somewhere to rent for the next six months…and he needs somewhere quiet but close to his friends in London. And old school. Yes, I think this could be the perfect place for us.'

Scott grinned up at Toni, who was staring at him with her mouth half open. 'What do you say, Toni? Will you rent your house to the Elstrom boys?'

Toni stared into his face for a second in total silence, with an expression that was part shock and horror and part bewilderment.

'You want to rent my house?'

He nodded once and gestured towards her with one hand. 'I can offer you top rates and a good deposit if that's what you're worried about and I promise that we won't trash the place.'

Toni's jaw had dropped slightly, which probably meant

that she was at least not dismissing the idea out of hand, so Scott dived in quickly to seal the deal. 'Think of me as your ideal tenant. Hardly here. Does the washing-up when he has to and is fairly orderly. And my dad has this thing for old books and paintings. He may not be the best businessman in the world but I know that he could feel at home here.'

'Scott, you are not making any sense whatsoever. You have only been here five minutes! How do you know what the rest of the house is like? The studio is stacked to the ceiling with canvases and painting stuff and the bathroom is going to be all modern and white and flash when it's done. Your dad might hate it.'

'Good. I like the sound of that already. As for the rest of the house? I would love a tour.'

And for the first time that morning Scott lifted his chin towards the window so that she could see his face in the sunlight instead of shadow.

Although his mouth was turned into a gentle half smile there was a deep crease between his eyebrows and, as she looked closer, the deep shadows under his eyes told her that he had probably had less sleep than she had. Those stunning, hypnotic blue eyes scanned her face over and over again, as though he was looking for a sign of how she was feeling about him.

And they looked at each other in silence for what seemed like minutes.

Then both of them started talking at the same time.

'Ladies first,' Scott chuckled, breaking the crackling electric current that was in the air between them.

'Okay,' Toni replied. 'Talk to me. What's this really all about, Scott?'

Scott looked at her then leant closer. 'My father needs something positive in his life. He's come out of this second divorce with health problems and the business has collapsed around him. We are totally different people in every way. But right now? I wouldn't mind spending some time with him when he comes back to London.'

He looked around and flashed her a grin. 'Sharing a house like this would be a blast. It reminds me of the early family house we used to have when we felt more like a family than strangers that passed in the hallway from time to time. I mean it. He would love it here. And think of it this way.' He flicked one hand into the air. 'Less clutter to sort out. He likes the clutter.' Then his overly confident smile faded a little. 'We haven't been very good friends since I left the business. Things were totally crazy back then and things were said which cannot be unsaid. Maybe it's time to move on.'

'By sharing this tiny house? I don't know, Scott.'

He flicked a tongue over his lips. 'If this is about the other night, I owe you an apology. I should not have kissed you and I am sorry that it has put us into an awkward situation.'

Toni took a deep breath and looked into his face. His last few words had come gushing out in one long rush and she knew how hard they must have been to say. 'No—it's nothing to do with that. You don't owe me an apology,' she replied. 'I was right there and I may even have kissed you at one time. Let's call it evens.'

Scott shook his head. 'I think I do. We had both worked hard, it was a lovely evening and I got caught up in the moment.'

He lifted both hands from the table. 'It certainly wasn't planned, but I don't want there to be any confusion. You are one hell of a beautiful woman and I cannot guarantee that I'll be able to keep my hands off you.'

Scott looked up at her and this time his face was pale

and serious and each and every one of the frown lines were frozen into sharp relief.

'I can understand it if you want to hit me over the head with one of those heavy books, but I'm hoping that you can forgive me and my overactive libido enough to work with me as a colleague over the next few days and think about renting me your home. How about it, Toni? Willing to give me a chance?'

Toni stared at Scott long enough to see beads of perspiration on his forehead.

It was probably only minutes but in the silence of the room all she had to listen to was the background soundtrack of birdsong and the thumping of her heart.

Because Scott had just told her in his own way that he felt just as much for her as she was feeling for him. He was trying to create some distance between them to protect them both from the pain of some crazy love affair.

And he clearly had no idea that she could see it in his face. And, if anything, his words only served to bind them more closely together instead of driving them apart. He was doing this for her as much as himself.

Toni pushed up from the sofa and put her coffee mug on the table, aware that Scott was still watching her every move.

'You'd better see the studio first. It would make a perfect workroom for your dad.'

CHAPTER EIGHT

'I KNOW. IT'S fantastic news, Freya! My friend must have taken fifty photos yesterday before she made up her mind but I had a feeling that she would, fast! What was that? How did Scott react to the news?'

Toni grinned and scanned through some of the images on her camera one-handed. 'Your brother gave that poor woman the benefit of his full-on charm offensive. I have never seen him so cooperative. He even shaved a little and changed into a smart shirt! I know! Amazing. She was putty in his hands. But it worked. We have a deal! I am so pleased for you both. In fact, Scott was so relieved that the building is safe for the rest of the year that he took off into the snow to bring back coffee and doughnuts. It's a dangerous mission but he refused to be deterred.'

Freya's laughter echoed down the phone as she described how it was positively balmy in Rome but she would be back in a few weeks to do more to help out. With a quick promise to meet up as soon as they could, Toni closed the call and put down the handset. Her fingers lingered on the phone as she breathed out slowly.

In a week and a half she would be back at work in some freezing photographic studio and this world of old maps and charts and wood-panelled walls would be a distant memory.

But what about Scott?

He was serious about renting out her house so there was no hope that she could be free of him. And that was the problem. She didn't want to be free of the man.

They had worked side by side over the past four days and the more time she spent with Scott the more she liked him.

Scott Elstrom was clever, quick and actually willing to listen to her ideas, which made a nice change from her normal work where she was still the minion girl Friday who did most of the running about for the guys with the professional qualifications and experience. Scott treated her like an equal.

The hard, brash exterior was a total front—the armour he wore to get by in his world. Gut instinct told her that he had been badly hurt at some time but she wasn't going to pry. If he wanted to tell her about it he would if and when he was ready. She still wasn't sure what his true reasons for coming back to Elstrom Mapping were but he was certainly working hard to save the business.

In four days, and with fingers which were still strapped up and obviously hurting, Scott had helped her to clear the main office, made an inventory of everything that had been left behind in the mapping room where the few staff used to work, and had passed her the first box of items to photograph.

Yesterday's visit from the location scout had been the icing on the cake!

She'd loved this old building and had immediately seen the potential for several historical documentaries and dramas already commissioned during the year.

It was a start and meant Scott could get to work on the inventory without having to worry about the lights being turned off. He might even be able to afford to replace the central heating boiler and the flaky electrics which made the lights flicker on and off.

Lifting her camera to her eyes, Toni captured a few images of this amazing room with all the rows of tools and the huge drawing tables.

She heard his footsteps pound up the staircase before the front door closed and slowly turned towards the office as Scott came bounding in and dropped his bakery bag on to the table in front of his office window.

There were snowflakes caught in his hair and on the shoulders of his coat and as Toni stepped into the office he lifted his chin and looked out of the window with a wistful smile on his face. As though he was looking out at the light snow and thinking of other people and other places.

Her breath caught in her throat and she pressed the shutter and kept on pressing it. Over and over again.

The tingles ran down her arms to her fingers. That was it. That was the image she had been looking for.

There was always a moment when she knew that she had taken the perfect shot of her subject. Sometimes it took days of careful staging to make the subject feel comfortable in the setting and other times it was completely spontaneous. Sometimes it never happened and they had to make the best of what they had taken.

Not today. The picture she was going to paint was already forming in her mind and she could practically see the way her paint was going to capture his swept back blond hair and dark eyebrows, damp now with melting snow.

Sniffing back a wave of emotion, Toni lowered her camera and smiled as Scott turned to face her.

It was as if every cell in her body was suddenly totally fascinated by the freckles across the bridge of his long straight nose and the way the crease lines at the sides of his eyes were white against his tanned skin.

Scott Elstrom was not a handsome man at all. He was gobsmacking gorgeous.

His presence jumped out at her, grabbed her by the bra straps and pulled her with such force that she could almost feel her body leaning forward towards him.

'Hey—' he grinned '—ready for coffee?'

A shot of pure lust hit her hot and wet in all of the wrong places.

Oh, my. Not now. Please, not now. This is not good.

'You bet,' she whispered in a quivering voice. 'Any time.'

He shot her a worried look. 'Sore throat? You have to watch these colds this time of year.'

Oh, please don't be nice to me, she willed. *Focus on the work instead.*

'Not at all,' Toni replied, lifting her chin. 'Just chattering too long on the phone to Freya. She's so pleased with the location deal she just couldn't wait to call.'

'Damn right,' Scott said and shrugged off his jacket. 'You did a great job, so today we have chocolate cream éclairs instead of doughnuts. Prepare for the sugar rush!'

His shirtsleeves were still rolled up and Toni couldn't stop herself from focusing on how the blond hairs on his arms prickled to attention as he dived into the bag and pulled out the coffees and pastries.

'Don't you mean that *we* did a great job? I only made that first call. It was your idea to dig out all of those old photos of the building and I know she loved those sepia prints with the horse-drawn carriages outside. Light bulbs were flashing inside her head with every new image.'

Toni reached out and wrapped a napkin around the piece of iced pastry which was in great danger of oozing fresh cream all over his desk and tried to ignore the way that Scott's lips closed around the top of his coffee. 'The shameless charm offensive didn't hurt either, you old smoothie.'

Scott replied with a low grunt but she could tell from the slight flush at the back of his neck that he was slightly embarrassed. 'So what have you been up to?' he asked, rapidly changing the subject between slurps of coffee and bites of pastry.

'Box number four. The instruments have been photographed from every angle and I was just about to start work on that stunning map you prepped this morning. Want to take a look?'

He nodded and, picking up his coffee, strolled out of the office and followed her into the map room, brushing sugar from his fingers as he walked.

'So tell me about this sea chart,' Toni said as she adjusted her camera settings on the tripod. 'The colours are amazing. Is it all hand-painted?'

Scott looked up from his coffee. 'Absolutely. I'm working on the catalogue entry next.' He pointed towards the mapping table where he had unfurled the leather scroll for Toni to photograph. 'This is a portolan from a Spanish cartographer who had a workshop on the Canary Islands in about 1730. He made it his business to collect every scrap of information from the captains and navigators who stopped there on the way back from trading journeys to the Caribbean or Far East. Each map took months but they were traded for huge sums.'

'I can understand why,' Toni replied, looking down her viewfinder. 'Such beautiful workmanship and what tiny writing. I will need to do something special for those sections.'

She stepped back and planted a hand on each hip as she

tilted her head. 'Are you going to sell it?' she asked as she walked around the chart and studied it from every angle.

Scott got slowly to his feet and stood next to her, the sleeve of his shirt bristling against her top as he pointed to dark marks on the corners of the leather and a strange stain right in the middle of the chart. 'If the price is right. My father intended to restore these pieces before he put them on the market. There is a specialist map dealer who begged us to sell it about ten years ago. A Russian oligarch wanted an original sea chart for his new office in London but my dad refused. It was too precious to him.'

A deep sigh made Toni look up at Scott and he smiled back at her.

'I love my father, Toni, but he is clueless when it comes to people. His world centres on books and research studies. He has published brilliant works on the history of sea charts. They're amazing! Elstrom men were sea captains whose mission was to create navigational charts on a sea journey and detailed land maps when they arrived on the east coast of America or Canada or around the top of the world into Russia. That was how the company got started. Men and paper and a hard life in the worst conditions where a lot of the crew didn't make it back. So my father used the family histories and documents to create a personal history of the exploration and how map-making is part of who we are.'

'What will your father do when he's feeling better?' Toni asked.

'What he loves to do. Restore charts and maps. Research books and be the expert he was always intended to be. He was never cut out to be a businessman and certainly not a husband or father. He is clueless when it comes to family life.'

'What do you mean, clueless? Freya seems to get on okay with him.'

'Two marriages and two divorces. No happy ending for anyone.'

Scott rolled his shoulders back as though he was trying to stretch out the knots from sitting hunched over his laptop for several hours. 'The only reason this collection is still in the archive at all was that my predecessor had no clue what was inside the leather scroll tubes and my father was too busy to explain. The really valuable pieces were sold about a year ago to pay the staff. They were top quality pieces in perfect condition. No catalogue needed.'

'Your predecessor?' Toni wrapped her hand on the tripod and turned to look at Scott. 'Did your dad employ a business manager? You haven't mentioned that before.'

There was a sharp cough and a low grunt from across the table. 'Not exactly. My stepbrother joined the company two years ago straight out of business school. Travis ran the business when I was working overseas. He was a disaster as a man and as a manager.'

Toni nodded very slowly. 'Ah. Stepbrother. That must have been difficult, for you and your dad.' Then she sniffed and waved her hand from side to side. 'I get it. You're back to show this Travis who is the better man. A lot of pressure on you to get the job done, but that makes perfect sense now.'

Instantly the air temperature seemed to drop several degrees and she pressed her lips together and pretended to be extra fascinated in the sea chart.

'Are you always so intuitive?' Scott asked in a low, hoarse voice but there was just enough humour in it that she felt that she could breathe again.

'Always. Only one of my many special gifts. Think of

it as a free bonus with the portrait painter and photographer special package deal.'

He gestured with his head towards the camera as though signalling that he wanted to change the subject. 'Speaking of which. How are we doing?'

Toni smiled and walked around to the laptop computer and full-sized monitor that she had brought from home. 'Why don't you take a look? I think this catalogue design works, but you're the expert!'

She perched on the end of the high stool and opened up the online digital catalogue that they had agreed was the best format for displaying the inventory. The images could easily be enlarged so that all of the stunning detail popped out in full colour alongside a full description and history for each piece.

Toni felt Scott's arm press against hers as he bent down to look at the screen so that as she turned to speak their faces were only inches apart.

His tanned forehead might be furrowed, rough and creased with life but his mouth was soft and wide.

Lush.

He already had the slightest hint of stubble at eleven a.m., so the rest of his body must be... No, she couldn't think about what was below the glimpse of blond chest hairs curling out from the V of his shirt.

He half opened his mouth to say something, grinned and then changed his mind.

Her brain screamed out that this was a huge mistake and that she should tell him the presentation needed a lot more work and that she needed to get back to the photography. But her heart was too busy getting worked up over the boyish smile on his face and the very manly look in those eyes that were smiling at her.

He was dazzling!

As she perched on the stool, his head was only inches from her face, her bosom pressed against his shirt. In a fraction of a second, Toni was conscious that his hand had slid slowly around her waist, moving under her top so his fingertips could feel the heat of her warm skin. She felt something connect in her gut, took a deep breath and watched words form in that amazing mouth.

'Did you know that Freya has a passion for baking?'

'She never mentioned it,' Toni whispered as Scott stepped a little closer into the gap between her legs.

Suddenly she wasn't so sure that her decision to wear a skirt and leggings today instead of her usual black trousers was such a good idea.

Because, as Scott moved closer, her skirt started to hitch higher up her legs and her hands were too busy holding her up to do anything about it.

'Cakes, mainly. Do you like cake, Toni?'

'Oh, yes. I love cake, especially…chocolate,' Toni replied, but the words were driven from her mind as Scott's fingers wound up into her hair and then the base of her skull. His gaze followed the line of his hand as though her hair was the most fascinating thing that he had ever seen.

His fingers slid forward and stroked her cheek with the gentlest of touches.

'You have cream and éclair on your face,' Scott whispered and, leaning forward, he raised one finger and brushed it along her upper lip. Then, as she watched, riveted, he slowly ran the tip of his tongue across his chocolate-covered fingertip.

It only took a fraction of a second but it was the hottest thing Toni had ever seen in her life. So hot she couldn't help herself taking a sharp breath in some feeble attempt to cool her suddenly burning cheeks.

'Perhaps we should stick to the doughnuts in future?' she squeaked. 'Messy eater.'

'I'll risk it.' He grinned and followed the outline of her jaw with his thumb.

Scott slanted his head and slid closer and just for one second she thought that he was going to kiss her neck.

Instead, she felt a breath of warm sweet air from his soft lips against her cheek.

And every hair on her body instantly stood to attention.

Before she could change her mind, Toni rested both hands lightly on his hips so that the scent and sensation of his body could warm every cell in hers before she finally pulled her head back.

She knew without looking that her nipples were alive and proud and probably doing crazy things to the front of her top, but she truly did not care.

Scott looked straight at her, his chest responding to his faster breathing, and whispered, 'Chocolate works for me,' before sliding his hands down the whole length of her back, the pressure drawing her forward as he moved his head into her neck and throat, kissing her with just the barest contact of his lips on her collarbone, then up behind her ears, his hands moving up and down in a gentle caress of both sides of her back, inside her sweater. As though he wanted to find out what her skin tasted like without the chocolate and cream chaser.

The stubble on his chin and sideburns made her burn with instant fire, and instinct rather than sensible thought took over.

And chocolate was not what Toni was thinking about. At all.

For a moment their eyes locked together.

The need in his took her breath away and left her floundering, helpless.

What if he wanted her as much as she wanted him at this minute?

That could only spell trouble. For both of them.

Toni tried to break the mood by looking away first.

And then she made the fatal mistake of glancing back and fell dizzyingly into Scott's startling blue flecked eyes. Eyes which called to her with a message that her heart could not ignore.

I like you. A lot.

Doomed.

Without a second's hesitation, she leaned forward just an inch and started to angle her head so that their noses wouldn't clash, their eyes still locked. His tongue moistened his upper lip, and she instinctively did the same. His eyes glanced from her mouth back to her eyes as his hand came up to cradle the back of her head, smoothing down the hair, caressing the warm skin between her neck and ear. And suddenly she wanted—needed—to crush her mouth against his and taste his sweetness and life and passion.

She could sense that her breathing sped up in anticipation for his kiss, her eyes half closed at the pleasure to come. *She wanted him to kiss her.*

But what he did instead made kissing seem tame in comparison.

Scott's fingers moved down from her waist on to the rough tweed fabric of her trendy skirt until they reached her exposed leggings-covered thighs.

Toni breathed out a sigh of shuddering delight as his palms cupped her thighs, his thumbs caressing back and forth on the sensitive area on the inside of her legs, moving just a little higher with each caress.

She blinked up into Scott's face and he smiled at her

with an expression that told her everything that she needed to know.

This man knew exactly what he was doing and how her body was reacting to his touch. But she wasn't the only one. His breathing was matching hers, hot and fast and snatched between gasps.

Just to prove the point, his gaze locked on to hers and his hands pushed her skirt just high enough for him to step closer so she could feel just how much his body was enjoying the moment.

Somewhere inside her head a voice was telling her that she should tell him to stop. Soon. Very…*oh, Lord*…soon. But maybe not straight away. Because this felt way too good to stop.

Toni was just about to arch her back over the drawing table when Scott suddenly moved his hands out from under her skirt, pressed them on to the table, stepped back and whispered, 'I have an idea.'

An idea? What? Now?

Licking her lips and forcing her brain to form something close to sense took a second but eventually Toni managed to whisper, 'Great. Although I was hoping that you might have more than just the one.'

'Ah, but this is a classic. How would you like to be my date for dinner this evening?'

What?

Toni felt as though someone had just thrown a bucket of cold water over her and she instantly pushed her bottom off the stool and tugged her skirt down.

'A date? You? Me? Are you serious?'

'Is that so outrageous?'

'No. I mean yes,' Toni blustered, desperately trying to come up with an excuse why she could not, dare not put her heart on the line again. 'Technically, I'm working for you. An employee, in fact. And you have a girlfriend. You told me about the girl you left behind in Alaska the other day in the coffee shop. I'm sure that your lovely blue-eyed Dallas wouldn't be too happy with that idea. I don't date other girl's boyfriends. Ever.'

Scott paused for a moment, grinned then pulled out his wallet and handed her a photograph. 'Good to know. Toni, meet Dallas.'

'Oh, you have to be kidding me? You keep a photo of…a very handsome husky dog.' Toni peered at it, rolled her eyes and passed the snapshot of the dogsled back to its owner. 'Tease. Dallas is one of your sled dogs, isn't she?'

'Hell, no.' Scott grinned. 'Dallas is my lead girl. She runs the rig. If she doesn't want to tug and run?' He sliced the air with his hand. 'We're grounded.' Then a warm loving smile crept up out of nowhere and hit her with its full power. 'But when she moves? That girl is poetry in motion. And smart. We get on just fine.'

'So I see.' Toni smiled. 'Well, it's obvious that any girl would have to work hard to compete with the lovely Dallas. That's a special relationship.' She sucked in air between her teeth. 'I wouldn't want to come between a man and his dog.'

Scott scowled at her then pressed his lips together, winced, and then slapped the heel of his hand to his forehead as he took several steps back towards the door. 'You already have a boyfriend. Of course you do. How stupid of me.'

He gave her a short bow. 'Apologies. I jumped to conclusions. Another one of those flaws I was talking about. I only hope your boyfriend doesn't turn up at the house and thump me for asking his girl out.'

There was just enough of a change in his voice to make her look up. Unless he was a very good actor and she was completely misreading the signals, she saw a glimmer of genuine regret and disappointment cross that handsome face before he covered it up.

Interesting.

Decision time. Pretend she was seeing someone and lie through her teeth...or not.

'You're safe. I broke up with someone a year ago and right now I'm on my own. What I meant was that I'm between boyfriends and I don't feel comfortable with starting a serious relationship right now. But thanks again for the invitation.'

It was astonishing to see how fast Scott could switch on that killer smile.

'Ha. So you are single. That makes two of us.' He looked at her quizzically, eyebrows high. 'But who said anything about a serious relationship? What I'm talking about is a fling. A sweet, short and fun fling.'

'A fling? Why on earth would you want a fling with me? You could have your pick of girls to fool around with.'

He stepped closer and ran his hands up both sleeves of her jacket and smiled as his gaze locked on to her eyes. 'I've been through one very difficult divorce and since then my focus has been totally on my work. The last thing I want is to rush into that sort of commitment again. But I would like to get to know you better. A lot better. Maybe even get used to the idea that I can start looking for love again. Do you understand that?'

'Looking for love again? Yes. Yes, of course I understand that. Isn't that what we all want?'

Scott gave a small shoulder shrug. 'Maybe. But in the meantime we're both adults who understand the difference between a casual arrangement and a long-term relationship. This way, we can have the benefits. Without the messy complications.'

Then the tone of his voice cooled. 'But I'll be back in Alaska by the autumn. I can't promise you anything but a good time for the next few months and I need to know that you understand that very clearly. No confusion or re-criminations. A fling. Short and sweet. Now. What can I do to tempt you to take up my offer?'

'Oh, Scott,' she replied, shaking her head. 'You're temp-tation on legs.'

A smile that could defrost icebergs warmed the air. 'It's been said. And you're a lovely girl, Toni. We seem to make a great team at work. Now that has to say something.'

Make a great team at work! Oh, Scott, if you only knew. That was the worst thing that you could possibly have said.

Those were the precise words that Peter had used, right before he'd whisked her off to his hotel room and off her feet. She had fallen hard and fast in weeks not months. Blind to all the warning signs that screamed out to her not to go there. Her head full of dreams of a wonderful future working together. And all the time he was using her to get the work done and be his dirty little fling at the same time.

Six months with Scott Elstrom? Oh, no.

Toni chuckled under her breath and slowly slid out of the warmth of his embrace, even though it killed her to do it.

'Lovely and convenient! Sheesh. I'm the one who ac-tually pushed to work in your office and take your pho-tograph.'

She flipped her right hand over from side to side. 'Painter. Client.' Then she blew out hard and shook her head. 'So many great artists have fallen into that trap. Di-saster waiting to happen.'

Then she gave a casual shoulder shrug. 'Sorry, Scott.

My answer is thank you but no. You're going to have to work harder and find yourself another fling partner.'

She braced her back and shoulders and lifted her chin as Scott formed a reply, but was saved by her cellphone.

It was Amy's personal ringtone.

Great timing, sis!

'Sorry,' she whispered to Scott, who was glaring at the phone as though he wanted to toss it out of the nearest window. 'Amy…Peru. I should really answer it. Really sorry.'

It took a moment for her to slide her body sideways and out of the circle of his arms but even as she lifted the phone she could feel his gaze burning a hole in her back.

Tugging down the hem of her top as if Amy could see her, she opened the call and, before she could say a word, an entire orchestral chorus of *Happy Birthday* belted out at huge decibels into the quiet room.

Oh, great! Amy had sent her a musical birthday card to add to the surprise birthday present of a tiny locket that she had left for their neighbour to deliver that morning.

Scrabbling with her phone, she quickly turned it off, took a breath and turned sideways to look at Scott, who was standing with his arms folded and a lazy grin plastered all over his face.

'Today is your birthday? You might have mentioned that earlier. I could have brought back extra chocolate.'

'I had my party on Saturday, remember? At Freya's house. No big deal.'

'Oh, no—' he shook his head and pushed out his lips '—you don't get away that easy. I would fail in my duty if I didn't take you out for a birthday dinner. What time do you want me to pick you up for your date?'

My date?

Her heart was thumping so loudly he could probably hear it from where he was standing. He smelt wonderful, his touch sent her brain spinning and he was so handsome that her heart melted just looking at him.

But a date? Oh, no. That was something else. What was she doing?

She had felt that wicked pull of attraction in the coffee shop and then working side by side and had forced it deep down. And she would have to do the same now, because the high tension wire that was pulling her closer and closer towards Scott would only lead one way—to heartbreak and pain.

She had learnt her lesson with Peter and dared not place her trust in a man like this again. She just couldn't risk being used then cast aside.

She wasn't ready to date anyone. Nowhere near.

'A dinner date? Thank you, but I don't think that would be a very good idea, Scott.'

'Elstrom Mapping just had a big success today. That's worth celebrating over hot food and a nice glass of wine. I might even run to a slice of birthday cake, seeing as I ate most of your brownies last Saturday night.'

Toni made the mistake of looking into those blue eyes. He was challenging her to take him up on his offer. And she didn't have any plans for her birthday.

'So this would be a business dinner? The hot food part does sound tempting.'

'If that is what you want. I can do hot food and talk business.'

She sniffed once then nodded. 'Okay, you're on. Throw in a tablecloth and cutlery and you have a dinner date. Not a fling, of course. Oh, no.' Then she opened up her smartphone. 'Do you want me to book somewhere?'

Scott covered her hand with his long clever fingers.

'Leave this to me. My treat. Let's make it a night to remember.'

Then he flashed her a cheeky wink and strode back to his office, his taut bottom teasing her with every step.

No messy complications and not a fling. Toni groaned to herself. *Right*.

CHAPTER NINE

SCOTT STOOD WITH his legs braced in front of the stone balustrade and looked out across the Thames to the south bank of the river. The early evening traffic was still fierce behind his back but he blocked it out and focused on the lights twinkling in the old stone buildings to the east that he knew led away towards the financial district and St Paul's Cathedral.

He was so engrossed at working through his mental map of the city he knew so well that it took a full second before he recognized the female voice behind him.

'Hello, handsome. I'm conducting a survey on people's favourite London walks and I'm keen to know what yours is. Do tell.'

Scott turned around just as Toni stepped forward. His reward for hanging around close to the busy road for the last ten minutes was the touch of her tantalising cold lips on his cheek. So, before she had a chance to move away, he grabbed her and kissed her on the side of the mouth. But pretended that he had been aiming for her cheek.

The kiss only lasted a second but he instantly felt the heat of her smile on his face.

'Cheeky,' she scolded, but then her eyes softened and that smile made him feel that it would have been worth running here through the snow.

He would love to touch her again and hold her in his arms. Instead, he held out his hand towards her and gave a low whistle.

'Hey, look at you, birthday girl! That colour is amazing!'

Toni held out the skirt of her long tailored Russian-style coat which was in a shade of bright cherry-red which he usually associated with Christmas decorations. And yet, with the black lace-up boots and black knitted hat pulled down over her ears, she somehow managed to look elegant and chic instead of too bright.

'You like? These boots are ancient but they're so warm and comfy I couldn't resist.'

'I like. Cute hat too.'

'Amy made it for me! We Baldonis are so talented.'

'It's a miracle that you stay so grounded and modest.' Scott laughed and when her gloved hand reached out for his, it seemed perfectly natural for him to mesh his fingers with hers. He couldn't recall the last time he'd held hands with a woman in the street. Alexa used to hate public displays of affection of any type. Maybe he should have taken a hint from that?

Either way, he liked this just fine. For the next few hours he was going to put aside the problems back in the business and do his best to enjoy himself.

'Now, about that walk,' he said in a casual tone. 'I have so many favourites it's hard to choose.'

'Um...I agree. I've lived in this city all my life and I still find parts which are completely new to me! It's astonishing.'

'Then here's a suggestion. Let's see where our feet take us. No particular direction or destination. Just free to go where we want. Then back to my very favourite place for dinner. And yes, hot food is on the menu.'

Toni gave his hand a squeeze. 'Somehow I suspect a map will be involved but that's okay. Lead the way, oh, great explorer.'

If someone had asked Toni to describe where they had walked and how long it had taken and what they had seen, she would not have been able to. Westminster Abbey was involved at one point and possibly Trafalgar Square because she did recall roaring with laughter about feeding bananas to the lions in London Zoo.

What mattered were the shared experiences of growing up in the same city. Their parents and their lives were so very different and yet the more they talked movies and music and the fun things they enjoyed the more connected she felt.

It was hard hearing Scott talk about his parents' divorce and how he and Freya had to struggle to keep in contact with their father when he'd remarried so quickly to a woman with a grown-up son.

With each step she felt that he was opening up to her, sharing his life and his love of the natural world. And all the time his hand kept a tight hold on her, taking her with him on the journey.

Scott was talking about his team of sled dogs and how he loved to watch them tug at the traces and take off on the trail across frozen forests and lakes. She looked up into his face and it was so alive and intense she could feel the heat and the passion for what he did burning in every word.

Maybe that was when a vague sense of unease started to creep into her thoughts.

What was she doing here? Sled dogs? Frozen lakes?

She didn't know whether to feel privileged that he felt able to talk to her about the precious things that mattered to him or overwhelmed by how quickly her fun birthday dinner stroll had turned into something much deeper.

He wanted her to know about his life, which was wonderful. But, if anything, it only made her feel inadequate and ill prepared for the new world she was facing in the coming months. She had never travelled or done any of these exciting things. The biggest challenge she faced every week was dragging Amy out of bed and now even that was gone. Lifting a camera might exercise a few arm muscles but that was it.

Their lives were so very different it wasn't funny. He had been to university and studied with the best in his field and she had barely survived college. She'd had Amy to take care of. But it didn't make it any easier.

It was foolish to compare her life with Scott's. They were such different people.

Problem was—she liked him more than was healthy.

A sudden flash of light snapped Toni out of her dream and she smiled at Scott as they strolled up to a road crossing. Suddenly a group of tourists ran across towards them and as she stepped left, Scott moved right and her gloved fingers slid from his. And she immediately missed that simple connection with the man.

Inhaling sharply and cursing her ridiculous crush, Toni quickly plunged her hand into her coat pocket so that Scott would not reclaim it, casually glancing from side to side.

Big mistake. Because in one step he had closed the gap between them and pressed his hand into the small of her back and then around her waist, holding her to him as they crossed the busy London road, which was a whirl of traffic and cyclists who apparently took red lights to mean go faster.

Her foolish heart relished that contact with the muscular

body that was so close to the surface of his relatively thin all-weather short jacket and how his hand felt on her back.

Crazy girl! It was madness to get her hopes up that they could ever be more than the casual friends that they had become.

The reality of their situation hit her like the cold wind blowing in from the river.

A fling. That was what he was offering her. A short-term, time-limited relationship.

Of course she was tempted. She had done nothing but think about his offer for most of the afternoon.

Stupid, really. She would be back at work in a week, and she knew that the diary would be filling in with lots of overseas trips. Scott was only here for six months and then he would be gone and she would probably never see him again.

But whenever she was within touching distance of Scott there was this tantalising tingle of something in the air that seemed to toss logical thought out of the window and replace it with the idea that maybe he was the boyfriend that Amy had imagined that New Year's morning.

Decision time.

She could enjoy her hot dinner and thank Scott for a lovely evening with a polite kiss on the cheek and then tell him that her time at Elstrom had run its course. She had given him a week. So thank you very much but she needed to work on his painting and the house now. Be in touch when the plumbing was all sorted out and he could move in. Goodnight.

She glanced up into Scott's face as he cheerily chatted on about the time he'd tried to make a map of London at junior school out of tape and glue and poster paint.

He *was* a great man and it would be only too easy to fall and fall fast. She was already halfway there!

Or there was the other option. Take a huge risk and follow her feelings and play the fun friends with benefits card and live with the consequences. That was what she had promised Amy that she would do. Just another single girl having a good time with a great man while she had the chance.

Toni shivered deep inside her coat. This could be her only chance.

After what had happened with Peter she had struggled with her colleagues. Not one of them looked at her as a professional who could be their equal and over these past twelve months she seemed to have been offered projects where she was always going to be the assistant.

A strange idea crossed her mind and she pressed one hand to her forehead. Had she deliberately been accepting work where she knew that she would be in the background? That was all part of her training, wasn't it? To be the apprentice learning her trade from the experts.

Just as she had done with…her father.

Toni exhaled slowly as that thought rattled around inside her head and made her feel sick. She had slipped into the old pattern and not even realized it.

Worse. She had actually looked for those jobs, afraid to put herself forward as already trained and ready to work alone. Just as she had done with the paintings.

Scott chose that moment to laugh out loud and grin down at her.

She was a coward! Scott had given up the work he loved to come back to London to try to save his family business and his relationship with his father. He wouldn't let the Elstrom name go down without a fight.

A man like that was worth taking a risk on, no matter what happened.

Decision made.

Toni tucked her arm tightly into his elbow so that their hips touched as they walked but she didn't mind one little bit.

'Of course you do realize that your terrible secret is now out in the open, Scott Elstrom.'

Scott looked around as though shocked by the very suggestion and swallowed hard. 'Which one? I have so many.'

'No doubt. I was, of course, referring to the route march we have been following for the last few hours.' Toni counted out the vices on her fingers. 'Mr Scott Elstrom, Company Director.' She waved her fingers around. 'Not averse to a little travel on foot. Does not use a GPS, or at least I've never seen him use electronic mapping devices but, from what I saw this evening, he knows every highway, street and lane in this city like the back of his hand. Yes, Scott, I realise that you have walked me back to the same street as the Elstrom building. So that only leaves one question: how many maps of London have you drawn up over the years?'

He laughed out loud now. A real belly laugh, displaying his perfect teeth. 'Eight worth printing. Nine if you include the one I painted on my bedroom wall when I was seven years old.'

Toni gave an over the top gasp and jogged around in front of him, forcing Scott to look down at her when he replied.

'Wait just one minute. You can paint? When were you planning to reveal this secret skill? Or was it going to be a surprise?'

'Wax crayons and coloured pencils are my media of choice. So vibrant, you know.'

'Seriously?'

He looked at her for a split second, still laughing. 'Not a bit. I like technical drawing. Black lines using a straight-edge ruler and circles made from saucers and plates. Now that I am computerised, the survey company allow me to colour in the big bits but only when it's not important. They can always correct it later.'

Now it was Toni's turn to laugh, before she thumped him gently on the arm.

'You might have warned me this afternoon that we would be coming back here tonight! I spent ages choosing something smart to wear for my posh birthday dinner. I should have guessed that you would choose a restaurant close to home. Research—so important.'

'Absolutely. Which is why I'm taking you somewhere very, very exclusive. Think of it as your birthday present.'

'Exclusive! I like the sound of that. Even if I wasn't expecting a present. Is it very far?'

He smiled, and surprised her by sliding around behind her so that his arms were wrapped around her waist, holding her tight against him. She felt the pressure of his head against the side of her face as he dropped his chin on to her shoulder, lifted his left arm and pointed.

She pretended not to notice as his fingertips gently moved against her skin to flick the imaginary ends of her hair back over the collar of her wool coat, which was being warmed by Scott's hot body.

'For one night only, Elstrom Mapping has become Elstrom Fine Dining.'

'We're eating here! Wait a minute,' she said and tried to turn around to face him but the wall of muscle wouldn't move an inch. 'I asked for hot food and a tablecloth. Cutlery would be nice too.'

He brushed his stubbly cheek next to her throat so that when he spoke the words were whispered, hot and moist, in her ear. 'The way I want to kiss you right now might get us arrested. Especially when I have something hot and spicy waiting inside. Would you like to find out more? Was that a nod? Excellent. Let's go, birthday girl.'

Ten minutes later, Toni was starting to reconsider whether this was such a good idea after all.

'You didn't mention that walking upstairs wearing a blindfold would be involved,' she giggled. 'I hope you don't think that my birthday party was my usual kind of social event. Please, tell me where I'm going. If fluffy handcuffs come out I may run.'

Or perhaps not. But she didn't want Scott to know that!

His reply was a truly filthy low chuckle and he took even tighter hold of her waist and pulled her closer to him.

'That would spoil the surprise.'

He kissed her quickly on the top of the head, which made her giggle even louder. 'Get ready,' he whispered and their steps slowed. 'We've arrived.'

She felt him stretch forward and suddenly a very cold breeze whirled around her legs. Even the warmth of Scott's body pressed along her side couldn't block out that icy blast.

Toni took a tight hold of her bag but gripped Scott's hand tighter.

'Is this going to be an igloo-style dining experience? Because I have to tell you that I left my thermals back at the house.'

'Glad to hear it. Stay close. You'll be fine, trust me.'

One final squeeze of her hand and she took a step forward and cuddled even closer to Scott. Trust him! If he was planning to make her get up close and personal he was certainly doing a good job. It was freezing!

'Promise not to peek for ten more seconds,' Scott murmured and she could feel the heat of his breath against her

neck and then the gentle tug of the ribbon covering her
eyes being untied at the back and lifted away.

She carefully half opened one eye and then instantly
blinked and stared in amazement, her eyes scarcely able
to take in what she was looking at.

They were standing on a rooftop terrace with panoramic views across the London skyline. All the lights
of the tall buildings and the winding curve of the River
Thames were laid out in front of her on this clear, cold
frosty night.

Every light twinkled and gleamed as though it had been
polished diamond-bright just for her. And above her every
star in the heavens was clear and sharp against the dark
night sky, with only a faint glow from the city below.

It was as though she had been transported to her own
personal roof garden overlooking London.

Scott took a step closer to an elaborate wrought iron
railing and they stood side by side for a second, their
breaths hot and fast and making faint clouds of mist in
the cold air.

'Oh, Scott,' was all she managed to say, one hand
pressed against her throat and the other still clutching on
to his arm.

'Happy birthday, Antonia.' He smiled and wrapped
his arm around her shoulders and hugged her. 'Happy
birthday.'

Scott grinned down at Toni, who was standing next to him
with a totally shocked look on her face, and was rewarded
with a stunning smile that seemed to reach into his heart
and unlock the heavy metal gates that he had constructed
since Alexa.

There wasn't a hint of artifice or pretence in this girl's

smile and everything he had been through to make this evening possible suddenly seemed a small price to pay.

'Hey, birthday girl. Let's get you out of the cold.'

Holding tightly on to Toni's waist, he nudged her back towards the door and heard her gasp of delight.

'What? I cannot believe it.' She laughed up into his face and then looked back to the enclosed conservatory area of the roof garden, where he had set up his father's simple bistro table for dinner for two.

Electric lamps flickered on each wall, there were candles on the table and a blast of warm air welcomed them the second they stepped inside.

'My dad isn't too keen on the cold so he built this extension from his third floor flat out on to our roof garden when we were kids. We can be out of the wind here but still get the view.'

'Oh, wait until I tell Amy about this place.' Toni chuckled as Scott guided her into the half glass conservatory. 'It is actually warm and cosy. In fact I'm thinking of moving in. I love it. Want to make a trade?'

'Not quite. I have two heaters on full power just for you. And. Hot. Food.'

Scott guided Toni to her chair and watched her eyes pop with delight at the hot tray he had plugged in before he'd set out.

It only took a moment to pour her a glass of red wine and then one for himself.

'How about a toast? To lamb tagine and rice, made by the brilliant Moroccan restaurant down the street. A decent French red from the cellar. And good company. Cheers.'

'Good company,' Toni breathed as they touched wine glasses and then she took a sip and closed her eyes in pleasure as she savoured the wine. 'That's wonderful. In fact—' she gazed around the conservatory, taking in the tiny sofa for one and the bookcases and plants '—this is all wonderful. When you do exclusive, you do it in style, Mr Elstrom. I approve.'

'Then my work is done,' he said, smiling. 'I'm pleased you like it. The roof garden used to be one of my favourite places, even before this conservatory was built. There were fewer skyscraper buildings then and the stars seemed brighter somehow.'

He knew that his voice must have trailed away because Toni had stopped gazing out to the balcony and her entire focus was on his face. Her soft brown eyes flickered with amber and gold to match the colours in her hair and the connection between them pulled them tighter and tighter until her sweet gentle voice broke the silence.

'I would rather look at you,' Toni whispered as she got to her feet, slipped off her coat and crossed the few steps between them.

Her soft lips pressed against his and he tasted sweet red wine and all of the heat and warmth that he'd thought would never be offered to him again.

'I've been thinking about your offer,' she breathed, her gaze scanning his face as her fingertips traced gentle circles at the back of his head. 'And do you know what? I've changed my mind. In fact, I like the idea of a fling. Very...' she kissed his forehead '...very...' then his temple '...much.' And nipped the corner of his top lip with her teeth. Then her mouth lifted into the sweetest, cheekiest grin that he had ever seen. 'If the offer is still open?'

Her fingers cupped the back of his head as she angled her face and stepped closer so that her kiss could deepen and deepen, overwhelming and passionate.

Clutching hold of her soft sweater, Scott rode the wave of sensation until the tip of her tongue found his. And the rules went out of the window.

In an instant her lush body was crushed against his and his hands were exploring every inch of that frame as his mouth took over, nibbling her upper lip, then moving down on to her throat and then lower until his cheek found a home next to her breast.

Breathing became a second priority for a few minutes but he didn't mind in the slightest. He was perfectly content to hold Toni in his arms and use his mouth to give her pleasure, knowing that she wanted him as much as he wanted her.

It was time to find out just where this journey would take them.

'Scott... The lights have gone out.' Toni's words were murmured in between gentle nibbles on his ears and in the hollow of his neck.

'Probably a power cut,' he whispered and wrapped his arms tighter around her body, drawing it closer to him and trying to find a comfier position on the narrow wicker sofa. The moon was higher and lighting the room but the candles had burnt out an hour ago.

She nodded and then lifted her head. 'I can smell something burning. Is it our dinner?'

He chuckled for a full second before the smile dropped from his lips and with a deep groan of regret he took hold of Toni's hands.

'Nope. Not the dinner. That's the smell of electric cable burning. Sorry, Toni. I need to find out where the problem is.'

'Not without me,' Toni said and they pulled on their clothes and Scott dashed out of the conservatory and into his father's apartment, the moonlight at their backs guiding their steps.

Scott was right. The burning smell grew stronger the

closer they got to the main staircase and when they opened the door to the apartment there was smoke in the hallway.

'I left a torch in the store room,' Toni called out as the lights started to flicker. 'Just inside the door to the right.'

'On it,' Scott called back and took the stairs two at a time and Toni saw the torchlight beam out only seconds before all the lights went out and she was left in the smoke and darkness.

'Scott! Are you okay?' she called out and blinked as the torchlight blinded her.

'It's in the fuse box,' a dark shape called out through the smoke which was so thick that she could hardly make out his face. 'No time to grab your coat. We're leaving and we're leaving right now. Before this whole building goes up in flames.'

CHAPTER TEN

TONI SHRUGGED HER arms into an old cardigan belonging to Scott's father that she had found hanging on the back of a chair. But it was no good. She still stank of smoke. All of her clothes and certainly her hair and skin were dirty with soot and grime and no amount of rinsing her face could clear her eyes of that horrible gritty feeling.

She peeked around the corner of the main office and watched Scott direct the electricians to the totally burnt-out junction box which was the source of all of the smoke. No actual flames, thank goodness. That would have been truly terrifying.

Scott was even filthier than she was!

Hardly surprising. He had been amazing. Once he had known that she was safe outside on the pavement, he had dashed back into the service room with only a small fire extinguisher and the torch held between this teeth.

That was a sight that she was not going to forget in a hurry!

Her heart had been in her throat for the whole ten minutes until he had emerged, coughing and smoky. Through the smoke, it was obvious that the ancient electrical system had finally given up and had been totally burnt out and would need to be replaced.

The emergency electrician who arrived to make the

building safe gave them the bad news in the middle of the night. The whole building would have to be rewired to bring it up to modern safety standards. In fact he was astonished that this had not happened earlier. He had never seen anything this old still in operation. Anywhere!

Sitting in a coffee shop in their stinky clothing at first light was not exactly how she had imagined her birthday dinner would end. Scott wasn't going to get another up close and personal second viewing of her new burgundy underwear after all. Not tonight, anyhow.

It hadn't taken long for the shock to wear off and the real impact of the damage to sink in and they had sat in silence for a lot of the time, deep in thought.

Neither of them was stupid. All of that work had been wasted! And what would this mean for the financial plans for the building? Rewiring a two-hundred-year-old building was no easy task. Wooden panels and flooring were not designed to be easily removed and replaced. The work could take weeks!

Any plans to use Elstrom Mapping as a film location were officially on hold.

The true extent of the smoke damage was only really obvious when they braved the smell and went back in to open every window to try and clear the smoke. And this time there was no way that she would stay outside and leave Scott to do the work alone.

Her camera and the precious maps and charts had all been safely locked away in the mapping room drawers before she left the previous evening but other paperwork and some of the archive papers had been covered in smoke and smelt horrible.

It was heartbreaking to see this fine building that she had come to care about so much looking so wrecked and damaged.

Heartbreaking to see Scott trying to sound positive on the phone to Freya and the insurance company. Heartbreaking to sit with him and look at the damage and know how much work was needed to restore the greatness of this fine place.

And heartbreaking to know that she only had one more week to help him. Her boss at the media company had already emailed her twice to make sure that she would be at the airport on Monday morning for a flight to Madrid and then on to Athens a few days later to shoot a three-week commercial campaign for a housewares company. Her time at Elstroms was coming to an end.

What was she going to do? What could she do?

It was almost a shock to hear the phone ringing on Scott's desk and she jogged around and picked up the handset, just as Scott strolled into the room.

'Elstrom Mapping.' Toni said, trying to sound professional, but her throat was still a little hoarse to pull it off. 'Good morning.'

'Not from what I've just heard,' a high-pitched male voice replied. 'I need to speak to Scott right now. Is he there?'

Toni beckoned Scott to her and he gave a quick nod and stretched out his hand for the phone. 'One moment, please. Who shall I say is calling?'

'Just tell him it's Travis. He'll take the call.'

Scott must have seen the surprise on her face and his eyebrows creased together for a second before he put the phone to his ear, but that was nothing compared to the look of absolute rage that seemed to transform his face the second he heard the other man's voice.

'I wondered when you would call. It didn't take long, did it?'

Scott was on his feet, walking back and forth in front

of the desk with exhaustion only too clear on his face. But, as Toni sat back in his office chair, every word that exploded from Scott's mouth sounded like cannon fire.

'Sell the building? Now, why should I do that? A bit of smoke damage only adds to the character.'

Something Travis said must have upset Scott even more because suddenly he froze. 'How the hell do you know what my father wants? When was the last time you even spoke to him? Oh, yes, I remember. Just after you started screwing my wife. Forget it, Travis. I'm not selling. You're going to have to find some easy money somewhere else. Now, get off my phone. I have a business to run.'

Toni leant back as the phone came sliding across the desk towards her and she could hear the sound of Scott's breathing as he continued to pace with one hand pressed hard to the back of his head.

'So that was Travis. He sounded intense. It's amazing how quickly bad news travels.'

Scott threw off the thick leather gloves and tossed them on to the desk and stomped closer to her, but Toni stayed exactly where she was.

Scott was furious; when he spoke, each word was like a dagger stabbing at her forehead and penetrating her skull.

'Intense? Is that how you would describe Travis? Intense? You want to know about my stepbrother?'

Scott was almost spitting out the words as he said the name.

'That man hated the fact that his widowed mother married someone who he thought was totally beneath her in every way. Yes, that's right. My dad was a boring academic type who wasn't worthy to marry a woman with a title. How pathetic was that! And, even worse, the man had two children and expected him to play nice.'

Scott coughed. 'Travis broke up his mother's marriage

and then used every trick in the book to turn my family against me, starting with my father and then my wife, Alexa. And I cannot forgive him for destroying something I thought was special.'

Toni sucked in some air. 'You're still in love with her. I understand. Really. You can't just wipe away all of those years of your life that you spent together.'

'Ah, Toni, believe me—I'm over Alexa. But memories have this habit of kicking you when you're down. I haven't forgotten what it felt like to find my stepbrother and my wife together in the boardroom. And what they were doing on that table had nothing to do with forward planning, unless it was to find a contract which would keep me as far away from London as they could come up with. Alaska fitted the bill nicely.'

'Oh, Scott, surely you don't think that they planned it?'

'No, I don't think—I'm sure of it. Travis told me to my face on the day we first met that he was determined to have everything that I had. Well, he got what he wanted.'

Scott stopped pacing long enough to count out the list using his fingers. 'A controlling interest in Elstrom Mapping. My father gave his new wife half of his shares as a little wedding present and Travis a few more on his twenty-first birthday. All Travis had to do was persuade his mother to put the shares in his name, for tax reasons or some other excuse, and he had the shares he needed to sit on the board.'

'But surely he couldn't do that. You and your father ran the business.'

'And how could I forget my father? He made sure that there was always some excellent excuse why my father should attend some function Travis had organised instead of seeing me. And when I complained? I was being childish and jealous. So, of course, when the position for CEO came up? He took my job. The only job that I had trained for and wanted since I could read a map.'

'Oh, Scott, I can't believe it.'

'Believe it.' He paused a moment and shook his head and blew out sharp and fast.

'And then there was the lovely Alexa. She was the final trophy in his little collection. When he had Alexa he had the full set. He had everything he wanted. Everything he thought that I wanted. He had taken everything that mattered to me.'

Scott was pacing now like a caged animal. 'But Travis had forgotten something rather important. Where do you go when you have everything that you have ever wanted?'

Scott whirled, one hand in the air.

'I remember coming into this room on the day before I left for Alaska. Travis was sitting at the head of the table. Master of all he surveyed. And I looked at him and laughed in his face. Do you know why? He had no clue. None. About any of it. He didn't know how to run a business. How could he? He had shadowed me for almost a year but that wasn't nearly long enough. Sad thing was, Travis was clever enough to realise that he taken on too much too soon. But too arrogant to admit that he had failed.'

'So what did he do? After you left?'

'He did what any desperate fool does. He threw money at the problem. Brought in top consultants. Experts in new mapping technology. Anybody and anything that could give him a rope to hold on to so he could try and climb out of this pit that he had dug for himself and for Elstrom Mapping and have someone else to blame when it all went wrong.'

Scott gazed out of the tiny squares of mullioned glass on to the busy London street and his voice dropped to a sad whisper.

'My father came back from Italy with Freya and walked in the front doors to find the bailiffs were already here to unplug all of the ludicrously expensive computer systems that Travis had ordered and never bothered to pay for or train anyone to use.'

Scott looked at Toni over one shoulder then turned back to gaze at the city street.

'Travis was gone. Resigned. Walked out. Leaving Freya and my father to try and sort out the chaos that he had created and left for other people to deal with.'

'Oh, no. That's so cruel.'

'Cruel and irresponsible,' Scott agreed. 'But if you're looking for someone to blame for my father's poor health, don't look to Travis. Start with me. Because I saw it coming and did not do one thing to stop it.'

'What do you mean, you saw it coming?' Toni asked as she stepped closer to Scott so that she could see his face.

'It was common knowledge that we desperately needed to invest in new mapping and survey technology. That was why I had spent three months studying the alternatives and putting together a proposal which would have taken us into the next generation of mapping.'

Scott turned and gazed at the imposing chair at the end of the table. 'I stood here and spent an hour going through the detail. Freya loved it. But she was the only one. Alexa and my father sided with Travis. He couldn't wait years. I wasn't being adventurous enough. I needed to wake up and be more experimental. I was not the man for the job.'

The pain in Scott's voice was so intense that Toni rested her hand over his in support and for a moment his gaze focused on her. 'I walked out, Toni. I was so angry and bitter that I wanted Travis to fail and for the world to see it. Why should I stay and try and save the business when my father had chosen to put his trust in Travis instead of me? Let Travis bankrupt the business. Then they would see who was wrong and who was right!'

Scott gave a low shuddering sigh. 'Not something I am proud of. He brought out an ugly side of me which I didn't know existed.'

'That was what he wanted to do, wasn't it? Make things so impossible that you had to leave him in charge of the company.'

Scott flashed her a closed mouth smile. 'Clever girl. He goaded me into it by forcing me to choose whether to stay and work with him or take off. So no, Travis Brooks is not my favourite person in the world. And now he's back and he needs money. The question is—what will he do to get it this time? My ex-wife soon outlived her usefulness and he moved on to the next wealthy woman a year later. He had no use for her any longer. And I cannot forgive the man for that.'

Toni paced up and down the parquet floor several lengths, her head down but her gaze was wild as she mentally worked through the question and tried to come up with an answer.

'Did Travis keep his shares in the company?' she asked, blinking.

'Not all of them,' Scott replied. 'Alexa was an expensive luxury so he sold a few to Freya when he needed some money.'

'Freya? Yes, of course. Neutral territory. I'm beginning to get the picture. One last question.' She licked her lips. 'What about Alexa? Does she still have a say in what happens to Elstrom?'

'Alexa wanted half my shares as part of the divorce but when she saw what was left after Travis was left in control, she changed her mind and walked away with the home that we had made together as final settlement.'

He strolled forward and tented his hands on the table. 'I can see where you're going with this. My dad might be ill but he has handed over his control of the company to me. Travis has some shares, but I control the decisions now. What I say goes and he had better get used to that.'

'Travis could still fight you.'

'I expect him to.'

Scott gestured towards the stairs. 'This fire is nothing. Just a small temporary setback. Your location scout won't even know that things have changed. I'll make sure of that.'

He broke into a strange and slightly scary grin. 'This is round two, Toni. Now it is his turn to feel excluded. And this time I get to win.'

'Win?' she repeated. 'So this is a battle. Oh, Scott. Don't you see what he's doing? Travis is pulling your strings again. Making you play his game and by his rules all over again.'

Toni stood in front of Scott and pressed the palms of both of her hands flat against his chest. 'Don't let Travis manipulate you into doing something you will regret, Scott. Because, if you do, he will have won.'

That caught Scott's attention. 'What do you mean—won?'

'You told me on my first day in this office that you had come back to save the family business from losing everything. But now I'm wondering if that was the only reason. Was it to do with Alexa and Travis?'

'You don't know what you're talking about, Toni. It has been a hell of a long night. Why don't you head off home and get some sleep and I'll catch up with you later?'

'No, Scott. I need to hear this. Please. Tell me now and I will never mention it again. Why have you come back to work for Elstrom? You told me that it was about your family legacy. I understand that better than you could know. But I'm beginning to think that there is a lot more to it than that. Why are you here, Scott? Why did you agree to come all the way from Alaska to save an old wooden building and a few rooms of maps and charts? Was this to spite Travis and get retribution for taking your place in your family?'

Scott gazed at her with a stunned expression on his face, jaw slack and his eyes dancing.

Then, just as quickly, he shook it off.

'Right now I am a lot more interested in making this building safe to work in. The junction box is fried and I don't intend to spend a minute longer than I have to on Travis when there is so much work to do.'

'All I am asking for is the truth. That's all.'

'The truth? You want to know the truth? Why don't you ask Travis? He will tell you his version of the truth. Oh, yes. Golden boy Travis could even convince my own father that I was responsible for throwing my wife at him. I neglected her, you see. Left her all alone while I was out working on every mapping project I could find. According to Travis, all that work had nothing to do with trying to save the company. It was all because I couldn't stand to see Travis in charge of Elstrom Mapping instead of me.'

He pushed both of his hands flat against the brick wall and closed his eyes for a second before speaking into the distance, his voice low and harsh and intent.

'And do you know the worst thing? He was right. I couldn't stand to see Travis at the head of the boardroom table with all of those portraits looking down at the back of his head. So yes, I took too many trips overseas to win some new business to pay for the extravagant lifestyle that my father's new family was living. There was no one else doing the work to bring in new business and for once I was determined not to see it go down with the crazy plans for expansion that Travis and Alexa came up with between them without even bothering to ask me first.'

'Was it so very bad?'

'Need you ask? It was a disaster. My father trusted them to turn the business around. Clever academic business degree Travis was going to rescue the company and bring it into the new technological age of map-making.'

Scott shook his head and coughed low in his throat. 'He had so many grandiose plans and no clue about what he was doing. So yes, I went out looking for new business, but don't you dare tell me that it gave him permission to seduce my wife behind my back and laugh about it to my face.'

'I would never do that,' Toni gasped. 'And I'm sorry that you had to go through that. It was inexcusable and cruel. I know…I know how it feels when someone you love betrays you.'

'You know? You have no idea what it felt like to walk into the boardroom and find my wife with Travis. You have no idea at all. Because it was one of the few times in my life when I understood why people commit crimes of passion. He was very lucky that day that I chose to walk out and leave the two people who I thought were my family to rot.'

The sound that Scott's fist made when it hit the wall made Toni jump with shock. 'No, Toni. You only think that you know. You don't have any idea at all.'

CHAPTER ELEVEN

EVERY ONE OF Scott's words hit Toni like a slap across the face and she flinched as though he had struck her.

She felt instantly overwhelmed by what had happened a year ago on her birthday.

An event which she had pushed firmly away as past history.

Her breath caught in the back of her throat and she gasped at the sudden flash of memory. Pain surged through her and she collapsed down on the hard wooden chair, her legs like jelly and unable to take her weight. Suddenly she felt sick and tearful and pathetic.

'You are wrong, Scott. I do know. Because exactly the same thing happened to me.'

'What are you talking about? How can the same thing have happened to you? Have you ever been married?'

'No. But I had a boyfriend who I trusted and cared about more than I should. We were together day and night for almost three months working on a documentary in France together. I thought I knew him and that he loved me and wanted to be with me. I was wrong. About both of those things.'

'No—' Scott started to speak but she held up one hand '—let me finish.'

She had to get it out and explain or she would go mad.

'I had worked like crazy for weeks to finish the film-ing and editing before the deadline and it still wasn't done. Peter was doing the networking and keeping the client happy; I was working the cameras. We were a great team. Then he asked me to help him out. He had been invited to a family wedding and really wanted to be there but that was going to be impossible unless we finished the final studio work that week. Could I help him by finishing it on my own? Then we could meet up back in London in time for my birthday that weekend.'

Toni dropped her head back. 'Of course I said yes. He was my boyfriend. I would do anything for him. I worked for forty-eight hours straight to make the deadline. And it was great work.'

She sniffed and gave a low laugh. 'The problem was, it was so good that the client offered me a free ride back to London on the company jet. Fantastic, I thought. I'll pop around to Peter's apartment and drop off the equip-ment then take a day's holiday to sleep. But something weird happened on the flight. The client asked if I could get hold of the talent agent for Peter's girlfriend. He had completely forgotten to ask Peter and they were looking for a lingerie model for another campaign. They were such a handsome couple!'

A low chuckle turned into a half cry. 'I started to tell the client that he was wrong and that I was his girlfriend but suddenly things started to click together in my mind. The fabulous clothes in Peter's wardrobe which he claimed belonged to his sister who used the apartment. The tele-phone calls he took at all hours of the day and night from clients. And the texting. The constant bloody texting, day and night. It all made sense.'

Her voice faded away. 'There was no family wedding. That was just an excuse that he had made up to get rid of me. Peter was having a clothes optional dinner for two with his Brazilian girlfriend when I turned the key and walked in on them in the shower.'

Even moistening her lips could not make the words come any easier.

'I am sorry. I had no idea.'

'Why should you? I keep these things to myself,' Toni replied. 'He used me because I was convenient and trusting and I fell for it. That hurts and it never completely goes away, does it?'

His answer was a small shake of the head.

Toni closed her eyes and luxuriated in the warmth of his body pressed against her side and, without thinking of the consequences, she leant sideways against him, daring to push the boundaries that they had set in the bedroom.

His left arm snaked around her waist and Scott drew her even closer to his body.

She could feel the pounding of his heart under his smart blue shirt as she pressed her fingertips to the soft fabric which separated his skin from hers, only too aware that one thin layer of mightily creased cardigan wasn't perhaps the best outfit she could have chosen to rescue smoke-damaged documents. She must stink of smoke.

Strange. Somehow, that didn't seem important any longer.

Who was she kidding? Scott meant more to her than any man she had ever known. She had never told anyone about that day. Not even Amy knew the real truth. Until this week she would never have thought it possible that she could forge so powerful a bond to this amazing man and feel that friendship and connection back in return.

Peter had been her lover and her colleague and for a few idyllic and heady months in one of the most romantic cities in Europe she thought that they had a future together. But, looking back, she knew now that Peter had never been her friend. Real friends didn't use one another.

'Tell me what you need me to do,' she whispered. 'I have to go back to work in a week but I have loads of pals who would be happy to help. We can bring a team in and start the clear-up. We can turn this place around in a week. You wait and see.'

She could stay this way for ever and not regret it. But, just as her head lolled back against the chair, she sensed his mood change, as though someone had opened the window wider and allowed a cool breeze into the room.

His arm slid away from behind her back and he moved, just an inch, then more, and their bodies slid apart, slowly at first then swiftly as Scott stepped sideways and bent over the paperwork on the table.

The shock of being separated was like a physical blow to Toni's poor heart. But it was the look on Scott's face that truly startled her as he turned to face her.

Desire, anguish, self-reproach and unmistakable desire. For her.

She had not been mistaken after all.

The way his hand had started to seek hers when they were out, the way she caught him looking at her when she least expected it, and the kiss on the roof terrace the night before had been real. The gentleness of his mouth on the nape of her neck which turned her legs to jelly had meant as much to him as it had to her.

And she didn't know whether to grin and shout in glee while she had the chance, or be patient and let him take the lead.

This was why, when he did speak, the words he used touched her heart and made her weep.

'A week? You think we can clear up this mess in a

week? Somehow, these past few days I had forgotten that you have your own life and another job. Oh, Toni.'

His finger stroked her cheek from her temple down to her chin. 'I can't do this, Toni. I thought a fling was what I needed—hell, what we both needed. But you're a lovely woman and any man would be honoured to have you in his life and we both know that I will be back in Alaska in a few months. It wouldn't be fair on either of us to make promises we can't keep. No matter how much we would like things to be different. You should go back to your work and make it the success it deserves.'

Well. That answered her question.

Two choices. She could accept what he said and let him go with a smile on her face or she could do something mad and challenge him.

Just the thought of not having Scott in her life sent a cold shiver down her back. He was hers and nobody else's. And she hadn't even realized that until this moment. She didn't want to lose Scott Elstrom. She couldn't lose him, not now, not after all they had shared together.

She wanted Scott and she wanted him badly enough to fight for him.

'Can't do what, Scott? Be friends with me? Like me and want to spend time with me? Want to hold me in your arms? Is that what you can't do, Scott? Please tell me the truth because I'm starting to get confused by what your body is telling me and the words coming out of your mouth.'

Before Toni realized what was happening, Scott had crossed the few steps that separated them and had wrapped his hand around the back of her neck, his fingers working into her hair as he pressed his mouth against hers, pushing open her full lips, moving back and forth, his breath fast and heavy on her face.

His mouth was tender, gentle but firm, as though he was holding back the floodgates of a passion which was on the verge of breaking through and overwhelming them both.

She felt that potential, she trembled at the thought of it, and at that moment she knew that she wanted it as much as he did.

Her eyes closed as she wrapped her arms around his back and leaned into the kiss, kissing him back, revelling in the sensual heat of his body as it pressed against hers. Closer, closer, until his arms were taking the weight of her body, enclosing her in his loving, sweet embrace. The pure physicality of the man was almost overpowering. The movement of his muscular body pressed against her, combined with the heavenly scent that she knew now was unique to him alone.

It filled her senses with an intensity that she had never felt in the embrace of any other man in her life. He was totally overwhelming. Intoxicating. And totally, totally delicious.

And, just when Toni thought that there could be nothing more pleasurable in this world, his kiss deepened. It was as though he wanted to take everything that she was able to give him and without a second of doubt she surrendered to the hot spice of the taste of his mouth and tongue.

This was the loving warm kiss she had never known. The connection between them was part of it, but this went beyond friendship and common interests.

This was a kiss to signal the start of something new. The kind of kiss where each of them was opening up their most intimate secrets and deepest feelings for the other person to see.

The heat, the intensity, the desire of this man was all there, exposed for her to see when she eventually opened her eyes and broke the connection. Shuddering. Trembling.

Then he pulled away, the faint stubble on his chin grazing across her mouth, as he lifted his face to kiss her eyes, brow and temple.

It took a second for her to catch her breath before she felt able to open her eyes, only to find Scott was still looking at her, his forehead pressed against hers. A smile warmed his face as he moved his hand down to stroke her cheek.

He knew. He knew the effect that his kiss was having on her body. Had to. Her face burned with the heat coming from the point of contact between them. His heart was racing, just as hers was.

'Is that the way you usually silence women who ask you tough questions?' Toni asked, aiming to keep her voice casual and light as she tried to catch her breath. And failing.

He simply smiled a little wider in reply, one side of his mouth turning up more than the other, before he answered in a low whisper. 'I save it for emergencies. And for when I need to answer tough questions.'

Scott pulled back and looked at her, eye to eye. 'You have to know that it is killing me to even think about leaving you here when I head back to Alaska, but that is where I belong. Freya will be back tomorrow to help me with the cleaning and organising the media companies and she's happy to do it, but she doesn't need me, Toni. There is no work for me here. You deserve a lot better than a part-time lover.'

He was nuzzling the side of her head now, his lips moving over her brow and into her hair as she spoke. 'Do I? I think that is the nicest thing that anyone has ever said to me.'

'And I mean every word. Your life is here, where you have a brilliant future as an artist and photographer. I can see it now.' His hand scrolled her name in the air. 'Portraits by Antonia Baldoni. It is going to be magic. Who knows, I might even come and have my photograph taken.'

'No need, Scott. I have all the photographs in the world. But they don't come close to the real you.'

Scott rested his forehead on her for one more second before he stood back and held out his hand. 'It's been a delight working with you, Miss Baldoni. Good luck in your future career.'

Then he turned and strode away from her, back to the second floor and the sound of sawing wood and drilling. Leaving her sitting there in her smoky clothes and hair with a broken heart. Bereft and alone. And already missing him more than words could express.

CHAPTER TWELVE

SCOTT STROLLED INTO the boardroom at Elstrom in the bright March sunlight and was immediately leapt on by Freya, who gave him such a warm hug that all of his fears and apprehensions for this day instantly vanished.

Holding her at arm's length, Scott moved his head slowly from side to side to check that they were the only two people in the room.

'I know that Dad is still in Italy because I spoke to him this morning. But where have you hidden Travis? I thought his ugly face was bound to turn up at any board-room meeting where money would be involved. Do I need to look under the table? That's the only place he would be out of reach of my fist.'

'Now don't be like that,' Freya scolded and wagged a finger at him. 'Travis sent me a very sweet email yesterday, telling me that he had decided to leave Elstrom behind for good and move on to pastures new.'

Freya must have caught the look in his eyes because she gave him a quick nod. 'Yes. That's right. Travis has sold all of his shares. And no, before you ask, I don't know who he sold them to. It certainly wasn't anyone in the family because I asked around. So don't give me that look. Who knows? It might be someone who has a real interest in the business. Think positive for once!'

'Positive! Right. Well, I can't say that I'm sorry to see him go. But I don't like the idea that we have an unknown investor. That makes me nervous.'

Freya hooked her arm through the crook of Scott's elbow and tugged him towards the back of the room.

'Then here is something to put a smile on your face.' She nervously licked her lips and Scott saw it.

'What's going on? I thought that you'd called me here for a board meeting?'

'I have.' Freya nodded. 'With my office manager hat on, I can tell you that everything is going splendidly, the building is booked for the next two years with more enquiries coming in every day and the finances have never looked rosier. The full report is on your desk. There. Done. Now, on to much more exciting stuff.'

She stepped back and slowly angled her head towards the wall behind the head of the table. 'Notice anything different?'

Scott rolled his shoulders back and followed her gaze, then blinked.

The full-length portrait of his uncle had been moved to the left, creating a gap which was occupied by a tall gold frame which matched the other portraits perfectly. What was inside the frame was covered by a plain grey dust sheet held up by a piece of tape, hiding the painting below.

It took a second for his brain to register what he was looking at.

'Toni finished my painting. Wow. I wondered about that.'

'Wonder no longer. That girl works fast! I have already seen it and paid the rest of her fee,' Freya whispered, then stepped to one side and kissed him on the cheek. 'This is your very own personal unveiling. Call me later. Love ya.'

With that, Freya swung her handbag over her shoulder

and strolled casually out of the room, leaving him standing there with his back against the table, staring up at the dust sheet.

Something close to nerves ran across his shoulders. This was so ridiculous! This was only paint on canvas. Why did he need a personal viewing?

He took a couple of calming breaths. Who was he kidding? This was paint brushed on to one of her father's canvases by the same clever fingers which had stroked his face and made him feel alive only a few weeks earlier. Until he blew it.

She had probably made him look like his grandfather. Complete with morning dress, sideburns and a handlebar moustache.

He deserved the worst.

Forcing the air from his lungs in one short blast, Scott tugged on the dust sheet and then gathered it up on to the floor.

Only then did he stand up, lift his chin and focus on the painting hanging on the wall in front of him.

What he saw took his breath away and Scott quickly pulled out a chair and collapsed down into it. Suddenly his legs were not quite as steady as they should be.

His portrait was astonishing.

Toni had painted him standing at the mullioned window of the office. His legs were braced and he was wearing cold weather gear and the fur-lined boots he had arrived in from Alaska. It was a side view and his left hand was resting on a wide decorated chart spread out on the mapping table in front of the window. Survey equipment and a dog sled harness were right there, on top of the map.

But that was not where the eye was drawn to. Scott's gaze was riveted by the expression on his face. He looked tanned, unshaven, with swept back hair but, with his chin up and his back straight, he looked the equal of any of the other Elstrom men captured on these walls. Strong, powerful and in control. Even down to the grey in his beard and stubble.

But this portrait was different.

Toni had seen something in him which nobody alive had ever truly noticed before.

Yearning. It was in the way his blond eyebrows came together in concentration as his eyes stared out of the window where gentle snowflakes blurred the hazy outline of the tall buildings opposite Elstrom. His mouth was curved into a small warm smile as though he was dreaming of somewhere else. She had painted his eyes a shade of blue that he knew from his reflection in the mirror every morning. The exact perfect shade.

Tears pricked the corners of Scott's eyes and he left them there.

Freya was right. This painting was intensely personal. Every single brush stroke screamed out to him that the hand that had painted his image cared about him so deeply and intensely that it was impossible to conceal.

It was a love letter in the shape of a painting.

Toni Baldoni was in love with him.

A bubble of happiness popped up from deep in his chest and he scrubbed his chin a couple of times. Men like him rarely got second chances and he had never imagined that it could happen twice.

Damn Toni for showing him how wrong he had been.

No way was he going to lose his chance of love again!

Leaping to his feet, Scott saluted the strong and intelligent-looking man in the painting before whirling around and striding to the door. 'Wish me luck. I have ten minutes to work out how to tell Toni what I feel. *And it had better be good!*'

* * *

'Oh, rollers,' Toni grunted through gritted teeth as a great splodge of white emulsion paint dropped off the end of her paint tray and on to the leg of her painting overalls. She didn't mind the paint; she was used to that. It was the wet patch she was not too keen on.

No time to get changed. She was determined to finish the studio walls today and that was precisely what she was going to do! It was the third coat and the last. From now on, the studio walls were going to reflect back every bit of the natural light she needed if she had any chance of working the way she wanted.

For the past three weeks Toni had filled her days and sometimes her nights with the perfect challenge. Transforming the Baldoni studio into a space which she could use for new clients and new portraits. She didn't need a photographic studio on the high street. Not any longer.

The first things to go were the cracked paint trays and old chewed paintbrushes which she knew that she would never use. She had broken up the old wooden cracked picture frames and battered shelving and used them as firewood. That little splash of linseed oil really helped warm the old stone walls. Papers went for recycling. Same with the dried-up paints and oil cans.

It was as though working on Scott's portrait had unleashed a cleaning demon which had been waiting inside to get out.

The portraits that her father had hung on the terracotta-coloured walls were the last things to be taken down. His hoarding of every receipt and invoice had actually come in useful for once and in three cases the client who had sat in this very studio so many years ago had been delighted to pop in and buy a copy of their portrait from the artist's family and at very good rates.

The nice thing was, the moment they'd taken a look at Scott's painting on the easel, they had been so delighted that they'd wondered if she might be available to paint their granddaughter or son who had just received a wonderful promotion at work.

Three new commissions in three weeks.

She would never have thought it possible.

Scott Elstrom had a lot to answer for, in more ways than one! No matter how many late nights she worked or how physically exhausted she was at the end of the day, Scott still filled her thoughts with dreams of what could have been and what had been lost.

It only took one glance at his portrait to take her instantly right back to Elstrom Mapping and the man who owned it.

It was gone now. Freya had collected it yesterday. All boxed up and packed away.

So why did Scott's face still flood her mind even now, halfway up a ladder with her arms stretching up to cover the walls with white paint?

Stepping down from the ladder for a moment to check for dark patches, Toni was suddenly aware that there was a cold draught from the kitchen but she was sure that she had closed the back door.

Wiping her hands, she stepped into the kitchen and was suddenly aware that there was someone standing in front of her.

It was Scott.

In the flesh.

He was here. Standing in front of her. All tall and gorgeous and clean and handsome and so attractive she could happily have dived into those blue eyes and warm arms and not come up for air.

The masculine strength and power positively beamed

out from every pore and grabbed her. It was in the way that he held his body, the way his head turned to face her and the way he looked at her as though she was the most fascinating woman he had ever met, and oh, yes, the laser focus of those intelligent blue eyes had a lot to do with it as well.

He was so close that she could touch him if she wanted to. She could practically feel the softness of his breath on her skin as he gazed intently into her eyes. The background noise of the radio she always played at full volume when she worked seemed to fade away until all of her senses were totally focused on this man who had captivated her.

She couldn't move.

She did not want to move.

There was an awkward gap and just then her resolve gave way and she felt that she simply had to say something—*anything*—to fill the silence. 'What are you doing here, Scott? What do you want from me?'

Her words blurted out in a much stronger voice than she had intended, and she instantly warmed them with a small shoulder shrug. 'I thought that you were travelling?'

Scott straightened his back and lifted his chin. 'What am I doing here? Well, I thought that was fairly obvious. I'm here to thank you for the portrait.'

Freya!

'Do you think it is a good likeness?' Toni asked as casually as she could.

'Perfect. It's me. All of me. Outside and inside too. I don't know how you did that with paint but you did. Clever girl.'

'It's in the blood. But I'm pleased that you like it. That means a lot.'

He tilted his head slightly to one side and gave her a lopsided grin which made him look about twelve years old.

And her poor lonely heart melted all over again.

She smiled back, her defences weakened by the wonderful charm and warmth of this man she cared about so very much, who was standing so very close and yet seemed beyond reach.

'What have you been doing with yourself these past weeks?' Scott whispered. 'Travelling the world with that camera of yours?'

'Actually, I've been working on my own projects, right here.' She waved her right hand in the air and looked up at the white-painted ceiling. 'I thought that I might stay in one place for a while.' Her voice quivered a little. 'In fact, I decided to take a year's leave from the media company and focus on painting for a while. See where it takes me.'

Scott glanced quickly over her shoulder before turning his gaze back to her face. 'You've worked wonders. It looks amazing.'

His fingers traced a line along her chin from ear to throat. 'My portrait is stunning. You should be very proud of your talents, Toni. I believe you have it in you to achieve amazing things with your work. Photographs, painting. It's all part of your creative genius. You're destined for wonderful things, my girl.'

His girl?

'Oh, Scott, I've been such an idiot,' she whispered.

His reply was to cup Toni's head between his hands, his long fingers so gentle and tender and loving that her heart melted even more.

'You were right, Scott. I did need to paint your portrait. And it wasn't just for the cash, although it has been very useful. It was more than that. A lot more.'

Her head dropped forward on to his chest so that when she spoke her words were swallowed up in the warmth of his fleece shirt.

His reply was a low sigh of contentment as he wrapped his arms tighter around her back and drew her even closer so that she was totally encased in his loving embrace.

'Ah. She finally admits that I am a genius in all things. Happy days.'

'You don't get everything right. You thought that I couldn't understand what it was like to see the Elstrom heritage slip away from you. But you are so wrong about that.'

Words and feelings whirled around inside her head and her heart so fast that she thought she might pass out if it wasn't for Scott's strong arms holding her upright.

But how could she explain without giving away a secret that she had sworn to her parents that she would never tell anyone unless she had to?

Toni closed her eyes and listened to the sound of Scott's heartbeat. It was strong and clear and it beat for her and only her. She was certain of that now.

It was so hard to step back from Scott but she could still feel his arms around her as she whispered, 'I need to show you something. Okay?'

Sliding away, she took hold of Scott's hand and with one quick smile she led him into the bedroom and gestured for him to sit on the bed.

'If this is a lingerie display I may have to call Freya and tell her that I'm missing dinner.'

With a quick chuckle, Toni shook her head. 'Sorry to disappoint you, but this is more of an art display.'

Toni knelt down next to her bed and tugged an old battered leather suitcase out from underneath. Taking a long juddery breath, Toni slowly pressed the metal sliders away and felt the lid of the suitcase spring up as the pressure was released.

Suddenly exhausted, Toni sat on the floor next to the

suitcase with her back pressed against the bed and her legs outstretched in front of her.

Slowly and with shaking hands, she lifted the suitcase lid and sat for a few moments in silence. Staring back at her was the sweet smiling face of the nine-year-old Amy. It was the last portrait that she had ever painted and signed under her own name. Lifting up the thin wooden light canvas, Toni smiled and stroked the edges as a freckle-faced happy girl with long hair and a turned-up nose and missing teeth grinned back at her.

When she finally found the words Toni was speaking more towards the picture than to Scott but she knew that he was listening.

'Every brush stroke of this painting was a delight. Our annual holiday had been in Cornwall for a couple of weeks the summer after I turned seventeen and we had all gone down to the beach for the afternoon. That was a rare event in itself. My father hated the sun and would much rather have stayed inside working on a commission he had to deliver the following week. It had been going too slowly and he couldn't seem to concentrate on the work so Mother had suggested that he take the afternoon off.'

Toni smiled to herself. 'It turned out to be a wonderful day of happy relaxed laughter and fun and sheer pleasure. Not too hot. Not too windy. Perfect blue skies and golden sandy beach. It was only natural that I should take some photographs of Amy and my parents. I had never intended them to become sketches or paintings. But somehow the moment I lifted the camera and pointed it towards Amy everything changed. I called out her name…Amy turned towards me.'

Toni flicked both hands in the air. 'And bam. Just like that, I knew that the photograph would be wonderful. Not just good. But special and amazing. And that feeling was so astonishing and overwhelming that I started to cry.'

'Cry? Why were you crying? Didn't that make you happy?'

'Yes. Amazingly, wonderfully happy. But it was sad at the same time. All my life I had been focusing and training on one thing—to be a painter and true artist like my parents. And in that moment, looking down that camera lens, I realized that it was all for nothing. Because I had never once felt that way with anything that I had painted. Not once. I could paint professionally any day of the week. And that's not being immodest. It was the truth. But taking that photograph changed everything.'

She glanced over her shoulder at Scott and smiled through the tears that were streaming down her face. 'Until then I was Antonia Baldoni, little daughter of Aldo and Emily Baldoni. Painters. Artists. But that moment made me realize that I could take everything I had learnt and apply it to creating portraits and paintings with more than canvas and paint. I had found my passion. Just like you found yours.

'I was so excited that I was jumping up and down and laughing and crying at the same time and generally making my parents fearful that something terrible had happened. I couldn't wait to tell them. I thought that they would be so excited that I had found the artist in me.'

'Oh, Toni. I know where this is going. My poor girl.'

Her head dropped. 'It came as a bit of a shock to realize that everything I believed about being part of a family of artists until that second was completely wrong. They were not excited for me at all. In fact they were horrified. Speechless with shock and horror. They felt it was a betrayal of my legacy. And then there was my dad's work…'

Her hands got busy lining up the edges of sheets of her

sketches and notebooks inside the suitcase. She focused on the gold-edged papers so that when Scott shuffled closer she could pretend that a collection of ragged teenage work was far more interesting than the man whose trouser leg was only inches away from her shoulder.

'What about your dad's work?'

She pulled out a sketchbook and started casually flicking through it, not ready to look into his face.

Her fingers paused at one particular drawing and she ran the pad of her forefinger down the edge of the smooth paper she liked to work on.

'Have you ever heard of the studio system? No? The old masters used to train young artists as a way of making some extra income. They all did it. The more famous you were, the more parents were prepared to pay to have their children study with you and work in the studio.'

She lifted her chin and gestured towards the next room where the art supplies were kept. 'I remember a time when there were always three or four art students from the local college hanging around, making tea and preparing canvases and now and again my dad would let them make sketches on a sitting with a client. So he could critique their work. Show them how to develop the idea into a painting. Maybe even work on a background for one of his portraits. If they were very good.'

Tears pricked the corners of her eyes and she wiped them away with the back of her knuckle.

'Fame is a fickle thing, Scott. One day everyone loves your work and the next? You're history and nobody wants to hire you because the exciting new style is all the fashion and who needs their portrait painted? That's why cameras were invented.'

She felt his body lift from the bed as the hard springs

squeaked in protest and suddenly Scott was sitting on the floor next to her, his back so tall against the divan.

His left hand slid sideways and as she glanced down all the weight and strength that Scott possessed seemed to flow through those fingers as they meshed with hers.

'He resented you for leaving him.'

She nodded. 'I was his last apprentice. The student who was going to make her mark in the world and show the art establishment just how powerful fine painting could be. I was going to lead the next generation of Baldoni portrait painters proudly forward.'

Her head dropped and she picked up Amy's portrait with her left hand. 'I painted this when I was seventeen. By then I was working every night after school in the studio and doing nearly all of my dad's canvases. My weekends and every day of the school holidays were spent in that studio.'

She shook her head and blew out hard. 'I was his apprentice so it made sense for me to be there for the sittings so that I could paint the backgrounds and clothing on his portraits. He always worked on the fine detail. Afterwards. But as I got older and he got more disillusioned and depressed about how much photography was taking over, I found that he was leaving me to work on the few commissions that were coming in.'

Scott breathed in through his nose. 'You were doing the work. Weren't you? You were painting those amazing portraits and he was passing them off as his work. Oh, Toni.'

His fingers squeezed hers for one last time then slid away and moved around her waist so that he could draw her to him.

'It didn't feel like that,' she replied and rested her head on his shoulder. 'I loved the work and wanted to learn everything I could. This was my real education. School work

was not important in the least. Not like it was to Amy.'
She chuckled deep in her throat. 'It was a bit of a shock
finding out that we had a scientist in the family. Her idea
of drawing was a flow chart and computer spreadsheets.'
Then she swallowed down a lump of guilt and regret.
'But of course that put even more pressure on me to fly
the flag for the family and carry on my legacy. So when I
announced that I was moving to photography…it hit them
hard. So very hard.'

'What did you do?'

'What could I do? For a while they did everything they
could to try and make me change my mind. That I was
making a huge mistake and throwing away my career and
that people would start commissioning portraits again. I
just had to carry on and learn my craft and be patient and
it would all work out.'

She glanced quickly over one shoulder towards Scott,
who was breathing hard and fast on to the top of her head.

'Ever wondered what proud artists do when they don't
have any work coming in? They borrow on the only real
asset they have left. This house must have been mortgaged
and re-mortgaged four times. A commission comes in,
they pay some of the loan off, then the money runs out
and they borrow again and…I learnt the hard way that
putting your home at risk to pay the gas bill is a stress-
ful way to live.'

'Your family? Other relatives? Couldn't they help out?'

'Oh, no. My father was a stubborn man and he would
never have contacted his Italian side of the family. A Baldoni would never sink so low. So he dropped his prices
and offered to paint children and local people. Said that it
was his way of being generous.'

She chuckled and sniffed. 'They needed me to work
and work hard to create commercial pictures they could

sell quickly to bring in some income. And that is what I did. Nights and weekends. There are children around here with a genuine Baldoni portrait on their walls!'

'Did you sign them?'

'Of course I did. *A. Baldoni*. They didn't know that it was an Antonia Baldoni and not an Aldo Baldoni work they were buying—why should they? Everyone called me Toni. The local mayor would have been very upset if he knew. I think he is still bragging about that painting to every visitor to his official office.'

She wiped away one tear and whispered, 'Very upset. Seeing it was the last one that my father claimed to have painted before he died. It's his claim to fame.'

'How did it happen?'

'A train crash in Italy. It was June. They had been invited to a family reunion and scraped together the rail fare with some sort of excuse about them hating flying. It was…brutal to lose them both at the same time. Horrible, really. I was just about to leave school…'

Her eyebrows squeezed together tight. 'And that was the end of my hopes and dreams. How could I go waltzing off to my dream course in New York to study photography when I had a sister to take care of? So I stayed in London and went to college when Amy was at school and did the best that I could with grants and loans. And we worked it out. The two of us together. I got a job with a media company which meant that I could stay in London as much as possible. It was fine. Until I got a call from a certain Freya Elstrom.'

'My sister is a well-known troublemaker.'

Toni nodded. 'I thought that I was ready to put all of the painting behind me. Amy and I spent Christmas sorting through so much rubbish and clutter so I could get the house ready to decorate and rent out. The only room I didn't touch was the studio.'

She flashed Scott a half smile. 'The plan was to donate the unused canvases and equipment to the local school. Amy's art teacher would have taken everything if she had the chance. But somehow I couldn't bring myself to do it. You were my excuse.'

'I like to be useful.' Scott smiled back.

'Amy is no fool. She saw through my little pretence straight away so I convinced her that this was going to be my last portrait. Ever. One more painting and I would be done. End of an era. But then I met you. And my world has never been the same since.'

Her hand swept out, her eyes hot and fierce, and she tapped the heel of her hand against the hard planes of his chest. 'I blame you for everything, Scott Elstrom. All of it. I was happy to leave painting behind until you came along. My life was all planned out. Neat and tidy. Until you walked into my birthday party and blew me away. I have done things this month that I never imagined possible.'

She pressed the fingers of both hands hard against her forehead. 'Because do you know what I have done? Exactly the same thing as my dad did. I have borrowed money on my house to invest in Elstrom. And it is all your fault!'

CHAPTER THIRTEEN

Scott stared at Toni for a few seconds before he finally made the connections.

'It was you! You bought the shares from Travis.'

He looked to one side for a second as though his mind was trying to process what she had done. But when his gaze locked on to her face it was full of warmth and utter astonishment.

'You put your home on the line. For me! That is the most amazingly generous thing that anyone has ever done for me. And I don't even know where to start to thank you. Those shares will give me...'

'Your freedom,' Toni interrupted. 'I wanted you to be free of the past, Scott. You are an Elstrom. Your destiny is to be travelling the world exploring trade routes to some distant shore, not sorting through old pamphlets. You can do what you want now, Scott. Stay. Go. Be with who you want, where you want. All I am doing is returning the favour. There is no need to thank me.'

'I cannot believe that you did that for me.'

Gulping down her fears about how this proud man might react to her working behind the scenes without his permission, Toni looked up into Scott's face and what she saw there wiped away any doubts.

'You know why I did it. I love you, Scott Elstrom, and a girl will do anything for the man she...'

Toni never got to finish her sentence because her lips were far too busy being crushed by Scott's hot mouth.

She reached up and stroked his cheek, her eyes brimming with tears.

'I haven't stopped thinking about what you said. And you were right. This is the biggest risk of my life, your life, anyone's life.'

She breathed in, her heart thudding so loudly that she suspected he must have heard it. 'I know now that I will always love you, Scott Elstrom, and it doesn't matter where you are in the world. And if that means that I have to let you go, to be free to do your work—' she licked her lips '—then that is the way it has to be. I want to be with you. Love you. If you still want me to wait for you?'

Scott stood very still, staring at her, and she bit her lower lip in fear. She might have just made the biggest mistake of her life but this was the way it had to be and she was prepared to be turned down.

'I could be away for six or seven months at a time, you know,' he told her gently, his voice low, sensual and intimate.

'Probably longer. But that is the way it has to be. I didn't fall in love with an office clerk; I fell in love with you. I have to let you go and do what you have to do, wherever that is, so that you can be true to who you are. Because, just maybe, we can still get back together one day. I love you, Scott, and that is not going to change whether you're in Alaska or the Himalayas or down the road.'

Scott didn't answer, but she slid her fingers from his so that he could caress her face, his gaze scanning from her grubby nose to her roughly tied back out-of-control hair.

'You love me, but you are willing to let me go and do this work which means so much to me? Is that right?'

She nodded, too afraid to trust her voice. 'As long as you are somewhere in this world loving me, then I shall be fine. My heart will be your beacon home to my love. You don't even need a map. You'll always know where to find me. Apparently, there are people who still want their portrait painted so I'm staying put after all. Who knew?'

'Then there's only one answer to your question. Looking back these past few weeks, I can see just how low Alexa and Travis took me. I couldn't believe that the woman I loved was capable of doing that to me. To us. I was in love with my wife, Toni, but she didn't love me. That's hard to come back from. So my answer is no. I don't want you to wait for me.'

Her heart caught in her throat but he pressed one finger on her lips and smiled, breaking the terror. 'You see, I'm not as brave as you are. As soon as I saw that portrait this morning, I knew that I couldn't leave the woman I have fallen in love with without trying to come up with some options.'

He grinned at her and slid forward so that both of his hands were cupped around her face as tears pricked her eyes. 'I love you way too much to let you go. I need you, Toni. I need you so much. Nothing else comes close. What would you say if I told you that Freya and I have come up with a plan which will make it possible for me to work out of London for the summer months?'

She shuddered out a chuckle of delight and relief. 'I would say, *Yes, please*, and then I would ask how you have managed it.'

'Freya has been fielding enquiries from location scouts from TV and movie companies all around the world. Your idea worked, Toni. It worked brilliantly. We already have bookings for most of the year and part of the next. Elstrom Mapping is safe for the next five years and I have a job as a location actor any time I want one.'

Scott took both of her hands in his, his voice suddenly full of life and excitement and enthusiasm. 'There was one extra condition before I signed my new contract with the survey company in Alaska. I told them that I would only do it if I could bring my girlfriend with me to Anchorage in October so that she could see the Northern Lights for herself. After all, she is a professional artist and one of the Baldoni family. She deserves first class travel all of the way.'

'Your girlfriend—' She breathed out the words, tears pricking her wide eyes, scarcely daring to believe what he was saying.

'You have given me the greatest compliment a man could wish for. You offered me your love and your confidence and the freedom to live my life. I never imagined I would find a woman who could love me as much as I loved her. I am not going anywhere without you and I mean that.'

Scott's voice faltered as he pressed his forehead to her flushed brow.

'I have travelled all over the world, Toni. I might have kidded myself that it was for work, but the truth is harder to accept. I needed to prove to myself that I was not a complete failure and that I hadn't let my family down when I walked away from the firm.'

'Oh, Scott. It was never your fault. Just as it wasn't mine. I know that now. You *have* made a difference because the man I love has given his life to his family. And I know how many sacrifices that takes.' She was stroking the hair back from his forehead now, her fingertips moving through the short curls as she stared into the depths of those stunning eyes.

'I have never felt such an overwhelming sense of belonging than in those few days I spent with you. I didn't even realize that I was looking for it. Your heart is my beacon home. Wherever you are is where I want to be. Bring me home, Toni. Bring me home.'

He knelt in front of her as he whispered in a husky intimate voice that she had only heard before in her dreams, 'I love you and want you to be part of my life, Toni. If you'll have me?'

Toni looked into a face so full of love that her heart broke.

'Oh, my sweet darling. How can you ask that? You have to know that I love you. I will love you for the rest of my life. You are the centre of my world.'

She choked with emotion as Scott stood, swung her up into the air, her arms linked behind his head, whirling her around and around until her feet connected with the chair.

In an instant Scott lowered her to the floor, grabbed her hand and threw her over his right shoulder as though she weighed nothing.

He was almost in the middle of the street before she managed to wriggle free and, holding hands, they pulled and twirled each other around and around, heads back, laughing and shouting in pleasure, thick snowflakes falling around them, before collapsing into each other's arms, their heads pressed together into a passionate kiss.

It was picture perfect.

* * * * *

UNFINISHED BUSINESS

CAT SCHIELD

For my parents.
Your love and support have
helped me follow my dreams.

One

"You." The word came out as an unfriendly accusation.

"Hello, Max."

Rachel Lansing had been bracing herself for this meeting all day, and now that it had arrived, it was so much worse than she'd imagined. Her heart stopped as the gunmetal gray of Max Case's gaze slammed into her with all the delicacy of a sledgehammer.

She dug her fingernails into her palm as his broad shoulders loomed closer, blocking her view of the tastefully decorated lobby with its soothing navy-and-olive walls and stunning original art.

Was it her imagination or did Max seem bigger, more commanding than the creative lover that haunted her memories? Or maybe his presence overwhelmed her because in a charcoal business suit and silver tie, he was less approachable than the naked fantasy man that frequented her dreams.

Only the public nature of this reunion enabled her to

subdue the flight impulse in her muscles. She rose from the comfortable couch in the reception area at a deliberate, unhurried pace. Keeping her body relaxed and her expression professional required a Herculean effort while her pulse jittered and her knees shook.

Pull yourself together. He won't appreciate you melting into a puddle at his feet.

"Thank you for seeing me." She stuck out her hand in a bid to restore her professional standing and wasn't disappointed when Max ignored it. Her sweaty palm would betray her nerves to him.

When he remained mute, Rachel plowed into the tense silence. "How great that Andrea had her baby. And two weeks early. Sabrina told me she had a boy. I brought her this." She raised her left hand to show him the pink and blue bag dangling from her fingers. She'd bought the gift for his assistant weeks ago and was disappointed she wouldn't get to see Andrea's expression when she opened it.

"What are you doing here?"

"I was supposed to meet with Andrea."

"You're with the employment agency?"

She whipped out a business card and extended it across the three feet that separated them. "I own it." She made no attempt to disguise her pride at what she'd accomplished.

He rubbed his thumb over the lettering on the business card before glancing down. "Rachel…Lansing?"

"My maiden name." She wasn't sure why she felt compelled to share this tidbit with him. It wasn't going to change how he felt about her now, was it?

"You're divorced?"

She nodded. "Four years."

"And now you run an employment agency here in Houston?"

She'd come a long way from the girl who was barely able

to support herself and her sister on the tips she made waitressing in a beach restaurant in Gulf Shores, Alabama. And yet, how far had she come when no matter how well her business did, she never felt financially secure?

"I like the freedom of running my own business," she said, pushing aside the worry that drove her day and night. "It's small, but growing."

And it would grow faster once she moved into larger offices and hired more staff. She had the space all picked out. A prime location that wouldn't have lasted on the market more than a few days. She'd signed the lease yesterday, gambling that the commission she'd get from placing a temporary assistant with Case Consolidated Holdings would give her the final amount she needed to move. Maybe then she could stop living day to day and start planning for the future. However, now that she'd run into Max, that fee seemed in jeopardy, and just to be safe, she'd better back out of the lease.

If only Devon had been able to come here in her stead. A skilled employment specialist, he was her right hand. Unfortunately, his mother had gone to the hospital yesterday with severe abdominal pain and had been rushed into surgery to remove her gall bladder. Rachel had told Devon to stay with his mother as long as she needed him. For Rachel, family always came first.

"How many assistants have you placed here?" Max's piercing stare didn't waver from her face as he slid her business card into his breast pocket. The effect of so much icy heat coming to bear on her was starting to unravel her composure.

"Five." She dropped her hand into her jacket pocket to keep from plucking at her collar, lapel or buttons and betraying her disquiet. "Missy was the first. Sebastian's assistant."

"That was your doing?"

Rachel blinked at the soft menace in his voice. Did Max have something against Missy? She'd been with Case Consolidated Holdings for four years and had worked out great. In fact, it was that placement that had jump-started her business.

"I heard she recently got promoted to communications director." And married Max's brother, Sebastian. Surely that proved how good Rachel was at her job.

"That means you've been in Houston four years?" The question rumbled out of Max like a guard-dog growl.

Anxiety spiked. "About that."

"Why here?"

When she'd left him in the Alabama beach town, he'd never wanted to see her again. Was he wondering if it was fate or determined stalking on her part that she'd shown up at Case Consolidated Holdings?

"I moved here because of my sister. She went to the University of Houston and has friends here. It made sense for us to settle in Houston after she graduated."

Inferring that Rachel hadn't had friends where she'd lived before. Curiosity fired in Max's eyes. The intensity of it seared her nerve endings. Five years had passed since she'd last seen him and her physical response to his proximity hadn't dimmed one bit.

"I have three clients in this building," she told him, her tone firming as she reclaimed her confidence. She'd been dealing with executives for over ten years and knew exactly how to handle them. "The fact that I've placed five assistants here and we've never run across each other should tell you that my interest in your company is purely professional."

He surveyed her like a cop in search of the truth. "Let's talk."

"I thought that's what we were doing." She bit the inside of her lip as the smart-ass remark popped out.

Once upon a time he'd liked her cheeky banter. She doubted he'd say the same thing today. Five years was a long time to stay mad at someone, but if anyone could manage, it would be Max Case.

"In my office."

Pivoting on his heel, he strode away from her down the hallway that led into the bowels of Case Consolidated Holdings. He didn't look back to see if she was following. He expected obedience. He'd always been bossy that way. Telling her where to put her hands, how to move her hips, the areas of his body that needed her attention.

Her skin flushed. Desire found a warm and welcoming home inside her. She couldn't move. What was she doing? Her memories of those four days with Max belonged in the tomb with all her girlish hopes and dreams. Her moratorium on men and sex remained in full force. Indulging in lusty thoughts of Max was the height of stupidity if she hoped to cultivate a professional relationship with him.

Max disappeared around a corner. This was her chance to run. She should make some excuse. Send Devon to do the interview tomorrow.

No. Rachel squared her shoulders. She could do this. She had to do this. Her future required this placement fee.

Five years ago, she'd learned a hard lesson about running from her problems. These days, she faced all difficulties head-on. Lansing Employment Agency needed this commission. She would do a fabulous job for Max, collect her money and treat herself to a bottle of champagne and a long bubble bath the day the agency moved into its bigger, better office. It all started with this meeting.

Rachel forced her feet to move. Step by step she gathered courage. For four years she'd been scraping and clawing her way upward. Convincing Max that Lansing was the agency for him was just one more hurdle, and by the time she reached the enormous office bearing Max's name, she had her chin set at a determined angle and her eyes focused on the prize.

"Did you get lost?" he asked as she crossed the threshold.

A long time ago.

"I stopped at Sabrina's desk and asked her to send the baby gift to Andrea."

Rachel glanced around Max's office, curious about the businessman. During their four days together, she'd learned about his family and his love of fast cars, but he'd refused to talk about work. In fact, until she'd met Sebastian four years ago, and noticed the family resemblance, she didn't know he was Max Case of Case Consolidated Holdings.

The walls bore photos of Max leaning against a series of racecars, helmet beneath his arm, a confident grin on his face. Her heart jumped in appreciation of how handsome he looked in his one-piece navy-and-gray racing suit, lean hips and broad shoulders emphasized by the stylish cut. A bookshelf held a few trophies, and books on muscle cars.

"You cut your hair." Max shut the door, blocking her escape.

She searched his expression, but he'd shut all emotion behind an impassive mask. His eyes were the blank stone walls of a fortress. Nevertheless, his personal comment aroused a tickle of awareness.

"Never liked it long." Her ex-husband had, however.

A softening of his lips looked suspiciously like the beginnings of a smile. Did he recognize her attempt to camouflage herself? Shapeless gray pantsuit, short hair, no jewelry of any kind, a sensible watch, flat shoes, minimal makeup. Dull as dirt to look at, but confident and authoritative about her business. She'd never been any man's fantasy. Too tall for most boys. Too flat-chested and skinny for the rest, the best she'd been able to hope for from her male classmates in high school was best friend or buddy. She'd grown up playing soccer, basketball and baseball with the guys.

Which is why it continued to blow her mind that a man

like Maxwell Case, who could have any woman he wanted, had wanted her once upon a time.

An enormous cherry desk dominated a position in front of the windows. The piece seemed too clunky for Max. Rachel pictured him behind an aerodynamic glass and chrome desk loaded down with the latest computer gadgets.

Instead of leading the way toward his desk, Max settled on the couch that occupied one wall of his office. With a flick of his hand, he indicated a flanking chair. Disliking the informality of the setting, Rachel perched on the very edge of the seat. Her briefcase on her lap acted as both a shield and a reminder that this was a business meeting.

"I need an executive assistant here first thing tomorrow."

Rachel hadn't been prepared for Andrea to have her baby two weeks early. She had no one available that was skilled enough to fill in starting in the morning. "I have the perfect person for you, but she can't start until Monday."

"That won't do."

With her commission slipping away, panic crept into her voice. "It's only two days. Surely you can make it without an assistant until Monday."

"With Andrea gone today, I'm already behind. We're up to our necks in next year's budgets. I need someone who can get up to speed swiftly. Someone with world-class organizational skills." His focus sharpened on her. "Someone like you. You're exactly what I need."

Her gut clenched at the flare of something white hot in his eyes.

A matching blaze roared to life inside her. Five years ago, that similar fire had charred her self-protective instincts and reduced her sensible nature to ash. She'd flung herself head-long into his arms without considering the repercussions.

The last time she'd lost herself that way, he'd ended up hating her. Meeting his gaze, she realized that his anger hadn't been blunted by the passing years. Time hadn't healed. It had honed his resentment into a razor-sharp tool for revenge.

Rachel braced herself against the earthquake of panic that threatened her peaceful little world and set her jaw. "You can't have me."

Her declaration hung in the air.

But he could have her...

As his assistant.

In any of the dozens of ways he'd had her before.

His choice. Not hers.

Energy zipped between them, fascinating and unsettling. The scent of her perfume aroused memories. Reminded him how sharp and sweet the desire was between them.

"Are you really ready to risk disappointing a client?"

"No." A rosy flush dusted her high cheekbones. Had she picked up on his thoughts? "But I can't abandon my business to be your assistant."

"Hire someone to fill in for you." He bared his teeth in an unfriendly grin. "Even you can see the irony in that."

For the last few minutes, cracks had been developing in her professionalism. "You're being unreasonable."

"Of course I am. I'll call someone else." The telltale widening of her eyes was gone so fast he nearly missed it. This is where he challenged her reputation for providing excellent customer service to test how badly she wanted his business. "I'm sure another agency would have what I need."

"Lansing Employment has what you need," she countered, the words muddy because she spoke through clenched teeth.

He held silent while she tried to stare him down. Every instinct told him to send her on her way as he would any other supplier who couldn't provide him with exactly what he wanted.

But they had unfinished business. At some point in the last five minutes he'd decided he needed closure. Four days with her hadn't been enough time for the passion to burn out. Much to his dismay, he still wanted her. But for how long was anyone's guess. From past experience he knew his interest rarely lasted more than two months.

And when he grew tired of her, he would end things on his terms. On his schedule.

"Fine." She glared at him. "I'll fill in for two days."

"Wonderful."

She stood, ready to stalk out of the office, but something held her in place. Her eyes were troubled as they settled on him. "Why are you doing this?"

"Doing what?"

"Demanding that I act as your assistant until I can find a replacement."

"You're here. It's expedient."

His current workload was crushing him. His managers had finalized their forecasts and forwarded next year's budget numbers a week ago. With the economy slow to recover, controlling spending and increasing sales was more important than ever. Case Consolidated Holdings owned over a dozen companies, each one with very different markets and operations. It was an organizational challenge to collect and analyze data from the various sources given that each entity operated in a completely unique environment with it's own set of parameters and strategic plans.

Andrea knew the businesses as well as he did. Losing her now threw off his entire schedule.

"Are you sure that's all it is?" Rachel demanded.

Max stopped worrying about deadlines and reminded himself that his desperate staffing situation was only half the reason he'd insisted Rachel fill in for a few days. "What else could it be?"

"Payback for how things ended between us?"

"It's business." That she was suspicious of his motives added spice to the game.

"So, you're not still angry?" she persisted.

Yes. He was still angry.

"After five years?" He shook his head.

"Are you sure?"

"Are you challenging whether or not I know my own mind?"

His irritation had little effect on her. "Five years ago, you made it very clear you never wanted to see me again."

"That's because you never told me you were married." He kept his tone smooth, but it wasn't enough to mask his dangerous mood. "Despite my telling you how I felt about infidelity. How it nearly destroyed my parents' marriage. You involved me in an extramarital affair without my knowledge."

"I'd left my husband."

He breathed deep to ease the sudden ache in his chest. "Yet when he showed up, you went back to him fast enough."

"Things were complicated."

"I didn't see complications. I saw lies."

"I was going through some tough times. Meeting you let me forget my troubles for a while."

"You used me."

She tipped her head and regarded him through her long lashes. "We used each other."

Max's gaze roamed over her. She wasn't the most beautiful woman he'd ever met. Her nose was too narrow. Her chin a bit too sharp. She hid her broad forehead with bangs. Boyishly slim, her body lacked the feminine curves he usually appreciated in a woman. But there was something lush about the fullness of her lips. And he'd adored nibbling his way down her long, graceful neck.

He wasn't surprised to be struck by a blast of lust so intense, it hurt. From the first, the chemistry between them had been hot and all consuming. The instant he recognized her in the lobby, he knew that hadn't changed.

For a second, doubts crept in. Would spending time with her open old wounds? The last time they'd parted, he'd been out of sorts for months. Of course, he'd been in a different place then. Full of optimism about love and marriage despite the painful lessons about infidelity he'd learned from his father's actions.

Thanks to Rachel, his heart was no longer open for business.

"What time should I be here tomorrow morning?"

"Eight."

She headed for the door and he let his gaze slide over her utilitarian gray suit. One word kept rolling over and over in his mind. Divorced.

Fair game.

She hesitated in the doorway, her back to him, face in profile. Her quiet, determined voice floated toward him over her shoulder. "Two days. No more."

Without a backward glance, she vanished from view. Sexy as hell. She'd always had an aura of the untouchable about her. As if no matter how many times he slid inside her, or how tight he wrapped her in his arms, she would never truly be his.

For a man accustomed to having any woman he wanted, that elusive quality intrigued him the way nothing else would have. He couldn't get enough of her. They'd been together for four days. He'd been insatiable. But no matter how much pleasure he gave her, no matter how many times she came apart in his arms, not once did he come close to capturing her soul.

It wasn't until she left him and went back to her husband that he'd understood why.

Her soul wasn't hers to give. It belonged to the man she'd pledged her life and love to.

Rage catapulted Max from his chair. He crossed to his door and slammed it shut, not caring what the office thought of his fit of temper. His hand shook as he braced it against the wall.

Damn her for showing up like this.

And damn the part of him that was delighted she had.

Two

Rachel hurried through the plate glass doors of Lansing Employment Agency and nodded to her receptionist as she passed. She didn't stop to chat as was her habit, but went straight to her office and collapsed into her chair. It wasn't until she'd deleted half her inbox that she realized she hadn't read any of the emails. Sagging forward, she rested her arms on the desk and her forehead on her arms. Reaction was setting in. She was frustratingly close to tears.

"That bad, huh?" a male voice asked from the hallway.

Rachel nodded without looking up. "It's worse than bad."

"Oh, you poor thing. Tell Devon all about it."

With a great effort, Rachel straightened and looked at the man who sat down across from her. In a stylish gray suit with lavender shirt and expensive purple tie, he dressed to be noticed. Only the dark circles beneath his eyes gave any hint of his sleepless night.

"How's your mother?"

"She's doing fine. My sister just arrived from Austin and is staying at the hospital with her." Devon leaned back in his chair and crossed one leg over the other. "How'd it go at Case Consolidated Holdings?"

"Worse than I'd hoped."

"Damn. They didn't hire us?"

"They hired us." Rachel's eyes burned dry and hot. As she blinked to restore moisture, it occurred to her that she'd cried a river of tears over Max five years ago. Maybe she'd used up her quota.

"Then what's the problem?"

"Max Case needs an assistant immediately."

"But we don't have anyone available."

Rachel grimaced. "That's why I'm filling in until we do."

"You?" The gap between Devon's front teeth flashed as a startled laugh escaped him.

No one knew what had happened between her and Max in Gulf Shores. She figured if she kept it to herself, no one could criticize her for running away from her farce of a marriage and jumping into bed with a virtual stranger, and those amazing four days could remain untarnished in her memory. But she'd been wrong to start something with Max before she'd legally ended her marriage. And she'd paid the price.

"I was the expedient choice." The word tasted bitter on her tongue. Why had it bothered her that she was merely a convenient business solution to Max? Had she really hoped he might still want her after she'd kept quiet about her marital status, and let him betray his vow never to get caught up in an affair?

Those days in Max's arms had been magical. She hadn't felt that safe since her father died. It was as if she and Max existed in a bubble of perfect happiness. Insulated from the world's harsh reality.

Heaven.

Until Brody showed up with his threats and dragged her back to Mississippi.

"I hope you told him no."

"Not exactly."

"Then what exactly?" Her second in command frowned as if just now grasping the situation.

"It's not like he left me any choice. I signed the lease for the new offices. We need this placement fee to move into them."

"You agreed?"

"He backed me against a wall." She leaned back in her chair, remembering too late that the ancient mechanism was broken. She threw her weight forward before the cursed thing tipped her ass over teakettle.

Devon oversaw her antics with troubled eyes. "I still don't understand why he wants you personally. There are a dozen agencies that he could call."

She hesitated. As much as she liked Devon, she wasn't comfortable talking about her past. Five years ago, she'd been a very different person. Explaining how she knew Max meant she had to own up to the mistakes she'd made. Mistakes that haunted her.

"Once upon a time we knew each other," she said.

"Knew…" Devon's focus sharpened. "As in business associates? Friends?" His eyes narrowed. "You dated?"

As much as she hated talking about her past screwups, she decided to put her cards on the table. She owed Devon the truth. He'd been with her since the beginning and had labored as hard as she had to grow the agency. In fact, she was planning on making him a partner when they moved into the new offices.

If they moved.

"Not dated, exactly." She played with her pen, spinning it in circles on her desk.

"You slept with him."

"Yes."

Rachel shifted her attention from the silver blur and caught Devon's stunned expression. He looked so thunderstruck she was torn between laughter and outrage.

"Don't look so surprised. I wasn't always the uptight businesswoman I am now. There was a time when I was young and romantic." And foolish.

"When?"

"A long weekend five years ago."

Devon's lips twitched.

"What?" she demanded.

"It's just that Max is well-known for the volume of women he dates. I'm a little surprised he remembered you."

"He probably wouldn't have," she muttered. The truth hit closer to her insecurities than she wanted to admit. The thought had often crossed her mind that she'd had a pretty brief interlude with Max. Since moving to Houston, she'd learned a lot about the man who'd swept her off her feet in a big way. She'd often wondered how she'd feel if she ran into him and he looked right through her without recognition. "Except he was pretty angry with me at the time."

"Why?"

"Because I didn't tell him I was married."

Now Devon really goggled at her. "We've worked together four years and this is the first I've heard about that."

Rachel rubbed her right thumb across the ring finger of her left hand. Even after four years, she recalled the touch of the gold band against her skin and remembered how wrong she'd been to ignore her instincts. She wouldn't make that mistake again.

"It's part of my past that I'd prefer not to talk about." And in five more years, she'd be completely free. At least financially. She'd live with the emotional scars for the rest of her life.

"Not even if I tell you I'll expire from curiosity if you don't dish?"

"Not even," Rachel said with a chuckle. She loved Devon's flare for the dramatic. Having him around was good for her. Kept her from taking herself, or her problems, too seriously. She'd done that all too often in the past and turned molehills into mountains.

"Do you think Max is trying to start up with you again?"

From one unwelcome topic to another. "Hardly."

"I don't know." Devon shot her an odd look, half surprised, half crafty. "Demanding you act as his assistant, even for a couple days, seems a little odd for a businessman with Max's no-nonsense reputation."

Rachel exhaled. "Well, there's not much I can do at the moment. He's set on having me there." She grimaced. "Besides, you'll do great without me. Lansing Employment Agency wouldn't be anywhere near profitable without all your hard work."

"Yes, yes, I'm wonderful but the success has been all yours. I've just been along for the ride."

And what a ride it had been. When she'd first started the agency, she'd been waitressing on the weekends to make rent and put food on the table.

Today, providing things went right with Case Consolidated Holdings, they'd be moving into larger downtown Houston offices. That's why she was willing to do whatever Max wanted of her to stay on his good side.

"I just hope you know what you're doing," Devon said, getting to his feet.

"I know exactly what I'm doing." Her stomach gave a funny little flip as she said the words. Rachel shoved the sensation away. She was a professional. She would not allow her emotions to get all tangled up in Max again. The first time had left her with a battered heart. Letting it happen again might lead to serious breakage.

"You're a first-rate bastard, you know that?"

Max Case looked away from the photo on his computer screen and smirked at his best friend. "I've been called that before."

It was late Friday morning. He'd spent the last day and a half alternating between admiration for Rachel's keen business mind and annoyance that he couldn't stop imagining her writhing beneath him on his couch.

"I've been after Sikes to sell me that car for five years," Jason Sinclair grumbled, his gaze riveted on the image of Max standing beside a yellow convertible. "And you just swoop in and steal it out from under me?"

"I didn't swoop, and I didn't steal. I offered the guy a good price. He went for it."

"How much?"

Max shook his head. He wasn't about to tell Jason the truth. In fact, he wasn't exactly sure what had prompted him to offer the sum. He only knew that Bob Sikes had driven the rare muscle car off the lot in 1971 and wasn't about to let it go without some major convincing. The Cuda 426 Hemi convertible was one of only seven made. At the time, convertibles were too expensive, too heavy and too slow to interest the true racing enthusiasts. Thus, with fewer produced, they'd become extremely rare.

And now, Max owned one of the rarest of the rare.

"Are you ready to get your ass kicked in tomorrow's race?" He meant for the question to distract his friend.

"You sound awfully confident for a man who lost last weekend." Jason continued to frown over the loss of the Cuda. "A win that put me ahead of you in points."

"For now."

Max and Jason had been racing competitively since they were old enough to drive. They were evenly matched in determination, skill, and financing, so on any given weekend, the win could go either way.

For the last two years, Max had beaten Jason in points over the course of the season. Like the street racers of old, Jason and Max competed for cars. The guy with fewer points at the end of the season forfeited his ride. But Max knew coming in second bothered his best friend more than the forfeit of his racecar two years straight.

Jason adopted a confident pose. "If you think you're going to have the most points again this year, you're wrong."

Before Max could answer, Rachel appeared in his office doorway. Despite her severe navy pantsuit and plain white blouse, his pulse behaved as if she wore a provocative cocktail dress and a come-hither smile.

"Excuse me, Max. I didn't realize you had company."

He waved Rachel in. "Did you get those numbers I needed?"

She took one step into the room and stopped. "I updated the report." She glanced in Jason's direction. "I also scheduled an interview for you at two this afternoon and emailed you the candidate's resume. Maureen has a background in finance and business analysis. I think you'll find she's a perfect fit."

"We'll see."

Her lips thinned. "Yes, you will."

Amusement rippled through him as she tossed her head and exited his office. Did she have any idea that annoyance gave her stride a sexy swing?

"Hell."

Max noticed Jason was also staring after Rachel. "What?"

"That was Rachel Lansing. What is she doing here?"

"Working as my assistant."

"Have you lost your mind?"

Probably. But Jason didn't know about his affair with Rachel. No one did. Those four days had been too short and too intense. The end too painful for him to share. And after badmouthing his father's infidelity for years, how could he admit to family and friends that he'd had an affair with a married woman and not be viewed as a hypocrite?

"What are you talking about?"

"Lansing is a matchmaker."

"A what?" Max searched his best friend's serious expression for some sign that Jason was joking around.

"Lansing Employment Agency is a matchmaking service."

"You're kidding, right?" He was deeply concerned that his friend might not be.

Jason glared at him. "Don't look at me like that. You have no idea what you're dealing with."

Rubbing his eyes, Max sighed. "Right now I'm dealing with a lunatic." Confusion and amusement jockeyed for dominance. He'd never seen his best friend exhibit such over-the-top behavior.

"It's not funny."

A gust of laughter escaped him. "Sit in my chair for a minute, and I think you'll see it's really funny."

"My dad used Lansing last year." Jason's eyebrows arched. "He married his executive assistant six months later."

"Your dad was a widower for fifteen years. I'm a little surprised he didn't remarry a lot sooner. Besides, Claire is a knockout."

"You're missing the point. They're all knockouts."

"So," Max drawled. "It's a conspiracy?"

"Yes." The thirty-two-year-old CFO stopped looking wild-eyed and his attention settled laser-sharp on Max. Jason's chest lifted as he pulled in an enormous breath. "You think I'm crazy?"

"Certifiable."

"I know of five other guys that have hired their assistants from Lansing and ended up marrying them. I know two more guys that met their future wives at work. Wives that got their jobs thanks to the Lansing Employment Agency. Including your brother." Jason's lips thinned. "Still think I'm nuts?"

"How did you find all this out?"

Jason shrugged. "Do you really need to ask? After Dad started looking all gooey-eyed at Claire, I did a little research on the agency."

"What did you find?"

"A spotless reputation. And one hell of a track record."

"For what?"

"For turning executive assistants into wives."

"Don't you think that eight marriages out of hundreds of placements is a little insignificant?"

"It's more worrisome when you take into consideration the ratio of single executives with single assistants to married executives with married assistants."

"You lost me."

"The bulk of the executives are already married, so when you look at the numbers in that way…"

"The ratio looks worse."

Jason flung his hands forward in a that's-what-I'm-talking-about gesture, before sinking back with a relieved smile. "Exactly."

Max was still having a hard time swallowing the notion of Rachel as a matchmaker. "Well, you don't need to worry about me. Where Cupid's arrows are concerned, I'm wearing Kevlar."

Jason pointed a finger at him. "You can't be sure of that."

"On the contrary, I'm very sure."

"I'm not really feeling convinced," the CFO said. "Maybe you'd care to make things more interesting."

Max buzzed with the same adrenaline that filled him at the start of every race. "What'd you have in mind?"

"Your '71 Cuda."

"Double my punishment, double your fun?" Max snorted. "I lose my freedom and the rarest car in my collection?" Suddenly, he wasn't feeling much like laughing. "What sort of best friend are you?"

"The kind that has your best interests at heart. I figure you might not fight to stay single for the sake of your sanity, but you'll do whatever it takes to keep that car."

Interesting logic. Max couldn't fault Jason's reasoning. "And what are you putting on the table in case you lose?"

Now it was Jason's turn to frown. "You want my '69 Corvette?" He shook his head. "I just got it."

And Max was looking forward to taking it away. "What are you worried about?"

"Fine. You've got a deal." Jason got to his feet and extended his hand across Max's wide cherry desk. When you've met the girl of your dreams and gotten married, I'm going to miss you, buddy. But at least I'll have the '71 Cuda to remember you by."

Rachel sat at her desk outside Max's office and tried to concentrate as her nerves sang a chorus of warnings. For the last two days, he'd been professional, making no further references to their past. But his gaze on her at odd moments held a particular intensity that promised he wasn't done with her. Not by a long shot.

Despite his assurances otherwise, she suspected that his motives for strong-arming her into becoming his temporary assistant were personal. She wouldn't put it past him to lure her into bed, enjoy his fill, and then walk away in the same fashion he believed she'd walked away from him. And that wasn't her paranoia talking. Max wasn't someone who forgave easily or at all in the case of his youngest brother, Nathan, and their father.

From what she'd gathered from her sources inside Case Consolidated Holdings, ever since Nathan had blown into town almost a year earlier, tension amongst the Case brothers had risen. She'd learned from Max five years ago that there was bad blood between the older Case brothers and their illegitimate brother that went way back. According to Andrea, however, things had recently gotten better between Sebastian and Nathan.

If Max couldn't let go of the past where his family was concerned, he would certainly never forgive a woman he barely knew.

Shoving personal concerns aside, Rachel concentrated on something she could control. Max had a trip scheduled next week. The hotel arrangements and flight had been made some time ago, but she needed to arrange for a rental car, to work on a PowerPoint presentation and fix a hundred problems that hadn't even come up yet.

The phone rang. Anxiety gripped her at the familiar number lighting up the screen. "Tell me everything's running smoothly," she said into the receiver.

"You sound edgy." Devon's amusement came through loud and clear. "Is Max on your case?"

While Devon laughed at his joke, Rachel signed on to the computer using Andrea's ID and password. At the moment, Max was interviewing a candidate for his temporary executive assistant. If all went well, Rachel wouldn't need to contact the IT department for her own computer access. She scanned the assistant's contacts, searching for the phone number of the restaurant downstairs. Apparently, Max had his lunches catered in most days. Andrea's contacts gave Rachel a pretty good sense of Max's activities.

Restaurants. Florists. Even a couple jewelry stores. He enjoyed entertaining women. Clicking one particular restaurant Rachel had been dying to try except that it was way beyond her means, she saw the manager's name, the particular table Max preferred, even the wine he enjoyed.

The man was a player. She hadn't seen that about him during those days on the beach, although she'd figured it out since coming to Houston. Max didn't know it, but she'd seen him in action during her early days in the big city.

Rachel stretched a barricade of caution tape around her heart. If Max wanted to start something with her with the express purpose of payback, she'd better be wary.

"...doing?"

Devon had been talking the whole time her mind had been wandering. Whoops.

"I'm sorry, Devon. I wasn't listening. What did you ask?"

"How is it going with Maureen?"

"She just went in ten minutes ago. Max kept her waiting for half an hour."

"I know that tone. Stop worrying. She's perfect. Max won't find anything wrong with her skills or her references."

"I hope not."

And she didn't have long to wait to find out. Five minutes after she'd hung up with Devon, Maureen exited Max's office. Unsure whether to be delighted or concerned at the shortness of the interview, Rachel stood as the assistant candidate headed her way.

"How'd it go?"

The beautiful redhead's mouth drooped. "He didn't seem to like me."

"Max is very hard to read. I'm sure he found your qualifications and your experience exactly what he requested."

Rachel kept her expression cheery. "I'll go have a chat with him now and give you a call later."

"Thanks."

As soon as Maureen disappeared around the corner, Rachel headed into Max's office. "Isn't Maureen great? She has a BA in business and five years of experience in a brokerage house. She's great with numbers—"

"Not a self-starter."

How had he come to that conclusion after a fifteen-minute interview? "That's not what I heard from her references."

"She's not going to work out. I need someone who takes initiative. Find me someone else."

Rachel hid her clenched hands behind her back and concentrated on keeping her shoulders relaxed and tension from her face as her mind worked furiously on an alternative candidate. "I'll set up someone for you to interview on Monday."

"Single?"

His question came out of left field and caught her completely off guard. "By law we don't discuss anyone's marital status."

"But they'd be wearing wedding rings. You'd know if they were single or married."

"I could guess..." She floundered. What did he want? Someone single he could hit on? That didn't seem right. Max might be a player, but he wouldn't be unprofessional at work. Seeing he awaited the answer to his earlier question, she heaved a sigh. "She's single. Does that matter?"

"Your agency has a certain reputation." He didn't make that sound like a compliment.

"For providing the best."

"For matchmaking."

Rachel wasn't sure if she'd heard him right. "Matchmaking? Are you out of your mind?" The words erupted before she considered how they might sound. Taking a calming breath, she moderated her tone. "I run an employment agency."

He nodded. "And how many of your clients have married the assistants you've sent them?"

What the hell sort of question was that? "I don't know."

"Eight, including Sebastian and Missy."

Rachel didn't know what to make of his accusation. Is that why he sounded so annoyed earlier? He thought... She didn't quite know what he thought. A matchmaking service? Was he insane?

"Don't look so surprised," he muttered.

"But I am. How did you know that?"

"A friend of mine has done a fair amount of research on your little enterprise." He sneered the last word, leaving no doubt about his opinion of her or her company.

Rachel inched forward on the sofa as she wavered between staying and disputing his claims and walking out the door. Fortunately, her business sense kicked in and kept her from acting impulsively.

"I assure you I'm not in the business of matchmaking." She straightened her spine and leveled a hard look at him. "My agency is strictly professional. If my ability to find the perfect match between executive and assistant means that they're compatible in other ways, then that's coincidence." Serendipity. She grimaced. If word got out that something unprofessional was happening between her clients and her employees, she was finished. "If you're worried about finding yourself in a similar predicament, I'll only send you married assistants."

She recognized her mistake the second the words were out of her mouth. Annoyance tightened his lips and hardened his eyes to tempered steel.

Once upon a time she'd been married, and he'd fallen for her. Well, maybe fallen for her was pushing it a little. They'd enjoyed a spectacular four days together and he'd been interested in pursuing her beyond the weekend.

"Or really old and ugly assistants," she finished lamely.

One eyebrow twitched upward to meet the lock of wavy brown hair that had fallen onto his forehead.

Rachel's professionalism came close to crumpling beneath the weight of his enormous sex appeal. Fortunately, the grim set of his mouth reminded her that they hadn't parted on the best of terms. He wouldn't appreciate the feminine sigh bottled up in her chest.

"I'll arrange some candidates for you to interview on Monday," she said, her heart sinking as she realized she was now stuck acting as Max's assistant for the indefinite future.

Three

Monday came and went and Max was no closer to liking any of the candidates she'd arranged for him to interview. By the time Rachel pulled into her driveway at six-thirty, she was half-starved and looking forward to her sister's famous chili. It was Hailey's night to cook, thank heavens, or they'd be eating around midnight.

She entered the house through the kitchen door and sniffed the air in search of the spicy odors that signaled Rachel was going to need three glasses of milk to get through the meal. No pot bubbled on the stove. No jalapeño cornbread cooled on a rack. Rachel's stomach growled in disappointment. No pile of dirty dishes awaited her attention in the sink. Why hadn't Hailey started dinner?

"I'm home," she called, stripping off her suit coat and setting her briefcase just inside the door. "I'm sorry I'm late. The new boss is a workaholic. Did you..."

Her question trailed away as she entered her small living

room and spied her sister's tense expression. Hailey perched on the edge of their dad's old recliner, her palms together and tucked between her knees. The chair was the only piece of furniture they'd kept after he died. That and the family's single photo album were all the Lansing girls had left of their dad.

Hailey's gaze darted Rachel's way as she paused just inside the room. Rachel's stomach gave a sickening wrench at the misery her sister couldn't hide. Only one person in the world produced the particular combination of alarm and disgust pinching Hailey's lips together.

Rachel turned her attention from her sister's stricken gaze to the tall man who dominated her couch. He'd grown fleshy in the four years since she'd last seen him, his boyish good looks warped by overindulgence and the belief that the world owed him something. He still dressed like the son of a wealthy and powerful business owner. Charcoal slacks, a white polo, blue sweater draped over his shoulders. He looked harmless until you got close enough to see the malicious glee in his eye.

"What are you doing here?"

He smiled without warmth. "Is that any way to greet the man you swore to honor and cherish until death you do part?" His gaze slid over her without appreciation. He ran an index finger across his left eyebrow. "You look good enough to eat."

Devour, more like. And not in a pleasant way. Brody Winslow enjoyed sucking people in with his smooth talk and clever charades, and using them up. Once upon a time, that had been her. She'd been taken in by the expensive car he drove and big house he lived in. Not until it was too late did she realize that some of the best liars came from money.

"What are you doing here?"

"I came to collect the money you owe me."

"You've been paid what I owe you this year. Nothing's due for another nine months."

"See, that's where we've got a little bit of a problem. I need the fifty grand now."

"Fifty…" She crossed her arms over her chest so he wouldn't notice the way her hands shook. "I can't pay you the full amount now."

He looked around her house. "Seems like you're doing pretty well."

"I bought the house through a special program that allowed me to put zero money down. I've barely got five percent equity and no bank is going to give me a second mortgage for that. You're just going to have to wait. I'll get the next installment to you in nine months."

"That's not working for me." He pushed himself off the couch and headed toward her.

She flinched as he brushed past her on his way to the window that overlooked her driveway.

"Nice car. It's got to be worth something."

"It's leased."

He shot her a look over his shoulder. "What about that business of yours?"

She bit her tongue rather than fire off a sharp retort. Making him mad wasn't going to get him out of her house or her life. The man was a bully, plain and simple. And he'd figured out where she lived and what she was doing for a living.

"The business is barely breaking even." A deliberate lie, but it wasn't as if her simple lifestyle betrayed the nest egg she'd been building. For so much of her adult life, she'd been on the edge of financial disaster. Having a bank balance of several thousand dollars gave her peace, and she'd fight hard not to give that up.

"I get it. Times are tough for you. But I need that money.

You're going to have to figure out how to get it for me or times are going to get even tougher for you and your pretty baby sister." He patted her cheek and she flinched a second time. "You hear what I'm saying?"

"I hear."

"And?"

"I'll get you what I can." As difficult as it would be to give up her financial cushion and postpone moving Lansing Employment Agency into a bigger, fancier office, she'd make the sacrifice if it meant keeping Brody out of her and Hailey's life. "Now, get out."

Brody laughed and headed for the front door.

Rachel followed him across the room and slid the deadbolt home before his tasseled loafers reached her front walk. She didn't realize how loud her heart thundered in her ears until Hailey spoke. She had trouble hearing her sister's apology.

"He must have followed me home from work," she said. "I'm so sorry."

"It's not your fault. We weren't going to hide from him forever."

"We've managed for four years."

"Only because he never came looking." Rachel sat down on the recliner's arm and hugged her sister. Hailey was shaking. Her confident, bright sister had been alone with Brody and afraid. "Why did you open the door to him?"

"He followed me into the house when I came home from work. I didn't realize he was there until he shoved me inside."

Rachel rested her cheek on her sister's head. "I'm sorry I didn't get home sooner."

Hailey shrugged her off. "Why do you owe him fifty thousand dollars?"

"I borrowed some money to start up the employment agency." It was a lie, but Rachel didn't want her sister to worry. The burden was hers and hers alone.

"Why would you do that?" Hailey demanded. "You know how he is."

Rachel shrugged. "No bank is going to lend a high school graduate with big ideas and a sketchy business plan the sort of money I needed. Besides, he owed me something for the five years I put up with him." She tried to reassure her sister with a smile, but Hailey had regained her spunk now that Brody was gone.

"Those years were worth a lot more than fifty thousand." Hailey levered herself out of the chair and whirled to confront Rachel. Her brows launched themselves at each other. "What are we going to do? How are we going to come up with the fifty grand?" Hailey's pitch rose as her anxiety escalated.

Rachel stood and took her sister's cold hands to rub warmth back into them. "There is no we, Hales. It was my decision to borrow the money and it's my debt to repay."

"But—"

"No." Rachel gave her head an emphatic shake and stood. She could out-stubborn her sister any day. "You are not going to worry about this."

"You never let me worry about anything," Hailey complained. "Not how we were going to get by after Aunt Jesse took off, not paying for college, not anything."

"I'm your big sister. It's my job to take care of you."

"I'm twenty-six years old," Hailey asserted, her tone aggrieved. "I don't need you to take care of me anymore. Why won't you let me help?"

"You already helped. You graduated from college with straight As and got a fabulous job at one of Houston's top CPA firms. You pay for half the groceries, do almost all the cooking and even your own laundry." Rachel grinned to hide the way her mind was already furiously working on a solution to the Brody problem. "I couldn't ask for more. Besides, once I pay Brody the money, he'll be out of our lives once and for all."

"But how are you going to come up with the money?"

"I'll try to get a bank loan. They might not have been willing to loan me money four years ago when I was starting up, but Lansing Employment Agency has a profitable track record now."

Perched on a guest chair in the loan officer's small cubicle, Rachel knew from the expression on the man's face what was coming.

"Economic times have hit us hard, Ms. Lansing." For the last four days she'd been listening to similar rhetoric, a broken record of no's. "Our small business lending is down to nothing. I wish I had better news for you."

"Thank you, anyway." She forced a smile and stood. A quick glance at her watch told her she'd run over her allotted hour lunch break.

This morning she'd wired her twenty-five thousand dollar nest egg to her lawyer with instructions to give the money to Brody. For the last five years, she'd been paying him ten thousand a year, double what she'd agreed to in their divorce settlement. Reimbursement for a debt she didn't owe. Punishment for divorcing him. No, Rachel amended, punishment for marrying him in the first place.

Returning to the Case Consolidated Holding offices, she slid into her desk and shoved her purse into a bottom drawer a second before Max's scowl peered at her from his office.

"You're late."

Rachel sighed. "Sorry. It won't happen again. Did you need something?"

"I need you to be at your desk for eight hours."

She tried again. "Something specific?"

"Get Chuck Weaver on the phone. Tell him I needed his numbers three hours ago."

"Right away."

As she was dialing, her cell started to ring. Since Chuck wasn't answering, she hung up without leaving a voice mail and answered her mobile phone.

Brody's voice rasped in her ear. "Did you get the money?"

"I wired twenty-five thousand to my lawyer this morning."

"I said fifty."

Demanding bastard. "It's all I could get." She kept her voice low to keep from being overheard. "You'll just have to be happy with that."

"Happy?" He chuckled, the sound low and forced. "You don't seem to get it. I need the whole fifty thousand now."

"I get it," she said. "You've been on a losing streak."

She hadn't known about his gambling until the second year of their marriage. A shouting match between him and his father clued her in to his destination when he vanished on the weekends. Frankly, she'd been disappointed. She'd thought he was having an affair. Had hoped he'd fallen in love with someone else and would ask for a divorce.

"That's none of your business."

"You need to get some help."

"You need to get me the rest of my money." He disconnected the call.

Rachel blew out a breath and pushed back from her desk. She had to clear her head. It wasn't until she stood up that she realized someone watched her. Max wore an inscrutable expression, but his shoulders bunched, tension riding him hard. He had the sexy overworked COO look going today. Coat off, shirt sleeves rolled up and baring muscled forearms. She stared at his gold watch to keep her gaze from wandering to his strong hands, and her mind from venturing into the memory of how gently he'd caressed her skin.

"Chuck Weaver wasn't in his office," she said, burying her shaking hands in her pockets. "I'm going to run to the ladies room. I'll have him paged when I get back."

Max shut off her torrent of words with a hard look. "Come into my office. We need to talk."

At his command, Rachel froze like an inexperienced driver facing her first spinout.

"Just give me a second," she protested, her eyes shifting away from him as if looking for an escape.

"Now." Max strode into his office and waited until she entered before he shut the door, blocking them from prying eyes. "Who was that on the phone?"

"No one."

"It sure sounds as if you owe no one a great deal of money." Her evasion irritated him.

He didn't want to care if she was in trouble, but couldn't ignore the alarm bells that sounded while he listened to her side of the phone call. With ruthless determination, he shoved worry aside and focused on his annoyance. The fact that she was in a bad spot wasn't his concern. Her ongoing distraction from her job was.

"You had no right to eavesdrop on my private conversation," she returned, belligerent where a moment earlier, she'd been desperate and scared.

He anchored one hand on the wood door to keep from launching across the room and shaking her until her teeth rattled. "You seem to forget whose name is on the door."

Her stubborn little chin rose, but she wouldn't make eye contact.

"It's none of your concern."

That was the wrong thing for her to say. "When they're calling here it becomes my concern."

Her defiance and his determination stood toe to toe, neither giving ground.

She broke first. Her gaze fell to his wingtips. "It won't happen again."

"Can you guarantee that?"

With her hands clenched to white-knuckle tightness at her side, she pressed her lips into a thin rosy line. Her nonanswer said more than words.

Frustration locked his vocal cords, making speech impossible. He sucked in a calming breath, keenly aware he was venturing into something that was none of his business. If he had an ounce of sense, he'd back off and let her deal with whatever mess she'd stepped in. Unfortunately for him, below his irritation buzzed a hornet of disquiet. He ducked the pesky emotion the way he'd dodge the stinging insect, but it darted around with relentless persistence.

"Do you need help?" He wrenched the offer free of his better judgment. The ramifications of involving himself in her troubles were bound to bite him in the…

"No." Her clipped response matched his offer in civility and warmth.

They glared at each other. Two mules with their heels dug in.

He should be glad she'd turned him down. Instead, her refusal made him all the more determined to interfere.

"Stop being so stubborn. Let me help you. How much do you owe?"

Her eyes never wavered from his, but she blinked twice in rapid succession. "I don't need your help."

"But I need things to run smoothly. I can't afford for you to be distracted by money problems. I assume that's what you've been dealing with on your extended lunch breaks."

"I've got everything under control."

"That's not the way it sounded just now." Max shoved

away from the door and stalked in her direction. He had no idea what he planned to do when he reached her. Something idiotic, no doubt, like take her in his arms and kiss her senseless.

The scent of her filled his nostrils. Some sort of nonfloral fragrance that made him think of clean sheets bleached by the sun. He was assailed by the image of her remaking the bed in their beach bungalow after their frantic lovemaking had ripped the sheets from the mattress.

His irritation faded. "You sounded upset."

Her eyes widened at whatever note of concern she heard in his voice. "I'm not going to let you help me."

Damned stubborn fool.

He caught her arm and pulled her across the gap between them. She came without resistance, her lips softening and parting as a rush of air escaped her. He wanted to sample those lips. Were they as pliant and intoxicating as ever?

"How are you going to stop me?" he demanded, cupping the back of her head to hold her still.

He dropped his head and claimed her mouth, swallowing her tart answer. He expected resistance. They'd been dancing around this moment for almost a week. The shoving match of his will against hers had inflamed his appetite for a similar battle between the sheets.

She moaned.

Her immediate surrender caught him off guard. It took him a second to change tactics, to stop taking and coax her instead to open to his questing kiss. She tasted like fruit punch, but went to his head like a Caribbean rum cocktail.

Long fingers darted into his hair. Her muscles softened. The flow of her lean lines against his frame was like waves on a beach, soothing, endlessly fascinating. With his eyes closed, the surf roaring in his ears, he remembered how it felt to hold her in his arms.

In a flash, all the memories of her that he'd locked away came back. Every instant of their time together played through his mind. His heart soared as he remembered not just the incredible sex, but the soul-baring connection they'd shared.

Then came her leaving. The ache that consumed him. His destructive anger.

Max broke off the kiss. Chest heaving, he surveyed the passion-dazed look in her azure eyes. Her high color. The flare of her nostrils as she scooped air into her lungs. He felt similarly depleted of oxygen. Surely that was the reason for his lightheadedness.

"That was a mistake," he said, unable to let her go.

Rachel took matters into her own hands. She shifted her spine straight and pushed on his chest. His fingers ached as she slipped free.

"That's supposed to be my line," she said, tugging her jacket back into order.

He inclined his head. "Be my guest."

Max retreated to the couch. Resettling his tie into a precise line down the front of his shirt, he laid his arm over the back of the couch and watched Rachel battle back from desire. She recovered faster than he'd hoped.

"That was a mistake." Crossing her arms over her chest, she leveled a narrow look his way. "One that won't be repeated."

"You misunderstand me," he said. "The mistake I referred to was letting the kiss happen here."

"What do you mean here? There's no place else it's going to happen."

He hit her with an are-you-kidding expression. "You're crazy if you think this thing between us is going to die out on its own."

"It will if you stop fanning the flames."

He had to fight from smiling at her exasperated tone. "Impossible. You set me on fire every time I get within twenty feet of you."

"I'm flattered."

Was she really? Her tight lips told a different story. "Don't be. I'm sure I get to you the same way." He plowed on, not giving her time to voice the protests bubbling in her eyes. "It's just a chemical reaction between us. Something ageless and undeniable. We can burn it out, but I don't see it just fizzling out."

"I really don't have the energy for this," she groused.

"Good. Stop fighting me and conserve your energy. I have a much better use for it."

Her arms fell to her sides. "Max, please be reasonable."

She'd stooped to pleading. He had her now.

"When have you ever known me to be reasonable?"

That wrung a grimace out of her. "Good point." She inhaled slow and deep; by the time the breath left her body, she'd changed tactics. "What'd you have in mind?" she questioned, retreating into humor. "A quickie in the copy room?" Pulling out her smart phone, she plied it like a true techno geek. "My schedule clears a bit at three. I can give you twenty minutes."

Max cursed. He should have anticipated she'd use humor to avoid a serious conversation. "I'll need more than twenty minutes for what I have in mind."

"You want more than twenty minutes," she corrected him, letting her thick southern accent slide all over the words. "You probably don't need more than…" She paused and peered at him from beneath her lashes. "Ten?"

Max rose from the couch and prowled her way. She turned her back as he stepped into her space. He loomed over her in order to peer at her phone's screen. So, she wanted to mess with him. Two could play at this game. A minute quiver betrayed her reaction to his proximity. Tension drained from his body. The chemistry between them was textbook and undeniable. His palms itched to measure her waist, reacquaint themselves with her breasts.

"I wasn't so much thinking of my needs as yours," he said, his voice low and intimate. "I know how much you like it when I take my time."

She sized him up with a sideways glance. "I thought this was the sort of thing you were trying to avoid doing with your assistant."

Max shook his head. "I was trying to avoid losing my freedom in one of your matchmaking schemes."

"You were trying to avoid marriage?" She slipped the phone back into its cradle at her waist. "Or falling in love?"

"Both."

"Because they don't always go hand in hand, you know."

"I'm all too familiar with that truth."

As she well knew. The four days they'd spent together hadn't been limited to learning about each other physically. Max had shared his soul, as well. Whether because they'd been two strangers sharing a moment with no thought of a future, or because being with her had thawed places long numb, he'd told her everything about his childhood and the problems with his family, delving into emotions he had no idea lurked beneath his skin.

She'd been a damn good listener. Made it easy to be vulnerable. He'd felt safe with her. And she'd left him. Gone back to her husband.

What an idiot he'd been.

"I'll go get Chuck Weaver on the phone," she said, retreating from his office.

It wasn't until he sat behind his desk and answered the call she put through that he realized she'd completely distracted him from getting answers about what sort of financial mess she was in.

Four

By six o'clock, the offices and cubicles around Rachel were dead quiet. Executing a slow head roll to loosen her shoulder muscles, she gusted out a sigh and saved the spreadsheet she'd been working on for the last couple of hours. Max had asked her to analyze the operations budget for one of the companies Case Consolidated Holdings owned in Pensacola, Florida. The company had been struggling with profitability for the last five years, and Max wanted her to figure out where they could trim expenses.

Whether Max knew it or not, she was the perfect person to figure out how to cut the fat. Ever since she'd lost her father and taken on the responsibility of her sixteen-year-old sister, money had been tight. She'd learned how not just to pinch a penny, but to turn it inside out and scrape every last bit of value out of the thing.

She cast a glance toward Max's office. Should she sneak out or say good-night? The kiss earlier had rattled her more than anything else she'd experienced in the last seven days and with Brody's unexpected reappearance and outrageous demand, it had been a doozy of a week.

As if summoned by her thoughts, Max appeared in the doorway.

"Leaving?" His low question boomed into the silence.

"It's six o'clock. We're the only ones here." She gulped as her words registered.

Pointing out to him that they were completely alone was probably not the brightest move after what happened between them today. The discovery that he intended to rekindle their affair made maintaining her cool a big challenge. If he'd decided this would be the perfect time to assault her willpower, it wouldn't be much of a skirmish.

That he still wanted her both worried and excited her. The heat between them remained as fierce as ever, and as much as he seemed to despise her for not being truthful five years ago, he was right when he said the passion between them hadn't been allowed to run its course back then.

Their four days together had been like an appetizer. One of those fancy ones that awakened the palate, but when you finish sampling, you're still hungry.

How long would the main course last?

A month?

Two?

Max leaned his shoulder against the door frame and regarded her through narrowed eyes. "I thought maybe we could have dinner and discuss your problem."

Translation, he wanted to probe her for more information about the phone call with Brody he'd eavesdropped on.

"You're the only problem I have," she muttered.

"I sincerely doubt that."

Rachel decided to let his remark pass unchallenged. "I can't have dinner with you. I have plans."

"A date?" His smooth tone gave away nothing, but his gaze gained an edge as he awaited her answer.

"Dinner with my sister." Why Rachel felt compelled to assure him she wasn't seeing anyone, she had no idea. Max wouldn't care if she was involved with someone. As long as she wasn't married, in his mind she was fair game. "She does all the cooking at home so I take her out once a week as a treat."

"I seem to recall she was in college when we first met. Did she graduate?"

"Right on schedule." Pride coated Rachel's voice. She might have done a lot of things wrong in her life, but somehow none of it had tainted Hailey. She'd turned out just fine. "She works for a CPA firm not far from here. Between work and her boyfriend, she's pretty busy, but we always make time one night a week."

An invitation to join them tickled the end of her tongue. Hailey would love to meet Max. Her sister fussed over Rachel's lack of a social life as if it was the worst thing in the world and would be giddy to know she'd spent four days in Gulf Shores, Alabama, having the most amazing sex of her life with a hottie like Max Case.

"I'll bet she's not as busy as you."

Was that a note of admiration in his voice? Rachel gripped her purse strap and fought the impulse to cross the five feet of space that separated them and smash her body against his. A throb of need pounded through her. Longing tightened her chest. Her breath grew shallow. If she met his gaze would she risk standing up Hailey for the first time ever?

His next words answered her question.

"Have a nice evening."

With her emotions a muddle of disappointment and relief, Rachel stood by her desk and watched him disappear into his office. Breathing became easier with him gone. Rachel muttered a curse.

She was way too infatuated with Max's tall, solid frame, smoky gray eyes and devilish smile for her own good. But as compelling as his sexy looks were, she could guard her heart against his outward charms. Her marriage to Brody had taught her that beauty was only skin deep.

A strong work ethic was another matter. His dedication to Case Consolidated Holdings touched a chord in her. A workaholic herself, she understood the need to put in long hours. It made her like him.

Which led her into dangerous waters.

This was bad. She'd been working for Max less than a week and almost every hour she caught herself featuring him in her daydreams. Pressure built beneath her skin every time they occupied the same space. How long could she hope to resist the hunger for his touch? Or should she?

That she'd asked the last question told Rachel it was only a matter of time before she wound up back in Max's bed.

She had to pass his open office door on her way to the lobby. Naturally she looked in as she went by. The image of him rubbing the back of his neck as exhaustion swept his features tugged at her, but she kept walking.

Nearing the elevator, she savagely shoved her thumb against the button with the down arrow. Damn him for getting under her skin. So what if he'd looked tired? So what if he'd been working late every night this week?

She cursed the urge to march back to his office and bully him into knocking off for the day even as she retraced her steps, poked her head into his office and asked, "Do you want to join us for dinner?"

Max looked up in surprise. For a split second, a smile tugged at his lips. "I don't want to intrude." But he was already getting to his feet.

"I'm sure Hailey won't mind." Her pulse accelerated as he advanced across the room. His gaze bored into her, and Rachel fought to subdue her body's reaction to the questions lurking in his gray eyes. "Aren't you going to grab your coat and briefcase?"

"I need to come back and finish up some things later."

A man after her own heart. "Okay."

With an entire elevator to themselves, he chose to set his back against the wall beside her. His shoulder grazed hers. The urge to lean against him swelled in her. How was it that four short days with him had left such an imprint on her body and soul? She knew without hesitation that they could tumble back into bed and pick up where they'd left off without a trace of awkwardness. The kiss this afternoon had proven that. He knew exactly how she liked to be touched. Remembered the precise spot on her back that made her knees turn to jelly.

"I've got a business trip to Pensacola scheduled Friday," he said, his brisk tone banishing her evocative musings. "I'd like you to come along."

Warning bells clanged. She cleared her throat. "Did Andrea accompany you on trips?"

"Rarely."

"Then you don't really need me, do you?" But she wanted to go. Wanted an excuse to spend more time alone with him. She knew the risks, but the thrill of being in his arms over-rode prudence.

"On the contrary. You have a reputation for being able to read people. Isn't that how you make your perfect matches?"

Refusing to defend herself against his mockery, she watched the numbers light up above the door and wondered if she could get the elevator to descend faster by willpower alone.

"I could really use your opinion," he coaxed, altering his approach.

Rachel's defenses dropped at his softer tone. A quick check told her he was completely in earnest. Against her better judgment, she let herself feel flattered that he took what she did seriously. Very seriously, in fact.

"I'm really not sure I can be much help," she said as the elevator door opened.

"Let me be the judge of that."

Grimacing her acceptance, she stepped into the lobby. Max joined her after a slight hesitation. "We're walking?"

She pointed straight ahead. "The pub is a couple blocks that way. The fresh air will do you good."

"Fresh air?" he echoed doubtfully.

The hot July sun no longer baked the downtown Houston sidewalks, but heat continued to linger even in the shadows cast by the towering buildings. Rachel and Max strolled in silence toward their destination three blocks away—an Irish pub with great food and a relaxed atmosphere.

As they neared the pub, laughter and loud conversation reached them. Despite the day's humidity, the bar's outdoor seating was packed with business people enjoying happy hour after a long day. Max glanced at the windows, hung with neon signs advertising Guinness and Harp, and then the oval sign dangling over the front door.

"I've never been here before."

"Why am I not surprised?"

Max hit her with a hard look. "What's that supposed to mean?"

"It doesn't really seem like your kind of place. And why would you come all the way down here when you've got Frey's in the lobby of your building. That's more your style."

"And what do you think my style is?"

Snooty. Overpriced. Pretentious. "Sophisticated."

He actually laughed. A surprised chuckle that transformed his features into blinding handsomeness. White teeth flashed.

His gray eyes sparkled like sunshine on water. And his lips…
those gorgeous lips relaxed into glorious, kissable curves.

Rachel almost groaned her appreciation.

"Did you forget the bar where we met? It was pretty low
key." He got a faraway look as if his thoughts went backward
to that moment five years earlier when they had locked gazes
across a crowded bar.

Just like in the movies. Rachel remembered that first jolt
of awareness from twenty feet away. Of course, it had been
nothing compared to the sizzle when he'd come over and
leaned close to tell her his name. Goose bumps broke out at
the memory. Two hours later they'd been in his hotel room
ripping each other's clothes off. She'd never experienced a
moment that intense or right with anyone else.

"The food is great here," she said. "The pints are cold.
What more do you need?"

Max opened the heavy wood door for Rachel. As she
passed, he asked, "Does your sister know about us?"

Us?

Rachel's heart stopped at Max's use of the pronoun.

Inside the pub's front door was a small foyer that led to a
second set of doors. The space kept the sultry outside from
infiltrating the air-conditioned inside. Rachel paused between
the doors and took advantage of the quiet to answer Max.

"Are you asking does she know that I had a four-day affair
with you that ended badly and that you've bullied me into
working as your assistant?"

"Yes."

"No."

"Hmmm." Max reached past her for the inside door
handle. His body bumped against hers and started a water-
fall of sparks running down her spine.

"What does that mean?" She stopped and half turned to
confront him.

"It means you keep a lot of stuff to yourself."

She knew he referred to the fact that she hadn't mentioned her marital status to him five years ago. Despite knowing he had a right to be furious about that, his censure stung. "And what's wrong with that?"

"People get hurt."

People or him?

Don't be silly. They'd known each other four days. Not long enough to develop deep feelings. It had been abundant chemistry that had made those four days sizzle. Sure, there'd been some sort of connection above and beyond the physical, but no one fell in love in four days.

"If I don't share everything that's only because I'm doing what I think is best." And she'd kept some whoppers from Hailey. Stuff that if it came out, her sister would be upset. Rachel didn't like keeping Hailey in the dark. She did it to protect her.

"Best for whom?"

Before Rachel could answer, the door behind them opened and three guys in their mid-twenties appeared in the doorway, their good cheer shattering the tension in the small space and forcing Rachel and Max to move forward.

She stepped into the crowded bar, conscious of Max pressed against her back. Happy hour was in full swing. The sounds of merrymaking bounced off the pale brick walls and dark paneling. The space was illuminated by etched glass chandeliers and lighted beer signs. The bartender waved hello as Rachel made her way past the bar in search of her sister. Hailey worked in the building so she was always first to arrive and secure a table. Rachel found her staking out a booth in the back corner. The noise level improved back here. A dark beer sat on the table in front of her. She stared into it as if reading her future in the mahogany foam.

Rachel stopped beside the table. "Hi," she croaked. "I brought company."

Hailey looked up in surprise, her eyes widening as she noticed the tall figure looming behind Rachel.

"I'm Max." A hand reached past Rachel, aimed toward her sister. "You must be Hailey."

Max's solid torso pressed against Rachel's back. She hummed as delight poured through her veins like warm caramel. Only when she saw the hundred unspoken questions setting fire to her sister's keen blue eyes did she stuff a cork in her wanton emotions.

"Nice to meet you," Hailey murmured, unable to tear her gaze from Max. "Very nice."

Regretting her invitation, Rachel slid into Hailey's side of the booth and nudged her toward the wall, leaving the opposite seat open. This meant she would have the pleasure of staring at Max the whole meal, but wouldn't need to endure the tantalizing brush of his arm, shoulder or thigh against hers.

"Rachel has told me all about you," Max said, shooting a smug look her way.

"Is that so?" Hailey plunged an elbow into Rachel's side. "I'm afraid she hasn't mentioned you at all. How do you two know each other?"

"She's working as my executive assistant."

"Why is she doing that?" Hailey quizzed. "She's in the business of placing people, not taking jobs herself."

Rachel felt the heat of her sister's curiosity. Her cheeks warmed as she glared at Max. "It's just for a little while."

"Rachel knows how very particular I am and offered herself until my regular assistant gets off maternity leave."

His double entendre was a cheap shot to Rachel's midsection. Her stomach clenched. She had not offered herself to him in any way, shape or form. Not yet. She clenched her teeth to contain a hiss of exasperation.

"How are you doing that and running your company?"

"I'm managing."

"Is this why you haven't been home all week?"

"I've been home. It's just been late." Rachel lifted her shoulders in an offhanded shrug. "And I've been heading out early. It only seems as if I haven't been there."

"How long do you intend to keep this up?"

"As long as I have to."

Hailey ran out of questions about the same time as Jane, their usual waitress, set a glass in front of Rachel then smiled expectantly at Max.

"I'll have what she's having." He indicated Rachel's drink.

"A black and tan it is," Jane said.

Hailey pushed a menu at him. "I already know what I'm having."

While Max glanced at the menu, Rachel exchanged a nonverbal warning with Hailey, who merely grinned.

Decision made, Max closed the menu and leaned his forearms on the table. Hailey received the brunt of his attention as he said, "Your sister tells me you're a CPA."

"For almost three years now."

"Is that how long you've been in Houston?"

"We came here a year before that. From Biloxi." Hailey leaned back and framed her glass in a circle made by thumbs and forefingers. "How about you, are you from Houston?"

"Born and raised. Except for the years I spent away at school."

"And what business are you in?"

"My family owns Case Consolidated Holdings. My brothers and I run it."

"I'm familiar with the company." Hailey nodded in approval and nudged her knee against Rachel's. "And what do you do there?"

"I'm the chief operating officer."

"Are you two done giving each other the third degree?" Rachel interrupted.

"Not quite," Max said, his gaze never leaving Hailey. "Your sister has been agitated for the last couple days. Is she in some sort of trouble?"

"Max! That's none of your concern."

Hailey's gaze clung to Max as if he was a knight on a white horse come to save the day. Rachel clamped her fingers around her sister's arm to keep her from spilling about Brody and his demands for money.

"I think your sister wants to tell me what's going on."

"It's not a big deal. I've simply had to postpone moving my offices into a better location." She kept her voice and expression as bland as white rice.

"Why is that?"

"I had a little financial setback. Nothing disastrous. It's something that comes with being an entrepreneur. You should know that. Aren't you having a little difficulty of your own since Nathan showed up? I've been hearing stories of arguments that almost came to blows."

Max blew out a disparaging breath. "It sounds worse than it was."

"Who's Nathan?" Hailey asked.

"My half brother. He came to work for the company a year ago and he's been a pain in my ass ever since." Max sipped at his drink, appearing as if he'd said everything he intended to on the subject.

Hailey rested her elbows on the table and her chin on her clasped hands. "Why is that?"

While Max explained about an acquisition they'd decided not to make, Rachel watched him unnoticed. Max's animation and the multilayered nuances of his tone and facial expressions were vastly different from his older brother's stoicism. His passion had captivated her from the start, stirring her enthusiasm for whatever he was interested in. Like some smitten female, she could sit in silence and let him go on and on just to enjoy the way his eyes glowed with excitement and the way he punctuated his words with hand gestures.

"But enough about me," Max declared abruptly. "Let's talk about your sister. Is she dating anyone?"

Rachel came out of the clouds with a thump. "That's none of your concern."

Max's eyes swung in her direction. "It is my concern." His tone had gone deadly serious. "I'd like a clear field this time."

His intensity roused goose bumps on Rachel's arms. She sat on her hands to avoid rubbing the telltale reaction away and gritted her teeth against the shiver tickling her spine.

"What do you mean a clear field this time?" Hailey asked, leaning forward. "How long have you two known each other?"

"We met five years ago," Max admitted.

"In Biloxi?"

"Gulf Shores."

Rachel squirmed as Hailey went completely still. She should have told her sister something about meeting Max in Gulf Shores. At the time, she didn't want Hailey to know how miserable she'd been with Brody.

Her marriage had been anything but a love match. Brody had offered her security and a way to get her sister through college, not his undying devotion. In exchange, she'd agreed to work as his executive assistant and turn her paycheck over to him. Since he took care of her needs, she had little use for the money she earned working for him.

It wasn't until she signed her first tax return that she got a glimpse of how much money she was making working for Brody's family business. She was earning almost three times what an executive assistant should. Way more than he was paying out for Hailey's room and board. And when she asked him where the money was going, she discovered the sort of situation she'd gotten herself into.

She wasn't in a marriage. She was nothing more than a pawn in Brody's desperate attempt to keep his father from finding out how his gambling addiction had taken over his life. When Rachel found out the truth, she was told in no uncertain terms that she'd better keep her mouth shut or her happy little world would vanish. She and her sister would be back out on the street. Rachel knew that keeping her husband's secret was a small price to pay to keep Hailey in college.

But then, things started to get worse.

Brody grew more erratic. He would disappear for days at a time and when he was home, he seemed hunted. He missed family events and Rachel covered for him, but his parents were relentless in their questions. He came home from one weekend with bruises and admitted that he owed a lot of money to a casino. Money grew tight. They were behind on their mortgage. Her credit cards were declined.

The summer before Hailey's senior year, Rachel had enough. She took off, determined to divorce Brody and figure out another way to pay for Hailey's last year of college. Without cash or a plan, she wasn't likely to get very far. Heading to Gulf Shores had made sense. She'd grown up there. It was home. For two days, she'd hung out and contemplated what a mess she'd made of her life.

Then, she'd met Max. Those four days with him gave her a taste of how love was meant to be. Supportive, deeply connected, full of endless possibilities. She'd been a fool to marry Brody. She'd taken the easy way out of her problems and instead, made things worse.

Brody had tracked her down through a call to Hailey. His arrival had shattered the peace Rachel had found. She'd returned home with him because he'd threatened to tell Hailey about their marriage. Rachel couldn't let that happen.

Hailey would feel horrible if she thought Rachel had sacrificed her own happiness and peace of mind so that Hailey could go to a good college. Rachel was no more going to burden her sister with guilt than she would burden her with four years of college debt.

An awkward silence had settled over the table. Rachel could almost hear Hailey's thoughts as she sifted through the subtext of the conversation.

"I remember that trip," Hailey said. "It was the summer before my senior year. You were really different when you came back. Quiet. Except when you were trying too hard to be upbeat. You never mentioned you met someone."

With Max watching her, his expression a cement wall, Rachel swallowed a mouthful of her drink. "Max and I met at The Lucky Gull and hung out for a few days. It was…"

Rachel's eyes slid sideways toward her sister. She kept her face as expressionless as possible. She'd kept the truth about her troubled marriage from Hailey for the same reason she'd protected her sister before and after their father died. As the big sister, Rachel was responsible for Hailey's well-being.

"Casual," Max supplied, his voice as smooth as butter. "No big deal. We enjoyed each other's company for a short time and went our separate ways."

If he intended for this description of their affair to cause her damage then his aim was flawless.

"Casual," Rachel agreed, increasingly worried that her feelings for Max were anything but.

Five

While the sisters talked about plans for the upcoming weekend, Max tucked into a delicious dinner of shepherd's pie and pondered what the hell he hoped to accomplish by digging into Rachel's life. What was it about her that kept him from just leaving well enough alone? Because as soon as he got her away from her sister, he intended to get to the bottom of what was going on.

Was he looking for ammunition to use against her because five years after the fact he was still angry about being an unwitting accomplice in her infidelity? Sure, he had a hard time letting go of things that bothered him, but he'd only known her four short days. Not enough time for his emotions to get engaged. They'd had fun. Lots of great sex. The connection between them might have seemed real, but it had been a vacation fantasy.

As the debate raged inside him, Max grew less certain of his rationalization.

He'd come away from that long weekend in Alabama a changed man. Before he'd met Rachel he'd been an easygoing bachelor, happy to date a series of women with no distrust of love. After their time together, he closed himself off to emotions and made sure anyone he dated knew he wasn't interested in getting serious.

Until recently, he'd assumed his motivation for doing so was born out of being lied to by Rachel. In the last few days, he'd come to realize it stemmed from the fact that he'd experienced the four most amazing days with her and couldn't imagine feeling that way with anyone ever again.

A shriek went up across the table from him. Max's gaze shot to Rachel. The delight that glowed in her sapphire eyes and flushed her creamy skin rosy catapulted her from merely lovely to truly gorgeous. Happiness banished the shadows masking her eyes. The genuine love for her sister revealed her true heart. She was as beautiful on the inside as on the outside.

Her effect on him put his chest in turmoil. Heart and lungs competed for space in his ribcage. As he contemplated what a foolish move it had been to pull her back into his life, Rachel threw her arms around her sibling.

"Where's the ring?" Rachel demanded, snatching her sister's left hand and frowning at her bare fingers.

"Being sized." Hailey wore a concerned frown as she peered at her sister. "Are you sure you're okay with this?"

"Okay?" Rachel echoed, her pitch lower as excitement gave way to confusion. "I'm thrilled. Leo is a great guy. You two have been dating for two years. Why wouldn't I be okay?"

"Because we won't be living together anymore."

"And you're worried about me being on my own?" Rachel laughed. "Are you kidding? I can't wait to turn your bedroom into a home office."

Whether or not Hailey picked up on her sister's bravado, Max heard it loud and clear. Rachel was thrilled for her sister, but that didn't mean that she was ready for the major change in her life. It didn't take a genius to see that the sisters were tight, or that Rachel regarded her younger sibling as a child she was responsible for.

"Congratulations," Max interjected when the sisters paused for breath. "Have you set a date?"

Hailey answered after a quick glance at Rachel. "November fifteenth."

"So soon?" Rachel sagged in dismay. "There's so much to do before then."

"No, there's not. We're going to have a small wedding, just immediate family."

"But that's not your dream. And you've been saving for a huge blowout wedding since the day Leo asked you out."

Hailey held her sister's gaze, her expression determined. "Leo and I discussed it and we really don't want a huge wedding."

"But that's what you've been saving for. Your dream wedding."

"We want you to have the money."

A-ha!

Max's palm hit the table hard enough to cause plates and glasses to bounce, but the sisters were so focused on their battle of wills, neither turned his way. Confirmation that something was going on with Rachel's finances.

"You're being ridiculous," Rachel insisted, her tone scolding. "I'm not taking your money. You earned it. If you don't want a big wedding, use it as a down payment on your dream house."

"But what about—"

"It's okay," Rachel interrupted, gripping her sister's arm. She followed it up with an emphatic, "Really."

Max leaned forward with interest and pinned Hailey with his gaze. "Why would your sister need money?"

"Quit poking your nose into my business," Rachel said before Hailey could answer. "She has this silly idea that she should repay me for taking care of her all these years and paying for her college. It's ridiculous. I love her. That's why I did it. I wasn't expecting anything back."

There was more to it than that. Max could tell from Hailey's sudden silence and Rachel's fierce scowl.

"If you need money, I can help you out." He'd expected her definitive head shake. "Call it a personal loan. No strings attached."

He couldn't resist adding the latter. The way Rachel glared at him sent his libido into overdrive. He imagined her thinking of all the ways he'd use the loan to gain the upper hand in their arguments, as well as other areas. Her expression had never been more transparent. He studied her, his level gaze causing her color to rise. At last she locked eyes with him. The hard glint in their depths warned him to back off.

Sensing Rachel would continue to deny him answers until he got her alone, Max dropped the matter. Then, deaf to the protests of the two independent career women across from him, he settled the bill.

They exited the restaurant only to discover the day's heat had lingered into evening. Rachel's gaze followed her sister as Hailey headed off to where she'd parked her car. The shadows were back in her eyes.

"She's on top of the world," Max remarked, pacing beside Rachel as she retraced the path they'd taken an hour earlier.

"She's really happy."

Max cursed the strong desire to put his arms around Rachel and kiss her sadness away. "But you're not."

"Of course I am." She adjusted her purse strap. "I'm thrilled."

"For her, but not for yourself."

She wrapped silence around her like a muffler and shot him a look that would have taken down a lesser man.

"Not that I blame you for feeling sad," he persisted. "You've taken care of her all her life. It's got to be hard to let go."

"My feelings don't belong in the conversation."

Impatience rose in Max. Five years ago, he'd found her mysteriousness appealing. Until he'd discovered the reason behind it. How bad were the secrets she was hiding today?

"Why not? Surely it can't hurt to talk to me about what's bothering you."

"Nothing is bothering me."

In other words, she wanted him to back off. Too bad his disquiet over her financial troubles was a pest he couldn't ignore.

"That's not true. You've got financial problems."

She stopped at an intersection and faced him. "I'm going that way." Her finger pointed up a street perpendicular to the one they'd been walking along. "You need to go that way."

"I'm not going to let you walk alone to your car."

Despite the storm brewing in her blue eyes, she smiled. "I walk alone to my car every day. I don't need your manly presence at my side to keep me safe."

"Whatever."

He snagged her arm just above the elbow and stepped into the crosswalk. She resisted his manhandling for three strides before breaking free.

"I don't need you to walk me anywhere."

"Stop being so damned independent and let me help you."

She was breathing hard as they reached the sidewalk on the other side. Frustration poured off her in waves. She whirled to confront him. "I don't need your help."

"How about Hailey's help? Why does she really want to give you—?"

She stopped the rest of his question with an open-mouth kiss that left him reeling. Up on her toes, her fingers fisted in his hair, she plunged her tongue into his mouth in a determined bid to divert his line of questioning.

It worked.

Max gathered her slim form tight against his body. He slipped one hand between their bodies, her breast his goal, when a horn honked nearby, reminding him they were standing in the middle of a city street.

Panting, he raked his lips across her cheek. The heavy air had coated her skin with a fine sheen of perspiration. She tasted salty.

"Come back to my place."

"I can't." Her hands retreated from his back, sliding away from his body with haste. "I have a ton of work to catch up on at the agency."

"Take tomorrow morning off and do it then."

"You don't understand." Heaving a sigh, she shook her head and turned aside. "My boss is a complete tyrant."

Max caught her arm and tugged her back into his arms. "A bear, is he?"

She arched her eyebrows and peered up at him. "Always roaring and throwing his arms around in a threatening manner. It's awful."

"Maybe there's a reason why he's like that."

"Such as?"

"Sexual frustration?"

A golden chuckle rippled through her. "Not possible. You should see all the women he dates. There's a list of them on my computer. All their preferences. Their favorite restaurants. Favorite flowers. Favorite music. Even their preferred jewelers. I think he's getting plenty of action."

At her recitation, Max's grip loosened enough that she was able to free herself and put several feet between them. He hadn't considered that she'd have access to Andrea's files and information about his personal life. Sure, he knew a lot of women. Dated a lot of women.

"Did it ever occur to you that he dates all those women because he's searching for something missing in his life?"

"Ms. Right?" She shook her head, tugged her suit jacket straight and raised her chin. "I don't think that's what he's looking for. He's a confirmed bachelor. No woman stands a chance of capturing his heart." Rachel sent a breezy smile winging toward him and headed away. "See you tomorrow, boss."

Max stood where she'd left him, a sour feeling in his gut. At some point today he'd set his toes on the line he'd drawn five years ago in the sand of an Alabama beach. He'd sworn then that he'd never forgive Rachel for her lies. He hadn't understood the powerful connection between them or his vulnerability to it.

Today, in the face of his compelling need for her, Max felt anger and resentment losing their grip on him. How long before his heart was in danger? The smartest thing would be to cut her loose and stop playing this dangerous game. But his whole body ached at the thought of never again tasting her kisses or hearing the sounds of her pleasure as he drove into her.

Max pivoted and headed toward the Case Consolidated Holdings offices.

Who said he had to deny himself the opportunity to enjoy her body? Making love to her. Forgiving her. Falling for her, even. None of these things would result in the loss of his '71 Cuda.

He'd only lose his bet with Jason if he married her. And that was a trap he could avoid with ease.

* * *

At four in the afternoon, a Pensacola, Florida parking lot was the last place Rachel wanted to be. No breeze stirred the stifling air radiating from the sun-baked blacktop. The sky was a perfect blue, unspoiled by clouds. Rachel brushed sweat from her brow and half trotted to keep up with Max's long stride. The dense Florida humidity made her white blouse stick to her skin. Every inch of her felt uncomfortably damp. Only her mouth was dry. The parched sensation had begun the instant they'd emerged into the harsh afternoon sunlight, and Max had transformed from Case Consolidated Holdings' difficult chief of operations to the charming devil she'd toppled into bed with five years ago.

"That's got them running scared," he declared, even, white teeth flashing in a rakish grin. He stripped off his suit coat and flipped it over his shoulder. "When you pulled out your analysis of their numbers, Carlton got so red in the face, I thought he was going to pass out."

Eyes glued to the large brown hand tugging at the knot on his tie, Rachel told her hormones to settle down. Her chastising had no effect on her unruly body. "Are you really going to transfer operations to the Birmingham plant if they don't bring their costs down?"

Bright shards of silver danced in his gray eyes. "Of course not." With a very un-Max-like flourish, he held the rental car door open for her. This was the most relaxed she'd seen him. "They just need to realize that things can't continue the way they've been going." He leaned his forearms on the door and watched as she tossed her briefcase into the back. "It's hotter than hell out here," he remarked, his gaze sliding over her. "Aren't you going to ditch that jacket you're wearing?"

Not on her life. The last thing she wanted to do was relax around Max.

"No need," she replied, ignoring the way his knowing smile made her pulse jerk. "The car has air-conditioning."

"Suit yourself."

Rachel kept her head turned toward the passenger window as Max drove the car back to the airport, but her attention wasn't on the streets of Pensacola. She was running the last week through her mind.

Since the dinner with Hailey and the kiss afterward, the tenor of their working relationship had changed. Max had become less professional and more friendly. His hand had developed a distracting habit of brushing her arm, landing on her shoulder, or sliding into the small of her back at odd moments. Nothing as overt as her action the other night when she planted a big kiss on him, but the subtle touches made her acutely aware of how sensitive she'd become to his every slow breath, sidelong glance, and nuance of posture.

"Are you hungry?"

Max's question snapped her out of her daydream. A glance at the dashboard clock told her she'd been lost in thought for half an hour. "Where are we? I don't remember the trip from the airport taking so long this morning."

"I thought we'd take a little detour before heading back to Houston."

A detour? What was he up to? She recalled his last question. Did he want to prolong their time together by taking her to dinner?

"You don't need to feed me. I can make it back to Houston."

"About that."

She wasn't sure if it was his words or his tone that sent her uneasiness into overdrive. "About what?" Before long, the sign appeared for Highway 292 confirming her unspoken fear. "Where are we going?"

"The beach."

"Which beach?" she asked.

"Gulf Shores."

She'd known the answer before he spoke. Naturally, he'd pick the place where it all began. He wanted closure. What better way to get that than recreate the fantasy of those four days and let their romance run its course? And fantasy is exactly what it had been. She'd been running from reality. Being with Max then had been a frantic grab at the joy her life had been missing since she'd married Brody. She'd never been happier before or since.

Curses exploded in her mind like fireworks. This was going to end badly for her. Worse than the first time when she'd convinced herself the magic of those days had been all about the best sex of her life. Now, she knew better. Max was a complex man who both frustrated and fascinated her. What she felt for him went way beyond the purely physical. She felt a spiritual connection to him. And when that was ripped away, she would no longer be whole.

"I can't." She surveyed his profile and noted the steely set of his jaw. His lips might be relaxed into a half smile, but he was not in a cooperative frame of mind. "I've got things I need to do."

"What sort of things?" He raised dark eyebrows, daring her to lie.

"Things."

"I thought you said your schedule was clear this weekend."

"I never told you that."

"True. I must have overheard you talking to Hailey about how much you were looking forward to a weekend with nothing to do."

"You eavesdropped?"

"Eavesdropped is such a negative word."

"Listened in. Snooped. Spied. Take your pick." Her accusations bounced off him like bullets off Superman.

"It's not like you left me much choice. Perhaps if you were more willing to tell me what's going on in your life."

Rachel ignored his not-so-subtle dig. "I'm not going to sleep with you if that's what you think is going to happen this weekend." With a disgruntled huff, she folded her arms over her chest.

He took his eyes off the road long enough to show her he didn't believe that for one second. "Who are you trying to convince? Me or you?"

She ground her teeth together because she had no snappy comeback. Already her body was softening in anticipation of the feel of his lips against her skin, his hands finding where she burned for him.

"I suppose with all the dating you do, you're pretty confident when it comes to getting a woman into bed," she muttered, unable to leave well enough alone.

"I'm confident you'll wear yourself out resisting what your body wants." He reached across and took her hand in his, fingers sliding over hers with intoxicating results. He lifted her hand and lightly brushed to his lips across her knuckles.

She sighed at the gentle tug of his warm, moist mouth against her skin. She felt a damp heat between her thighs and resisted the urge to squirm on her seat as he ministered to the inside of her wrist, tongue flicking out to probe her staccato pulse.

"Pay attention to your driving." She used her free hand to pry herself out of his grasp. Much more of that delicious sucking and nibbling and she would put that hand of his where it would do her the most good. "I don't want to get into an accident."

With a low, sexy chuckle, he returned his full attention to the traffic around them.

Even with the air conditioner running at full blast, Rachel felt uncomfortably warm. Since willing her body to cool and settle wasn't working, she peeled off her jacket and released the top two buttons on her blouse. Raking her fingers through her hair, she disturbed the gel she'd used to restrict the waves into a sleek hairstyle. She rolled up her sleeves, took off her clunky jewelry, kicked off her shoes and shed her professional image.

"I suppose I'm falling right into your trap by saying I have nothing to wear but the clothes on my back."

"Normally, this would be where I'd tell you that I intend to keep you naked all weekend." Max glanced over at her, eyes burning with carnal promises. "But I had Hailey pack a bag for you. It's in the trunk."

Her own sister had betrayed her. Rachel's chest ached as she rested her elbow on the door and her head on her palm. "You thought of everything."

"I like to prepare for all contingencies."

Off to their left, sunlight sparkled on the Gulf of Mexico. A familiar sight from her childhood. Rachel flinched away from the sharp stab of nostalgia. Was it possible her father had been dead ten years? She missed him every time she sat in his scruffy old recliner or pan fried grouper the way he'd taught her.

They'd been a happy family—she, Hailey and their dad. Both Rachel and her father had worked hard to make sure Hailey never missed the mother that had run out shortly before Hailey turned two. Rachel remembered her as a sharp voice and little else. Her dad hadn't talked about her and there weren't any pictures of her in the house. The lack of a mother hadn't bothered Rachel until she turned thirteen and realized she didn't know much about becoming a woman. If she'd had a mother to advise her, would she have made so many stupid choices?

"Are you all right?" Max had caught her wiping away a tear.

"The sun's in my eyes." She lowered her visor and blinked

rapidly to clear moisture so she could see. "I wish I hadn't forgotten my sunglasses back in Houston."

Max whipped his off. "Take mine."

"You need them to drive."

"I'll be okay."

"Thanks." She slipped them on, appreciating the UV protection as well as the shield against Max's curiosity. "I'll buy a pair when we stop."

It was an hour's drive from Pensacola to Gulf Shores. Rachel recalled making the trip in reverse with her high school friends in those happy days before her father died. They'd head up to the "big city" to catch a movie or go shopping. There'd been a huge sense of freedom in getting in the car and going.

Her decision to take Hailey to live with Aunt Jesse in Biloxi after their dad died had robbed her sister of those sorts of fun times. If only she hadn't been so afraid to take on the responsibility of supporting her and her sister. At the time it seemed sensible to seek out the help of an adult. Of family. Too bad she didn't know what a loser their aunt was until it was too late.

Max's warm fingers stole over the fist balled on her thigh. "You know, it won't kill you to talk to me."

The soothing slide of his skin against hers caused her to release the breath she'd bottled up. She loved holding hands with him. They'd done a lot of that during those days at the beach. In fact, she doubted they'd gone more than five minutes at a time without touching. When they'd been out in public, most people had taken them as newlyweds, asking if they wanted their picture taken together.

To Rachel's surprise, Max had played along. Despite his claims that he never intended to marry, he'd sure enjoyed playing the part of smitten bridegroom.

What he never knew was that she'd asked one couple to

take their picture and email it to her. She'd stared at it every day until Brody found it on her computer and deleted it.

"I didn't tell you last time, but Hailey and I grew up around Gulf Shores. Dad was a deep-sea fishing guide. The best in the county."

He cocked his head. "How come I didn't know that?"

She shrugged. "You did most of the talking that weekend."

"I guess I did." His forehead creased. "That's not going to happen again."

"Are you sure?" she teased, forcing lightness she didn't feel into her tone. "You're kind of an egomaniac."

Rachel's doubts about spending this weekend with Max were coming to a boil once more. Last time, they'd been able to drop their guards and completely enjoy each other with no reservations or baggage between them. Intimacy had come easy because they'd been strangers.

Max's fingers tightened on hers. "Don't do that."

"What?" Her stomach crashed to her toes.

"Push me away with humor."

"Was I funny? You'd be the first person to say so." Rachel heard herself and ejected a sigh. "You're right. I'm sorry. I've never been good at playing with others." Amusement stirred at Max's impatient snort. "You know, now that I've gotten started, I don't think I can stop."

"I think you can," Max said, all serious. "Why don't you start by telling me why you and your sister left Gulf Shores?"

Max could try to dig up all the details about her past he wanted in an effort to rediscover the connection they'd briefly enjoyed five years ago, but he'd find out pretty quickly that the walls she'd spent the last ten years erecting wouldn't come down without a prolonged siege. And time was something they didn't have. A couple days, a couple weeks maybe, and he'd lose interest in her.

"Our dad died when I was eighteen and Hailey was sixteen. He was shot during a convenience-store robbery in Foley, Alabama. He had a girlfriend up there that he visited a couple times a month. They hadn't been dating long, but I had the feeling he really liked her."

"Had you met her?"

Rachel shook her head. "No, he didn't like bringing anyone around. He didn't want us to get attached to anyone in case things didn't work out." She watched beach houses slide past the window, barely recognizing the area with all the new construction that had taken place, but she knew they were getting close. "Our mom left when we were little. Dad didn't want to set us up to get hurt again."

"He sounds like a great father."

"The best." Remembering there had been tension between Max and his father, she didn't elaborate on all the wonderful things about her dad. "He put his life on hold to look after Hailey and me. I didn't realize how much until after he was dead and all his friends started telling stories of job offers he'd turned down because he wanted us to grow up in a community like Gulf Shores. There'd even been a woman he'd wanted to marry, but she had a big career somewhere up north and he wanted to keep us down here."

"Sometimes there are obstacles to a relationship that can't be overcome."

Like how she'd neglected to tell Max she was married? She probably should have ended things with him when she'd learned about his father's affair. After twenty years, Max couldn't let go of his resentment that his father had loved someone other than Max's mother. Even worse, Brandon Case had loved the child of that union as much as he'd loved his legitimate sons.

"And sometimes people are just plain stubborn. Hailey and I could have grown up anywhere and been just fine. I think Dad was afraid to trust anyone after the way my mom left us."

"Trust once broken is often impossible to heal."

And yet, here they were. Rachel let her head fall back against the headrest. This weekend was going to be a disaster. Why hadn't she pitched a fit until she convinced Max to take her home?

Because she wanted to be with him, no matter the cost to her heart and soul? She was a fool.

"You're right about that," she said. "Especially when people refuse to change." The sun dipped into the clouds looming on the horizon and Rachel pulled off the sunglasses. She handed them back to Max. "Looks like we might get some rain tonight."

"I checked the forecast for the weekend and it promised sunshine both days."

"Forecasts aren't always accurate."

"Let's just say, I'm feeling optimistic."

Was he, now. "Optimistic enough to only book one hotel room?"

Max answered her question with a blazing smile.

<u>Six</u>

Letting her stew about their destination amused Max for the next half hour. The silence gave him time to mull over what he'd learned about her. He'd known she'd taken care of Hailey and helped her by paying for college. It just never occurred to him how young she'd been when she'd taken on the responsibility of her sister.

As they entered the city limits of Gulf Shores, Rachel sat forward in her seat, her expression growing animated. Had she been back in the last five years? Many times he'd imagined her here. Pictured her long blond hair whipping around her face as she walked the beach or sat having breakfast at Jolene's Hideaway.

The car streaked past the beach cottages where they'd spent their four days together. Rachel's gaze snagged on the cluster of pale peach structures, her head turning as she kept her sights locked on them. Curiosity and confusion melded in the turbulent blue depths of her eyes as they came to rest on him.

"We're not staying there?"

"No."

"Then where?"

"You'll see."

They quickly left the main strip behind, hotels, restaurants and shops giving way to beach homes. Leggy structures built on pilings lined the road, their colors pale representations of the surrounding landscape.

"I thought you said we're staying in Gulf Shores," she persisted.

"We are."

"But the hotels are all back there." She gestured over her shoulder, indicating the town now a mile behind them.

"I own a house here." He didn't need to glimpse her expression to know he'd surprised her. Beside him, her body tensed. "I bought it four years ago."

A year after they'd met. It made sense to purchase property since he'd taken to visiting the town once a month. All in the hopes of finding her again. Proof positive that he was a fool. She'd been married. She'd returned to her husband. Yet he'd returned to the scene of the crime like some lovestruck idiot. Over and over.

When it occurred to him that he was behaving exactly like his father's mistress—a woman he despised for her weakness—that he was willing to take whatever scraps of Rachel's life he could because living without her made him miserable, he'd stopped coming to Gulf Shores for three months. But in the end, his longing for her had been too strong.

Naturally, all this was wrapped up in logic and justified by sound reasoning about rising property values and his need for a vacation home. But each time he returned to the beach house, he couldn't hide the truth from himself. He was here because he hoped Rachel would return to him.

"This is yours?" Rachel's question broke the quiet. She'd rolled down her window and a light breeze wafted in, bringing the rhythmic crash of surf and the scent of brine. "I don't get it. Your weekends are filled with racing. Why'd you buy a house out here? It's a lot of money for something you never use."

"I like the beach." More than ever now that she was here. "Let's go inside, I'll show you around."

Max had chosen the house for it's open floor plan and the location, but as Rachel exclaimed over the granite countertops and stainless appliances in the gourmet kitchen, he decided he might have had a woman in the back of his mind when he'd had the kitchen and bathrooms updated.

As they concluded the tour of the main part of the house and headed toward the bedrooms, Rachel tugged her overnight bag from his grasp and marched into the guest bedroom. He saw that she expected him to argue. Why bother when words would have little effect on her? She was afraid of what the chemistry between them would lead to. Oh, not the lovemaking. The hungry look in her eye told him that her desire for him matched his longing for her. But she was worried how their relationship would change after this weekend.

"I'm going to grab a shower," he told her. "See you in thirty."

When he returned to the small bedroom, he found Rachel in the midst of unpacking. She'd also showered and now wore a pale blue sundress that bared her slender arms and showed off her delicate collarbones. Her damp hair lay flat against her head, the bright gold darkened to bronze. Tiny silver butterflies swooped below her ears.

"Nice," he murmured, gaze snagged on the frothy scrap of red satin and black lace laid out beside her suitcase.

"That is not mine." She shook her head. "And I wouldn't have packed it for a weekend getaway with you."

"Why not?" He made no effort to resist a grin.

She rolled her eyes. "Because it wouldn't have lasted more than ten seconds, so what would be the point in putting it on?"

"Try it on and I'll demonstrate the point."

Max gathered her into his arms and dropped his lips onto hers. He'd meant it to be just a hot, quick kiss, a suggestion of what would come later, but she melted against him and he lingered. He tasted yearning and reluctance in her kisses. Both excited him. He couldn't wait for that moment when passion torched her hesitation and she let herself go.

Dropping his hands to her backside, he cupped his palms over her sweet curves and pulled her hard against the unruly tension in his groin. Her shiver told him she was on the verge of surrender. His stomach took that inopportune moment to growl.

A different sort of growl rumbled his throat as she laughed and flattened her hands against his chest to push him away.

"Sounds like the beast is hungry," she said.

Before she could move out of reach, he caught her hand and pressed it over the erection straining against his zipper. "The beast is starving."

For a series of heart-pounding seconds she cupped him, fingers trailing along his length, and Max found his knees starting to give way. But before he could swoop in for a deep, exploring kiss even hotter than the last one, she twisted free and fled out the door.

"Come on, Max," she called over her shoulder, cheeks flushed, her half smile taunting him. "You promised me dinner."

Ten minutes later, her eyes glowed as they drove into the parking lot of the restaurant she'd recommended. Reluctance, eagerness, anxiety and yearning passed across Rachel's features, and Max wondered what memories this place roused. He took her hand as they started up the steps to the enormous deck that wrapped around the outside of the waterfront restaurant. With spectacular views of the Gulf of Mexico, the deck was wide enough to accommodate two rows of tables set for four and a generous aisle between. Despite the heat, families and couples occupied every table.

Weathered wood boards squeaked beneath their weight as Max held the door open for her to enter the restaurant. Once inside, the cries of gulls and the soothing pulse of the gulf gave way to the chatter of the crowd occupying the tables in the enormous restaurant. Walls of windows on three sides provided stunning views of the beach and offered the opportunity to watch the day draw to a close in spectacular shades of orange and red.

Rachel approached the hostess stand and spoke to the woman who was directing her wait and bussing staff with crisp instructions. "Hi, Mary."

The woman looked around and her face lit up with astonishment. "Rachel Lansing. You darling girl. Come here and give me a hug."

At first Rachel looked overwhelmed by the warm welcome, but adapted with enthusiasm.

"Max. This is Mary. She owns the Pelican's Roost. I used to work here back in my high school days."

"She was one of our most popular girls."

"Yes," Max murmured. "I'm sure she was."

Mary lifted a disapproving eyebrow at his dry remark. "Not like that. She was a good waitress. Always smiling. Never got an order wrong and she could charm the crankiest customers. And we get a lot of those during season."

"I wasn't all that," Rachel demurred. "Dad taught me the value of hard work, that's all."

"Yes," Mary said with a sigh. "God rest his soul. So, where are you living these days? The last time you were here was five or six years ago, wasn't it? You were living in Biloxi, I think."

"I live in Houston now. I run my own business. Lansing Employment Agency."

"And is this handsome fellow your husband?"

Color brightened Rachel's cheeks as she shook her head. "He's a client, actually. We were in Pensacola on business."

To Max's bemusement, he resented being described as Rachel's client. But what did he expect, that she'd announce to the world that they were soon to be lovers? Or ex-lovers? Their relationship, past, present and future, was too complicated to be easily labeled.

"Do you want to sit inside or on the deck?" Mary gathered menus.

"Outside." Rachel grabbed Max's hand as the restaurant owner headed off and tugged to get him moving. "Is that okay with you?"

"Outside's fine."

He squeezed her hand and shook off his pensive mood. This weekend was supposed to be about two uncomplicated days of sex, conversation and laughter. No need to muck it up with a bunch of pesky emotions that would confuse things. Keep it light. Keep it casual.

"Everything looks good," he said, scanning the menu with only half his attention. The rest was caught, spellbound, by the whimsical curve of her lips as she set her arm on the railing and peered at the water. "What do you recommend?"

"I'm having the raw oysters, followed by the pan-fried grouper." She leaned forward and whispered, "Don't tell Mary, but it's not as good as my dad used to make." Then, she resumed speaking in her regular tone. "And for dessert, peach cobbler because nobody makes cobbler like the Pelican's Roost."

"Sounds good."

And it was. Thirty minutes later, Max set down his fork after cleaning up every last peach cobbler crumb and exhaled. "Everything was fantastic. Why didn't we come here five years ago?"

"We had a hard time getting dressed and going anywhere," she reminded him with a cagey grin.

That was true. They'd been insatiable. But looking back with a clearer head, he remembered it was Rachel who'd resisted his offers to investigate the local restaurants. The one time they had gone out for dinner, she'd directed him to a town fifteen miles farther along the coast. He realized now that she hadn't wanted to explain being with a man not her husband.

Then it struck him that this was how Nathan's mother must have felt. Always hidden away. Always coping with the fact that she was the dirty little secret in her lover's closet. Max had spent most of his teenage years hating his father's mistress, blaming her for the problems in his parents' marriage. With twenty years of resentment propping up his perception, he was dismayed to feel a twinge of sympathy for the woman.

As he drove back to his house, Rachel's nerves became more and more obvious. She half jumped out of her skin after he parked the car in the driveway and touched her arm.

"How about we take a walk on the beach?" he offered.

"But I thought…?" she began, obviously flabbergasted.

"That I was going to pounce on you the second we got back?" He wrapped his arm around her slim waist and pulled her snug against his side. He had no intention of telling her that his body was revved up to make love, but his emotions were playing sentimental tricks on him. "I thought you'd be more receptive after a sunset stroll."

"How thoughtful of you to consider my romantic needs." Beneath her dry tone he heard a throb of anxiety.

Max dropped a kiss on her head. "Just shut up and enjoy the moment."

Her chuckle vibrated against his ribs, easing the tension. They shed their shoes by the beachside stairs that led to his deck and stepped onto the warm sand. Fine white grains slipped between his toes as they strolled along the beach. The moon had risen early and shone as a narrow, white crescent against the deepening blue of the eastern sky. Max estimated it was somewhere close to low tide because they were able to walk on the hard, packed sand near the water's edge. The breeze was too light to push the waves onto the beach with any force.

"Thank you for bringing me here this weekend," Rachel said. "I didn't realize how much I missed the beach until now."

"Why'd you move away?"

She paused so long before answering, Max began wondering if she'd heard his question.

"After Dad died we went to live with his sister in Biloxi." She settled into her story like someone perched on the edge of a soft couch, too afraid to get comfortable. "Hailey wanted to stay and graduate with her friends, but I insisted we'd be better off if we were close to family."

"So, you don't have any family around here? What about your mother?"

"I barely remember her. She left when I was four and Hailey was two. Didn't have much use for us. At least that's what Daddy said." She slipped into a drawl that sounded very much like the local accent.

That's when he realized she'd stripped as much Alabama out of her accent as she could at some point since leaving here.

"And you never knew your grandparents?"

"I never knew anyone from Mom's side of the family. Sometimes it felt as if Hailey and I had been left on Daddy's doorstep."

"What about your other grandparents?"

"We met them a few times. They lived in Iowa and came down to visit from time to time until my grandmother got Alzheimer's and had to be put in a nursing home."

This was more of her background than she'd shared before. Five years ago, she'd sidestepped every question he'd directed at her. She'd been so accomplished at keeping the conversation focused on him that he hadn't been aware how little he knew about her until she was gone.

What had prompted her to open up to him now? Was she starting to trust him a little? Trust him enough to tell him about her problems?

They walked west in companionable silence, enjoying the play of rich oranges and purples across the sky. The clear night allowed the sun to glow red for a long time before it disappeared below the horizon. As daylight faded, they retraced their steps.

As peaceful as he felt with a soft, curvaceous Rachel relaxed against his side, the closer they got to his beach house, the more anticipation tightened his nerves into bowstrings. His earlier decision to take things slow now became the biggest mistake he'd made in months. Why had he taken Rachel first to dinner then on this long walk on the beach when they could have grabbed takeout and eaten dinner off each other's naked bodies?

Need tightened his gut as he watched Rachel dust sand off her feet on the deck. Patience snapping, he caught her hand and pulled her into the house.

"I can't wait another second to kiss you," he said, closing and locking the sliding glass door. Putting his arms around her, he tugged her hard against his body.

A breathy laugh escaped her. "Then I guess we'd better get started."

His lips captured hers in a fervent kiss that paid homage to her vulnerability while giving her a glimpse of how waiting had fueled his impatience. She met his demand with no sign of her earlier hesitation. Her arms came around his neck. He cupped her head and held her still for a deep, exploring kiss hotter than any they'd exchanged. She arched her back, pushing her lower half against his erection, letting him feel her urgency.

"Make love to me, Max." She tugged his shirt free of his pants and found his skin burning for her. "The romance has been nice, but I need you inside me."

In complete agreement, he drew her down the hall toward the master bedroom. Flinging aside the comforter, Max stripped off his shirt and kicked off his shoes. Despite the cool air blowing across his naked shoulders, he felt feverish. Kissing Rachel set him on fire. Making love to her threatened to reduce him to ash.

"Max."

He turned at the sound of his name and caught Rachel staring at him, her hand behind her, sliding down the sundress' zipper. The look in her eyes stopped his breath. The uncertainty lurking in their velvet blue depths was gone, replaced by confidence. She looked radiant in the rapidly fading evening light.

The smile she offered him was equal parts bold and encouraging. "Are you going to stand there and watch or help?"

She didn't need to ask twice. He brushed the straps off her shoulders and the dress fell to a pool at her feet. Clad in a lavender bra and matching panties, she stood still for his inspection, her chest heaving with each ragged breath.

"Beautiful." He played his fingertips along her collarbones

and then dragged reverent caresses along the bra straps to the edge of the bra. "Your skin is like silk."

She placed her palms on his abs and fanned the fire banked these five years. But he'd promised himself he'd take it slow. He wanted to learn every inch of her skin again.

Her fingers crept down his stomach, past his belly button to the low ride of his waistband. Beneath the buttons that held his jeans together his erection strained toward her questing touch. A groan erupted as she freed him. His hard length speared at her belly, searching for the soft, hot sheath that awaited him. Before he guessed her intentions, she grasped him in her hands.

Sensation exploded through him. A guttural moan tore from his throat as she closed her hand around him. The years fell away. There was no awkwardness in her caresses. She remembered exactly how he liked to be touched. Before her ministrations could cause a premature end to their fun, he swept her into his arms and deposited her on the bed.

"I get to play first," he told her, rolling her beneath him and pinning her hands above her head.

Her thighs parted as he inserted one leg between them. She bent her knee and rocked her hips, grinding her pelvis against him in a slow, sexy wiggle that short-circuited his willpower.

He captured her mouth with his again, his tongue easing past her full lips to sample the exotic pleasures that awaited him beyond. Frantic mewling noises erupted in her throat as she tugged to free her hands. He released her, having better uses for his fingers than holding her captive.

"Better," she murmured, hands riding his shoulders and back with provocative flair.

Taking his time, he drove her mad with feather-light kisses across her soft, fragrant skin. Inch by inch, he eased his way down her body, revisiting all her ticklish spots and the ones that made her gasp. Five years had gone by, but he knew her body as well as he knew his own. Maybe better.

His teeth latched on to the lace edge of her bra. Tugging at the material caused her to hiss impatiently through her teeth. He buried his smile between her breasts, trailing his tongue up one round curve just above the line of silk. He wrapped his fingers around her straps and eased them off her shoulders, but made no attempt to draw the material lower. Her breath came in erratic pants as he retraced his tongue's path, this time dipping below the fabric.

"You're being awfully darned slow about getting me naked," Rachel complained, arching her back to reach her bra catch.

It loosened, but kept her covered. She pushed hard on his shoulder, rolling him onto his back. He grabbed her hips and brought her with him. The bra fell, exposing her small, perfect breasts.

Max palmed them with a sigh of sheer joy. Her bra sailed somewhere off to his left as he began relearning the shape of her. Already her nipples had peaked into dark buds. Max half closed his eyes in satisfaction at the hitch in her breath as he fondled her.

Below where she sat, his erection prodded against her lavender panties, seeking entrance. She leaned forward and rocked her hips. His sensitive head slid against the silk of her underwear, so close to her heat he thought he might go mad with wanting.

She reached behind her and seized him. Max's mouth fell open in shock at the intense pleasure that washed over him. A groan ripped from his chest as her fingers played over the head of his erection. His focus narrowed to her hand and the acute agony denying himself the satisfaction his body craved.

He pulled her hands away and meshed her fingers with

his. He closed his eyes to block out her happy smile and the passion glowing in her half lidded gaze.

Not one of the women he'd been with since the day she'd left had brought him to the edge this fast. Control had never been a problem for him until Rachel had entered his life. Max sucked air into his lungs, struggling to clear the fog of passion before something happened they would both regret.

"Condom," he rasped out.

"Where?" She sounded as impatient as he felt.

"Front pocket."

She stabbed both hands into his pockets and plucked out a condom. "You came prepared," she said, dismounting.

The bed sagged to his left. Max shoved down his pants and opened his eyes in time to see a naked Rachel rip open the foil packet with her teeth and poise the condom over the tip of his erection. Clenching his teeth, Max let her finish the task without his help while his hands fisted into the bed sheets.

The time for subtlety and patience ended. With his heart thundering a frantic cadence, Max sat up, flipped Rachel onto her back and slid into her with one long thrust.

The perfection of Max buried deep inside her robbed Rachel of breath. Five years was a long time to go without being complete. And complete was how she felt in Max's arms. No other man reached past her defenses and captured her heart the way he did.

"You feel amazing," he said, voice husky and raw as if overused. The timbre rasped against her nerve endings with delightful results. "I'm sorry I didn't take it slower. I wanted to."

"You always wanted to delay the good stuff," she groused, but couldn't hide her smile.

He dropped a kiss on her mouth. "And you were always rushing me."

"Like this?" She placed her feet on the mattress and rocked her hips into his.

"Exactly like that."

But he began to move with her and the incredible slide of his thick length in and out of her body transported her beyond speech. She peaked fast, the climax shocking her with its intensity and duration.

"What the hell?" she muttered as his body continued to move against hers, stronger now. "Where did that come from?"

"Where they all come from."

He kissed her hard and long, the play of his tongue mimicking the movements of his lower body. To her intense disbelief, pleasure began to spiral upward again. Impossible. She was sated, exhausted by the intensity of her orgasm, yet another loomed on the horizon. Max slipped his hand between their bodies, finding the knot of sensitive nerves and plying it to great effect.

"Come for me again," he demanded. "Come hard. I want to hear it."

Faster and harder he thrust. Teeth bared, breath coming in heavy pants, he moaned her name, sounding as if it ripped from deep within his soul.

"Yes," she clutched his shoulders, driving her nails in as another orgasm rippled outward from her womb. "Yes, Max. Now."

And he came. She watched it unfold. Her inner muscles clenched in aftershocks as he bucked against her, wild and ferocious in his release. It thrilled her that she'd done this to him. For him.

He collapsed onto her with a gush of air and rolled them onto their sides. With Max still locked deep within her body, she bound his legs with her thigh, needing to keep them connected as long as possible.

"I'd forgotten how it was," he murmured, his palm damp against her sweat-soaked cheek.

She laughed then. It burst from her like the trill of a happy songbird. "So did I."

Time and self-preservation had dulled her memories of him. Of this. How else could she have gotten on with her life? And now that she'd tasted the amazing passion between them again, how was she supposed to walk away a second time?

When he pulled out of her arms and headed into the bathroom, she rolled onto her stomach and buried her face in the pillow. The sight of so much male perfection had aroused her all over again. She tingled with glee at the thought that he was hers, and hers alone, all weekend.

And after that?

The question clawed its way out of her subconscious and roosted in the front of her mind. Max was never going to marry. Even if his father's infidelity and mother's acceptance of it hadn't given him a sour view of the institution, there'd always been misgivings lingering in the back of his mind. Hesitations that had bloomed into full-blown skepticism after she'd made him an unwitting participant in betraying her marriage vows. Which meant, even if he changed his mind about marriage, he'd never change his mind about her.

Sunday morning, Max leaned his forearms on the balcony railing off the master bedroom and watched the rising sun shift the color of the sky from soft pinks and lavenders to a bright coral and gold. The wind had picked up overnight, and blew against his face, carrying the scent of brine to his nostrils. A jogger went by, nodding to a couple walking hand in hand as he passed. Farther east along the beach, a black lab chased a stick into the surf, bounding into the water with great enthusiasm.

Behind him, Rachel slept like someone who'd spent an exhaustive night making passionate love. He caught himself grinning. He'd worn her out. And she'd worn him out, but not enough to still the thoughts circling and bashing together in his head like bumper cars.

Last night, his mother had called. She was working on the seating arrangements for her thirty-fifth wedding anniversary party next weekend and wondered whether or not he was bringing a date. He should have told her he was flying solo; that had been his plan when he'd first learned his parents were renewing their vows and planning a big celebration.

His thoughts coasted to the naked woman slumbering in the room behind him.

If he asked Rachel to accompany him, the invitation would alter the texture of their relationship. No longer could he pretend that his interest was purely driven by sexual need. If he introduced her to his family, they'd be approaching something that resembled dating. Is that what he wanted?

Five years ago, before finding out she was married, he'd been ready to head down that road. Four short days with her had caused him to consider what his future would be like with her in it.

This weekend wasn't supposed to be about starting fresh. It was supposed to be about settling old business and Rachel seemed on board with that. Why alter course and sail into a storm when the skies before him were a calm blue?

He could tell himself that he was simply taking her for moral support. Both his brothers would be accompanied by their wives, and there was something about the way Sebastian and Nathan regarded him these days that felt a whole lot like pity. As if life was so much better for them. Both of their wives had them wrapped around their slender fingers. With children on the way, they were as trapped as two men could be. So why the hell did they seem so damned blissful?

Slender arms circled him from behind. Against his back, the soft press of Rachel's breasts, encased in thin silk, jump-started his body. Her hands played over his chest as her lips trailed over his shoulder. He closed his eyes, savoring the sweet seduction of her caresses until her teeth grazed the tender skin below his armpit and her fingers dove below the waistband of his pajama bottoms.

Lust surged, but instead of losing himself in sensual oblivion, he caught her wrists to stop the sexy exploration and trapped her hands in his. "Come with me to my parents' anniversary party next weekend."

"I don't think that's a good idea." Her body tensed as he dragged her around to face him. "You don't want your family getting to know me."

No, he didn't.

"My mother thinks I'm bringing a date." He drew a fingertip along her spine and felt her shiver.

She pushed against his chest. "I'm sure you can find someone to take in the next few days."

At her resistance, every bit of his ambivalence vanished. "I asked you."

Bending down, he hoisted her onto his shoulder and strode back toward the rumpled king-size bed, her fists hammering on his back all the while. He dumped her onto the mattress and slid his gaze from her ankles to her well-kissed mouth and stormy gaze. Gorgeous.

He set his knee on the mattress beside her right hip and pinned her in place with a stern look. "And we're not leaving this room until you agree."

Seven

Rachel hid a yawn behind her hand as Max turned the corner and arrived on her street. With her work schedule, she was accustomed to sleeping less than eight hours a night. But usually she lazed in bed on Sunday mornings and caught up on her rest. This Sunday morning she'd been in bed, but it hadn't exactly been lazy or restful.

As they neared her house, she automatically checked for Hailey's car in the driveway. She didn't really expect to see it there. Hailey had been spending more and more time with Leo. It wouldn't be long before they moved in together. Especially now that they were engaged.

Rachel sighed. She was going to miss having her sister around. The years Hailey spent at college were different. Then, Rachel had acted as parent. She'd shouldered financial responsibility for her sister's schooling, worried about how her studies were going, and planned for the future. Now, Hailey was a capable, accomplished woman in charge of her life. She'd taken charge of her dreams. Soon, she would be making plans with her husband. Rachel's role had been reduced to that of loving sister and nothing more.

It left her feeling a little lost.

Enter Max. Was she using him to fill a void? Being with him certainly filled a place inside her that had been empty for a long, long time.

He swung into her driveway and stopped behind her car. He stared through the windshield in silence for a long moment. "I don't want to drop you off and go home to an empty house."

Why did he always know exactly what to say to melt her insides?

"Inviting you in is not an option." She rushed a shaky hand through her tousled hair. "We'll just end up…" She flipped her hand in a circular motion. "You know."

He laughed. Her heart expanded at his relaxed expression and the silver shards that sparkled in his gray eyes. Max happy was like watching the most gorgeous sunrise ever. Just being in proximity to him in his current mood made her feel lighter than air.

"What if I promise to keep my hands off you?"

"You can stay for dinner," she said. "Although, it might have to be pizza because I don't know if we have any food in the house."

"Why don't you see what's there. We can always run to the store."

Rachel got out of the car, amused by the thought of Max in a grocery store. He had a housekeeper to shop, cook and clean for him. She had a hard time picturing him pushing a cart down the pasta aisle and deciding between linguini and bow ties.

"What's so funny?" he demanded, snaking his hand around her waist as they headed toward the side door that led into her kitchen. He crowded her on the steps, his solid muscles bumping her curves in tender affection.

Her body reacted accordingly, awakening to each cunning brush of hip and shoulder. "The thought of you shopping for groceries." She dug her keys out of her purse and slid her house key into the lock. It had been acting up lately so she needed to jiggle it a bit to get the tumbler to align properly.

Beside her, Max stiffened. "Someone slit your tires."

"What?"

Before she could turn around, he was off the steps and prowling around her car like a pride leader who'd had his territory invaded by a stray.

"All four of your tires are flat." His gaze shot to her. Worry pulled his mouth into a hard line. "You need to call the police."

"No." Her mind worked furiously. Brody had sounded more intense than usual during his last phone call, pushing her because the guy he owed money to wasn't satisfied by a partial payment. Did her slashed tires mean Brody's debt had become hers?

"What do you mean *no?*"

Seeing Max's surprise, she scrambled for an explanation. "I'm sure it's just neighborhood kids acting up. I'll call a tow truck and get new tires."

"This is serious vandalism," Max persisted. "You need to report it."

And explain her troubles in front of Max? Not likely. Besides, she didn't know for sure this had anything to do with Brody and his money problems. "It's not worth the hassle. The police won't be able to track down the culprits."

"You don't know that."

"It probably happened in the middle of the night when everyone was asleep so there won't be any witnesses. I'll have the tires replaced. It's no big deal."

Max set his hands on his hips. "Has this sort of thing happened in your neighborhood before?"

"Not to me," she hedged.

"Something's going on that you're not telling me. I don't like it."

"Nothing is going on. It's just some stupid vandalism." Her voice grew more strident as Max continued to press. Rachel gathered a long breath and aimed for calmer speech. "Let's go inside. I need to find someone who can fix the car or I won't make it to work on time tomorrow. And you know how difficult my boss is if I'm late." She tried for humor but it fell flat in the face of Max's scowl.

He took her by the elbow and walked her into the house. Once the door was shut and locked, he pulled out his cell phone and dialed a number. It turned out to be a friend that owned a repair shop. Rachel retreated to her bedroom while Max arranged to have her car picked up and the tires replaced.

Her heart pounded with vigorous force against her ribs as she dropped her overnight bag on the bed. A quick check told her Max was still on the phone. She shut the door and took her cell into the adjoining bathroom.

"Someone slashed my tires," she said when Brody answered.

"Yeah, well, I told you this guy plays rough."

"This is your problem, not mine. Did you tell him where I live?"

"It was that or he was going to beat me up."

Coward. She let her disgust come through in her tone as she said, "You're a bastard for making me a part of your problem. Did you explain to him that I don't have any more money to give you or him?"

"You could ask that rich boyfriend of yours," Brody responded, sounding so much like a whiney six-year-old that it was all Rachel could do to not hang up on him.

How had Brody found out about Max? And if her ex had told the goon about her, would Brody send him in Max's direction next? She had to stop that from happening.

"I already asked him," she lied. "He broke up with me over it, so there's no money coming from him."

"Ask again. Do whatever you have to do to convince him to give you the money."

"He won't speak to me and I'm done talking to you. If anything else happens, I'm going to the police."

"You're a bitch," Brody snarled, changing tactics. "He won't stop coming after you."

"You tell him he'd better." Or she'd what? Rachel's hands shook, making the phone bump against her ear. She couldn't believe this was her talking. But then, she'd never been this mad before, and with Max in the other room, she felt safe. "And if you don't," she continued, "he will be the least of your problems. I'll come after you myself."

Now, she did hang up. And her knees gave out. She sat on the toilet seat until her hands stopped shaking. Then, she returned to the kitchen where Max stood beside her small breakfast table, feet spread, arms crossed, a determined expression on his face.

She ignored his militant stance and peered into the refrigerator. Hailey had gone shopping at some point during the week. Rachel sighed in relief. She couldn't face going past her car's four flat tires right now.

She pulled out two plastic-wrapped packages and turned toward Max. "Steak or pork chops?" she asked with false brightness. Either could be grilled and served with red potatoes and a fresh salad.

"It doesn't matter. We're not staying here for dinner. Grab some clothes. You're coming home with me."

Dismay flooded her. She stuck the pork chops back in the refrigerator, hiding her expression from him. "Steak it is."

"Didn't you hear me?"

"I heard you, but I'm not going anywhere."

"You could be in danger."

"Because my tires were slit?" she scoffed, but very real panic fluttered in her gut.

"Because I don't think it was a random bit of vandalism."

"And why is that?"

"Who'd you go into the bathroom to call, Rachel? I heard you talking to someone when I came in to see if you were all right."

Of course he'd followed her into the bedroom. He was worried about her. Warmth pooled in Rachel's midsection. No one had worried about her since her father had died. It would be so easy to drop her guard and tell Max all her troubles. He would help her take care of Brody. And then he would walk away because when he found out she was keeping secrets from him about her ex-husband a second time, he would be angry with her all over again.

"I was talking to Hailey."

"And you had to go into the bathroom and shut the door to do that?" He scowled. "What sort of fool do you take me for?"

Rachel worried the inside of her lower lip. "I can't talk about this with you."

"Can't or won't?"

She couldn't face the cold fury in his eyes. Her heart worked hard in her chest as the silence stretched. "Both," she said at last, her voice catching on a jagged breath. "It's none of your concern."

His eyes narrowed. "I care about you. Why don't you think it's my concern?"

"Care?" Her heart swelled as hope poured into it. But what did Max's admission mean?

"You sound surprised."

"More confused. I don't know what you expect of me."

"I don't expect anything."

"But you do. You expect me to let you into my life."

"I want to help with whatever's going on."

"I don't need your help."

Frustration built inside him like a sneeze. She watched it pull his lips into a tight line and bunch his muscles. He frowned. He glared.

"You're getting it whether you like it or not. Pack."

This wasn't going well. "No."

"Rachel."

"Look, this thing between us. It's supposed to be about hot sex until the passion burns out. You didn't sign up for providing moral support and I didn't ask for a white knight to rescue me."

"That's what you think I'm doing?"

"Isn't it? After what happened between us five years ago, you admitted you don't trust me. Are you saying you've changed your mind?"

His stony stare gave away none of his thoughts. "The way you've been behaving tonight gives me no reason to."

She couldn't let him see how much his admission hurt. "Maybe we should return our relationship to that of boss and assistant without benefits."

"Is that what you want?" He asked the question in a deadly tone, soft and calm.

Rachel shivered. If she gave him a truthful answer, she'd open her heart up to be hurt. He'd know how much she cared for him, what having him in her life meant to her.

"It might be for the best." She turned back to the refrigerator, unsure her whopping big lie would stand up to his scrutiny.

Max came up behind her and held the door closed. "Might be?" His breath tickled her nape. The sensation raised the hairs along her arm. "Are you saying you don't care if I walk out the door and we never see each other again? Because that's what's going to happen. And if I go, don't bother showing up at work tomorrow. Consider your contract terminated."

"That's unfair."

"Maybe, but that's the way I roll."

"All because I won't let you take charge of my problems? That's ridiculous."

"No, what's ridiculous is that you won't let me help you."

She turned and put her back against the counter, feeling the bite of the Formica in the small of her back. "I don't let anyone help me."

"Not your employees?"

"I pay them to do a job."

"Hailey?"

Rachel shook her head. Crossing her arms gave her a little breathing room as his chest loomed closer. "I've taken care of her all my life."

"Who takes care of you?"

"I do." And she was damned proud of that fact.

His voice softened. "Everyone needs help from time to time."

"Not me."

"Why?"

"Because, every time I turn to someone for help they take advantage of me." She slid sideways away from him putting some distance between them.

"You think I'm going to take advantage of you?"

"Maybe." She didn't really. Of course, she hadn't thought

Aunt Jesse or Brody would leave her worse off financially than before she'd accepted their help, either.

"You can't be serious?"

Fool me once, shame on you. Fool me twice, shame on me. She'd be a complete idiot if she got fooled a third time.

"Given my financial situation, you probably think that it's far more likely that I'd take advantage of you than the other way around." She hardened her heart against the longing to fling herself into his arms and tell him everything. Once upon a time it had been so easy to trust. But she'd learned the hard way not everyone had her best interests at heart. "But I can't take that chance."

"You don't trust me?"

Instead of answering, she shrugged.

Max blew out his breath. "If anyone in this relationship deserves not to trust, it's me."

"I never asked you to trust me," she reminded him. "I'm sorry if I've upset you, but I need to do this myself." She tried a smile. "And what's wrong with that? You and I both know this thing between us is going to burn out eventually. It'll be easier to part ways if I don't owe you anything."

"I wouldn't expect you to owe me."

"I wouldn't feel comfortable taking help without being able to pay you back."

Max wasn't usually, at a loss for words, but he seemed to be struggling with what to say to her now. Rachel imagined he was sorting through his conflicting impulses. Continue to push into her life and become the guy she could rely on, the one who would be there when things got difficult or uncomfortable. Or just enjoy the physical side of their relationship and be the guy that moved on before things got too complicated.

"Do you want me to find someone to come in for me starting tomorrow?"

The way his eyes widened, he hadn't expected her to be so matter-of-fact about ending things. He didn't know how much armor she'd wrapped around her heart or how many times she'd smiled in the face of heartbreak.

"No." He scrubbed at his unshaven cheek and studied her from beneath long, dark lashes. "Get in when you can. We're not done with this. Not by a long shot."

Rachel nodded, her throat too tight to speak as she watched him disappear out her door. For a long time her legs were too unsteady to move. By the time she walked to her large front window and sank to the floor, Max's car was long gone. She rested her chin on the sill and wished he could hear her silent plea for him to come back, take her in his arms and tell her everything was going to be okay.

A half an hour ticked by before she gave up hope. Max couldn't help her because she wouldn't let him. If she was miserable, she had only herself to blame.

Max drove out of Rachel's neighborhood, his gut on fire. He hadn't been this mad since Nathan decided to join the family business a year ago. But at least then, his anger made sense. His half brother had been pushing his way into a family where he didn't belong since their father brought him home twenty years ago.

Max had no real reason to be mad at Rachel. She didn't want his help. So what? She had an independent streak a mile long. He'd known that about her since they first met.

Did he really think she owed him an explanation about the things going on in her life? What were they to each other? Lovers. Casual ones at that. He'd told her they had no future. He'd given her a clear picture of his boundaries. Now he was upset because she didn't need him?

Max gunned the engine and pulled out into traffic.

This was for the best. It would be easier in the long run if they didn't draw out the goodbyes. A clean break. Just like last time.

Only here he was. In deeper than last time. On fire. Singed body and soul by emotions only she aroused. Around every corner, more secrets. More lies. And his need for her showed no sign of abating any time soon.

The next morning he arrived at the office tired and cranky. However, his surly mood brightened slightly at the sight of Rachel at her desk looking just as exhausted. She didn't greet him as he neared, but her tight expression told him she was acutely aware of his presence. To his dismay, he was relieved to see her. Happy, in fact. The sight of her shouldn't lift his spirits. He was still mad at her.

"I told you to take your time getting in this morning," he said, accepting the cup of coffee she held up to him.

"I know. And I appreciate it, but Hailey brought me in."

"Did you tell her what happened?"

Rachel shook her head. "She saw my car and she was no more happy about it than you were."

"Why am I not surprised?"

She appeared so miserable it took all his considerable willpower to keep from sweeping her into his arms and kissing away the worry lines between her brows. Instead, he jerked his head toward his office.

"Come in for a second."

She hesitated. "Is this about work? Because from here on out, that's all I want to talk to you about."

"Yes. It's about work. I have a difficult situation with an employee and I'd like your opinion on how to handle it."

Once he had her inside his office, he shut the door and gestured her into one of his guest chairs. Then he strode to the window and stood staring out over downtown Houston. Behind him, he heard her soft sighs and the creak of wood as she shifted in the chair, impatient for him to begin.

"Last night you said people had taken advantage of you. What happened?"

"You said you had a situation with an employee."

"You're an employee." Max turned and let his gaze catch on hers. "We have a situation."

"I'm a contractor working for you."

"Same difference."

"And nothing about this situation has to do with our professional relationship."

"It has everything to do with my ability to concentrate on work."

"I'll quit."

"It won't change my ability to get my job done. Five years ago, you walked out of my life and never looked back. That's not going to happen again."

"What are you saying?"

Yes, what was he saying? "That I want to see where this goes. And I want to start by learning about your past and your present. Maybe that way we can have a future."

"It will never work between us."

He snorted. Any other woman he'd ever dated would have been dancing for joy at what he'd just offered. He had to pick the one woman more skittish about commitment than he was. "What makes you so certain of that?"

"The biggest problem is you can't trust me."

"And you don't trust me," Max countered, still smarting from that revelation. "That puts us on the same page."

She crossed her arms over her chest. "We're not even in the same bookstore."

"Let's see if we can change that. Tell me who took advantage of you that makes you so skittish about accepting help."

She opened her mouth, but no words came out. A second later, she bit her bottom lip. Max waited while she grappled with what story to tell him and how much to tell. Letting her sort it out without prompting tested his patience, but he kept silent. At last, she seemed to come to some sort of decision. Her breath puffed out.

"Aunt Jesse." She closed her eyes. "My dad's sister."

"What happened?"

Instead of forcing intimacy by sitting in the chair next to her, Max gave her space by keeping his big executive desk between them.

"I was eighteen when my dad died and still in my senior year of high school. Hailey was two years younger. Since our mom left when we were both young, I'd always thought of Hailey as my responsibility. She was diagnosed with asthma when she turned six. The first time she collapsed and turned blue, I don't think I've ever been so scared in my whole life. After that, I watched her like a hawk, making sure she had her inhaler with her at all times. She was my baby sister. I couldn't lose her, too."

Too? Max wondered if she knew what she'd given away with that one word. Her mother had disappeared when she was four. Rachel had felt the loss no matter what she was willing to admit to herself. And then her father died. Max suspected protecting herself against loss had become second nature. Pity the man who tried to break down those walls.

"Who took you in after your dad died?"

Rachel stared at her hands. "No one. I dropped out of school and went to work full-time to make ends meet until we received the money from Dad's insurance policy. He took it out because you can be as careful as anything when you're out on the gulf, but accidents happen. No one expected he'd be shot during a convenience-store robbery twenty minutes from home."

"You never graduated?"

She shook her head. "I got my GED. I needed to take care of Hailey. Only it was a lot more expensive than I was expecting. And I was working all the time. By the time we got the insurance money, I was exhausted and worried about how I was going to handle everything. We had no medical insurance and Hailey's asthma had been flaring up a lot more since Dad died. The medication was expensive. That's when I called Aunt Jesse."

"Was she able to help?"

"She told us to come live with her in Biloxi. We'd have a place to stay while Hailey finished high school. I could work and maybe go to a community college. The rest of the money could go toward a real college for Hailey. She was always the smarter one."

"So, what happened?"

"For a while everything seemed okay. Then one day Aunt Jesse came home and asked if she could borrow Dad's life insurance money for a couple days."

"And you gave it to her."

"It was supposed to be a loan until she got paid at the end of the week. I probably should have said no, but she took us in when we needed help and she was family." Rachel's bitter smile said more than her expression. "She took the money and disappeared. We were stuck in Biloxi with no money, no friends and no family."

Her story would have wrung sympathy out of the most jaded heart.

"Did you call the cops?"

"And tell them what? That I'd lent money to our aunt and she'd disappeared?"

"Did you look for her?"

Rachel shook her head. "For all she was our closest living relative, we knew nothing about her life or her friends. Or, we didn't until people showed up looking for her. That's when we found out she was dealing drugs and had some rather scary acquaintances."

"Did any of them hurt you?"

"No. After the first guy came knocking, we didn't stick around."

"What happened?"

"I had a waitressing job. I picked up more hours. We found a small studio apartment in a relatively safe neighborhood and scraped by." Rachel downplayed what must have been a scary time for her with a single shoulder shrug and a self-deprecating smile.

Max's admiration for her went up several dozen notches. "I'm sorry you had such a tough time of it."

Rachel's eyes hardened into sapphire chips. "It was my fault we were in the mess."

"How do you figure that?"

"Hailey begged me to stay in Gulf Shores. She wanted to finish high school with her friends. But I was too scared about being solely responsible for her to listen. I wasn't ready to be an adult. Don't you get it? I screwed up. If we'd stayed put, Aunt Jesse wouldn't have stolen the insurance money. It would have been so much easier."

"You were eighteen. Cut yourself some slack."

"Life doesn't cut you slack," she said. "Life comes at you hard and fast and you either meet it head-on, duck, or get blindsided. I've promised myself not to get blindsided again."

Yet Max had the sense that something had blindsided her recently. Something that wasn't him. Something she wouldn't let him help her with.

"You said people *helped* you."

"What?"

"Last night. You said people. That's plural. Who else took advantage of you?"

She offered him a sad smile. "Sorry. I only reveal one major mistake from my past at a time. Tune in next week for the continuing saga of Rachel Lansing's journey into bad judgment."

"Don't shut me out. I want to know everything about you." Max hated the way she kept deflecting his questions. It created a chasm between them when all he wanted was to get close to her. "You know you can trust me."

"Of course I do. It's just that I get depressed when I think about all the mistakes I've made. Can't we talk about something else?"

As much as he wanted to push harder, he recognized the stubborn set of her mouth and knew they would only end up fighting if he bullied her for answers.

He tossed a file across the desk toward her. "Take a look at the Williamsburg numbers in their strat plan. They don't add up. I didn't have time to check it over this weekend and I'm supposed to be on a conference call with them at eleven."

Her relief at being back on professional footing was so palpable she might have stood up and given a double fist pump. Max watched her head out of his office, a slim silhouette in her long pencil skirt and fitted jacket. He wanted to take her in his arms and promise he wouldn't let her down the way others in her life had. But was that something she'd believe when he wasn't sure himself if it was something he could deliver?

Eight

Rachel sat down at her desk and opened the file she'd been working on before Max summoned her into his office. The numbers blurred on the page. She sat back and rubbed her eyes, then reached for her tall coffee with the three shots of espresso. Max was a bad influence on her in more ways than one.

What had possessed her to tell him about Aunt Jesse?

She owed him no explanations. The intimacy they'd developed was physical, not emotional. Yet, she couldn't deny that sharing the story had lifted a little weight off her shoulders. Not much, but enough to help her get through the day. To clear her mind for how she would handle things with Brody. She simply had to find the twenty-five thousand she still owed him.

You could borrow the money from Max. If you asked, he'd help.

And have to explain to him about Brody and why she'd

married him. As if his opinion of her wasn't bad enough already, Max could add opportunist and user to her list of flaws. Besides, she didn't want her ex-husband to come between them again. Although, at the rate she was screwing things up on her own, it wouldn't matter what she told Max. Given the way their conversation had gone last night, he was probably done with her right now.

Rachel made notes on the file Max had asked her to look at and checked in with Devon to see if anything had come up. He was proving to be a great manager despite his reservations about taking on the responsibility. Maybe this meant she could take a long weekend for herself after everything was over. Four days with nothing to do and no worries sounded like heaven.

But was it reality? Since coming to work for Max, she'd been drifting in a fantasy world. The time for daydreams was over.

Right at eleven, Max's conference call began with the general manager of their Williamsburg operations. While he was asking the questions she'd posed about their numbers, his second line lit up. Rachel answered the call. It was Andrea.

"How are things going?" Rachel winced in sympathy at the loud cries in the background.

"As well as can be expected with a baby who's up all hours of the night with colic."

"I hope things get better soon."

"Me, too."

"Max is on a conference call at the moment. Do you want me to have him call you?"

A long pause preceded Andrea's response. "No. I'll try him again later."

Rachel picked up on the other woman's change of tone. "Is something wrong?"

"Not wrong." But something was up. Rachel could hear it in Andrea's voice.

"Anything I can help you with?"

"Look, I don't exactly know how he persuaded you to fill in for me, but you should probably find someone to take over on a permanent basis."

"You're not coming back?"

"Ned and I discussed it on and off since the middle of my pregnancy. Max is great, but he works such long hours." Andrea tried for cheerful but her tone fell flat. "Now with Ben not sleeping, I'm even more exhausted than I was before he was born. We just think it would be better if I stayed home for his first year. Maybe longer if we decide to get pregnant again right away."

"That makes sense to me." Rachel's mind raced. She needed to call Devon right away about possible candidates for a permanent position. "You have to make your family your priority." If anyone understood that, she did.

Andrea's laugh released some of her tension. When she spoke next, she sounded less like she was carrying fifty pounds of salt on her shoulders. "Thanks, Rachel. I hope Max hasn't been too hard on you. I know what he's like when things don't go exactly to his plan."

"Well, don't worry about that anymore. You just concentrate on that baby of yours. He's the important one."

"Thanks."

Rachel ended the call and dialed Devon, giving him the heads-up that they were now dealing with a permanent placement.

"What are you up to now?" a deep voice demanded from behind her.

Rachel glanced over her shoulder and spied Max standing in his doorway. Her pulse jumped as it always did when he was around. He had an annoying habit of sneaking up on her.

"I've got to go," she said to Devon, and hung up. She glanced toward the phone and noticed his line was no longer lit up. "That was a short conference call."

"After I used your notes to point out to them where their numbers still weren't good enough, they decided to go back and reassess. We're scheduled to talk this afternoon. Who was that on the phone?"

"Devon. Andrea called a few minutes ago. She's not coming back. We've got three candidates for you to interview."

His gaze swept her features, settled on her mouth for a moment longer than the rest, then reconnected with her eyes. "How fast can you get them here for interviews?"

"It would go faster if I could work from my office. I need access to my files. My notes. Those are at my office."

"Then go."

And just like that it was over. His abrupt dismissal left her floundering in dumbfounded silence.

What was it about Max that turned her from a hardheaded business woman into a sentimental fool?

A lean, muscular body made to drive a woman mad in bed.

A personality that was one-third angry bear, one-third stubborn mule and one-third cuddly tiger.

But it was the way he looked at her as if she was the only woman he'd ever desired that turned her insides to mush. How could she help but fall under his spell?

It was a short three blocks back to the building that housed Lansing Employment Agency, and Rachel used the time to gather her scattered emotions into a nice neat ball. Sharp pains began in her stomach as she swallowed the desire to cry or shout out her unhappiness. Max was done with her. What had she expected? A tearful goodbye?

Devon was on the phone as she went past his office. Knowing he would be full of questions, she took a deep breath and tucked all emotion away.

"What are you doing here?" he asked from her doorway moments after she dropped into her executive chair. "Did you quit or did we get fired?"

"Neither." After playing assistant for Max these last four weeks, she'd forgotten how wonderful it felt to be the one in charge. "Max wants to interview potential candidates as soon as possible. It'll go faster if I'm here."

"You're on the verge of netting us another big commission and yet you don't look happy."

"Of course I'm happy."

But to her intense dismay, tears filled her eyes. Devon stared at her in stunned silence, before rushing in and kneeling beside her chair.

"What happened? Was it Max? Did he upset you? Do you need me to go kick his ass?"

The thought of five-foot, nine-inch Devon kicking anyone's ass, much less Max's, made her chuckle. Shaking her head, she straightened her shoulders and shook off her melancholy.

"No. Nothing like that. I did something really stupid."

"I don't believe that for a second. You're one of the most savvy businesswomen I've ever met."

"I slept with Max."

"Ah," Devon said cautiously.

"What do you mean, *ah?*"

"I'm not surprised, that's all. You said you'd known him before. So what happened?"

Telling Max about Aunt Jesse earlier today had caused a crack in her self-imposed isolation. She'd felt better, lighter, after sharing her struggles in the aftermath of her father's death. Drawing on Max's strength had helped make the memories less painful. No matter how much she isolated herself, she wasn't alone. Telling Devon about Max could provide the same sense of relief.

"He and I met five years ago in Alabama."

The whole story poured out of her. She explained about her affair with Max. She talked about her financial problems with Brody. She told Devon about keeping everything from Hailey and about her slashed tires. Max's offer of help and her subsequent refusal.

"I understand everything," Devon said. "Except the part where you won't tell Max about the trouble your ex-husband is causing."

Rachel dabbed at the tears that had overflowed onto her cheeks. "My being married to Brody is what caused Max to despise me the last time. I don't want him involved in case Brody sets the loan shark on him."

"So, all your problems stem from the fact that you're trying to keep your sister and Max from worrying about you and pushing them away in the process."

"That's not fair."

"But it's what you're doing."

"So, what am I supposed to do? Explain to Hailey that I stayed married to Brody even though he was stealing from me to pay his gambling debts? That I was then so desperate to get free that I let myself agree to a ridiculous divorce agreement that compelled me to pay back the hundred thousand dollars it cost for her college education? And that I'm being harassed by Brody and whatever goon he owes money to?"

"For starters."

"I can't. I've spent my entire life protecting her. Don't ask me to stop now."

Devon shook his head. "She was a kid back when all the bad stuff happened. She's an adult now. Tell her the truth and let her be someone you can lean on."

"She's getting married. She's starting a fresh new life." Rachel shook her head and dried her eyes. "I don't want her to have to worry about the past."

Devon blew out a breath. "I can see why Max got angry with you."

Despite his neutral, slightly sad tone, Rachel felt as if she'd been slapped. "He wanted nothing from our relationship except sex."

That was a cop-out. She didn't really believe that's all she and Max had. But it was more comfortable to cling to that notion than to open herself up to hope and end up getting hurt.

"He invited you to his parents' anniversary party."

Part of her longed to believe Devon's optimistic take on her and Max. Spending time with him made her happier than she'd ever been. But he'd insisted from the start that he wasn't with her for the long term. And his track record bore that out.

"He's between women at the moment."

Devon stared at her for a long time. "Or maybe he's found the one he wants."

"Or maybe," she countered stubbornly, "he hasn't. And he just likes to stick his nose in where it doesn't belong."

"You don't really believe that's all there is to it."

"I can't afford to believe anything different." Despair was close to swallowing her unsteady composure.

"So, you're going to push him away?"

Rachel picked up her pen and twirled it. "After what happened last night and today, I don't think I'm going to have to."

To her surprise and despite their rocky week, when Saturday night rolled around, Rachel found herself at Max's side as they ascended the steps of his parents' home in the western suburb of Houston, a gated community with wall-to-wall mansions. She had no clear idea how she had arrived at this moment. Sure, she'd given her grudging acceptance that morning in Gulf Shores so he'd stop torturing her body with seductive caresses that got her motor revved up, but took her nowhere.

But after their argument at her house and how disinterested he'd been about her leaving Case Consolidated Holdings...

She figured he was done with her.

Then late Wednesday night, he'd shown up at her office with the sea glass bracelet he'd bought her five years earlier. When she'd gone back to Mississippi, she'd left the bracelet behind because it was a talisman representing hope and joy. By returning to her marriage, she didn't believe she deserved such a keepsake.

She couldn't stop wondering why Max had kept the bracelet all these years. Did it mean he'd never stopped caring about her? What if it had no significance at all? Every question battered the armor surrounding her heart. Sleep came only after hours of tossing and turning. Her appetite had dropped off. She caught herself daydreaming at work while Devon worked harder than ever.

And Brody called her often to remind her how impatient he was.

Her life felt like it was spinning out of control and she wasn't sure how much longer she could hang on.

"Stop fidgeting," Max advised. He set his hand at the small of her back, his touch soothing. "You look fine."

Rather than let him see how ragged her emotions were, Rachel retreated into sarcasm. "Fine?" She glazed the word with contempt. "What makes you think any woman wants to be told she looks fine?"

To her intense annoyance, his lips twitched. His relaxed

mood made it hard to keep her glare in place. Why did the man have to make her so damned happy?

"You look gorgeous."

Her harrumph resulted in a full-blown grin.

"I really shouldn't be here," she said for about the hundredth time. "This isn't a business associate or a group of friends, this is your family."

He'd never given her a satisfying answer about his true motive for badgering her to accompany him. In the end, she'd let him convince her to attend the party, but dug in her heels when he insisted she also be there for the family-only renewal of vows that had taken place earlier that afternoon at the church where his parents had originally been married.

"You're here because I didn't want to go through this alone."

His explanation made perfect sense. She was a stand-in because he was between women. She knew better than to call them girlfriends. Max dated, but he didn't get involved. Casual affairs were more his style.

So, what were they doing?

Since Wednesday, she'd gone home with him after work and spent the night at his house. They watched TV. They made dinner. They made love. Playing house. Getting to know each other better with each hour that passed. The chemistry wasn't burning out the way he'd said it would. In fact, it was getting hotter by the day.

Nor was either of them trying to cool things off or slow things down.

Two months, she kept telling herself. That's how long his relationships usually lasted according to the notes in Andrea's computer. She wouldn't think any further into the future than that.

A maid opened the front door as they approached. The grand, two-story foyer Max nudged her into was half the size of her house. She gaped like a girl from a small beach town. Meeting wealthy executives at their offices didn't prepare her for the reality of what money could buy.

"Did you grow up here?" she asked, trying to imagine three energetic boys roughhousing around the expensive furniture and exquisite antiques.

"No. Mom and Dad downsized after they kicked the chicks out of the nest."

Her breath rushed out. "Downsized?"

"This house only has four bedrooms."

"Only." Apparently, her answers were limited to two syllables.

"Come on. Let's go congratulate the happy couple." The mischief vanished from his eyes as he steered her deeper into the house.

With Max's arm around her waist, Rachel floated through the large, perfectly decorated rooms in a haze of anxiety and awe. Her nervousness was tempered by a couple things. First, the beige silk cocktail dress she'd splurged on might have come off the rack of her favorite consignment store, but it was a designer original and she needed that boost of confidence as they passed by women wearing thousands of dollars worth of gowns and jewelry. Second, most of the furniture had been upholstered in tones of cream, beige and gold. That meant she could sit down and virtually disappear.

"There's Mom. Let me introduce you."

She hung back as Max leaned forward and kissed his mother on the cheek. Dressed in a beaded cream gown with diamonds at her ears, wrist and around her neck, Susan Case looked every inch a wealthy socialite, but the smile she beamed at her son looked warm and genuine enough to put Rachel at ease.

"Mom, this is Rachel Lansing. Rachel, my mother, Susan."

Rachel stretched her lips into a smile, hoping her nerves didn't show, and shook the soft hand Susan Case offered. "It's really nice to meet you," she said. "Max talks about you a lot."

"Have you two been dating long?"

"Oh, we're not dating," Rachel insisted in a rush. "I own an employment placement service. I'm helping him find an assistant to replace Andrea."

"I see." But it was obvious she didn't.

Rachel didn't miss the curious glance Susan sent winging toward her son. Beside her, Max radiated displeasure. Well, what did he expect? That she was going to explain the complicated arrangement between them when she wasn't exactly sure how to define it herself?

"How is the hunt for a new assistant going?"

"He's turning out to be a difficult man to please." She shot Max a warning look to shut down whatever protest he was about to make.

"Is he, now," Susan murmured wryly. "Well, I'm sure you'll figure out how to make him happy."

Rachel flushed at the subtext of Susan's remark and wished a sinkhole would develop beneath her feet. Before she mustered a response, a tall man with dove-gray eyes stepped into the trio's circle and wrapped a possessive arm around Susan.

"Good evening." Brandon Case extended his free hand to Rachel. "My son is lucky to have such a lovely companion this evening."

Rachel smiled at Brandon Case as she shook his hand, unable to stop herself from basking in the man's charm. At her side, Max stiffened slightly.

"Congratulations on your thirty-fifth anniversary," she said. Max's tension heightened her own anxiety and the next words that came out of her mouth, she wished back immediately. "What's your secret?"

Susan dipped her head in acknowledgement. "To a long marriage?" She gazed up at her husband. A gentle smile curved her lips. She was obviously very much in love with the man she'd married. "I think you need to be able to forgive each other and laugh together."

Such simplicity took Rachel's breath away. Was that really all there was to it? She thought about her own marriage. She and Brody had failed at both. She couldn't recall a single time when they'd laughed together. In the beginning, they'd gotten along, but it had never been joyful the way it was with Max.

A slight indent had developed between Max's brows at his mother's words. "And that's it? All the pain just magically melts away? Trust is restored with a chuckle?"

Rachel put her free hand on Max's arm and squeezed in sympathy. She'd been so busy thinking about herself this week, she hadn't considered how hard this renewal of vows and anniversary celebration would be on Max. He'd never gotten over his father's infidelity. And now she saw that he was also angry with his mother for staying with a man who'd betrayed her.

"Of course not," Brandon retorted, his gray eyes hard as they rested on his son. "What I did to your mother wasn't forgiven overnight. It took years before she began to trust me again. And now that she does, I would never do anything else to hurt her."

"Max, this is a party," his mother said, her voice showing no signs of stress. "My anniversary party. Please behave."

As the tableau played out before her, Rachel had a hard time swallowing past the lump in her throat. Seeing Max's expression darken and knowing why he was so upset made her realize she'd been a fool to wonder if the passion they shared might lead to something more.

If twenty years had passed without him forgiving his parents their shortcomings, she'd been a fool to hope he would ever forgive her.

Laughter and forgiveness.

His mother was kidding herself. For years she'd turned a blind eye to her husband's second life with the woman he couldn't bring himself to live without. She should have included sacrifice in the mix of ingredients that kept a marriage going. Because, in his opinion, if she hadn't sacrificed her pride, her self-confidence, and her peace of mind, she would have divorced Brandon a long time ago. Instead, her husband had violated her trust with his infidelity and yet she'd stayed.

She'd stayed because she loved him.

And she'd taught Max a valuable lesson about trust, marriage and love. He wouldn't make his mother's mistakes. He wouldn't trust. He wouldn't marry. He wouldn't love.

The first two he could control. It was the last that worried him.

Coming here tonight with Rachel brought home his own weakness. He'd grown preoccupied with a woman who behaved like his father, keeping secrets, sharing only the surface of her life, not the emotions that drove her actions. How could he trust her? What hidden bombs lurked beneath her composed exterior, waiting to detonate at the worst possible time?

A couple weeks ago he'd wagered an extremely valuable car that he wouldn't marry. Falling in love had been the furthest thing from his mind. But that's before Rachel had brought up all the unresolved issues between them. Telling himself that it was nothing more than passion that needed to run its course was a speech he was having a harder and harder time selling. What he felt for her ran deeper than desire. It had sunk its claws into his soul.

He couldn't control his fierce need for her. Just like his father couldn't control whatever had made him stay married to one woman and love another for more than twelve years. Max had become just like his father. He'd grown up despising Brandon because he'd let his emotional need for Nathan's mother damage his marriage, and in Max's eyes, destroyed his credibility and his character.

Her hand slipped into his to draw him along to the buffet. The simple contact tugged his pulse into a sprint.

Being with Rachel made a mockery of his principles. Yet the idea of walking away was sheer agony. He'd believed the only solution would be to purge his need for her. And the only way he knew to do that was to keep her in his bed until he grew tired of her.

Who was he kidding? He grew more attached to her every day.

On their way to the backyard where a dining tent had been set up to accommodate the guests, they were intercepted by a dateless Jason.

"I don't believe we've met." Max's best friend took Rachel's hand and bent forward to smile into her eyes. "I'm Jason Sterling, and you are way too gorgeous to waste your time on my friend here."

Max stiffened at his friend's flirtatious manner. They'd competed over women a time or two, but once either staked his claim, the other immediately backed off. A growl started building in Max's chest as Jason's gaze dropped from Rachel's face to scope out the rest of her.

"Rachel Lansing," she said. "I know your father. How are he and Claire doing?"

"They're doing great, thanks to you. My father's never been happier." Jason's keen eyes surveyed them. "Are you two dating?" A vile grin curved his lips as he looked to Max for confirmation.

"Something like that." Max stared down his friend, warning Jason to keep further comments to himself, and slid his hand into the small of Rachel's back.

Jason looked positively delighted. "How long has this been going on?"

"We're just old friends," Rachel said, offering her own version of their relationship.

"Are you, now?" Jason looked entirely too pleased with himself as he turned to Max. "I got an offer on my '69 Corvette yesterday. Looks like I should take it. I have a feeling there's a new car in my near future."

The taunt infuriated Max. "I've got room in my garage for the 'Vette. Maybe I'll take it off your hands."

Jason just laughed and turned his charm back on Rachel. "Will you sit next to me at dinner?"

"She's with me," Max growled.

"I thought you two were just old friends."

Max stepped between Rachel and Jason, bumping his best friend in the process. "You're supposed to bring a date to events like this, not poach someone else's." It wasn't until he'd settled Rachel at the table and taken his place beside her that his annoyance with Jason dulled to a nagging irritation.

Snarling like a guard dog was not the usual way he kept other men from sniffing around his dates. On the other hand, he wasn't sure he'd ever cared enough to warn anyone off before.

Rachel's hand settled on his thigh. His attention jerked in her direction.

Her eyes were soft with questions. "What was that about?"

"It was just Jason being Jason." For some reason he didn't want to explain about the bet.

"Why did you tell him we were just old friends?"

"I guess it's a little bit of a stretch." Her lips thinned as she pressed them together. "Why did you give him the impression we're dating?"

"Aren't we?"

"I don't think so." She settled her napkin on her lap. "The term seems too tame for what we're doing."

And wasn't she right about that. He remembered how she'd looked this morning in his robe, the dark blue terrycloth contrasting with her pale skin and matching the midnight blue of her eyes. With her hair soaked from her shower, she'd let him pull her close then shook herself like a dog after a swim. He'd retaliated by dumping her onto the mattress and making her all sweaty again. Then, he'd joined her for her second shower of the morning.

Desire seared him, hot and consuming. He laid his arm across the back of her chair and leaned close. When she glanced his way, he captured her gaze and gave her a glimpse of his hunger. To his intense satisfaction, her lips parted and her cheeks flushed.

With the amount of time they'd spent together in the last week, his body shouldn't be clamoring to ditch the party and take her home, but her touch set off a chain reaction inside him. Two things kept him in place. His mom would kill him if he left, and he was eager to take Rachel in his arms on the dance floor.

He covered her hand with his. Their fingers meshed. His emotions settled. The temperature of his desire dipped from raging boil to slow simmer.

On the opposite side of the table Jason watched him through narrowed eyes. Max knew what his friend was thinking, but he was dead wrong. As Sebastian stood to deliver the first toast, Max let his gaze roam around the tent. All the usual suspects had been invited. Immediate family, extended family and friends. About two hundred people in all. Including his illegitimate half brother, Nathan, who sat two tables over with his very pregnant wife, Emma.

For a moment, Max fought irritation. Nathan's presence shone a spotlight on Brandon's infidelity and made a mockery out of celebrating thirty-five years of marriage. Max had never understood how his mother had allowed her husband to bring Nathan into her home after his mother died. Sure, it was the decent thing to do and his mother was kind and generous, but it had to have killed her to explain to all her friends about the twelve-year-old boy with Brandon's gray eyes. Yet to the best of Max's recollection, he'd never heard a cross word between his parents on the subject. He'd never know if his mother had forgiven her husband, or if she'd just decided to bear the humiliation for the sake of her marriage.

He and Sebastian hadn't followed her example of tolerance toward Brandon and their half brother. Even now, twenty years later, Max couldn't come to peace with his father or Nathan. The anger and resentment bubbled far below the surface like a dormant volcano.

And caught up in all those negative emotions were his feelings for Rachel. He couldn't completely let go of the way she'd deceived him all those years ago. Nor could he turn a blind eye to the secrets he knew she kept from him now.

The secrets that were bound to tear them apart.

"What are you doing out here?"

Max looked up from the steering wheel of the '71 Cuda and spied Rachel standing in the doorway that led from the garage into his back hallway. They'd returned from the party fifteen minutes ago and while she'd disappeared into the bathroom to change clothes and brush her teeth, he'd retreated to the one place in the house that had the most soothing effect on him.

"I'm enjoying my latest purchase."

Rachel stepped into the garage, her three-inch heels giving her long legs a positively sinful appearance. She wore the red and black baby-doll nightie Hailey had packed for the trip to Gulf Shores. That weekend, his appetite hadn't afforded her the chance to wear it. He recalled her opinion about the futility of wearing the thing. That he would have it off her in ten seconds.

"Wouldn't you enjoy it more if you took it for a drive?" She stopped near the front of the car and bent down to slide her palms up the hood. The black lace edging her neckline gaped, baring her round breasts. Beneath his intent regard, her nipples puckered against the gown's thin fabric.

The combination of muscle car and half-dressed Rachel was irresistible. He was instantly hard.

"Feel like going for a ride?" He got out of the car and prowled toward her.

She plucked a condom from inside her bodice and held it up. "Maybe later."

He put his arms around her, hands riding the sexy curve of her butt to the nightgown's hem. "How about now?"

He loved the flow of the material over her warm curves and the contrast between the scratchy lace and her silky skin. But he adored the heat between her thighs even more. And the low moan of longing that rumbled through her as he dipped his fingers into the moisture awaiting him there.

She pressed hot kisses to his neck as her fingers dipped inside the elastic waistband of his underwear and slid them down his thighs. He kicked free of the material, groaning his appreciation as her hands rolled the condom on his hot shaft.

Her mouth was open and awaiting his kiss as he lifted her off her feet, savoring the damp slide of her hot, sweet center against his belly. Gently, he placed her on the car's hood, past caring what damage he might do to the very expensive collectible. He only gave himself a second to enjoy the sight of

Rachel splayed across the yellow hood, but the mental snap-shot was unforgettable.

The elastic band kept the bodice snug against her chest and allowed the rest of the material to billow around the top of her thighs. However, the nightie was so short that when he'd set her on the car, the fabric rode up, exposing her con-cave belly and the thatch of dark blond curls at the juncture of her thighs. Nothing looked as gorgeous as she did at the moment.

He stepped between her legs and gathered her butt in his hands. Fastening his mouth on her, barely hearing her gasp past the roar in his ears, he feasted on her. She tasted incred-ible. Mewling sounds erupted from her parted lips as her fingers clutched his shoulders. He laved her with his tongue, penetrating deep while she writhed within his grasp. He drove her toward orgasm without mercy, ignoring her incom-prehensible protests. Maybe later he would give her a turn at him. Right now, he wanted to put his mark on her body and soul.

When she was close to the edge, he slipped two fingers inside her and watched her explode. She screamed his name. Her nails bit into his shoulders as her back arched and her heels found purchase on the bumper. Shudder after shudder pummeled her body, wringing every single sensation pos-sible out of her. Only when she went completely limp did he cease his erotic assault and kiss his way up her body.

Sliding his hands under the elastic beneath her breasts, he rode the material up over her head. She blinked and stared at him, dazzled.

"No fair," she complained. "I was going to do that for you."

"Later," he promised, riding the curve of her breast with his lips.

"It'll have to be much later," she agreed, sifting her fin-gers though his hair. "Because I can't move at the moment."

"That's okay. You just lie back and let me do all the work." He opened his mouth over her nipple, swirling his tongue around and flicking it over the sensitive tip. Her body jerked as he grazed his teeth against her flesh.

"Whatever you say." She closed her eyes. A half smile curved her lips. She looked the picture of utter contentment.

His heart turned over. It was happening to him all over again. He was falling beneath her spell. Her palms glided along his biceps as he nudged against her entrance. She was so slick, he almost drove straight in. But a week of intense lovemaking had taken the sharp edge off his driving need. He intended to savor every inch of their joining. To take his time enjoying the tight sheath that seemed made just for him.

And to watch her expression as he did so.

For it seemed the only time she truly dropped her guard and let him in was when he was buried inside her. That's when she couldn't fight what she needed or hide her thoughts.

He eased forward, delighting in the play of happy emotions across her features. When he was fully embedded, she surrendered a smile of sheer delight and opened her eyes. Plummeting into their blue depth, Max sank past her doubts and fears to her true heart. Jewel bright, her joy welcomed him. Pure and fierce it connected him to her.

"Again," she coaxed, cradling his face between her hands. "I love the feel of you sliding inside me."

He was happy to oblige her. She crooned her delight as he completed another long slow thrust. It was then that she wrapped her legs around his hips and began moving with him. He increased his rhythm. Pleasure built in slow waves as he took his time and gave her more of exactly what she liked.

And when he came, the pressure, swelling low in his back, exploded through him like a concussion bomb. The waves of pleasure caught Rachel and pulled her into bliss along with him. He lowered his head and touched his lips to hers, fusing their mouths together in a kiss of tender passion.

"Best ride of my life," he murmured against her neck as his heart labored and his lungs pumped.

Her nails grazed along his back to the base of his spine. "Better than racing around the track at a hundred twenty miles an hour?"

"Much, much better."

With his body mostly recovered, he gathered her in his arms and carried her back to bed. Once there, she snuggled at his side, her head on his shoulder, hand on his chest. Peace swept over him. He liked falling asleep next to this woman. Sleepovers were something he usually frowned on. They suggested a level of intimacy he avoided with all the women he dated.

Rachel was different. She knew they had no future. Only the present. They weren't dating. They were lovers. Lovers without expectations. She understood and accepted the limits of their relationship.

Because after much soul-searching tonight, he'd decided it was all he could offer her.

Nine

Max finished interviewing the last of the candidates Rachel had sent him. His respect for her ability to match employer to employee had increased over the last two days. She'd even scheduled the four women in order of their compatibility for both him and the type of work he would have them do, starting with the most likely candidate first and finishing with the woman he liked least.

They were all beautiful. Single. Intelligent. A month ago, fantasizing about any one of them could have occupied him for hours.

Today, his thoughts centered around one woman. Rachel. With her wise and witty opinions of the four candidates melding with his impression of them, he couldn't help but appreciate their similar thought patterns. Already he missed her sitting outside his door. He hadn't realized how often he'd walked past her desk so that he could deliver a remark guaranteed to make her grin or frown at him.

"Thank you for coming by on such short notice," he told the last candidate as he handed her off to his temporary assistant. A capable woman in her fifties, she'd been sent by Rachel to fill in for a few days. "Cordelia, can you show her out?" To his chagrin, he'd already forgotten the candidate's name.

"Of course." Cordelia stood. "And there's a young woman waiting for you in the lobby. Hailey Lansing."

Curious why Rachel's sister would have come to see him, Max headed for the lobby.

"Hailey?" He approached her with a smile. "To what do I owe the honor of your visit?"

Rachel's sister rose to her feet and took the hand he extended. Her brows darted together. "Thanks for seeing me like this. I probably should have called."

Something about Hailey's grave expression and obvious agitation put Max's instincts on red alert. Here was his chance to find out what was really going on with Rachel. She might never forgive him for going behind her back, but if he had to lose her, at least he could say that he'd done everything he could to straighten out whatever had gone wrong in her life.

"Let's get out of here." He gestured toward the elevator. Whatever Hailey had to say involved her sister and he thought it might go down easier with a single-malt scotch.

As the elevator door closed on them, Hailey twisted her engagement ring around and around on her finger and shot him an uncomfortable half smile. "You're probably wondering why I came to see you."

"You could say that."

Given Rachel's proclivity for keeping her problems hidden from everyone in her life, he was dying to know what had brought Hailey to his doorstep. And why she was wringing her purse strap like a dishcloth.

He escorted her across the lobby to the restaurant that occupied a large chunk of the first floor. Known for its fabulous cuisine and rich ambiance, it was a favorite place for those in the surrounding buildings to bring clients. It was also packed for happy hour, but at three in the afternoon, it was early enough that Max was able to find them a table in a quiet corner of the bar.

The waiter brought his usual and Hailey surprised him by ordering a martini.

At his expression, she offered him a weak smile. "It's been a long week."

Even though it was only Wednesday, Max agreed. "What can I help you with?"

"My sister."

Of course. "I thought that might be why you came by." He let an ironic smile kick up one side of his lips. "She's no longer working for me directly."

"I know."

"Then, I'm not sure what I can help you with."

The waiter placed their drinks before them. Hailey took a long sip of her martini before answering. "I found out from our neighbor last night that someone slashed Rachel's car tires."

Max stared into the amber depths of his drink. "Yes, I know. It happened sometime between Friday night when I picked her up and Sunday evening when I dropped her off."

"I knew it." Hailey flashed her straight, white teeth in a triumphant grin.

"Knew what?"

"That you two were involved. The sexual tension between you that night at dinner was hot."

Max leaned back and redirected the conversation where he wanted it. "Rachel said the neighborhood kids slashed her tires."

"That's what she told me, too, but I know better." Hailey's hunched shoulders suggested she was worried.

Alarm sizzled along his nerve endings. "Then who do you think is responsible?"

"Her stupid ex."

"I didn't realize he lived in Houston." Why hadn't Rachel told him? Why did he even bother asking? She held secrets tighter than a cold-war spy.

"As far as I know, Brody still lives in Biloxi. And my sister doesn't like admitting past mistakes. Brody was a big one."

"Why is that?"

"Because he was a complete jerk. You'd never know it to look at him. He dresses like he's harmless and he can turn that boyish charm of his on and off like a faucet, but beneath the surface, he's creepy."

Something beyond sisterly loyalty tightened Hailey's expression into a stiff mask. Seemed she had a few secrets of her own. But it was the fear that Max glimpsed in her eyes that pumped him full of adrenaline.

"You're not as good at hiding things as your sister. Tell me why he was a complete jerk."

"I didn't spend much time around him, just my last year of high school. And even then, I was cheerleading and on the yearbook staff so I wasn't home much." She took a deep breath and continued. "I didn't like the way he treated Rachel when I wasn't around."

"How did you know how he treated her if you weren't there?"

"Sometimes they didn't know I was home. I spent a lot of time in my room with the door closed. Brody was always on her about putting me first. He said that he was her husband and she should make his needs her priority. I'm ashamed to admit that I was really glad to head off to college. And once I was gone, I stayed away as much as I could, taking summer courses and working." Her chin sank toward her chest. "Part of me hated to leave Rachel alone in that house, but I knew if I showed her I could take care of myself, she could concentrate on her marriage."

"So, he was abusive."

"Not physically. He was too much of a coward to go after her. But I heard them fighting a couple times." Hailey's expression hardened. "Nothing Rachel couldn't handle. My sister's tough. But that's no way to live."

Max acknowledged that with a weary exhalation. "I agree." He didn't like the picture developing in his head. And it made him rethink how angry he'd been with her all those years ago for going back to her ex-husband.

"I guess it's wrong of me to say bad things about him when he paid for my education and everything. That's why I've been paying him back a little every year. I don't want to feel indebted to him at all."

"How much have you paid him?"

"Not much. About twenty thousand."

Max whistled. "That's a pretty big chunk for someone just out of school."

"I still owe him almost eighty." Hailey drew circles around the rim of her martini glass with her finger. "I wish I had it so I could be done with the guy."

"Why did you agree to pay him anything?"

"When Rachel asked him for a divorce he made it pretty clear that he wasn't going to let her go." Hailey winced. "He agreed to let her have a divorce if I paid him back the money he'd shelled out for college."

"That's blackmail."

"It was the only way he'd let her go without a major battle."

Max was liking Rachel's ex-husband less and less with each bombshell Hailey dropped. How had Rachel fallen for a guy like that? Granted, she'd been young, and probably a bit desperate, but had she mistaken gratitude for love? Or was he only hoping that her feelings for such worthless scum hadn't run deep?

"Let me lend you the money to pay off Rachel's ex-husband."

Hailey looked appalled. "That's not why I wanted to talk to you. What you must think of me."

She looked ready to walk out on him. Max put a hand on her arm to calm her. The sisters were very much alike. He hoped her fiancé had a clue what he was getting into. "I think you're charming. And crazy to repay someone like your ex-brother-in-law."

Her features settled into a mutinous expression she'd learned from her sister. "I pay my debts."

"Of course you do," he soothed. "And that's why I offered you the loan. Rachel's ex sounds unstable. I would just feel better if he was out of both of your lives for good."

Hailey shook her head. "Forget about me. It's not me he's harassing. Would you be willing to help Rachel in the same way?"

"Of course." He was insulted she even needed to ask. "But she won't tell me what's wrong much less accept my help. In fact, we had a big fight about it."

"But enough to break up over?"

"No." But it was why he feared their relationship might be over. Pain stabbed his chest. "Why do you ask?"

"Because she's been moping around lately like you two were done." The look she leveled at him was fierce and concerned. "I hope you mean to stick around. The last time you walked away she was different."

"I didn't walk away. She did. She got in a car with her ex-husband. She left me." Was he going to let her walk away from him again? The decision to fight for her had been gaining momentum in his subconscious. He might have noticed sooner if he'd stopped behaving like a pigheaded idiot. "Why did you assume I left her?"

"When we met, I recognized you from a picture she kept on her computer of the two of you. She hadn't looked that happy since before Dad died. I couldn't imagine her giving that up." Hailey's voice trailed away. She looked rattled.

As rattled as Max felt. Those days with Rachel had been the best moments of his life. But Rachel had gone back to her husband. And now he was back in her life again.

Max couldn't lose her this time. "How can I help?"

"She borrowed money from Brody to start the business. He showed up a couple weeks ago to collect the full amount. She paid him, but I don't think she had enough to pay him all of it."

"Is that why he's harassing her? How much is left to pay?"

"I think around twenty-five thousand."

Peanuts. Such a small amount shouldn't cause this much drama.

"Are you sure Brody's hanging around because of the money she owes him?"

"Why else?"

"Maybe he wants her back. You said he was possessive and gave her a hard time about the divorce. So much that you two left town to escape him. If he tracked her down after five years only to call for the money she owes him, why hasn't he come after you, too?"

Hailey's eyes widened. "Do you think he might come after me?"

He hadn't meant to upset her further. "Not if he hasn't already. No. I think this is personal." And if it was, Max was going to make sure Brody stayed out of Rachel's life for good. "Do you have a phone number for this guy?"

"I took it off Rachel's cell."

"Give it to me. I'll take care of him."

Ten

Rachel's office phone rang and her stomach dropped. Ten days had gone by since she'd gone with Max to his parents' anniversary party. Two days ago Max had hired his new assistant. She hadn't heard from him once since. Had her contact with him started and ended with his employment needs? If so, what had the amazing sex on Saturday night been about? Good-bye?

Hearing the phone ring had become torture. Any call could be Max. How should she act with him? Professional? Friendly? What should she say? Were they moving to a different level?

But he never called and she wasn't sure where they stood.

Nevertheless, every time she picked up the phone, her heart lurched as if it was trying to escape her chest.

"Rachel Lansing."

"Well, if it isn't my beautiful girl."

Rachel shuddered. Brody had always called her that and

never meant it. She'd never been his idea of beautiful. Just his idea of someone he could manipulate.

"What do you want, Brody?"

"I want you to meet me."

She rolled the phone cord around her finger. "Why? I already told you I can't pay you anything. There's no need for us to meet."

"The guy I owe money to isn't going to give up unless you tell him that."

"Why do I need to tell him anything? And what makes you think he's going to believe me any more than he believed you?"

"He just wants to meet you."

Rachel didn't like this one bit. "It has to be somewhere public." With lots of security guards within earshot.

"How about that place in the lobby where your boyfriend works? We could have drinks. Catch up."

"He's not my boyfriend." The restaurant in the lobby of Max's building? "Not there. Choose some other place."

"Can't. I already told the guy we'd meet in the bar. Be there at three."

He hung up. Rachel stared at the phone in her hand, consumed by the urge to slam it repeatedly on the edge of her desk. Acid burned her stomach. What was going on? Had Brody told the guys about her connection to Max? Would they follow him to his car one night and slash more than his tires?

Rachel wanted to scream in frustration. She couldn't let anything happen to Max. If that meant meeting Brody and the thug he owed money to, so be it.

Exactly at three, she pushed through the lobby doors and headed toward her rendezvous with Brody and his loan shark. For about the hundredth time she wondered what the hell she was doing. These were dangerous men. But it was a public place. And if it got her off the hook then it would be worth her trouble.

She spotted Brody before she reached the restaurant. He was deep in conversation with another man who faced away from her. She'd recognize those broad shoulders and the arrogant stance anywhere. Max. Her heart hit her toes as the worst of her imagined scenarios began to play out.

Max handed Brody a thick envelope and slid a folded piece of paper into an inner pocket of his suit coat before heading toward the elevator without ever noticing her standing in stunned immobility in the middle of the enormous lobby.

Brody spotted her as soon as Max headed for the elevator. A broad smirk transformed his boyish good looks into engaging handsomeness. The effect was lost on Rachel. She stalked over to him.

"What were you doing with Max?" She pitched her voice low, conscious that Max stood twenty feet away waiting for the elevator.

Brody waggled the envelope. "Collecting the money you owe me."

"Give me that." She made a swipe at the envelope, but Brody lifted it out of her reach.

"I don't think so."

"That money doesn't belong to you."

"The hell it doesn't." Brody's smug smile made her grind her teeth.

"Where's the guy who's been threatening me?"

Brody laughed. "You're such a sap. There never was anyone. I knew you needed motivating so I made him up."

"No guy?" She shook her head, confused. "But you owe someone the money?"

"Nope. I needed the fifty grand to buy into this poker game a buddy of mine is running. I knew you wouldn't give me the money unless you thought I needed help. I remember how scared you were when I owed money to Chuckie back when we were married."

"Poker?" Was she that much of a sucker? Shame overrode her other emotions for a moment. Then she grasped what Brody had done. "You terrorized me and my sister over a stupid poker game?"

Rachel saw red. She raised her fists, ready to beat him silly, but spotted Max returning across the lobby toward them. Her hands fell to her sides, the fight draining out of her.

Max stepped between her and Brody. "Get out of here," He addressed the command to her ex. "And don't let me catch you anywhere near Rachel or her sister ever again."

He might be a bully with her, but Max's threat made him pale. However, when Max made no further move against him, Brody sneered at Rachel and departed across the lobby toward the street.

Frustration surged as Rachel watched her ex-husband getting away. "Damn it, Max." She turned the full brunt of her irritation on him. "What the hell did you do?"

"I paid your debt with your ex. You don't have to worry about the guy ever showing up again."

Dismay consumed her. "You paid my debt? I didn't ask you to do that." Now she was in his debt. Someplace she'd sworn never to be.

"Yours and Hailey's. He's out of both of your lives forever."

Rachel stared at him, some of her anger draining away. "Hailey didn't owe him any money."

Max nodded. "She did. She was paying him back for her schooling."

"What?" Rachel struggled to breathe as the weight of these new revelations crushed her.

"It was the only way she could get him to leave you alone. He agreed to stay out of your life if she reimbursed him the hundred thousand for her college education." Max frowned down at her. "Only you had to go and borrow money to start your agency and bring him back in."

She ripped her wrist from his grasp. "I didn't borrow money from him," she snarled. "I told Hailey that so she wouldn't know what was really going on." Bitter laughter tore from her throat. "What a bunch of idiots we all are. I was already paying Brody back for her schooling. It was part of our divorce decree. He played all of us. You. Me. Hailey." She set her back against a nearby pillar as strength left her limbs. "How much did you give him?"

Max didn't look the least bit worried about what she'd just told him. "A hundred and five thousand dollars."

Rachel gaped at him. "What? Why so much?"

"The twenty-five you owed him plus the eighty Hailey still owed."

"How much had she paid him already?" She shut her eyes, fought tears, and awaited the answer.

"Twenty."

Helpless fury welled up inside her, but she didn't have the energy to vent it. Hailey had been paying Brody behind Rachel's back? That hurt.

"Rachel?" Concern tempered Max's tone. "What the hell is going on?"

She looked up at him. His brows had come together in a concerned frown that made her stomach turn cartwheels. From deep inside her mind, Devon's words surfaced.

Or maybe he's found the one he wants.

Her heart ached for it to be true, but Rachel shied away from the foolish hope.

"I need to get out of here," she said. "I need to find Brody and get that money back."

Max caught her arm. "I don't want you anywhere near him."

"I can't owe you."

"You don't."

"I do. You paid my debt."

"To get him out of your life, forever. If you hadn't shown up today you'd never have known about our deal." Max's steel gray eyes sliced at her. "Isn't that the way you work? Keeping everyone in your life in the dark about what's going on with you."

"That's not fair. I was only trying to protect Hailey."

"Fair? Do you think it was fair of you to keep the truth from your sister? She was paying your ex-husband a hundred thousand dollars to protect you."

Rachel gasped. "She didn't need to do that. I had everything all worked out."

"Only she didn't know that, did she? You were too busy keeping her wrapped in cotton to realize that by isolating her, you made her vulnerable."

"I was trying to keep her safe."

"And she was trying to help you. But you couldn't let her. You can't accept help from anyone."

Max's accusations lashed at her. Unable to deny that they made sense, she retreated into her convictions. What he said rang true, but it was only half the story.

"For good reason."

"Care to share?"

She recoiled. Telling Max about the mistakes she'd made with Brody would substantiate every negative thought he'd ever had about her. Rachel wasn't convinced she was strong enough to watch his concern die, but what choice did she have?

"So you agreed to pay him for Hailey's education."

"I didn't borrow money from Brody to start up the business. I was paying him so he would agree to a divorce."

"How much?"

"A hundred thousand dollars."

"Why so much?"

"That's how much it cost to put Hailey through college."
All at once, the secrets she'd lived with for years could no
longer be contained. "Brody used me to keep his gambling a
secret from his father. While I was married to him, he put me
on the payroll for more than what I should have been earning. I was supposed to use the money for Hailey's school, but
most of the time, there wasn't enough because he was losing
the money playing poker. To get what I needed, I waitressed
on the weekends he was gone."

"He was stealing money from the company."

"I guess."

"How much of Hailey's education did you pay for by waitressing?"

"By the end, I was paying for all of it." She circled her
hand in a vague gesture. "That's when I wanted out. But
Brody hired the best divorce attorney in Biloxi and contested
everything. I was desperate enough to agree to anything to
get away from him."

"I don't understand why you let him do that to you."

"Because I was young and scared. When I met Brody, I'd
been taking care of Hailey by myself for a year and slipping
a little further behind every month. Our apartment was a
dump. We clipped coupons and barely scraped by. Most days
I didn't see how I was going to make it to the next paycheck.
Then Brody swept into my life. He seemed like a dream come
true. Wealthy, handsome, charming, and he saw me as the
perfect patsy. Stupid and gullible." Rachel turned away from
Max, unable to face her failure reflected in his eyes. "I guess
some things haven't changed. I came here today because he
said that I needed to meet with the guy who slashed my tires
and convince him that I wasn't going to be able to come up

with any more money. Only there wasn't any guy threatening Brody."

"He lured you here to see me giving him the money. He wanted to hurt you."

He wanted to humiliate her. To demonstrate he'd always be smarter than her. "How did you know about him? About the money I owe him?"

"Hailey. She was worried about you and came to me for help. Did you know she was paying your ex for her tuition?"

"What?" This was a complete disaster. Now she had to have a long, painful talk with her sister. "Why would she do that?"

"Brody convinced her the only way he would give you a divorce is if she paid him back for tuition."

"She did it because we were worried about you. Why can't you just say thank you for the help?"

Failure buzzed around her head like a swarm of black flies. She'd screwed up again. Self-loathing flared, setting fire to her irritation.

"I didn't ask for her help or yours."

"Maybe everything would have turned out better if you had." Max's gaze warned her to stay silent as she opened her mouth to disagree. "You brought this whole mess on yourself and on us because you had to do it all yourself. You couldn't reach out for help. You couldn't accept assistance when it was offered. Instead, you alienated Hailey and me and made it so your ex-husband could cheat both of us."

"You'll get every penny back," she retorted, her face hot while the rest of her body shivered with chill. "If it takes me until the day I die, I'll pay you back every cent."

"I don't care about the money. I only care about you." He reached for her, but Rachel flinched back. It was instinctive reaction to Max's earlier scolding, but his gray eyes became like a wintry sky, dense and ominous. "Only you won't let me do that."

And to Rachel's profound dismay, he turned on his heel and walked away from her. She wrapped one arm around her waist and ground the knuckles of her other hand against her lips to keep from calling him back. The set of his shoulders told her he was completely done with her.

As he should be.

He was right. This was all her fault. She'd made nothing but one mistake after another since the day her father died. She'd trusted the wrong people. She'd allowed fear to make her weak. And when she learned to be strong, she swung so far in the other direction that she'd put up walls that kept out even the people she loved.

She didn't blame Max for walking away. In fact, she was a little surprised he hadn't run as far and fast as he could to get away from her. She owed him more than she could repay. Not just the money he'd given Brody, but for stepping in on her behalf as well as on Hailey's.

What a fool she was to have shut him out. She was an even bigger fool to let fear of rejection stand in the way of her chasing after him now.

Max went straight to the parking garage. His footfalls ricocheted around the concrete structure, mimicking the echo in his empty chest. He'd called his new assistant and warned her he'd be gone the rest of the day. Taking off in the middle of the afternoon wasn't like him, but what was the point in trying to work when there was no way he could concentrate?

He eased his car up the exit ramp and rolled down the window to activate the garage's electronic gate. Heavy, humid air, stinking of exhaust, washed over him as his tires reached the street. He longed for the clean scent of the beach. But even that wouldn't soothe him for long. The fragrance would forever remind him of Rachel and their time together.

How could two people be so right for each other and so wrong at the same time?

The question made him think of his parents' past troubles, and before he knew his intention, the car was heading to the suburbs. He called ahead to make sure someone was home and his mother met him at the door.

"Your father is golfing," she said, drawing him through the house with her arm linked through his. "He appreciates playing so much more now that he's back to work part-time. I've never seen him so relaxed. He'll be back in an hour or so if you can wait around that long."

"I didn't come about business. I need to talk to you."

"Really?" Her surprise faded to concern as she scanned his face. "Is it something serious? You're not ill, are you? You look awfully pale. Are you sleeping?"

"Nothing like that." Max patted her hand to reassure her. "It's about Dad's affair." Max felt his mother's whole body stiffen. He kicked himself for being so blunt. "If it's too hard for you to talk about, I'll understand."

"No." The word swept out of her on a gust of air. "It's okay. I should be able to talk about it after twenty years, right?"

"It's okay if you can't."

She didn't speak until they'd entered the kitchen and she'd pushed him onto a stool at the breakfast bar. In his childhood home, the kitchen had been separate from the rest of the house, a place where the housekeeper prepared meals and he and Sebastian snuck snacks. In this house, the kitchen opened onto a large great room with overstuffed couches and an enormous flat-screen television. A sunroom had been transformed into a semiformal dining area for eight and a breakfast nook held a table that seated four.

Although the house possessed a formal dining room designed to entertain on a grand scale, the room was used infrequently. For holidays, birthdays and spontaneous dinners, the family gathered in this casual space.

From the refrigerator, his mother brought out white cheddar cheese, pâté, and olives. From the pantry, two types of crackers. By the time she handed Max a glass of crisp chardonnay, an empty plate and a napkin, he was grinning.

"What's so funny?" she demanded, handing him a cracker spread with pâté.

"I didn't realize it was happy hour."

"It's five o'clock somewhere." She waved her hand at him and sipped her own wine. "I tried a new recipe for the pâté. I'd like your opinion, but only if you rave about my wonderful cooking. Now, what did you want to know about your father's relationship with Marissa?"

Nathan's mother's name slipped off her tongue with ease as if she'd spoken it a thousand times.

"It really isn't the affair I'm interested in. I wanted to know why you forgave Dad after what he'd done to you." Max popped the cracker into his mouth and chewed. "Or maybe I should ask how you forgave him."

"I loved him."

"That's all there was to it?" Max couldn't shake his disappointment. He wanted a concrete, step-by-step plan that he could apply to his own difficulties with Rachel. "You didn't weigh your options then decide do it to keep the family together or because he promised never to do anything like that again?"

His mother shook her head. "No. I forgave your father for purely selfish reasons. I didn't want to live without him."

"Even knowing he hadn't been honest with you?" The question struck at the heart of what he couldn't grasp. "What assurance did you have that he wouldn't lie again?"

"None." His mother cocked her head. "I went on faith."

"That's it?" Damn it. The answer to such a complex problem couldn't be that simple. "After everything that happened you didn't want a guarantee?"

"What assurance do you have that someone will love you forever or that they ever intended to keep vows they made? 'Til death do us part. How many people believe in that anymore? The vows should say, ''til we're no longer willing to work on our marriage.'"

His mother's pragmatism left Max momentarily speechless.

"But you and Dad just renewed your vows. Why did you do that if you didn't believe in them?"

"Did I say I didn't believe in them? I took my vows to your father very seriously." She handed him a slice of cheese. "And just so you know, it was his idea to renew our vows. It's taken us a lot of work to get to where we are today. But I can say with confidence that your father and I are more in love and more committed to each other than we were the day we got married."

Max chewed on the cracker and pondered his mother's words.

He loved Rachel. There was no sense in denying it any longer. Her stubborn need to reject all outside help had given him the excuse he needed to hide from the truth in his heart. No matter how many secrets she kept from him, she wasn't deceitful because she was a bad person. She merely struggled to trust anyone. And after what she'd been through, could he blame her? He had his own issues with trust.

"Is this about that woman you brought to the party?" his mother asked, stepping into the silence. "I liked her very much." Her lips curved in a wry grin. "I got the distinct impression you did, as well. You two left here early enough."

Max felt a little like a teenager caught in the backseat of

the car with a half-naked girl. "We've been seeing each other for a few weeks."

"And she's important to you."

"Yes."

"But there's a problem of trust between you?"

"We met five years ago. She was married at the time, although I didn't find that out until after we…" He paused, groping for a delicate way to put it.

His mother played with her diamond tennis bracelet. "Spent some time together naked?" While he regarded her in dismay, she chuckled. "Oh, I wish you could see the look on your face right now."

Max dove back into the story. "I was so angry when I found out. With everything that happened with Dad you know I wouldn't have gotten involved with her if I'd known." Or would he? The chemistry between them had been hot and all consuming. Would he have walked away if she'd told him up front that she was in an unhappy marriage?

"She's divorced now, I take it."

"For four years. When we met, she didn't tell me she was married. I found out when her husband showed up to bring her home."

"And you overreacted because you've always taken issue with your father for cheating on me. If you love her, you can't continue to punish her for mistakes she made."

"I don't want to punish her." But wasn't his inability to trust her just as detrimental to their relationship?

"If you can't forgive her, you might have to give up and let her go."

But his mother hadn't given up and Max needed to know why. "Why didn't you leave?"

"Some things are worth fighting for. Your father was one of them."

"Even after he'd lied to you and had an affair?"

"Not just an affair," she told him, her voice and eyes steady. "He loved Marissa. I don't know why he never left me for her."

Max's temper simmered at the old hurts. "You didn't ask?"

"It was enough that he stayed."

He remembered those days. His mother had been depressed and on the verge of tears much of the time. Max hadn't understood what was happening between his parents until Nathan appeared, but he'd been mad as hell at his dad for upsetting his mom.

Max still didn't understand his mother's ability to forgive his father. Sure, she loved him and wanted to keep her family together, but she wasn't bitter or angry about the past. It was as if she understood she needed to let it go in order to be happy in the future.

"And he promised it would never happen again," his mother continued.

"You believed him?"

"Yes." She lifted her hand and showed off the five carat diamond ring Brandon had bought to renew their vows. "And we're still married because I did."

"I'm not sure I have it in me to forgive Dad."

"I wish you would. Hanging on to the past isn't healthy. You've let what happened between your father and me keep you from falling in love and getting married. Rachel seemed like a lovely woman. I can't imagine that you would care for her if she wasn't wonderful. Forgive them both. I think you'll find doing so will set you free."

"I'll think about it," Max muttered, but even as he said the words, he felt himself resist.

Rachel hadn't wanted to interrupt Hailey at work, but she desperately needed to talk to her sister. She called Hailey and invited her to dinner. Then, she went to the grocery store and bought what she needed to make their father's famous pan-fried grouper.

The domestic routine soothed her. She'd been rushing around so much these last few weeks, between her business and Max's office, fitting in a couple hours to cook and eat a meal hadn't been a priority.

It was time she slowed down.

By six o'clock when Hailey arrived, Rachel had made a mess of the kitchen but had fun doing it.

"Whoa. What's with this? You're cooking?" Hailey dropped her purse on the small breakfast table and surveyed the mess Rachel had made. She wrinkled her nose at the spilled flour, puddles of buttermilk and the array of spices and bowls that occupied every square inch of countertop. "Now I remember why I took over cooking. You are a disaster in the neatness department."

"Don't I always clean up when I'm done? Get changed and come open a bottle of wine."

"I'll be right back."

Only a twinge of guilt pinched Rachel as she directed her sister to the bottle in the refrigerator.

Hailey pulled it out and peered at the label. "Champagne? What are we celebrating?"

"I had some good news today."

"A new client?" Hailey worked off the foil and pried at the cork.

"Better." Rachel waited until her sister was fully engaged in wiggling the cork free before she unloaded her bombshell. "Max paid off Brody."

The bottle jerked. The cork shot out with a loud pop and dented the ceiling. Hailey stared at Rachel with her mouth open as foam flowed down the side of the bottle onto the floor.

"He did?"

"Any idea how Max found out that Brody was hassling me about money?"

"I told him." Hailey looked one part anxious and one part resolute. "Are you mad?"

Damn right she was mad. But confronting Hailey about seeking Max's help wasn't satisfying. Tension flowed out of her, leaving behind nothing. Not even regret.

"No. I'm angry with myself. I should have told you the truth instead of trying to protect you." Rachel's eyes burned as she reached into the cupboard and brought out two water glasses. The only pair of champagne glasses she'd ever owned had been bought for her wedding toast. She'd smashed them not long after her first anniversary.

Hailey poured the champagne. "I wish you had. It would have made things a lot easier for both of us."

"Here's to honesty between sisters from here on out." Rachel clinked her glass against Hailey's.

"I'll drink to that," Hailey said. "Tell me what happened today."

"Why don't you start by telling me what possessed you to go to Max."

Hailey shot her an accusing look over the rim of her glass. "You are mad."

"I'm not," she started, but her sister's impatient huff reminded her of their toast. "Okay, I'm not exactly mad at you. I get why you did it. I just wish you hadn't."

"I had to. Someone slashed your tires. That scared me."

Rachel flinched. "I had it under control."

"No, you didn't." Hailey's voice was hot as she countered Rachel's claim. "Just like you didn't have it under control after Dad died and Aunt Jesse took off on us. I know I wasn't out of high school, but you should have let me help."

"I was trying to protect you."

Hailey shook her head. "You always treated me like I was

made of glass. Just once I wanted you to lean on me, but you never did."

"I didn't realize it was that important to you," Rachel said, holding up her hands to fend off her sister's verbal battery. She'd always been proud of her sister, but never more than now. "Thank you for going to Max."

Hailey's temper evaporated. Her lips formed a half grin. "Wow, how'd that taste?"

"Bitter." Rachel finished the rest of her champagne in one swallow and held her glass out for a refill. "If you hadn't gone to him, Brody would have continued to pester us. He'd have taken more of your money. And I would forever be hopeful that Max might someday forgive me for not telling him I was married five years ago. I don't need to worry on any of those accounts any more."

"You and Max will make it work. That man has it bad for you."

"You didn't see him today. He never wants to see me again. Thanks to me he paid a hundred and five thousand dollars to a lowdown stinking liar."

"Why so much? You only owed him twenty-five."

"But you told Max that you'd promised to pay Brody for your college education."

Hailey gasped. "He wasn't supposed to do that."

"Now do you understand why I kept this from Max?" She slid the cooked fish onto two plates and dished out the broccoli she'd steamed. "He's not the sort of man to stand on the sidelines when he could save the day." Another reason why she loved him. Rachel blew out a breath. "He settled both our debts. I told him I'd pay him back the money. The problem is, you and I were both paying Brody off for your schooling. He was double dipping."

"I thought you were paying him back for a loan to start your business."

"No. Brody was cheating us. We paid him for your schooling twice."

"Twice?" Hailey looked horrified.

"I was paying him as part of our divorce decree. Now paying back Max will make it three times."

"That's insane. You're not going to do that. I'm not going to let you."

Rachel shoved a plate into her sister's hands. "Yes, I am."

"No, you're not. It was my mistake. I'm going to pay Max back."

"It was my fault for not telling you about my arrangement with Brody from the beginning. I'll pay Max back. You're getting ready to start your life with Leo. You don't want this sort of debt hanging over your head."

"And you've got a business to run. You shouldn't have to shoulder it, either."

Rachel had never seen her sister look so fierce or so determined. New respect bloomed. While she'd struggled with her business and finances, Hailey had become a strong, independent-minded young woman. Rachel was ashamed she hadn't noticed sooner.

"Okay."

Hailey's eyebrows shot up. "What do you mean, okay?"

"You're absolutely right that I don't want to be the one to pay Max back."

"You're going to let me do it?" Hailey nodded in satisfaction.

"Nope. I have a different idea altogether." Rachel rubbed her hands together and sent an evil grin winging toward her sister.

Hailey cracked a smile. "Anything you'd care to share?"

"Grab some silverware. We'll talk while we eat."

Eleven

Rachel stood on Max's front porch, her finger hovering over the doorbell. Her enthusiasm for the plan she talked over with Hailey had faded as she'd driven the twenty minutes to his house. What was she doing here? Max wouldn't want to help her after what had happened earlier today. Even if he answered the door, he'd probably slam it in her face as soon as he spotted her standing here.

Maybe he wasn't home. It was a Thursday night. Didn't he get together with his friends and go clubbing on Thursdays? She should have called. But what if he refused to answer?

She should have waited until Monday and caught him at his office. Of course, he might refuse to see her there, as well.

The door opened while lose-lose scenarios played through her mind like an action movie.

"Are you planning on standing out here all night?" Max asked. He blocked the doorway with his arm and nothing about his hard expression or his tense body language gave her hope. But suddenly Rachel's spirits rose.

"I guess I'll have to if you don't let me in."

His eyebrows rose. "What's the password?"

"You were right."

"That's three words."

She dug deeper. "I'm sorry."

"That's two words." A twitch at the corner of his mouth told her she was getting close.

"Help."

He reached out and dragged her inside. "That's it."

Lowering his head, he captured her mouth in a hard, unyielding kiss that melted away her worries. She wrapped her arms around his neck and kissed him back, giving full rein to her angst and fear of losing him.

He stripped off her shirt and dove his fingers beneath the elastic waistband of her skirt, pushing it down her hips until she stood before him in bra, panties and sneakers. Then, he scooped her into his arms and carried her down the hall to his bedroom.

The long walk gave her time to summon explanations or apologies, but Max's grim expression tied her tongue into knots. Make love to him now. Fight with him later. At least they would make another incredible memory for her to relive after they parted ways for good.

When he set her on her feet beside the bed, she grabbed the hem of his T-shirt and raised it past his flat stomach and powerful chest. He helped her by tearing it over his head. A purr-like sound vibrated her throat as she set her palms against his chest and backed him toward the bed.

Her fingers worked at the button and zipper of his jeans. She needed to taste him. The urgency made her clumsy and she let him rid himself of the rest of his clothes. Once he was naked, she dropped to her knees in front of him and sucked him into her mouth without finesse or preliminaries. He released a hoarse groan as her tongue circled him, discovering his texture and the best way to give him pleasure.

Before she brought him all the way to release, he stopped her and pulled her back to her feet. Placing a hot, sizzling kiss on her lips, he lifted her and deposited her on her back in the middle of the mattress. She kicked off her shoes. He followed her down and as his weight pressed her into the mattress, she ran the sole of her foot along his calf.

His fingers hooked around her underwear, stripping it down her legs. While he cast it aside, she took off her bra. The contact between her sensitized nipples and his hard chest set off a chain reaction of desire.

She lifted her hips toward the hand that teased between her legs, urging him to touch her with wild gyrations and garbled pleas. A half sigh, half moan broke from her as he slid his finger into her wetness and penetrated deep. She shuddered as he began to stroke her, each movement of his hand driving her further toward fulfillment. But that's not the way she wanted to go. Her nails bit into his wrist.

"Not like this," she gasped as his teeth grazed her throat. "Make love to me."

"If you insist."

He moved between her thighs, impaling her with one swift thrust. Hard and thick, he filled her over and over, the friction driving her crazy with wanting. Together they climbed. Higher and faster than ever before. When she came, the sensation rolled over her, wave after wave of intense pleasure. She floated back to earth in slow motion, the thundering of her heart keeping time with Max's thrusts as he surged toward his own climax.

Fascinated, she watched him come. His facial muscles locked in concentration. His eyes, half-closed, snagged with hers. He set his mouth against hers and plunged his tongue deep in a sexy kiss that stole her breath. Then his body drove into hers one last time and spasmed in release.

With her arms wrapped around his shoulders, Rachel held on to him and absorbed his aftershocks. Loving Max like this was easy. They knew exactly how to communicate in bed. She'd lost hope at being able to do so anywhere else.

All too soon, Max pushed away and dropped onto his back beside her. He lay with his forearm across his eyes, his chest rising and falling as his body recovered. Unsure if he would welcome her touch now that their frantic coupling was through, Rachel rolled onto her side and tucked her arm beneath her head.

Five minutes passed before he spoke.

"I'm glad you stopped by." Voice neutral. Expression hidden behind his arm. His mood an enigma.

"Me, too."

As much as she longed to cuddle up beside him and feel the reassuring weight of his arm settle around her, she'd made too many mistakes to hope that he felt tender or affectionate toward her.

"I was hard on you earlier," he continued. "I'm intolerant when I don't agree with someone. It's a bad habit of mine." He shifted his arm off his face and set it above his head. His gaze locked on the ceiling. "Or so my mother tells me."

"You were right to be angry. I screwed up. I should have been more up front with Hailey and with you. If I had, none of this would have happened." She paused. "It's my fault that Hailey gave Brody twenty thousand dollars. It's my fault that you gave him a hundred and five thousand. It's not right that he cheated you and I intend to get that money back."

At last, Max looked at her. The iron in his gray eyes made her wish he hadn't.

"How do you intend to go about that?" he demanded, his hard tone warning her he'd better like her answer.

She drew her knees up and bumped his thigh with them. The grazing contact eased the tension between them. "I'm going Biloxi to ask for it back."

"He went to a great deal of trouble to get the money in the first place," Max said, rolling onto his side so that they faced each other. "Have you considered what you'll do if he won't just give it back?"

She offered him a wan smile. "I was hoping you'd come along. I need your help." She held her breath and waited for some sign that he wasn't going to kick her and her crazy idea to the curb. "Please."

"You're asking me to help you?"

"Yes. I need you. I can't do this alone."

Max's arms snaked around her body, pulling her flush against him. With her thigh trapped between his and her head settled on his shoulder, his lips glanced off her forehead. "I'm glad you finally realized that."

The closer they got to Biloxi, the quieter Rachel became. And it wasn't just that she stopped talking. Her entire body stilled as if by remaining frozen, she could become invisible. Max kept glancing her way as they picked up a rental car at the airport and drove through the city.

He longed to reach out and offer her comfort, but she'd locked herself away and drawn the shutters. His fingers beat a tattoo on the steering wheel. The previous evening's connection had faded with the advent of dawn. She'd stood at the foot of his bed and worried the inside of her lip while he made arrangements for their flight to Biloxi.

"Say the word and we'll get right back on the plane and go home to Houston," Max offered.

In the seat beside him, Rachel started as if he'd jumped out and yelled "boo." Beneath his scrutiny she struggled a long moment before mastering the trace of panic in her dark blue eyes. Seeing her vulnerable for even that short second disturbed Max. She was awash in anxiety and trying like crazy to hide it. He was used to her strength and determination. Is this why she was so scared to ask for help?

"We've come all this way," she said. "We're not going back without that money."

Max nodded. He liked the way she said *we,* including him as part of her team, and appreciated what it had taken her to let him in.

"It's going to be okay. I won't let him hurt you ever again."

"I'm counting on that."

To Max's surprise, she reached out and grabbed his hand.

"Is that why you brought me along?" he teased. "Muscle?"

She stroked up his biceps, wrapping long fingers around his upper arm. "Well, you certainly have enough of them to qualify for that. But that's not why you're here."

"Then why?"

"Because I knew you'd want to come." She glanced his way and encountered his frown. Her elaborate sigh filled the car. "Fine. Because I wanted you to come. You make me feel safe in ways that no one ever has before." She pulled a face. "Happy now?"

"Deliriously."

Rachel's directions brought them into a commercial section of Biloxi. Max parked the car in a visitor's spot in front of Winslow Enterprises. As they entered the front door, he watched her gather courage. By the time they'd arrived at the front desk, her spine was straight and her eyes glinted with determination.

"Hello," he said to the receptionist. "I have an eleven o'clock meeting with Carson Winslow."

Rachel jerked in surprise. He could feel her gaze upon him.

"And your name?"

"Max Case."

While the receptionist spoke into the phone, Rachel grabbed on to Max's arm and drew him toward a seating area. "Why are we meeting with Brody's father?"

"I called him with a business proposition."

"Why?"

"You didn't seriously think Brody was going to just return the money because we asked him to, did you?"

From the expression on her face, she hadn't planned beyond demanding the money back.

Max shook his head. "You told me he's been gambling for years. He used you and the huge salary he paid you to hide his problem from his father. Why do you think he was so reluctant to give you a divorce?"

"Because any financial problems we had he could blame on me." Rachel blinked in dazed disbelief like a prisoner coming out of a dark cell. "What has he been doing since then?"

"I don't imagine he's quit gambling."

"Obviously not if he came to me for the cash he needed to get into a high-stakes poker game."

"Mr. Winslow said he'd be right up," the receptionist said with a polite smile before returning to stuffing envelopes.

"So, what's your plan? You're not going to ask Carson for the money, are you? Brody works hard to keep his father completely in the dark."

"And that will work to our advantage."

She frowned at his cryptic reply, but had no chance to ask for clarification because a thin, gray-haired man in his mid-sixties appeared in the doorway that led to the rest of the building.

"Follow my lead," Max murmured as he stepped forward with his hand extended. "Max Case. Thank you for taking a meeting with me on such short notice."

"Not at all. I was intrigued by your call."

"This is my associate." Max stepped to one side so Rachel came into view.

"Rachel?" Carson's smile faltered. "How are you?"

"I'm wonderful. And you?"

While pleasantries were exchanged between Rachel and her former father-in-law, Max observed the interplay with interest. There was no obvious animosity between the pair. Did that mean Carson had no idea what had transpired in his son's marriage?

"Let's head back to my office," Carson said.

Once inside the spacious corner office, Max wasted no time in getting to the point. "You've probably figured out by now that Rachel was the one who pointed me in the direction of Winslow Enterprises."

"I'll admit it clears up how we came to your attention."

Max smiled. "After doing some research on your company, I was able to determine that it's positioned to break out, but you lack the capital and the skilled management to take you to the next level."

Frustration and resignation tightened Carson's mouth into a grim line. Beside him, Rachel had gone so still, Max wondered if she was holding her breath. He matched her immobility, letting his words penetrate Carson's defenses. From what Max had gathered from his sources in Biloxi, ever since Carson had handed the business operations over to his son, the company was floundering.

Carson was at a crossroads. He needed to decide if he was going to let his son take over and risk the company's future, or sell the business and enjoy his retirement.

"What's going on in here?" an unfriendly voice demanded from the doorway.

Rachel shifted in her seat to confront her ex-husband. Her knees bumped Max's thigh. A tremor passed through her, heightening his determination to give her closure with her ex. By the time Max finished with Brody, the guy wouldn't dare bother Rachel or her sister again.

Carson hit his son with a meaningful look. "Max has come to us with a proposition."

"Is that so." Brody's lip curled. "And what is she doing here?"

Rachel inclined her head, all nervousness mastered. With a half smile, she said, "If it wasn't for me, Max would never have become interested in Winslow Enterprises."

The return of Rachel's confidence eased Max's tension.

"Of course, my brothers are not convinced that your company is large enough for us to pursue. But after we get a look at your books, I'm sure they will be persuaded."

Brody's gaze bounced between his father and Max. Anger melted into uncertainty. "Well, it's not for sale."

"You don't get to make that decision," Carson reminded him, his voice tight with reproof.

"Why not? You've put me in charge, haven't you?" Brody seemed to have forgotten that this family squabble was in front of witnesses.

His father's gaze flicked in Max's direction. "We'll discuss this later. Right now I'm going to take Max on a tour of the facility."

"Let me do it," Brody said.

The tension between father and son tainted the air like exhaust as Brody led the way out of the office. But instead of taking Max and Rachel on the tour his father had suggested, Brody steered them into a conference room and shut the door.

"You've got a lot of nerve showing up here," he snarled.

"*We've* got a lot of nerve?" Rachel began, her fingers curled into claws as if she'd like to rip her ex-husband's eyes out. "You bastard. I want the money you stole from Hailey."

"I don't know what you're talking about."

"She's been paying you for her college."

"So?"

"We agreed as part of our divorce settlement that I would pay you for her education. You had no right to go behind my back and demand money from her, as well."

Brody laughed. "Too bad."

"I want every penny back that she gave you."

"Not going to happen."

"You haven't had time to lose all of it."

"I haven't lost any of it."

"Good. Then you can return the hundred thousand you stole from my sister."

"I didn't steal anything from Hailey or you. She agreed to pay me."

"Because she didn't know I was already paying you."

"And whose fault is that? You were always so determined to keep her in the dark about everything. Our marriage. Her education. You made it so easy for me to tell her anything I wanted and have her believe it."

Max decided it was time to step in. "Return the money."

Brody heard the threat loud and clear. "Or what?"

"Or I'm going to make your father an offer on his business he can't refuse and a team of accountants will show up to do due diligence and your father will learn just how much money you've embezzled from this company over the years."

"I don't know what you're talking about." But Brody's bluff fell flat.

Max snorted in disgust. "I can see why you lose at poker as often as you do," he said. "What do you think is going to happen when your father realizes that you haven't kicked your little problem the way you claim you have?"

"You've been stealing from the company?" Rachel looked almost sorry for her ex-husband.

"More so after you two divorced," Max interjected.

"Have you lost your mind?" Rachel questioned. "After he paid off your gambling debt with the Menks brothers, he swore if you gambled again he would sell the company and cut you off without a cent."

Max chipped in. "Imagine how unhappy he would be to hear that you never had any intention of quitting."

"You have no idea what you're talking about."

"Don't I?" Max couldn't believe the guy thought anyone would believe the words coming out of his mouth. "My brother used to be a professional gambler. When he reached out to his contacts they put him in touch with a number of people you've borrowed money from. Your associates were happy to shed light on your past dealings with them." Max shouldn't have enjoyed twisting the knife as much as he was, but this guy had mistreated Rachel and deserved everything he was getting. "And they've agreed to have a chat with your father if I ask them to."

"You're bluffing." Brody's eyes were blind with panic.

"I don't gamble," Max told him. "That means I never bluff. Every negotiation I go into, I'm holding a royal flush. I never lose."

"Everyone loses sometimes."

"The only one who loses today is you. Get the money."

"I don't have it with me." Brody's tone was close to a whine. Despite the air-conditioned comfort of the room, a bead of sweat trickled down his temple.

"Pity." Max set his hand on the small of Rachel's back and turned her toward the conference-room door.

"Wait."

Max turned the knob and opened the door to reveal Carson Winslow. The older man was frowning.

"I thought Brody was going to take you on a tour."

"He's been telling us how much the company means to

him," Max said. "I didn't realize he was so passionate about the business."

From the way Carson regarded his son, the current owner of Winslow Enterprises hadn't, either. "Well, that's good to know."

"Thank you for your time."

Carson shook his head in confusion. "You're leaving? But we never discussed the reason for your visit."

"I had hoped for a more amiable meeting." Max shook hands with the elder Winslow. "However, Brody made his position clear. He's not interested in doing business with me. I'm sure in time he'll regret making such a rash decision." He hit Rachel's ex with a hard stare.

It took a couple seconds for Brody to understand that Max intended to carry out his threat of informing Carson of his son's gambling. Brody glared at Max.

Seeing the unfriendly exchange, Carson turned on his son. "That wasn't your decision to make."

"Take it easy, Dad." Brody put up his hands. "Max just misunderstood my reservations. If I can have a couple minutes with him in private, I'll explain myself better."

While Rachel and Carson headed for the reception area, Max followed Brody down the hall and into his office, wondering what sort of scheme Rachel's ex would come up with now to save his hide.

To Max's surprise, Brody opened his briefcase and took out an envelope.

He tossed it at Max. "Here it is. A hundred grand. Count it if you want."

Max did. "Looks like it's all here."

"This means we're done. You'll leave me alone?"

"As long as you leave Rachel and Hailey alone, you'll never hear from me again."

"Good."

As he neared the lobby, Max caught Rachel's eye and gave her a tiny nod. Her eyes brightened with unshed tears. His heart turned over in his chest. He wanted nothing more than to wrap her in his arms and hug her hurt away. But with Carson looking on, Max limited himself to a brief smile.

"Did you get Hailey's money back?" she quizzed the instant they emerged into the hot Mississippi afternoon.

He handed her the envelope. "A hundred thousand. Just what you asked for."

She pulled out twenty thousand and gave him back the balance.

"I don't think Brody wants to risk his comfortable little world collapsing around him," he said, watching her face as she held her sister's money.

"I probably could have gotten back all the money you paid him."

Rachel shook her head. "I couldn't spend the rest of my life looking over my shoulder, waiting for him to reappear because he thinks he was cheated out of what's rightfully his." She gave him a sad smile. "You won't be around to protect me forever."

They started their relationship again with the understanding that it was temporary, but it stung hearing her talk about a future without him in it.

"If he's so bad, why did you go back to him after we met?"

"I went back to him because he said he'd tell Hailey why I really married him. I didn't want her to be ashamed of me."

"Sweetheart, she loves you, and she's proud of you. Nothing you did could change that."

"But I couldn't take care of her. She was my responsibility and I was failing."

"You were barely able to take care of yourself." Max wrapped his arm around her shoulders and hugged her. "Cut yourself some slack. You did the best you could. No one could fault you for that."

They hadn't gone more than a mile before Max glanced over and saw Rachel's cheeks were wet with tears. He pulled into the first parking lot he came to and parked the car. The instant he shut off the ignition, she leaned against his shoulder. Max twisted in his seat and drew her into his arms.

"It's going to be okay now," he said. "He'll never bother you again."

Cupping her head, he nuzzled her cheek and absorbed her shudders against his chest. He soothed her with long caresses up and down her back until her breath settled into a steady rhythm.

"I can't believe it's really over." She rested her head on his shoulder for a minute longer, before pushing away and wiping her cheeks. "Take me home."

While Max drove back to the airport, Rachel got on her cell phone and gave Hailey a blow-by-blow of the confrontation with Carson and Brody. He only half listened to her voice. The other half of his attention chewed on his reaction to Rachel asking him to take her home.

He knew she meant home to Houston and her house. But he couldn't shake the bone-deep longing to take her back to a home that they'd make together. What was he thinking? Living together? Marriage? Was he ready to take that step? And with Rachel?

His mind cleared.

Of course with Rachel. He'd loved her since the moment they'd met. He'd been thinking of a future with her. No wonder he'd been so crushed to discover she was already married. That she loved someone else.

And now?

Was he ready to let go of past mistakes and start anew? He was. But first he had to settle a little unfinished business with his father. Max knew he'd never be able to move into the future with the old resentment chained to his ankles like a concrete block. He owed Rachel a fresh start.

As the plane lifted off the ground and low clouds obscured her view of Biloxi, Rachel let her head fall back against the seat. She could have been one of those clouds, as light as she felt at the moment. Today, a chapter of her life had ended. A door closed between past and present. She never had to return to Biloxi or think about Brody ever again.

She glanced at the man beside her. Seeing him in action earlier had made her glad he was on her side. He'd been decisive and intimidating. She'd enjoyed watching him outclass her ex-husband. For the first time in ten years she felt completely free.

"You're smiling," Max said, taking her hand and grazing his lips across her knuckle.

"Savoring the victory."

"I had no idea your divorce had been that contentious."

"My entire marriage was that way. When Brody was losing, he was miserable and made everyone around him the same way."

"No wonder you got out."

"I didn't love him."

Max nodded. "After all you'd been through, I understand why you wouldn't."

"Not in the end." The need to unburden herself was probably going to backfire, but he had seen part of the truth. He might as well know it all. "From the start." She plunged on, needing Max to understand what she'd gone through. "I know it was wrong, but you have to understand how it was. I was afraid. I didn't know how much longer I was going to be able to keep feeding us, much less send Hailey to college. When Brody came along, he seemed nice and wanted to help. I told myself I was in love with him when he proposed, but I think I was so relieved at the idea of having a real home again, I lied to myself and to him. I used him."

"People get married for all sorts of reasons. Not all of them are right." Max's eyes were clear and free of reproach.

"You don't hate me?" Rachel couldn't believe she'd been wrong all along. "I married a man I didn't love because I was scared and wanted financial security. Don't you think that makes me a terrible person?"

"No." Max frowned. "Is that what you've been worried about all this time? That if I knew you'd made a mistake at twenty that it would somehow diminish you in my eyes?"

"You already hated me for not telling you I was married five years ago."

"Hated." He echoed the word and rubbed his eyes. "I never hated you. I said some harsh things when I found out because I was angry. But I never hated you."

"Not even a little?"

When he didn't answer right away, Rachel waited, her breath lodged in her chest. He had something on his mind, an emotion that he needed to distill into words.

"You know my father cheated on my mother."

"Yes."

"It nearly destroyed our family. Mom went through a really tough time when Sebastian and I were kids. I had a hard time watching her be unhappy and not being able to do anything about it. I swore I would never involve myself in any sort of extramarital affair. It's one of the reasons I don't want to marry. I can never cheat on my wife if I don't have one."

Rachel stared at their linked fingers. "I never should have started anything with you."

"Don't say that. This isn't your problem, it's mine. And I'm not sure if I'd known from the start that you were married if I would have been able to walk away."

"Of course you could have. You just said that having an affair was something you swore never to do."

"That's what eats at me. When tested, my convictions failed."

"But they didn't. You didn't know I was married until the end."

"And when I did know, that didn't stop me from wanting you." Max's bitter half smile tore at Rachel's heart.

"So, what are you saying? That if I'd stayed, we could have had a future together." She couldn't help the doubt that crept into her tone. "That's a nice happy ending, Max, but you and I both know that it never would have happened. You would have forever resented me for luring you into something that deep down you didn't want."

"You don't know that."

"I saw your face at your parents' anniversary party. You haven't forgiven your father for what he did to your mother twenty years ago. Those same resentments would have colored our relationship. Every time you look at me you see my infidelity. Just like you see your father's."

She saw the truth in his eyes. It sliced deep into her heart. To conceal the wound, she leaned forward and kissed his cheek.

"I don't want that between us," he said.

"Neither do I." Her throat tightened. "It just is."

Twelve

The conversation on the plane ride home ate at Max long after he dropped Rachel at her house. The lingering kiss she'd given him had tasted like goodbye. Her sad smile, a sign marking a dead end.

Being told that he was an unforgiving bastard had never bothered him before. Only Rachel could make him question what good he was doing himself or anyone else by holding twenty-year-old mistakes against his father.

Restless and unable to face his empty house, he called his dad and found him at the golf course once again. However, when Max arrived, Brandon had just finished the round and was having a drink at the clubhouse before returning home.

"Max," Brandon said, getting up to shake his son's hand. "What brings you here?"

"I wondered if we could talk privately."

"Sure." Brandon excused himself from his friends and led the way to the bar. An Astros game filled the television screen behind the bartender. As soon as Max had ordered a whiskey, Brandon asked, "What's wrong? Problems with your brothers again?"

"Nothing like that."

Despite the fact that Max had recently decided a cease fire in the office was more conducive to productivity, his resentment toward the relationship between Nathan and their father persisted. Brandon had always favored Nathan. And why not? He'd been born to the woman Brandon adored. Unlike his first two sons.

Max wondered if that's what had bothered him all these years. His father had never seemed present when Max and Sebastian were kids. And then Nathan came along and suddenly there were family dinners and vacations. Brandon was around more because he preferred Nathan to his older sons and wanted to spend time with him. At least that's what Max's young mind had decided. He saw now that jealousy had buried that idea in his subconscious and tainted his relationship with his father.

"Your mom told me you came by and asked about my affair with Marissa."

Max and his father had always been blunt with each other. Mostly because Max lacked Sebastian's diplomatic skills or Nathan's charm.

"Your affair hurt her."

"I know." Brandon stared into Max's eyes without flinching. "It's something I'll never be able to make up for, even if I spend the rest of my life trying."

"But she forgave you."

"She's a saint. That's one of the reasons why I love her." Brandon's gaze turned to flint. "And don't for a second think I don't. I was wrong to promise her my fidelity and break that trust, but I loved her when we married and I've loved her every day since. Some days better than others."

For the first time ever, Max saw his father's remorse and the conflict that must have raged in him all those years. He hadn't had a string of affairs. He'd loved two women. One he'd married. The other he'd been unable to give up despite knowing his affair hurt both the women in his life.

"Why is this coming up now?" Brandon asked.

Because he'd hung on to his anger at his father and let the woman he loved walk away. He thought about what his mother had said about him overreacting to Rachel being married. If he'd gone after Rachel and found out the sort of bad situation she was in, he might have convinced her to return with him to Houston. If he'd supported her instead of turning his back in anger, she could have started fresh with him. How much pain could have been avoided if he hadn't been so quick to judge her?

"I'm sorry," he told his father. "I should have followed Mom's example and let go of my anger years ago."

For a long moment, Brandon looked too stunned for speech. "You shouldn't apologize," he said at last, his deep voice scored with regret. "I'm sorry I put you, your brother and my wife through hell." Brandon looked older than he had in the year since his surgery. "I've been waiting a long time for you to stop hating me."

"It took falling in love with a very stubborn woman to make me understand that my anger hasn't done me any good."

"Rachel." Brandon's head bobbed in approval. "I was glad to see you two together at our anniversary party. She brought Missy and Sebastian together, you know. If she hadn't found Missy to be his assistant, I don't know what would have happened to your brother. He's happier than I've ever seen him. We have Rachel to thank for helping make that happen."

And that was it in a nutshell, Max realized. Rachel had helped Sebastian. She'd found him the perfect assistant. The perfect mate. Helping was what she did best. Behind the scenes, often at great personal sacrifice.

His heart expanded as an idea took hold.

It was past time someone did something for her in return.

A new client, Devon had said. He'd sent a text to her phone with an address and suite number, but no contact name. She'd called him back, but he hadn't picked up at work and wasn't answering his cell phone. Not surprising. It was past five o'clock on a Friday night. He had a social life. As did Hailey and pretty much everyone else on the planet.

Everyone except her.

In the two weeks since returning from Biloxi, she'd thrown herself into work. Exhaustion helped her sleep, but nothing prevented the dreams where she chased Max through a maze of long, dark hallways, following the sound of his voice, but never able to catch up to him.

She didn't need a professional to analyze her dreams. As much as she longed to be with him, Max was out of reach.

Stepping out of the humid Houston afternoon into the cool comfort of the building's enormous lobby, Rachel felt the first tingle of excitement in weeks. Landing a client in this building would mean big commissions. This was prime downtown real estate, the sort of place she'd hoped to lease for Lansing Employment Agency.

In fact, six months ago, she'd looked here, but the available space, perfect for her needs, had been snapped up the day after she'd toured. With a gym and a whole host of retail and service providers on the first floor, it was a huge step up from the older building near the edge of downtown that she was in now. Rachel let a wistful sigh escape as she rode the elevator to the eighth floor.

The suite had no identifying name on the outside. Not surprising. She'd passed quite a few unmarked offices on the way. Pushing through the door, she hesitated just inside.

No one occupied the reception desk. The space beyond had an empty feel to it. Granted, it was after the normal workday on a Friday, but she'd expected some sign of life.

"Hello?" She felt uncomfortable searching out her contact in the empty office. "It's Rachel Lansing, I believe we had an appointment."

"Surprise!" Out of two offices burst Hailey and Devon. They threw their arms around each other's shoulders and laughed, enjoying her shock.

"What are you doing here?" she demanded, confusion making her cross.

"I work here," Devon explained. "Come see my new office."

"You quit?" Tears popped into her eyes. She couldn't lose Hailey, Max and Devon in the space of a month.

"No." Devon shook his head, his smile bigger than ever.

Rachel took a deep breath, her hurt easing toward confusion. "I don't understand."

"These are our new offices."

She must have misheard him. "Our new what?"

"Offices," Hailey chimed in, rushing forward to enfold Rachel in an enthusiastic hug. "What do you think?"

"That I've died and heaven is an office suite in the best building in downtown Houston."

A pop came from behind Devon, the distinct sound of a cork leaving a champagne bottle.

"Come see your office," Hailey said.

Rachel resisted her sister's tugging. "This is a great idea," she said. "But I've crunched the numbers a hundred different ways and I can't afford to move in here."

"You can," a deep, masculine voice assured her. Max came

down the hall, carrying four flutes of champagne. "Thanks to your sister."

Seeing him wrenched her heart in six different ways. The days of no communication had been excruciating. She had reached for the phone a hundred times and dialed his number at least a dozen. Loving him and knowing that he could never forgive her was agony.

She turned away from his handsome face and stared at her sister. "Hailey, what does he mean?"

"He means that I took the money I got back from Brody and put it toward your offices."

Rachel's spirits plummeted. "Hailey, no. You shouldn't have done that."

"Don't even go there. You put me through school. You suffered with Brody for five years. Let me do something for you."

"But you're getting married. You should use the money for your wedding or a house."

"I'm marrying a man who understands how amazing my sister is and supports my desire to help her with something she's been working toward for four years."

"In other words," Devon piped up. "Say thank you, Rachel."

"Thank you," Rachel echoed, with the slightest touch of irony. Tears burned her eyes. Emotion tightened her throat. She wrapped her arms around Hailey and hugged her hard. "Thank you," she repeated, unable to speak above a whisper.

"Here," Max handed her a glass of champagne, his eyes glinting with satisfaction. Devon handed Hailey a glass. "To Lansing Employment Agency. May it continue matching executives with assistants for many years to come."

They clinked glasses. Rachel sipped her champagne, and then watched the bubbles to avoid staring at Max. Two weeks and two feet separated them. She felt as giddy as a teenager, and just as awkward.

"I have you to thank for this, as well, don't I?" she asked him.

"I might have made a few inquiries."

She suspected he'd done more than that. She wouldn't be surprised if he'd vouched for her, as well. What prompted him to help her? Heaven knew she'd been nothing but a thorn in his side since reappearing in his life. He'd been eager enough to drop her off after their trip to Biloxi. She'd put every scrap of love she felt for him into that kiss and he'd walked away without a backward glance.

"Thanks." She put her hand on his arm. Lightning shot from her fingertips to her toes, awakening every nerve it passed. "You have no idea what this means to me."

"I think I do."

The room fell away as she got lost in the possibilities swimming in his eyes. He took a half step closer, filling her nostrils with his crisp masculine scent, swamping her with the heat from his body and the pull of his charisma.

"Max, I'm sorry about everything."

He plucked her glass from her numb fingers and set it on the receptionist desk. "You have nothing to be sorry for."

"Brody. The money."

"Gone and returned." His hands slid around her waist, drawing her against him. "I'm the one who's sorry."

"For what?"

"For making you the scapegoat for my problems with my father." He drew his thumb against her cheek. "Being with you, I felt things that made me question what I believed was right. For years I'd been angry with my father for cheating, and with his mistress for refusing to give him up. I resented my mother because she clung to love when self-preservation should have told her to walk away. Wanting you demonstrated that I was no better than them. I was ready to sacrifice my principles to have you in my life."

"But you were so angry when you found out I was married."

"I was angry because you went back to your husband."

"I didn't think I had a choice." And now she understood what a mistake she'd made.

"You put Hailey's needs above your own. How can I be angry about that?"

Rachel snuggled against his chest, hiding her tears from him. For the first time in forever, her life was perfect. She wanted to savor the moment. All too soon, Max pushed her to arm's length. She dabbed at the corners of her eyes with the back of her hand and sniffled.

Glancing around, she realized the offices were empty. "What happened to Hailey and Devon?"

"I think they had someplace else to be."

"Is this really all mine?" She still couldn't believe what Hailey and Max had done for her.

"All yours."

"When I didn't hear from you after getting back from Biloxi, I thought we were done."

"I needed a little time to settle my past where it belonged."

"And now?"

"Put to rest."

As nice as all this sounded, she wasn't sure what happened next. "I'm glad." She pushed aside her doubts about the future and concentrated on enjoying her present. "Can I buy you dinner to celebrate?"

"I have an errand to run, but after that, I'm free."

"How long will it take? Shall I meet you somewhere?"

"Not long. I could use your help, if you don't mind."

"Sure."

They exited the suite, Rachel taking care to lock the door

behind her. The hand Max placed against the small of her back spread warmth throughout her entire body. Contentment radiated to every nook and cranny, bringing light to the darkest recesses of her soul.

He gave her an address and directions before they parted on the downtown street. Still floating in her happy bubble, she scarcely noticed the rush-hour traffic as she crept toward the suburbs. By the time she parked in front of an elegant colonial in one of Houston's older, affluent neighborhoods, she'd decided whatever form Max wanted their relationship to take, she'd enjoy being with him as long as he wanted her around.

While she wondered who lived in the house, Max drove up past her in a familiar yellow convertible and parked in the driveway. Her cheeks heated as she recalled what had happened on the hood of that car. Mystified by the reason he was driving one of his rare cars, she crossed the lawn toward him.

He'd discarded his suit coat and tie and rolled up his sleeves. She took the hand he held out to her and let him lead her toward the front door.

"What are we doing here?" she asked as they waited for the owner to answer their knock.

"You'll see."

His mischievous grin told her he wasn't giving anything away. A second later, she was distracted by the blond man who opened the door. Jason Sterling, Max's best friend. His gaze bounced from Max to her to the car in the driveway.

He paled beneath his tan.

"Oh, man, I never thought I'd see the day." Jason stepped back to let them enter the house. "Are you sure you want to do this?"

"Never more sure of anything in the world." He tossed his keys to Jason and wrapped his arm around Rachel's waist, guiding her into the foyer.

She gazed up at him, deciding she'd never seen him so relaxed. "Why did you give Jason your car keys?"

"Not just the keys," Jason said.

"The car."

"But you love that car," she exclaimed. "Why would you sell it?"

Max raised his eyebrows. "I didn't sell it."

"I won it."

Rachel regarded the two men for a long moment, watching the silent interaction between them. "Won it how?"

Before Max could answer, Jason waggled his head in dismay. "I thought you loved that car."

"I love this woman more."

Rachel's breath stopped. Without his arm propelling her forward, her feet would have stopped as well. Instead, she kept going, stumbling over the transition from hardwood floor to area rug. Max's strong arm supported her. His steady calm soothed her flustered emotions.

She regained her balance, physically and spiritually, and stared up at him in awe. "You do?"

"Of course he does," Jason grumbled. "He's giving up the find of a lifetime because of you."

Max shot his best friend a sour look. Jason retaliated with a disgruntled glare of his own. The undercurrents in the room darted around her like agitated birds. Rachel wasn't sure what was going on, but she sensed she was at the heart of it.

"You don't have to give up your car for me."

Max took her hands in his and deposited kisses in both palms. "I'm not giving it up for you. I'm giving it up because I lost a bet."

"What sort of bet?"

"I bet him he'd marry whoever your agency placed as his assistant," Jason explained.

The absurdity of it made her laugh. "You were serious

about all that?" she asked him. "I thought for sure you'd made it all up as payback for what I did to you five years ago."

"No," Jason said. "We were completely serious. Do you have any idea how many men have married the assistants you've placed with them?"

"You're both insane."

"Nine." Jason crossed to a table with three crystal decanters and poured himself a shot out of one. When he gestured toward them with the bottle, both she and Max shook their heads. "Nine perfectly happy bachelors have fallen in love. Including my father. His brother. And now my best friend. All because of you."

"I wasn't perfectly happy," Max insisted.

Rachel turned on Jason. "You're behind his idiotic idea that I run a matchmaking service? You can't seriously think I have anything to do with those couples falling in love."

Jason scowled at her. "You match executives and assistants. A lot of them get married."

His claim was so preposterous she didn't know how to refute it. "That's crazy."

"Is it?" Jason gestured behind her.

Rachel turned. To her astonishment, Max dropped to one knee and produced a ring from his pocket. "Rachel Lansing. Will you marry me?"

Rachel covered her gasp with both hands as she stared from the man she adored to the ring he held out to her. The large diamond sparkled, hypnotizing her. Her thoughts began to circle. Max wanted to marry her. He loved her. They would live together in his big house and have lots of babies. At least she hoped they would. She had no idea of his views on children. Or any of a hundred things that couples heading toward marriage talked about.

"Answer him," Jason bellowed, his impatience spilling over.

"Yes."

Grinning, Max slid the ring on her finger. He got to his feet and cupped her face, drinking from her lips, long and deep.

By the time they came up for air, Jason had collapsed onto the couch and was staring at the empty glass in his hand.

"What's wrong with him?" Rachel whispered, nudging her head toward Jason. "He looks like he's lost his best friend."

Max's grin was pure mischief. "He's sad because he's a miserable, lonely bachelor."

"Does he need an executive assistant?"

Jason came off the couch with a roar. "Don't you dare."

Laughing, Max and Rachel retreated from the house. As Max drove her car back to his place, Rachel leaned her head against the seat rest and admired the ring on her hand. "Do you think there's anything to Jason's claim of matchmaking?"

"No." His scoffing tone was at odds with his uncertain frown. "But maybe in the future all the assistants you place at Case Consolidated Holdings should be old and married."

Rachel laughed. "I think that can be arranged."

* * * * *

LET'S TALK
Romance

For exclusive extracts, competitions
and special offers, find us online:

f facebook.com/millsandboon

○ @millsandboonuk

▾ @millsandboon

Or get in touch on 0844 844 1351*

For all the latest titles coming soon, visit
millsandboon.co.uk/nextmonth